PENGUIN MODERN CLASSICS

AFTER MANY A SUMMER

Born in 1894, Aldous Huxley belonged to a family of great talent: he was the grandson of the famous Thomas Henry Huxley; the son of Leonard Huxley, the editor of *The Cornhill Magazine*; and the brother of Sir Julian Huxley. He was educated at Eton and Balliol, and before devoting himself entirely to his own writing worked as a journalist and dramatic critic.

Aldous Huxley first attracted attention with a volume of stories called *Limbo* (1920) and followed this up with his novel *Crome Yellow* (1921). *Antic Hay* and *Those Barren Leaves* followed in 1923 and 1925 respectively. Possibly his three most outstanding novels are *Point Counter Point* (1928), *Brave New World* (1932), and *Eyeless in Gaza* (1936). His travel books include *Jesting Pilate* (1926) and *Beyond the Mexique Bay* (1934). *Grey Eminence* and *The Devils of Loudun* are historical studies, and in *The Doors of Perception* and *Heaven and Hell* he discussed the nature and significance of visionary experience. He died in 1963.

His last books were *Brave New World Revisited* (1959), *Collected Essays* (1960), *On Art and Artists* (1961), *Island* (1962), and *Literature and Science* (1963).

Cover drawing by Leonard Rosoman

BY ALDOUS HUXLEY

Limbo, 1920
Leda, 1920
*Crome Yellow, 1921
*Mortal Coils, 1922
*Antic Hay, 1923
On the Margin, 1923
Little Mexican, 1924
*Those Barren Leaves, 1925
Along the Road, 1925
Two or Three Graces, 1926
Jesting Pilate, 1926
Proper Studies, 1927
*Point Counter Point, 1928
Do What You Will, 1929
*Brief Candles, 1930
*Music at Night, 1931
The Cicadas, 1931
The World of Light, 1931
*Brave New World, 1932
Texts and Pretexts, 1932
*Beyond the Mexique Bay, 1934
*Eyeless in Gaza, 1936
The Olive Tree, 1936
Ends and Means, 1937
Grey Eminence, 1941
The Art of Seeing, 1943
Time Must Have a Stop, 1945
The Perennial Philosophy, 1946
Science, Liberty and Peace, 1947
The Gioconda Smile, 1948
Ape and Essence, 1948
Themes and Variations, 1950
The Devils of Loudun, 1952
*The Doors of Perception, 1954
The Genius and the Goddess, 1955
*Heaven and Hell, 1956
Adonis and the Alphabet, 1956
Collected Short Stories, 1957
Brave New World Revisited, 1959
Collected Essays, 1960
On Art and Artists, 1961
*Island, 1962
Literature and Science, 1963

Published in Penguin Books

ALDOUS HUXLEY

AFTER MANY A SUMMER

A NOVEL

PENGUIN BOOKS

IN ASSOCIATION WITH CHATTO & WINDUS

Penguin Books Ltd, Harmondsworth, Middlesex, England
Penguin Books Australia Ltd, Ringwood, Victoria, Australia

—

First published by Chatto & Windus 1939
Published in Penguin Books 1955
Reprinted 1959, 1961, 1964, 1967, 1971

—

—

Made and printed in Great Britain
by Hazell Watson & Viney Ltd
Aylesbury, Bucks
Set in Monotype Fournier

The woods decay, the woods decay and fall,
The vapours weep their burthen to the ground,
Man comes and tills the field and lies beneath,
And after many a summer dies the swan.

TENNYSON

PART ONE

*

Chapter One

IT had all been arranged by telegram; Jeremy Pordage was to look out for a coloured chauffeur in a grey uniform with a carnation in his button-hole; and the coloured chauffeur was to look out for a middle-aged Englishman carrying the Poetical Works of Wordsworth. In spite of the crowds at the station, they found one another without difficulty.

'Mr Stoyte's chauffeur?'

'Mr Pordage, sah?'

Jeremy nodded and, his Wordsworth in one hand, his umbrella in the other, half extended his arms in the gesture of a self-deprecatory mannequin exhibiting, with a full and humorous consciousness of their defects, a deplorable figure accentuated by the most ridiculous clothes. 'A poor thing,' he seemed to be implying, 'but myself.' A defensive and, so to say, prophylactic disparagement had become a habit with him. He resorted to it on every sort of occasion. Suddenly a new idea came into his head. Anxiously he began to wonder whether, in this democratic Far West of theirs, one shook hands with the chauffeur – particularly if he happened to be a blackamoor, just to demonstrate that one wasn't a pukka sahib even if one's country did happen to be bearing the White Man's burden. In the end he decided to do nothing. Or, to be more accurate, the decision was forced upon him – as usual, he said to himself, deriving a curious wry pleasure from the recognition of his own shortcomings. While he was hesitating what to do, the chauffeur took off his cap and, slightly over-acting the part of an old-world Negro retainer, bowed, smiled toothily and said, 'Welcome to Los Angeles, Mr Pordage, sah!' Then, changing the tone of his chanting drawl from the dramatic to the confidential, 'I should have knowed you by your voice, Mr Pordage,' he went on, 'even without the book.'

Jeremy laughed a little uncomfortably. A week in America had made him self-conscious about that voice of his. A product of Trinity College, Cambridge, ten years before the War, it was a small, fluty voice, suggestive of evensong in an English cathedral.

At home, when he used it, nobody paid any particular attention. He had never had to make jokes about it, as he had done, in self-protection, about his appearance for example, or his age. Here, in America, things were different. He had only to order a cup of coffee or ask the way to the lavatory (which anyhow wasn't called the lavatory in this disconcerting country) for people to stare at him with an amused and attentive curiosity as though he were a freak on show in an amusement park. It had not been at all agreeable.

'Where's my porter?' he said fussily in order to change the subject.

A few minutes later they were on their way. Cradled in the back seat of the car, out of range, he hoped, of the chauffeur's conversation, Jeremy Pordage abandoned himself to the pleasure of merely looking. Southern California rolled past the windows; all he had to do was to keep his eyes open.

The first thing to present itself was a slum of Africans and Filipinos, Japanese, and Mexicans. And what permutations and combinations of black, yellow and brown! What complex bastardies! And the girls – how beautiful in their artificial silk! 'And Negro ladies in white muslin gowns.' His favourite line in *The Prelude*. He smiled to himself. And meanwhile the slum had given place to the tall buildings of a business district.

The population took on a more Caucasian tinge. At every corner there was a drug-store. The newspaper boys were selling headlines about Franco's drive on Barcelona. Most of the girls, as they walked along, seemed to be absorbed in silent prayer; but he supposed, on second thoughts, it was only gum that they were thus incessantly ruminating. Gum, not God. Then suddenly the car plunged into a tunnel and emerged into another world, a vast, untidy, suburban world of filling-stations and billboards, of low houses in gardens, of vacant lots and waste-paper, of occasional shops and office buildings and churches – Primitive Methodist churches built, surprisingly enough, in the style of the Cartuja at Granada, Catholic churches like Canterbury Cathedral, synagogues disguised as Hagia Sophia, Christian Science churches with pillars and pediments, like banks. It was a winter day and early in the morning; but the sun shone brilliantly, the sky was without a cloud. The car was travelling westwards, and the sunshine, slanting from behind them as they advanced, lit up each building, each skysign and bill-board, as though with a spot-light, as though on purpose to show the new arrival all the sights.

EATS. COCKTAILS. OPEN NITES.

JUMBO MALTS.

DO THINGS, GO PLACES WITH CONSOL SUPER GAS!

AT BEVERLY PANTHEON FINE FUNERALS ARE *NOT* EXPENSIVE.

The car sped onwards, and here in the middle of a vacant lot was a restaurant in the form of a seated bulldog, the entrance between the front paws, the eyes illuminated.

'Zoomorph,' Jeremy Pordage murmured to himself, and again, 'zoomorph.' He had the scholar's taste for words. The bulldog shot back into the past.

ASTROLOGY, NUMEROLOGY, PSYCHIC READINGS.

DRIVE IN FOR NUTBERGERS – whatever they were. He resolved at the earliest opportunity to have one. A nutberger and a jumbo malt.

STOP HERE FOR CONSOL SUPER GAS.

Surprisingly, the chauffeur stopped. 'Ten gallons of Super-Super,' he ordered; then, turning back to Jeremy, 'This is our company,' he added. 'Mr Stoyte, he's the president.' He pointed to a billboard across the street. CASH LOANS IN FIFTEEN MINUTES, Jeremy read; CONSULT COMMUNITY SERVICE FINANCE CORPORATION. 'That's another of ours,' said the chauffeur proudly.

They drove on. The face of a beautiful young woman, distorted, like a Magdalene's, with grief, stared out of a giant billboard. BROKEN ROMANCE, proclaimed the caption. SCIENCE PROVES THAT 73 PER CENT OF ALL ADULTS HAVE HALITOSIS.

IN TIME OF SORROW LET BEVERLY PANTHEON BE YOUR FRIEND.

FACIALS, PERMANENTS, MANICURES.

BETTY'S BEAUTY SHOPPE.

Next door to the beauty shoppe was a Western Union office. That cable to his mother . . . Heavens, he had almost forgotten! Jeremy leaned forward and, in the apologetic tone he always used when speaking to servants, asked the chauffeur to stop for a moment. The car came to a halt. With a preoccupied expression on his mild, rabbit-like face, Jeremy got out and hurried across the pavement, into the office.

'Mrs Pordage, The Araucarias, Woking, England,' he wrote, smiling a little as he did so. The exquisite absurdity of that address was a standing source of amusement. 'The Araucarias, Woking'. His mother, when she bought the house, had wanted to change the name, as being too ingenuously middle-class, too much like a joke by Hilaire Belloc. 'But that's the beauty of it,' he had protested. 'That's the charm.' And he had tried to make her see how utterly right it would be for them to live at such an address. The deliciously comic incongruity between the name of the house, and the nature of its occupants! And what a beautiful, topsy-turvy appositeness in the fact that Oscar Wilde's old friend, the witty and cultured Mrs Pordage, should write her sparkling letters from The Araucarias, and that from these same Araucarias, these Araucarias, mark you, at *Woking*, should come the works of mingled scholarship and curiously rarefied wit for which her son had gained his reputation. Mrs Pordage had almost instantly seen what he was driving at. No need, thank goodness, to labour your points where she was concerned. You could talk entirely in hints and anacoluthons; she could be relied on to understand. The Araucarias had remained The Araucarias.

Having written the address, Jeremy paused, pensively frowned and initiated the familiar gesture of biting his pencil – only to find, disconcertingly, that this particular pencil was tipped with brass and fastened to a chain. 'Mrs Pordage, The Araucarias, Woking, England,' he read out aloud, in the hope that the words would inspire him to compose the right, the perfect message – the message his mother expected of him, at once tender and witty, charged with a genuine devotion ironically worded, acknowledging her maternal domination, but at the same time making fun of it, so that the old lady could salve her conscience by pretending that her son was entirely free, and herself the least tyrannical of mothers. It wasn't easy – particularly with this pencil on a chain. After several abortive essays he decided, though it was definitely unsatisfactory, on: 'Climate being subtropical shall break vow re underclothes stop Wish you were here my sake not yours as you would scarcely appreciate this unfinished Bournemouth indefinitely magnified stop.'

'Unfinished what?' questioned the young woman on the further side of the counter.

'B-o-u-r-n-e-m-o-u-t-h,' Jeremy spelled out. He smiled; behind the bi-focal lenses of his spectacles his blue eyes twinkled, and, with a gesture of which he was quite unconscious, but which he always, automatically, made when he was about to utter one of his little jokes, he stroked the smooth bald spot on the top of his head. '*You* know,' he said, in a particularly fluty tone, 'the bourne to which no traveller goes, if he can possibly help it.'

The girl looked at him blankly; then, inferring from his expression that something funny had been said, and remembering that Courteous Service was Western Union's slogan, gave the bright smile for which the poor old chump was evidently asking, and went on reading: 'Hope you have fun at Grasse stop Tendresses Jeremy.'

It was an expensive message; but, luckily, he reflected, as he took out his pocket-book, luckily Mr Stoyte was grossly overpaying him. Three months' work, six thousand dollars. So damn the expense.

He returned to the car and they drove on. Mile after mile they went, and the suburban houses, the gas-stations, the vacant lots, the churches, the shops went along with them, interminably. To right and left, between palms, or pepper trees, or acacias, the streets of the enormous residential quarter receded to the vanishing point.

CLASSY EATS. MILE HIGH CONES.

JESUS SAVES.

HAMBURGERS.

Yet once more the traffic lights turned red. A paper-boy came to the window. 'Franco claims gains in Catalonia,' Jeremy read, and turned away. The frightfulness of the world had reached a point at which it had become for him merely boring. From the halted car in front of them, two elderly ladies, both with permanently waved hair and both wearing crimson trousers, descended, each carrying a Yorkshire terrier. The dogs were set down at the foot of the traffic signal. Before the animals could make up their minds to use the convenience, the lights had changed. The Negro shifted into first, and the car swerved forward, into the future. Jeremy was thinking of his mother. Disquietingly enough, she too had a Yorkshire terrier.

FINE LIQUORS.

TURKEY SANDWICHES.

GO TO CHURCH AND FEEL BETTER ALL THE WEEK.

WHAT IS GOOD FOR BUSINESS IS GOOD FOR *YOU*.

Another zoomorph presented itself, this time a real estate agent's office in the form of an Egyptian sphinx.

JESUS IS COMING SOON.

YOU TOO CAN HAVE ABIDING YOUTH WITH THRILLPHORM BRASSIÈRES.

BEVERLY PANTHEON, THE CEMETERY THAT IS *DIFFERENT*.

With the triumphant expression of Puss-in-Boots enumerating the possessions of the Marquis of Carabas, the Negro shot a glance over his shoulder at Jeremy, waved his hand towards the billboard, and said, 'That's ours too.'

'You mean, the Beverly Pantheon?'

The man nodded. 'Finest cemetery in the world, I guess,' he said: and added, after a moment's pause, 'Maybe you's like to see it. It wouldn't hardly be out of our way.'

'That would be very nice,' said Jeremy with upper-class English graciousness. Then, feeling that he ought to express his acceptance rather more warmly and democratically, he cleared his throat and, with a conscious effort to reproduce the local vernacular, added that it would be *swell*. Pronounced in his Trinity-College-Cambridge voice, the word sounded so unnatural that he began to blush with embarrassment. Fortunately, the chauffeur was too busy with the traffic to notice.

They turned to the right, sped past a Rosicrucian Temple, past two cat-and-dog hospitals, past a School for Drum-Majorettes and two more advertisements of the Beverly Pantheon. As they turned to the left on Sunset Boulevard, Jeremy had a glimpse of a young woman who was doing her shopping in a hydrangea-blue strapless bathing-suit, platinum curls and a black fur jacket. Then she too was whirled back into the past.

The present was a road at the foot of a line of steep hills, a road flanked by small, expensive-looking shops, by restaurants, by night-clubs shuttered against the sunlight, by offices and apartment houses. Then they too had taken their places in the irrevocable. A sign proclaimed that they were crossing the city limits of Beverly Hills. The surroundings changed. The road was flanked by the gardens of a rich residential quarter. Through trees, Jeremy saw the façades of houses, all new, almost all in good taste – elegant and witty pastiches of Lutyens manor houses, of Little Trianons, of Monticellos; light-hearted parodies of Le Corbusier's solemn machines-for-living-in; fantastic Mexican adaptations of Mexican haciendas and New England farms.

They turned to the right. Enormous palm trees lined the road. In the sunlight, masses of mesembryanthemums blazed with an intense magenta glare. The houses succeeded one another, like the pavilions at some endless international exhibition. Gloucestershire followed Andalusia and gave place in turn to Touraine and Oaxaca, Düsseldorf and Massachusetts.

'That's Harold Lloyd's place,' said the chauffeur, indicating a kind of Boboli. 'And that's Charlie Chaplin's. And that's Pickfair.'

The road began to mount, vertiginously. The chauffeur pointed across an intervening gulf of shadow at what seemed a Tibetan lamasery on the opposite hill. 'That's where Ginger Rogers lives. Yes, *sir*,' he nodded triumphantly, as he twirled the steering-wheel.

Five or six more turns brought the car to the top of the hill. Below and behind lay the plain, with the city like a map extending indefinitely into a pink haze.

Before and to either hand were mountains – ridge after ridge as far as the eye could reach, a desiccated Scotland, empty under the blue desert sky.

The car turned a shoulder of orange rock, and there all at once, on a summit hitherto concealed from view, was a huge sky sign, with the words, BEVERLY PANTHEON, THE PERSONALITY CEMETERY, in six-foot neon tubes and, above it, on the very crest, a full-scale reproduction of the Leaning Tower of Pisa – only this one didn't lean.

'See that?' said the Negro impressively. 'That's the Tower of Resurrection. Two hundred thousand dollars, that's what it cost. Yes, *sir*.' He spoke with an emphatic solemnity. One was made to feel that the money had all come out of his own pocket.

Chapter Two

A_N hour later, they were on their way again, having seen everything. Everything. The sloping lawns, like a green oasis in the mountain desolation. The groves of trees. The tombstones in the grass. The Pets' Cemetery, with its marble group after Landseer's 'Dignity and Impudence'. The tiny Church of the Poet – a miniature reproduction of Holy Trinity at Stratford-on-Avon complete with Shakespeare's tomb and a twenty-four-hour service of organ music played automatically by the Perpetual Wurlitzer and broadcast by concealed loudspeakers all over the cemetery.

Then, leading out of the vestry, the Bride's Apartment (for one was married at the Tiny Church as well as buried from it) – the Bride's Apartment that had just been re-decorated, said the chauffeur, in the style of Norma Shearer's boudoir in *Marie Antoinette*. And, next to the Bride's Apartment, the exquisite black marble Vestibule of Ashes, leading to the Crematorium, where three super-modern oil-burning mortuary furnaces were always under heat and ready for any emergency.

Accompanied wherever they went by the tremolos of the Perpetual Wurlitzer, they had driven next to look at the Tower of Resurrection – from the outside only; for it housed the executive offices of the West Coast Cemeteries Corporation. Then the Children's Corner with its statues of Peter Pan and the Infant Jesus, its groups of alabaster babies playing with bronze rabbits, its lily pool and an apparatus labelled The Fountain of Rainbow Music, from which there spouted simultaneously water, coloured lights and the inescapable strains of the Perpetual Wurlitzer. Then, in rapid succession, the Garden of Quiet, the Tiny Taj Mahal, the Old World Mortuary. And, reserved by the chauffeur to the last, as the final and crowning proof of his employer's glory, the Pantheon itself.

Was it possible, Jeremy asked himself, that such an object existed? It was certainly not probable. The Beverly Pantheon lacked all verisimilitude, was something entirely beyond his powers to

16

invent. The fact that the idea of it was now in his mind proved, therefore, that he must really have seen it. He shut his eyes against the landscape and recalled to his memory the details of that incredible reality. The external architecture, modelled on that of Boecklin's 'Toteninsel'. The circular vestibule. The replica of Rodin's 'Le Baiser', illuminated by concealed pink floodlights. With its flights of black marble stairs. The seven-story columbarium, the endless galleries, its tiers on tiers of slab-sealed tombs. The bronze and silver urns of the cremated, like athletic trophies. The stained-glass windows after Burne-Jones. The texts inscribed on marble scrolls. The Perpetual Wurlitzer crooning on every floor. The sculpture . . .

That was the hardest to believe, Jeremy reflected, behind closed eyelids. Sculpture almost as ubiquitous as the Wurlitzer. Statues wherever you turned your eyes. Hundreds of them, bought wholesale, one would guess, from some monumental masonry concern at Carrara or Pietrasanta. All nudes, all female, all exuberantly nubile. The sort of statues one would expect to see in the reception-room of a high-class brothel in Rio de Janeiro. 'Oh, Death,' demanded a marble scroll at the entrance to every gallery, 'where is thy sting?' Mutely, but eloquently, the statues gave their reassuring reply. Statues of young ladies in nothing but a very tight belt imbedded, with Bernini-like realism, in the Parian flesh. Statues of young ladies crouching; young ladies using both hands to be modest; young ladies stretching, writhing, callipygously stooping to tie their sandals, reclining. Young ladies with doves, with panthers, with other young ladies, with upturned eyes expressive of the soul's awakening. 'I am the Resurrection and the Life,' proclaimed the scrolls. 'The Lord is my shepherd; therefore shall I want nothing.' Nothing, not even Wurlitzer, not even girls in tightly buckled belts. 'Death is swallowed up in victory' – the victory no longer of the spirit but of the body, the well-fed body, for ever youthful, immortally athletic, indefatigably sexy. The Moslem paradise had had copulations six centuries long. In this new Christian heaven, progress, no doubt, would have stepped up the period to a millennium and added the joys of everlasting tennis, eternal golf, and swimming.

All at once the car began to descend. Jeremy opened his eyes again, and saw that they had reached the further edge of the range of hills, among which the Pantheon was built.

Below lay a great tawny plain, chequered with patches of green and dotted with white houses. On its further side, fifteen or twenty miles away, ranges of pinkish mountains fretted the horizon.

'What's this?' Jeremy asked.

'The San Fernando Valley,' said the chauffeur. He pointed into the middle distance. 'That's where Groucho Marx has his place,' he said. 'Yes, *sir*.'

At the bottom of the hill the car turned to the left along a wide road that ran, a ribbon of concrete and suburban buildings, through the plain. The chauffeur put on speed; sign succeeded sign with bewildering rapidity. MALTS CABIN DINE AND DANCE AT THE CHÂTEAU HONOLULU SPIRITUAL HEALING AND COLONIC IRRIGATION BLOCKLONG HOT DOGS BUY YOUR DREAM HOME *NOW*. And behind the signs the mathematically planted rows of apricot and walnut trees flicked past – a succession of glimpsed perspectives preceded and followed every time by fan-like approaches and retirements.

Dark-green and gold, enormous orange orchards manœuvred, each one a mile-square regiment glittering in the sunlight. Far off, the mountains traced their uninterpretable graph of boom and slump.

'Tarzana,' said the chauffeur startlingly; there, sure enough, was the name suspended, in white letters, across the road. 'There's Tarzana College,' the man went on, pointing to a group of Spanish-Colonial palaces clustering round a Romanesque basilica. 'Mr Stoyte, he's just given them an auditorium.'

They turned to the right along a less important road. The groves gave place for a few miles to huge fields of alfalfa and fusty grass, then returned again more luxuriant than ever. Meanwhile the mountains on the northern edge of the valley were approaching and, slanting in from the west, another range was looming up to the left. They drove on. The road took a sudden turn, aiming, it seemed, at the point where the two ranges must come together. All at once, through a gap between two orchards, Jeremy Pordage saw a most surprising sight. About half a mile from the foot of the mountains, like an island off a cliff-bound coast, a rocky hill rose abruptly, in places almost precipitously, from the plain. On the summit of the bluff and as though growing out of it in a kind of efflorescence, stood a castle. But what a castle! The donjon was like a skyscraper, the bastions plunged headlong with the effortless swoop of concrete dams. The thing was Gothic, mediaeval, baronial – doubly baronial, Gothic with a Gothicity raised, so to speak, to a higher power, more mediaeval than any building of the thirteenth century. For this ... this Object, as Jeremy was reduced to calling it, was mediaeval, not out of vulgar historical necessity, like Coucy, say, or Alnwick, but out of pure fun and wantonness, platonically, one might say. It was mediaeval as only a witty and irresponsible modern architect would wish to be mediaeval, as only the most competent modern engineers are technically equipped to be.

Jeremy was startled into speech. 'What on earth is that?' he asked, pointing at the nightmare on the hill-top.

'Why, that's Mr Stoyte's place,' said the retainer; and smiling yet once more with the pride of vicarious ownership, he added: 'It's a pretty fine home, I guess.'

The orange groves closed in again; leaning back in his seat, Jeremy Pordage began to wonder, rather apprehensively, what he had let himself in for when he accepted Mr Stoyte's offer. The pay was princely; the work, which was to catalogue the almost legendary Hauberk Papers, would be delightful. But that cemetery, this ... Object – Jeremy shook his head. He had known, of course, that Mr Stoyte was rich, collected pictures, owned a show-place in California. But no one had ever led him to expect *this*. The humorous puritanism of his good taste was shocked; he was appalled at the prospect of meeting the person capable of committing such an enormity. Between that person and oneself, what contact, what community of thought or feeling could possibly exist? Why had he sent for one? For it was obvious that he couldn't conceivably like one's books. But had he even read one's books? Did he have the faintest idea of what one was like? Would he be capable, for example, of understanding why one had insisted on the name of The Araucarias remaining unchanged? Would he appreciate one's point of view about ...?

These anxious questionings were interrupted by the noise of the horn, which the chauffeur was sounding with a loud and offensive insistence. Jeremy looked up. Fifty yards ahead, an ancient Ford was creeping tremulously along the road. It carried, lashed insecurely to roof and running-boards and luggage-rack, a squalid cargo of household goods – rolls of bedding, an old iron stove, a crate of pots and pans, a folded tent, a tin bath. As they flashed past, Jeremy had a glimpse of three dull-eyed, anaemic children, of a woman with a piece of sacking wrapped round her shoulders, of a haggard, unshaved man.

'Transients,' the chauffeur explained in a tone of contempt.

'What's that?' Jeremy asked.

'Why, *transients*,' the Negro repeated, as though the emphasis were an explanation. 'Guess that lot's from the dust bowl. Kansas licence plate. Come to pick our navels.'

'Come to pick your navels?' Jeremy echoed incredulously.

'Navel oranges,' said the chauffeur. 'It's the season. Pretty good year for navels, I guess.'

They emerged once more into the open, and there once more was the Object, larger than ever. Jeremy had time to study the details of its construction. A wall with towers encircled the base of the hills, and there was a second line of defence, in the most approved post-Crusades manner, half-way up. On the summit stood the square keep, surrounded by subsidiary buildings.

From the donjon, Jeremy's eyes travelled down to a group of buildings in the plain, not far from the foot of the hill. Across the façade of the largest of them the words, 'Stoyte's Home for Sick Children', were written in gilded letters. Two flags, one the stars and stripes, the other a white banner with the letter S in scarlet, fluttered in the breeze. Then a grove of leafless walnut trees shut out the view once again. Almost at the same moment the chauffeur threw his engine out of gear and put on the brakes. The car came gently to a halt beside a man who was walking at a brisk pace along the grassy verge of the road.

'Want a ride, Mr Propter?' the Negro called.

The stranger turned his head, gave the man a smile of recognition and came to the window of the car. He was a large man, broad-shouldered, but rather stooping, with brown hair turning grey and a face, Jeremy thought, like the face of one of those statues which Gothic sculptors carved for a place high up on a

West front – a face of sudden prominences and deeply shadowed folds and hollows, emphatically rough-hewn so as to be expressive even at a distance. But this particular face, he went on to notice, was not merely emphatic, not only for the distance; it was a face also for the near point, also for intimacy, a subtle face, in which there were the signs of sensibility and intelligence as well as of power, of a gentle and humorous serenity no less than of energy and strength.

'Hullo, George,' the stranger said, addressing the chauffeur; 'nice of you to stop for me.'

'Well, I'm sure glad to see you, Mr Propter,' said the Negro cordially. Then he half-turned in his seat, waved a hand towards Jeremy, and with a florid formality of tone and manner said, 'I'd like to have you meet Mr Pordage of England. Mr Pordage, this is Mr Propter.'

The two men shook hands, and, after an exchange of courtesies, Mr Propter got into the car.

'You're visiting with Mr Stoyte?' he asked, as the chauffeur drove on.

Jeremy shook his head. He was here on business; had come to look at some manuscripts – the Hauberk Papers, to be precise.

Mr Propter listened attentively, nodded from time to time and, when Jeremy had finished, sat for a moment in silence.

'Take a decayed Christian,' he said at last in a meditative tone, 'and the remains of a Stoic; mix thoroughly with good manners, a bit of money and an old-fashioned education; simmer for several years in a university. Result: a scholar and a gentleman. Well, there were worse types of human being.' He uttered a little laugh. 'I might almost claim to have been one myself, once, long ago.'

Jeremy looked at him inquiringly. 'You're not *William* Propter, are you?' he asked. 'Not *Short Studies in the Counter Reformation*, by any chance?'

The other inclined his head.

Jeremy looked at him in amazement and delight. Was it possible? he asked himself. Those *Short Studies* had been one of his favourite books – a model, he had always thought, of their kind.

'Well, I'm jiggered!' he said aloud, using the schoolboyish locution deliberately and as though between inverted commas. He had found that, both in writing and in conversation, there were exquisite effects to be obtained by the judicious employment, in a solemn or cultural context, of a phrase of slang, a piece of childish profanity or obscenity. 'I'll be damned!' he exploded again, and his consciousness of the intentional silliness of the words made him stroke his bald head and cough.

There was another moment of silence. Then, instead of talking, as Jeremy had expected, about the *Short Studies*, Mr Propter merely shook his head and said, 'We mostly are.'

'Mostly are what?' asked Jeremy.

'Jiggered,' Mr Propter answered. 'Damned. In the psychological sense of the word,' he added.

The walnut trees came to an end, and there once more, on the starboard bow, was the Object. Mr Propter pointed in its direction. 'Poor Jo Stoyte!' he said. 'Think of having *that* millstone round one's neck. Not to mention, of course, all the other millstones that go with it. What luck we've had, don't you think? – we who've never been given the opportunity of being anything much worse than scholars and gentlemen!' After another little silence, 'Poor Jo,' he went on with a smile . 'he isn't either of them. You'll find him a bit trying. Because of course he'll want to bully you, just because tradition says that your type is superior to his type. Not to mention the fact,' he added, looking into Jeremy's face with an expression of mingled amusement and sympathy, 'that you're probably the sort of person that invites persecution. A bit of a murderee, I'm afraid, as well as a scholar and gentleman.'

Feeling simultaneously annoyed by the man's indiscretion and touched by his friendliness, Jeremy smiled rather nervously and nodded his head.

'Maybe,' Mr Propter went on, 'maybe it would help you to be less of a murderee towards Jo Stoyte if you knew what gave him the original impulse to get damned in just *that* way' – and he pointed again towards the Object. 'We were at school together, Jo and I – only nobody called him Jo in those days. We called him Slob, or Jelly-Belly. Because, you see, poor Jo was the local fat-boy, the only fat-boy in the school during those years.' He paused for a moment; then went on in another tone, 'I've often wondered why people have always made fun of fatness. Perhaps there's something intrinsically wrong with fat. For example, there isn't a single fat saint – except, of course, old Thomas Aquinas; and I cannot see any reason to suppose that he was a real saint, a saint in the popular sense of the word, which happens to be the true sense. If Thomas is a saint, then Vincent de Paul isn't. And if Vincent's a saint, which he obviously is, then Thomas isn't. And perhaps that enormous belly of his had something to do with it. Who knows? But anyhow, that's by the way. We're talking about Jo Stoyte. And poor Jo, as I say, was a fat-boy and, being fat, was fair game for the rest of us. God, how we punished him for his glandular deficiencies! And how disastrously he reacted to that punishment! Over-compensation. . . . But here I am at home,' he added, looking out of the window as the car slackened speed and came to a halt in front of a small white bungalow set in the midst of a clump of eucalyptus trees. 'We'll go on with this another time. But remember, if poor Jo gets too offensive, think of what he was at school and be sorry for him – and don't be sorry for yourself.' He got out of the car, closed the door behind him and, waving a hand to the chauffeur, walked quickly up the path and entered the little house.

The car rolled on again. At once bewildered and reassured by his encounter with the author of the *Short Studies*, Jeremy sat inertly looking out of the window. They were very near the Object now; and suddenly he noticed, for the first time, that the castle hill was surrounded by a moat. Some few hundred yards from the water's edge, the car passed between two pillars, topped by heraldic lions. Its passage, it was evident, interrupted a beam of invisible light directed on a photo-electric cell; for no sooner were they past the lions than a drawbridge began to descend. Five seconds before they reached the moat, it was in place; the car rolled smoothly across and came to a halt in front of the main gateway of the castle's outer walls. The chauffeur got out and, speaking into a tele-phone-receiver concealed in a convenient loophole, announced his presence. The chromium-plated portcullis rose noiselessly, the double doors of stainless steel swung back. They drove in. The car began to climb. The second line of walls was pierced by another gate, which opened automatically as they approached. Between the inner side of this second wall and the slope of the hill a ferro-concrete bridge had been constructed, large enough to accommodate a tennis-court. In the shadowy space beneath, Jeremy caught sight of something familiar. An instant later he had recognized it as a replica of the grotto of Lourdes.

'Miss Maunciple, she's a Catholic,' remarked the chauffeur, jerking his thumb in the direction of the grotto. 'That's why he had it made for her. We's Presbyterians in *our* family,' he added.

'And who is Miss Maunciple?'

The chauffeur hesitated for a moment. 'Well, she's a young lady Mr Stoyte's kind of friendly with,' he explained at last; then changed the subject.

The car climbed on. Beyond the grotto all the hill-side was a cactus garden. Then the road swung round to the northern slope of the bluff, and the cactuses gave place to grass and shrubs. On a little terrace, over-elegant like a fashion-plate from some mythological *Vogue* for goddesses, a bronze nymph by Giambologna spouted two streams of water from her deliciously polished breasts. A little farther on, behind wire netting, a group of baboons squatted among the rocks or paraded the obscenity of their hairless rumps.

Still climbing, the car turned again and finally drew up on a circular concrete platform, carried out on cantilevers over a precipice. Once more the old-fashioned retainer, the chauffeur taking off his cap, did a final impersonation of himself welcoming the young master home to the plantation, then set to work to unload the luggage.

Jeremy Pordage walked to the balustrade and looked over. The ground fell almost sheer for about a hundred feet, then sloped steeply to the inner circle of walls and, below them, to the outer fortifications. Beyond lay the moat, and on the farther side of the moat stretched the orange orchards. '*Im dunklen Laub die goldn' Orangen glühen,*' he murmured to himself; and then: 'He hangs in shades the orange bright. Like golden lamps in a green night.' Marvell's rendering, he decided, was better than Goethe's. And, meanwhile, the oranges seemed to have become brighter and more significant. For Jeremy, direct, unmediated experience was always hard to take in, always more or less disquieting. Life became safe, things assumed meaning, only when they had been translated into words and confined between the covers of a book. The oranges were beautifully pigeon-holed; but what about the castle? He turned round and, leaning back against the parapet, looked up. The Object impended, insolently enormous. Nobody had dealt poetically with *that*. Not Childe Roland, not the King of Thule, not Marmion, not the Lady of Shalott, not Sir Leoline. Sir Leoline, he repeated to himself with a connoisseur's appreciation of romantic absurdity, Sir Leoline, the baron rich who had – what? A toothless mastiff bitch. But Mr Stoyte had baboons and a sacred grotto, Mr Stoyte had a chromium portcullis and the Hauberk Papers, Mr Stoyte had a cemetery like an amusement park and a donjon like . . .

There was a sudden rumbling sound; the great nail-studded doors of the Early English entrance porch rolled back, and from between them, as though propelled by a hurricane, a small, thick-set man, with a red face and a mass of snow-white hair, darted out on to the terrace and bore down upon Jeremy. His expression, as he advanced, did not change. The face wore that shut, unsmiling mask which American workmen tend to put on in their dealing with strangers – in order to prove, by not making the ingratiating grimaces of courtesy, that theirs is a free country and you're not going to come it over *them*.

Not having been brought up in a free country, Jeremy had automatically begun to smile as this person, whom he guessed to be his host and employer, came hurrying towards him. Confronted by the unwavering grimness of the other's face, he suddenly became conscious of this smile – conscious that it was out of place, that it must be making him look a fool. Profoundly embarrassed, he tried to readjust his face.

'Mr Pordage?' said the stranger in a harsh, barking voice. 'Pleased to meet you. My name's Stoyte.' As they shook hands, he peered, still unsmiling, into Jeremy's face. 'You're older than I thought,' he added.

For the second time that morning Jeremy made his mannequin's gesture of apologetic self-exhibition.

'The sere and withered leaf,' he said. 'One's sinking into senility. One's . . .'

Mr Stoyte cut him short. 'What's your age?' he asked in a loud peremptory tone, like that of a police sergeant interrogating a captured thief.

'Fifty-four.'

'Only fifty-four?' Mr Stoyte shook his head. 'Ought to be full of pep at fifty-four. How's your sex-life?' he added disconcertingly.

Jeremy tried to laugh off his embarrassment. He twinkled; he patted his bald head. '*Mon beau printemps et mon été ont fait le sault par la fenêtre*,' he quoted.

'What's that?' said Mr Stoyte, frowning. 'No use talking foreign languages to me. I never had any education.' He broke into sudden braying of laughter. 'I'm head of an oil-company here,' he said. 'Got two thousand filling-stations in California alone. And not one man in any of those filling-stations that isn't a college graduate!' He brayed again, triumphantly. 'Go and talk foreign languages to *them*.' He was silent for a moment; then, pursuing an unexplicit association of ideas, 'My agent in London,' he went on, 'the man who picks up things for me there – he gave me your name. Told me you were the right man for those – what do you call them? You know, those papers I bought this summer. Roebuck? Hobuck?'

'Hauberk,' said Jeremy, and with a gloomy satisfaction noted that he had been quite right. The man had never read one's books, never even heard of one's existence. Still, one had to remember that he had been called Jelly-Belly when he was young.

'Hauberk,' Mr Stoyte repeated with a contemptuous impatience. 'Anyhow, he said you were the man.' Then, without pause or transition, 'What was it you were saying, about your sex-life, when you started that foreign stuff on me?'

Jeremy laughed uncomfortably. 'One was implying that it was normal for one's age.'

'What do *you* know about what's normal at your age?' said Mr Stoyte. 'Go and talk to Dr Obispo about it. It won't cost you anything. Obispo's on salary. He's the house physician.' Abruptly changing the subject, 'Would you like to see the castle?' he asked. 'I'll take you round.'

'Oh, that's very kind of you,' said Jeremy effusively. And, for the sake of making a little polite conversation, he added: 'I've already seen your burial-ground.'

'Seen my burial-ground?' Mr Stoyte repeated in a tone of suspicion: suspicion turned suddenly to anger. 'What the hell do you mean?' he shouted.

Quailing before his fury, Jeremy stammered something about the Beverly Pantheon and that he had understood from the chauffeur that Mr Stoyte had a financial interest in the company.

'I see,' said the other, somewhat mollified, but still frowning. 'I thought you meant . . .' Stoyte broke off in the middle of the sentence, leaving the bewildered Jeremy to guess what he had thought. 'Come on,' he barked; and, bursting into movement, he hurried towards the entrance to the house.

Chapter Three

THERE was silence in Ward Sixteen of the Stoyte Home for Sick Children; silence and the luminous twilight of drawn venetian blinds. It was the mid-morning rest period. Three of the five small convalescents were asleep. A fourth lay staring at the ceiling, pensively picking his nose. The fifth, a little girl, was whispering to a doll as curly and Aryan as herself. Seated by one of the windows, a young nurse was absorbed in the latest issue of *True Confessions*.

'His heart gave a lurch,' she read. 'With a strangled cry he pressed me closer. For months we'd been fighting against just this; but the magnet of our passion was too strong for us. The clamorous pressure of his lips had struck an answering spark within my melting body.

' "Germaine," he whispered. "Don't make me wait. Won't you be good to me now, darling?"

'He was so gentle, but so ruthless too – as a girl in love wants a man to be ruthless. I felt myself swept away by the rising tide of . . .'

There was a noise outside in the corridor. The door of the ward flew open, as though before the blast of a hurricane, and someone came rushing into the room.

The nurse looked up with a start of surprise which the completeness of her absorption in 'The Price of a Thrill' rendered positively agonizing. Her almost immediate reaction to the shock was one of anger.

'What's the idea?' she began indignantly; then she recognized the intruder and her expression changed. 'Why, Mr Stoyte!'

Disturbed by the noise, the young nose-picker dropped his eyes from the ceiling, the little girl turned away from her doll.

'Uncle Jo!' they shouted simultaneously. 'Uncle Jo!'

Starting out of sleep, the others took up the cry.

'Uncle Jo! Uncle Jo!'

Mr Stoyte was touched by the warmth of his reception. The face which Jeremy had found so disquietingly grim relaxed into a smile. In mock protest he covered his ears with his hands. 'You'll make me deaf,' he cried. Then, in an aside to the nurse, 'Poor kids!' he murmured. 'Makes me feel I'd kind of like to cry.' His voice became husky with sentiment. 'And when one thinks how sick they've been . . .' He shook his head, leaving the sentence unfinished; then, in another tone, 'By the way,' he added, waving a large square hand in the direction of Jeremy Pordage, who had followed him into the ward and was standing near the door, wearing an expression of bewildered embarrassment, 'this is Mr . . . Mr . . . Hell! I've forgotten your name.'

'Pordage,' said Jeremy, and reminded himself that Mr Stoyte's name had once been Slob.

'Pordage, that's it. Ask him about history and literature,' he added derisively to the nurse. 'He knows it all.'

Jeremy was modestly protesting that his period was only from the invention of Ossian to the death of Keats, when Mr Stoyte turned back to the children and in a voice that drowned the other's faintly fluted disclaimers, shouted: 'Guess what Uncle Jo's brought you!'

They guessed. Candies, bubble gum, balloons, guinea-pigs. Mr Stoyte continued triumphantly to shake his head. Finally, when the children had exhausted their power of imagination, he dipped into the pocket of his old tweed jacket and produced, first a whistle, then a mouth-organ, then a small musical box, then a trumpet, then a wooden rattle, then an automatic pistol. This, however, he hastily put back.

'Now play,' he said, when he had distributed the instruments. 'All together. One, two, three.' And, beating time with both arms, he began to sing, 'Way down upon the Swanee River.'

At this latest in a long series of shocks and surprises, Jeremy's mild face took on an expression of intenser bewilderment.

What a morning! The arrival at dawn. The Negro retainer. The interminable suburb. The Beverly Pantheon. The Object among the orange trees, and his meeting with William Propter and this really dreadful Stoyte. Then, inside the castle, the Rubens and the great El Greco in the hall, the Vermeer in the elevator, the Rembrandt etchings along the corridors, the Winterhalter in the butler's pantry.

Then Miss Maunciple's Louis XV boudoir, with the Watteau and the two Lancrets and the fully equipped soda-fountain in a rococo embrasure, and Miss Maunciple herself, in an orange kimono, drinking a raspberry and peppermint ice-cream soda at her own counter. He had been introduced, had refused the offer of a sundae and been hurried on again, always at top speed, always as though on the wings of a tornado, to see the other sights of the castle. The Rumpus Room, for example, with frescoes of elephants by Sert. The library, with its woodwork by Grinling Gibbons, but with no books, because Mr Stoyte had not yet brought himself to buy any. The small dining-room, with its Fra Angelico and its furniture from Brighton Pavilion. The large dining-room, modelled on the interior of the mosque at Fatehpur Sikri. The ballroom, with its mirrors and coffered ceiling. The thirteenth-century stained-glass in the eleventh-floor W.C. The morning-room, with Boucher's picture of 'La Petite Morphil' bottom upwards on a pink satin sofa. The chapel, imported in fragments from Goa, with the walnut confessional used by St François de Sales at Annecy. The functional billiard-room. The indoor swimming-pool. The Second Empire bar, with its nudes by Ingres. The two gymnasiums. The Christian Science Reading Room, dedicated to the memory of the late Mrs Stoyte. The dentist's office. The Turkish bath. Then down, with Vermeer, into the bowels of the hill, to look at the cellar in which the Hauberk Papers had been stored. Down again yet deeper, to the safe-deposit vaults, the power-house, the air-conditioning plant, the well and pumping-station. Then up once more to ground level and the kitchens, where the Chinese chef had shown Mr Stoyte the newly arrived consignment of turtles from the Caribbean. Up again to the fourteenth, to the bedroom which Jeremy was to occupy during his stay. Then up another six stories to the business office, where Mr Stoyte gave orders to his secretary, dictated a couple of letters and had a long telephone conversation with his brokers in Amsterdam. And when that was finished, it had been time to go to the hospital.

Meanwhile, in Ward Sixteen, a group of nurses had collected and were watching Uncle Jo, his white hair flying like Stokowski's, frantically spurring his orchestra to yet louder crescendos of cacophony.

'He's like a great big kid himself,' said one of them in a tone of almost tender amusement.

Another, evidently with literary leanings, declared that it was like something in Dickens. 'Don't you think so?' she insisted to Jeremy.

He smiled nervously and nodded a vague and non-committal assent.

More practical, a third wished she had her Kodak with her. 'Candid Camera portrait of the President of Consol Oil, California Land and Minerals Corporation. Bank of the Pacific, West Coast Cemeteries, etc., etc. . . .' She reeled off the names of Mr Stoyte's chief companies, mock-heroically, indeed, but with admiring gusto, as a convinced legitimist with a sense of humour might enumerate the titles of a grandee of Spain. 'The papers would pay you good money for a snap like that,' she insisted. And to prove that what she was saying was true, she went on to explain that she had a boy friend who worked with an advertising firm, so that he ought to know, and only the week before he had told her that . . .

Mr Stoyte's knobbed face, as he left the hospital, was still illuminated with benevolence and happiness.

'Makes you feel kind of good, playing with those poor kids,' he kept repeating to Jeremy.

A wide flight of steps led down from the hospital entrance to the roadway. At the foot of these steps Mr Stoyte's blue Cadillac was waiting. Behind it stood another, smaller car which had not been there when they arrived. A look of suspicion clouded Mr Stoyte's beaming face as he caught sight of it. Kidnappers, blackmailers – one never knew. His hand went to the pocket of his coat. 'Who's there?' he shouted in a tone of such loud fury that Jeremy thought for a moment that the man must have suddenly gone mad.

Moon-like, a large, snub-featured face appeared at the car window, smiling round the chewed butt of a cigar.

'Oh, it's you, Clancy,' said Mr Stoyte. 'Why didn't they tell me you were here?' he went on. His face had flushed darkly; he was frowning and a muscle in his cheek had begun to twitch. 'I don't like having strange cars around. Do you hear, Peters?' he almost screamed at his chauffeur – not because it was the man's business, of course; simply because he happened to be there, available. 'Do you hear, I say?' Then, suddenly, he remembered what Dr Obispo had said to him that time he had lost his temper with the fellow. 'Do you really *want* to shorten your life, Mr Stoyte?' The doctor's tone had been one of cool amusement; he had smiled with an expression of politely sarcastic indulgence. 'Are you absolutely *bent* on having a stroke? A second stroke, remember; and you won't get off so lightly next time. Well, if so, then go on behaving as you're doing now. Go on.' With an enormous effort of will, Mr Stoyte swallowed his anger. 'God is love,' he said to himself. 'There is no death.' The late Prudence McGladdery Stoyte had been a Christian Scientist. 'God is love,' he said again, and reflected that if people would only stop being so exasperating he would never have to lose his temper. 'God is love.' It was all their fault.

Clancy, meanwhile, had left his car and, grotesquely pot-bellied over spindly legs, was coming up the steps, mysteriously smiling and winking as he approached.

'What is it?' Mr Stoyte inquired, and wished to God the man wouldn't make those faces. 'Oh, by the way,' he added, 'this is Mr . . . Mr . . .'

'Pordage,' said Jeremy.

Clancy was pleased to meet him. The hand he gave to Jeremy was disagreeably sweaty.

'I got some news for you,' said Clancy in a hoarse conspiratorial whisper; and, speaking behind his hand, so that his words and the smell of cigar should be for Mr Stoyte alone, 'You remember Tittelbaum?' he added.

'That chap in the City Engineer's Department?'

Clancy nodded. 'One of the boys,' he affirmed enigmatically and again winked.

'Well, what about him?' asked Mr Stoyte; and in spite of God's being love, there was a note in his voice of renascent exasperation.

Clancy shot a glance at Jeremy Pordage; then, with the elaborate by-play of Guy Fawkes talking to Catesby on the stage of a provincial theatre, he took Mr Stoyte by the arm and led him a few feet away, up the steps. 'Do you know what Tittelbaum told me today?' he asked rhetorically.

'How the devil should I know?' (But no, God is love. There is no death.)

Undeterred by the signs of Mr Stoyte's irritation, Clancy went on with his performance. 'He told me what they've decided about . . .' – he lowered his voice still further – 'about the San Felipe Valley.'

'Well, what *have* they decided?' Once more Mr Stoyte was at the limits of his patience.

Before answering, Clancy removed the cigar-butt from his mouth, threw it away, produced another cigar out of his waistcoat pocket, tore off the cellophane wrapping and stuck it, unlighted, in the place occupied by the old one.

'They've decided,' he said very slowly, so as to give each word its full dramatic effect, 'they've decided to pipe the water into it.'

Mr Stoyte's expression of exasperation gave place at last to one of interest. 'Enough to irrigate the whole valley?' he asked.

'Enough to irrigate the whole valley,' Clancy repeated with solemnity.

Mr Stoyte was silent for a moment. 'How much time have we got?' he asked at last.

'Tittelbaum thought the news wouldn't break for another six weeks.'

'Six weeks?' Mr Stoyte hesitated for a moment, then made his decision. 'All right. Get busy at once,' he said with the peremptory manners of one accustomed to command. 'Go down yourself and take a few of the other boys along with you. Independent purchasers – interested in cattle-raising; want to start a Dude Ranch. Buy all you can. What's the price, by the way?'

'Averages twelve dollars an acre.'

'Twelve,' Mr Stoyte repeated, and reflected that it would go to a hundred as soon as they started laying the pipe. 'How many acres do you figure you can get?' he asked.

'Maybe thirty thousand.'

Mr Stoyte's face beamed with satisfaction. 'Good,' he said briskly. 'Very good. No mention of my name, of course,' he added, and then, without pause or transition: 'What's Tittelbaum going to cost?'

Clancy smiled contemptuously. 'Oh, I'll give him four or five hundred bucks.'

'That all?'

The other nodded. 'Tittelbaum's in the bargain basement,' he said. 'Can't afford to ask any fancy prices. He needs the money – needs it awful bad.'

'What for?' asked Mr Stoyte, who had a professional interest in human nature. 'Gambling? Women?'

Clancy shook his head. 'Doctors,' he explained. 'He's got a kid that's paralysed.'

'Paralysed?' Mr Stoyte echoed in a tone of genuine sympathy. 'That's too bad.' He hesitated for a moment; then, in a sudden burst of generosity, 'Tell him to send the kid here,' he went on, making a large gesture towards the hospital. 'Best place in the State for infantile paralysis, and it won't cost him anything. Not a red cent.'

'Hell, that's kind of you, Mr Stoyte,' said Clancy admiringly. 'That's real kind.'

'Oh, it's nothing,' said Mr Stoyte, as he moved towards his car. 'I'm glad to be able to do it. Remember what it says in the Bible about children. You know,' he added, 'I get a real kick out of being with those poor kids in there. Makes you feel kind of warm inside.' He patted the barrel of his chest. 'Tell Tittelbaum to send in an application for the kid. Send it to me personally. I'll see that it goes through at once.' He climbed into the car and shut the door after him; then, catching sight of Jeremy, opened it again without a word. Mumbling apologetically, Jeremy scrambled in. Mr Stoyte slammed the door once more, lowered the glass and looked out. 'So long,' he said. 'And don't lose any time about that San Felipe business. Make a good job of it, Clancy, and I'll let you have ten per cent of all the acreage over twenty thousand.' He raised the window and signalled to the chauffeur to start. The car swung out of the drive and headed towards the castle. Leaning back in his seat, Mr Stoyte thought of those poor kids and the money he would make out of the San Felipe business. 'God is love,' he said yet once more, with momentary conviction and in a whisper that was audible to his companion. 'God is love.' Jeremy felt more uncomfortable than ever.

The drawbridge came down as the blue Cadillac approached, the chromium portcullis went up, the gates of the inner rampart rolled back to let it pass. On the concrete tennis-court the seven children of the Chinese cook were roller-skating. Below, in the sacred grotto, a group of masons were at work. At the sight of them, Mr Stoyte shouted to the chauffeur to stop.

'They're putting up a tomb for some nuns,' he said to Jeremy as they got out of the car.

'Some nuns?' Jeremy echoed in surprise.

Mr Stoyte nodded, and explained that his Spanish agents had bought some sculpture and iron-work from the chapel of a convent that had been wrecked by the anarchists at the beginning of the civil war. 'They sent some nuns along too,' he added. 'Embalmed, I guess. Or maybe just sun-dried: I don't know. Anyhow, there they are. Luckily I happened to have something nice to put them in.' He pointed to the monument which the masons were in process of fixing to the south wall of the grotto. On a marble shelf above a large Roman sarcophagus were the statues by some nameless Jacobean stonemason of a gentleman and lady, both in ruffs, kneeling, and behind them, in three rows of three, nine daughters diminishing from adolescence to infancy. '*Hic jacet Carolus Franciscus Beals, Armiger . . .*' Jeremy began to read.

'Bought it in England, two years ago,' said Mr Stoyte, interrupting him. Then, turning to the workmen, 'When will you boys be through?' he asked.

'Tomorrow noon. Maybe tonight.'

'That's all I wanted to know,' said Mr Stoyte, and turned away. 'I must have those nuns taken out of storage,' he said, as they walked back to the car.

They drove on. Poised on the almost invisible vibration of its wings, a humming-bird was drinking at the jet that spouted from the left nipple of Giambologna's nymph. From the enclosure of the baboons came the shrill noise of battle and copulation. Mr Stoyte shut his eyes. 'God is love,' he repeated, trying deliberately to prolong the delightful condition of euphoria into which those poor kids and Clancy's good news had plunged him. 'God is love. There is no death.' He waited to feel that sense of inward warmth, like the after-effect of whisky, which had followed his previous utterance of the words. Instead, as though some immanent fiend were playing a practical joke on him, he found himself thinking of the shrunken leathery corpses of those nuns, and of his own corpse, and of judgement and the flames. Prudence McGladdery Stoyte had been a Christian Scientist; but Joseph Budge Stoyte, his father, had been a Sandemanian; and Letitia Morgan, his maternal grandmother, had lived and died a Plymouth Sister. Over his cot in the attic room of the little framehouse in Nashville, Tennessee, had hung the text, in vivid orange on a black background: 'IT IS A TERRIBLE THING TO FALL INTO THE HANDS OF THE LIVING GOD.' 'God is love,' Mr Stoyte desperately reaffirmed. 'There is no death.' But for sinners, such as himself, it was only the worm that never died.

'If you're always scared of dying,' Obispo had said, 'you'll surely die. Fear's a poison; and not such a slow poison either.'

Making another enormous effort, Mr Stoyte suddenly began to whistle. The tune was, 'I'm making hay in the moonlight in my Baby's arms', but the face which Jeremy Pordage saw and, as though from some horrible and indecent secret, immediately averted his eyes from, was the face of a man in a condemned cell.

'Old sour-puss,' the chauffeur muttered to himself as he watched his employer get out of the car and walk away.

Followed by Jeremy, Mr Stoyte hurried in silence through the Gothic portal, crossed a pillared Romanesque lobby like the Lady Chapel at Durham, and, his hat still pulled down over his eyes, stepped into the cathedral twilight of the great hall.

A hundred feet overhead, the sound of the two men's footsteps echoed in the vaulting. Like iron ghosts, the suits of armour stood immobile round the walls. Above them, sumptuously dim, the fifteenth-century tapestries opened windows upon a leafy world of phantasy. At one end of the cavernous room, lit by a hidden searchlight El Greco's 'Crucifixion of St Peter' blazed out in the darkness like the beautiful revelation of something incomprehensible and profoundly sinister. At the other, no less brilliantly illuminated, hung a full-length portrait of Hélène Fourment, dressed only in a bearskin cape. Jeremy looked from one to the other – from the ectoplasm of the inverted saint to the unequivocal skin and fat and muscle which Rubens had so loved to see and touch; from unearthly flesh-tints of green-white ochre and carmine, shadowed with transparent black, to the creams and warm pinks, the nacreous blues and greens of Flemish nudity. Two shining symbols, incomparably powerful and expressive – but of what, of what? That, of course, was the question.

Mr Stoyte paid attention to none of his treasures, but strode across the hall, inwardly cursing his buried wife for having made him think about death by insisting that there wasn't any.

The door of the elevator was in an embrasure between pillars. Mr Stoyte opened it, and the light came on, revealing a Dutch lady in blue satin sitting at a harpsichord – sitting, Jeremy reflected, at the very heart of an equation, in a world where beauty and logic, painting and analytical geometry, had become one. With what intention? To express, symbolically, what truths about the nature of things? Again, that was the question. Where art was concerned, Jeremy said to himself, that was always the question.

'Shut the door,' Mr Stoyte ordered; then when it was done, 'We'll have a swim before lunch,' he added, and pressed the top-most of a long row of buttons.

Chapter Four

MORE than a dozen families of transients were already at work in the orange grove, as the man from Kansas, with his wife and his three children and his yellow dog, hurried down the line towards the trees which the overseer had assigned to him. They walked in silence, for they had nothing to say to one another and no energy to waste on words.

Only half a day, the man was thinking; only four hours till work would be stopped. They'd be lucky if they made as much as seventy-five cents. Seventy-five cents. Seventy-five cents; and that right front tyre wasn't going to last much longer. If they meant to get up to Fresno and then Salinas, they'd just have to get a better one. But even the rottenest old second-hand tyre cost money. And money was food. And did they eat! he thought with sudden resentment. If he were alone, if he didn't have to drag the kids and Minnie around, then he could rent a little place somewhere. Near the highway, so that he could make a bit extra by selling eggs and fruit and things to the people that rode past in their automobiles, sell a lot cheaper than the markets and still make good money. And then, maybe, he'd be able to buy a cow and a couple of hogs; and then he'd find a girl – one of those fat ones, he liked them rather fat: fat and young with . . .

His wife started coughing again; the dream was shattered. Did they eat! More than they were worth. Three kids with no strength in them. And Minnie going sick on you half the time so that you had to do her work as well as yours!

The dog had paused to sniff at a post. With sudden and surprising agility the man from Kansas took two quick steps forward and kicked the animal squarely in the ribs. 'You goddam dog!' he shouted. 'Get out of the way!' It ran off, yelping. The man from Kansas turned his head in the hope of catching in his children's faces an expression of disapproval or commiseration. But the children had learnt better than to give him an excuse for going on from the dog to themselves. Under the tousled hair, the three pale, small faces were entirely blank and vacant. Disappointed, the man turned away, grumbling indistinctly that he'd belt the hell out of them if they weren't careful. The mother did not even turn her head. She was feeling too sick and tired to do anything but walk straight on. Silence settled down again over the party.

Then, suddenly, the youngest of the three children let out a shrill cry. 'Look there!' She pointed. In front of them was the castle. From the summit of its highest tower rose a spidery metal structure, carrying a succession of platforms to a height of twenty or thirty feet above the parapet. On the highest of these platforms, black against the shining sky, stood a tiny human figure. As they looked, the figure spread its arms and plunged head foremost out of sight behind the battlements. The children's shrill outcry of astonishment gave the man from Kansas the pretext which, a moment before, they had denied him. He turned on them furiously. 'Stop that yellin',' he yelled; then rushed at them, hitting out – a slap on the side of the head for each of them. With an enormous effort, the woman lifted herself from the abyss of fatigue into which she had fallen; she halted, she turned, she cried out protestingly, she caught her husband's arm. He pushed her away, so violently that she almost fell.

'You're as bad as the kids,' he shouted at her. 'Just layin' around and eatin'. Not worth a damn. I tell you, I'm just sick and tired of the whole lot of you. Sick and tired,' he repeated. 'So you keep your mouth shut, see!' He turned away and, feeling a good deal better for his outburst, walked briskly on, at a rate which he knew his wife would find exhausting, between the rows of loaded orange trees.

From that swimming-pool at the top of the donjon the view was prodigious. Floating on the translucent water, one had only to turn one's head to see, between the battlements, successive vistas of plain and mountain, of green and tawny and violet and faint blue. One floated, one looked, and one thought, that is, if one were Jeremy Pordage, of that tower in *Epipsychidion*, that tower with its chambers

> Looking towards the golden Eastern air
> And level with the living winds.

Not so, however, if one were Miss Virginia Maunciple. Virginia neither floated, nor looked, nor thought of *Epipsychidion*, but took another sip of whisky and soda, climbed to the highest platform of the diving-tower, spread her arms, plunged, glided under water and, coming up immediately beneath the unsuspecting Pordage, caught him by the belt of his bathing-pants and pulled him under.

'You asked for it,' she said, as he came up again, gasping and spluttering, to the surface, 'lying there without moving, like a silly old Buddha.' She smiled at him with an entirely good-natured contempt.

These people that Uncle Jo kept bringing to the castle. An Englishman with a monocle to look at the armour; a man with a stammer to clean the pictures; a man who couldn't speak anything but German to look at some silly old pots and plates; and today this other ridiculous Englishman with a face like a rabbit's and a voice like Songs without Words on the saxophone.

Jeremy Pordage blinked the water out of his eyes and, dimly, since he was presbyopic and without his spectacles, saw the young laughing face very close to his own, the body foreshortened and wavering uncertainly through the water. It was not often that he found himself in such proximity to such a being. He swallowed his annoyance and smiled at her.

Miss Maunciple stretched out a hand and patted the bald patch at the top of Jeremy's head. 'Boy,' she said, 'does it shine. Talk of billiard-balls. I know what I shall call you: Ivory. Good-bye, Ivory.' She turned, swam to the ladder, climbed out, walked to the table on which the bottles and glasses were standing, drank the rest of her whisky and soda, then went and sat down on the edge of the couch on which, in black spectacles and bathing-drawers, Mr Stoyte was taking his sun-bath.

'Well, Uncle Jo,' she said in a tone of affectionate playfulness, 'feeling kind of good?'

'Feeling fine, Baby,' he answered. It was true; the sun had melted away his dismal forebodings; he was living again in the present, that delightful present in which one brought happiness to sick children; in which there were Tittelbaums prepared, for five hundred bucks, to give one information worth at the very least a million; in which the sky was blue and the sunshine a caressing warmth upon the stomach; in which, finally, one stirred out of a delicious somnolence to see little Virginia smiling down at one as though she really cared for her old Uncle Jo, and cared for him, what was more, not merely as an old uncle – no, *sir*; because, when all's said and done, a man is only as old as he feels and acts; and where his Baby was concerned did he feel young? did he *act* young? Yes, *sir*. Mr Stoyte smiled to himself, a smile of triumphant self-satisfaction.

'Well, Baby,' he said aloud, and laid a square-thick-fingered hand on the young lady's bare knee.

Through half-closed eyelids Miss Maunciple gave him a secret and somehow indecent look of understanding and complicity; then uttered a little laugh and stretched her arms. 'Doesn't the sun feel good!' she said; and, closing her lids completely, she lowered her raised arms, clasped her hands behind her neck, and threw back her shoulders. It was a pose that lifted the breasts, that emphasized the inward curve of the loins and the contrary swell of the buttocks – the sort of pose that a new arrival in the seraglio would be taught by the eunuchs to assume at her first interview with the Sultan; the very pose, Jeremy recognized, as he had chanced to look her way, of that quite particularly unsuitable statue on the third floor of the Beverly Pantheon.

Through his dark glasses, Mr Stoyte looked up at her with an expression of possessiveness at once gluttonous and paternal. Virginia was his baby, not only figuratively and colloquially, but also in the literal sense of the word. His sentiments were simultaneously those of the purest father-love and the most violent eroticism.

He looked up at her. By contrast with the shiny white satin of her beach clout and brassière the sunburnt skin seemed more richly brown. The planes of the young body flowed in smooth continuous curves, effortlessly solid, three-dimensional, without accent or abrupt transition. Mr Stoyte's regards travelled up to the auburn hair and came down by way of the rounded forehead, of the wide-set eyes, and small, straight, impudent nose, to the mouth. That mouth – it was her most striking feature. For it was to the mouth's short upper lip that Virginia's face owed its characteristic expression of childlike innocence – an expression that persisted through all her moods, that was noticeable whatever she might be doing, whether it was telling smutty stories or making conversation with the Bishop, taking tea in Pasadena or getting tight with the boys, enjoying what she called 'a bit of yum-yum' or attending Mass. Chronologically, Miss Maunciple was a young woman of twenty-two; but that abbreviated upper lip gave her, in all circumstances, an air of being hardly adolescent, of not having reached the age of consent. For Mr Stoyte, at sixty, the curiously perverse contrast between childishness and maturity, between the appearance of innocence and the fact of experience, was intoxicatingly attractive. It was not only so far as he was concerned that Virginia was both kinds of a baby; she was also both kinds of baby objectively, in herself.

Delicious creature! The hand that had lain inert, hitherto, upon her knee slowly contracted. Between the broad spatulate thumb and the strong fingers, what smoothness, what a sumptuous and substantial resilience!

'Jinny,' he said. 'My Baby!'

The Baby opened her large blue eyes and dropped her arms to her sides. The tense back relaxed, the lifted breasts moved downwards and forwards like soft living creatures sinking to repose. She smiled at him.

'What are you pinching me for, Uncle Jo?'

'I'd like to eat you,' her Uncle Jo replied in a tone of cannibalistic sentimentality.

'I'm tough.'

Mr Stoyte uttered a maudlin chuckle. 'Little tough kid!' he said. The tough kid stooped down and kissed him.

Jeremy Pordage, who had been quietly looking at the panorama and continuing his silent recitation of *Epipsychidion*, happened at this moment to turn once more in the direction of the couch, and was so much embarrassed by what he saw that he began to sink and had to strike out violently with arms and legs to prevent himself from going under. Turning round in the water, he swam to the ladder, climbed out and, without waiting to dry himself, hurried to the elevator.

'Really!' he said to himself as he looked at the Vermeer. '*Really!*'

'I did some business this morning,' said Mr Stoyte when the Baby had straightened herself up again.

'What sort of business?'

42

'Good business,' he answered. 'Might make a lot of money. *Real* money,' he insisted.

'How much?'

'Maybe half a million,' he said cautiously, understating his hopes; 'maybe a million; maybe even more.'

'Uncle Jo,' she said, 'I think you're wonderful.' Her voice had the ring of complete sincerity. She genuinely did think him wonderful. In the world in which she had lived it was axiomatic that a man who could make a million dollars must be wonderful. Parents, friends, teachers, newspapers, radio, advertisements – explicitly or by implication, all were unanimous in proclaiming his wonderfulness. And besides, Virginia was very fond of her Uncle Jo. He had given her a wonderful time, and she was grateful. Besides, she liked to like people if she possibly could; she liked to please them. Pleasing them made her feel good – even when they were elderly, like Uncle Jo, and when some of the ways in which she was called upon to please them didn't happen to be very appetizing. 'I think you're wonderful,' she repeated.

Her admiration gave him an intense satisfaction. 'Oh, it's quite easy,' he said with hypocritical modesty, angling for more.

Virginia gave it him. 'Easy, nothing!' she said firmly. 'I say you *are* wonderful. So just keep your mouth shut.'

Enchanted, Mr Stoyte took another handful of firm flesh and squeezed it affectionately. 'I'll give you a present, if the deal goes through,' he said. 'What would you like, Baby?'

'What would I like?' she repeated. 'But I don't want anything.'

Her disinterestedness was not assumed. For it was true; she never did want things this way, in cold blood. At the moment a want occurred, for an ice-cream soda, for example, for a bit of yum-yum, for a mink coat seen in a shop-window – at such moments she did want things, and wanted them badly, couldn't wait to have them. But as for long-range wants, wants that had to be thought about in advance – no, she never had wanted like that. The best part of Virginia's life was spent in enjoying the successive instants of present contentment of which it was composed; and if ever circumstances forced her out of this mindless eternity into the world of time, it was a narrow little universe in which she found herself, a world whose farthest boundaries were never more than a week or two away in the future. Even as a show-girl, at eighteen dollars a week, she had found it difficult to bother much about money and security and what would happen if you had an accident and couldn't show your legs any more. Then Uncle Jo had come along, and everything was there, as though it grew on trees – a swimming pool tree, a cocktail tree, a Schiaparelli tree. You just had to reach out your hand and there it was, like an apple in the orchard back home in Oregon. So where did presents come in? Why should she want anything? Besides, it was obvious that Uncle Jo got a tremendous kick out of her not wanting things; and to be able to give Uncle Jo a kick always made her feel good. 'I tell you, Uncle Jo, I don't want *anything*.'

'Don't you?' said a strange voice, startlingly close behind them. 'Well, I do.'

Dark-haired and dapper, glossily Levantine, Dr Sigmund Obispo stepped briskly up to the side of the couch.

'To be precise,' he went on, 'I want to inject one-point-five cubic centimetres of testosterones into the great man's *gluteus medius*. So off you go, my angel,' he said to Virginia in a tone of derision, but with a smile of unabashed desire. 'Hop!' He gave her a familiar little pat on the shoulder, and another, when she got up to make room for him, on the white satin posterior.

Virginia turned round sharply, with the intention of telling him not to be fresh; then, as her glance travelled from that barrel of hairy flesh which was Mr Stoyte to the other's handsome face, so insultingly sarcastic and at the same time so flatteringly concupiscent, she changed her mind and, instead of telling him, loudly, just where he got off, she made a grimace and stuck out her tongue at him. What was begun as a rebuke had ended, before she knew it, as the acquiescence in an impertinence, as an act of complicity with the offender and of disloyalty to Uncle Jo. Poor Uncle Jo! she thought, with a rush of affectionate pity for the old gentleman. For a moment she felt quite ashamed of herself. The trouble, of course, was that Dr Obispo was so handsome; that he made her laugh; that she liked his admiration; that it was fun to lead him on and see how he'd act. She even enjoyed getting mad at him, when he was rude, which he constantly was.

'I suppose you think you're Douglas Fairbanks Junior,' she said, making an attempt to be scathing; then walked away with as much dignity as her two little strips of white satin would permit her to assume and, leaning against a battlement, looked down at the plain below. Ant-like figures moved among the orange trees. She wondered idly what they were doing; then her mind wandered to other, more interesting and personal matters. To Sig and the fact that she couldn't help feeling rather thrilled when he was around, even when he acted the way he had done just now. Some day, maybe – some day, just to see what it was like and if things got a bit dull out here at the castle . . . Poor Uncle Jo! she reflected. But then what could he expect – at his age and at hers? The unexpected thing was that, in all these months, she hadn't yet given him any reason for being jealous – unless, of course, you counted Enid and Mary Lou; which she didn't; because she really wasn't that way at all; and when it did happen, it was nothing more than a kind of little accident; nice, but not a bit important. Whereas with Sig, if it ever happened, the thing would be different; even though it weren't very serious; which it wouldn't be – not like with Walt, for example, or even with little Buster back in Portland. It would be different from the accidents with Enid and Mary Lou, because, with a man, those things generally did matter a good deal, even when you didn't mean them to matter. Which was the only reason for not doing them, outside of their being sins, of course; but somehow that never seemed to count very much when the boy was a real good looker (which one had to admit Sig was, even though it was rather in the style of Adolphe Menjou; but, come to think of it, it was those dark ones with oil on their hair that had always given her the biggest kick!). And when you'd had a couple of drinks, maybe, and you felt you'd like some thrills, why, then it never even occurred to you that it was a sin; and then the one thing led to another, and before you knew what had happened – well, it *had* happened; and really she just couldn't believe it was as bad as Father O'Reilly said it was; and, anyhow, Our Lady would be a lot more understanding and forgiving than he was; and what about the way Father O'Reilly ate his food, whenever he came to dinner? – like a hog, there wasn't any other word for it; and wasn't gluttony just as bad as the other thing? So who was he to talk like that?

'Well, and how's the patient?' Dr Obispo inquired in the parody of a bedside manner, as he took Virginia's place on the couch. He was in the highest of spirits. His work in the laboratory was coming along unexpectedly well; that new preparation of bile salts had done wonders for his liver; the rearmament boom had sent his aircraft shares up another three points; and it was obvious that Virginia wasn't going to hold out much longer. 'How's the little invalid this morning?' he went on, enriching his parody with the caricature of an English accent; for he had done a year of post-graduate work at Oxford.

Mr Stoyte growled inarticulately. There was something about Dr Obispo's facetiousness that always enraged him. In some not easily definable way it had the quality of a deliberate insult. Mr Stoyte was always made to feel that Obispo's apparently good-natured banter was in reality the expression of a calculated and malignant contempt. The thought of it made Mr Stoyte's blood boil. But when his blood boiled, his blood-pressure, he knew, went up, his life was shortened. He could not afford to be as angry with Obispo as he would have liked. And what was more, he couldn't afford to get rid of the man. Obispo was an indispensable evil. 'God is love; there is no death.' But Mr Stoyte remembered with terror that he had had a stroke, that he was growing old. Obispo had put him on his feet again when he was almost dying, had promised him ten more years of life even if those researches didn't work out as well as he hoped; and if they did work out – then more, much more. Twenty years, thirty, forty. Or it might even be that the loathsome little kike would find some way of proving that Mrs Eddy was right, after all. Perhaps there really and truly wouldn't be any death – not for Uncle Jo, at any rate. Glorious prospect! Meanwhile . . . Mr Stoyte sighed, resignedly, profoundly. 'We all have our cross to bear,' he said to himself, echoing, across the intervening years, the words his grandmother used to repeat when she made him take castor oil.

Dr Obispo, meanwhile, had sterilized his needle, filed the top off a glass ampoule, filled his syringe. His movements, as he worked, were characterized by a certain studied exquisiteness, by a florid and self-conscious precision. It was as though the man were simultaneously his own ballet and his own audience – a sophisticated and highly critical audience, it was true; but then, what a ballet! Nijinsky, Karsavina, Pavlova, Massine – all on a single stage. However terrific the applause it was always merited.

'Ready,' he called at last.

Obediently and in silence, like a trained elephant, Mr Stoyte rolled over on to his stomach.

Chapter Five

JEREMY had dressed again and was sitting in the subterranean store-room that was to serve as his study. The dry acrid dust of old documents had gone to his head, like a kind of intoxicating snuff. His face was flushed as he prepared his files and sharpened his pencils; his bald head shone with perspiration; behind their bifocal lenses his eyes were bright with excitement.

There! Everything was ready. He turned round in his swivel-chair and sat for a while quite still, voluptuously savouring his anticipations. Tied up in innumerable brown-paper parcels, the Hauberk Papers awaited their first reader. Twenty-seven crates of still unravished brides of quietness. He smiled to himself at the thought that he was to be their Bluebeard. Thousands of brides of quietness accumulated through centuries by successive generations of indefatigable Hauberks. Hauberk after Hauberk; barony after knighthood; earldom after barony; and then Earl of Gonister after Earl of Gonister down to the last, the eighth. And, after the eighth, nothing but death-duties and an old house and two old spinster ladies, sinking ever deeper into solitude and eccentricity, into poverty and family pride, but finally, poor pets! more deeply into poverty than pride. They had sworn they would never sell; but in the end they had accepted Mr Stoyte's offer. The papers had been shipped to California. They would be able, now, to buy themselves a couple of really sumptuous funerals. And that would be the end of the Hauberks. Delicious fragment of English history! Cautionary perhaps, or perhaps, and more probably, merely senseless, merely a tale told by an idiot. A tale of cut-throats and conspirators, of patrons of learning and shady speculators, of bishops and kings' catamites and minor poets, of admirals and pimps, of saints and heroines and nymphomaniacs, of imbeciles and prime ministers, of art collectors and sadists. And here was all that remained of them, in twenty-seven crates, higgledy-piggledy, never catalogued, never even looked at, utterly virgin. Gloating over his treasure, Jeremy forgot the fatigues of the journey, forgot Los Angeles and the chauffeur, forgot the cemetery and the castle, forgot even Mr

Stoyte. He had the Hauberk Papers, had them all to himself. Like a child dipping blindly into a bran pie for a present which he knows will be exciting, Jeremy picked up one of the brown-paper parcels with which the first crate was filled and cut the string. What rich confusion awaited him within! A book of household accounts for the year 1576 and 1577; a narrative by some Hauberk cadet of Sir Kenelm Digby's expedition to Scanderoon; eleven letters in Spanish from Miguel de Molinos to that Lady Ann Hauberk who had scandalized her family by turning papist; a collection, in early eighteenth-century handwriting, of sickroom recipes; a copy of Drelincourt *On Death*; and an odd volume of Andréa de Nerciat's *Félicia, ou Mes Fredaines*. He had just cut the string of the second bundle and was wondering whose was the lock of brown pale hair preserved between the pages of the Third Earl's holograph Reflections on the Late Popish Plot, when there was a knock at the door. He looked up and saw a small, dark man in a white overall advancing towards him. The stranger smiled, said, 'Don't let me disturb you,' but nevertheless disturbed him. 'My name's Obispo,' he went on, 'Dr Sigmund Obispo: Physician in ordinary to His Majesty King Stoyte the First – and let's hope also the last.'

Evidently delighted by his own joke, he broke into a peal of startlingly loud metallic laughter. Then, with the elegantly fastidious gesture of an aristocrat in a dust-heap, he picked up one of Molinos's letters and started, slowly, and out loud, to decipher the first line of the flowing seventeenth-century calligraphy that met his eyes. ' "*Ame a Dios como es en sí y no como se lo dice y forma su imaginación.*" ' He looked up at Jeremy with an amused smile. 'Easier said than done, I should think. Why, you can't even love a woman as she is in herself; and after all, there is some sort of objective physical basis for the phenomenon we call a female. A pretty nice basis in some cases. Whereas poor old Dios is only a spirit – in other words, pure imagination. And here's this idiot, whoever he is, telling some other idiot that people mustn't love God as he is in their imagination.' Once again self-consciously the aristocrat, he threw down the letter with a contemptuous flick of the wrist. 'What drivel it all is!' he went on. 'A string of words called religion. Another string of words called philosophy. Half a dozen other strings called political ideals. And all the words either ambiguous or meaningless. And people getting so excited about them they'll murder their neighbours for using a word they don't happen to like. A word that probably doesn't mean as much as a good belch. Just a noise without even the excuse of gas on the stomach. "*Ame a Dios come es en sí,*" ' he repeated derisively. 'It's about as sensible as saying "hiccough *a* hiccough *como es en* hiccough". I don't know how you *litterae humaniores* boys manage to stand it. Don't you pine for some sense once in a while?'

Jeremy smiled with an expression of nervous apology. 'One doesn't bother too much about the meanings,' he said. Then, anticipating further criticism by disparaging himself and the things he loved most dearly, 'One gets a lot of fun, you know,' he went on, 'just scrabbling about in the dust-heaps.'

Dr Obispo laughed and patted Jeremy encouragingly on the shoulders. 'Good for you!' he said. 'You're frank. I like that. Most of the Ph.D. boys one meets are such damned Pecksniffs. Trying to pull that high-moral culture stuff on you! You know: wisdom rather than knowledge; Sophocles instead of science. "Funny," I always say to them when they try that on me, "funny that the thing you get your income from should happen to be the thing that's going to save humanity." Whereas you don't try to glorify your little racket. You're honest. You admit you're in the thing merely for the fun of it. Well, that's why I'm in *my* little racket. For the fun. Though, of course, if you'd given me any of that Sophocles stuff, I'd just have let you have my piece about science and progress, science and happiness, even science and ultimate truth, if you'd been obstinate.' He showed his white teeth in a happy derision of everybody.

His amusement was infectious. Jeremy also smiled. 'I'm glad I wasn't obstinate,' he said in a tone whose fluty demureness implied how much he objected to disquisitions on ultimate truth.

'Mind you,' Dr Obispo went on, 'I'm not entirely blind to the charms of your racket. I'd draw the line at Sophocles, of course. And I'd be deadly bored with this sort of stuff' – he nodded towards the twenty-seven crates. 'But I must admit,' he concluded handsomely, 'I've had a lot of fun out of old books in my time. Really, a lot of fun.'

Jeremy coughed and caressed his scalp; his eyes winkled in

anticipation of the deliciously dry little joke he was just about to make. But, unfortunately, Dr Obispo gave him no time. Serenely unaware of Jeremy's preparations he looked at his watch; then rose to his feet. 'I'd like to show you my laboratory,' he said. 'There's plenty of time before lunch.'

'Instead of asking if I'd like to see his bloody laboratory,' Jeremy protested inwardly, as he swallowed his joke; and it had been such a good one! He would have liked, of course, to go on unpacking the Hauberk Papers; but, lacking the courage to say so, he rose obediently and followed Dr Obispo towards the door.

Longevity, the doctor explained, as they left the room. That was his subject. Had been ever since he left medical school. But, of course, so long as he was in practice he hadn't been able to do any serious work on it. Practice was fatal to serious work, he added parenthetically. How could you do anything sensible, when you had to spend all your time looking after patients? Patients belonged to three classes: those that imagined they were sick, but weren't; those that were sick, but would get well anyhow; those that were sick and would be much better dead. For anybody capable of serious work to waste his time with patients was simply idiotic. And, of course, nothing but economic pressure would ever have driven him to do it. And he might have gone on in that groove for ever. Wasting himself on morons. But then, quite suddenly, his luck had turned. Jo Stoyte had come to consult him. It had been positively providential.

'Most awfully a godsend,' Jeremy murmured, quoting his favourite phrase of Coleridge.

Jo Stoyte, Dr Obispo repeated, Jo Stoyte on the verge of breaking up completely. Forty pounds overweight and having had a stroke. Not a bad one, luckily; but enough to put the old bastard into a sweat. Talk of being scared to death! (Dr Obispo's white teeth flashed again in wolfish good-humour.) In Jo's case it had been a panic. Out of that panic had come Dr Obispo's liberation from his patients; had come his income, his laboratory for work on the problems of longevity, his excellent assistant; had come, too, the financing of that pharmaceutical work at Berkeley, of those experiments with monkeys in Brazil, of that expedition to study the tortoises on the Galapagos Islands. Everything a research worker could ask for, with old Jo himself thrown in as the perfect guinea-pig – ready to submit to practically anything short of vivisection without anaesthetics, provided it offered some hope of keeping him above ground a few years longer.

Not that he was doing anything spectacular with the old buzzard at the moment. Just keeping his weight down; and taking care of his kidneys – and pepping him up with periodical shots of synthetic sex hormone – and watching out for those arteries. The ordinary, commonsense treatment for a man of Jo Stoyte's age and medical history. Meanwhile, however, he was on the track of something new, something that promised to be important. In a few months, perhaps in a few weeks, he'd be in a position to make a definite pronouncement.

'That's very interesting,' said Jeremy with hypocritical politeness.

They were walking along a narrow corridor, white-washed and bleakly illuminated by a series of electric bulbs. Through open doors Jeremy had occasional glimpses of vast cellars crammed with totem poles and armour, with stuffed orang-utans and marble groups by Thorwaldsen, with gilded Bodhisattvas and early steam-engines, with lingams and stage-coaches and Peruvian pottery, with crucifixes and mineralogical specimens.

Dr Obispo, meanwhile, had begun to talk again about longevity. The subject, he insisted, was still in the pre-scientific stage. A lot of observations without any explanatory hypothesis. A mere chaos of facts. And what odd, what essentially eccentric facts! What was it, for example, that made a cicada live as long as a bull? or a canary outlast three generations of sheep? Why should dogs be senile at fourteen and parrots sprightly at a hundred? Why should female humans become sterile in the forties, while female crocodiles continued to lay eggs into their third century? Why in heaven's name should a pike live to two hundred without showing any signs of senility? Whereas poor old Jo Stoyte . . .

From a side passage two men suddenly emerged carrying between them on a stretcher a couple of mummified nuns. There was a collision.

'Damned fools!' Dr Obispo shouted angrily.

'Damned fool yourself!'

'Can't you look where you're going?'

'Keep your face shut!'

Dr Obispo turned contemptuously away and walked on.

'Who the hell do you think you are?' they called after him.

Jeremy meanwhile had been looking with lively curiosity at the mummies. 'Discalced Carmelites,' he said to nobody in particular; and enjoying the flavour of that curious combination of syllables, he repeated them with a certain emphatic relish. 'Discalced Carmelites.'

'Discalced your ass,' said the foremost of the two men, turning fiercely upon this new antagonist.

Jeremy gave one glace at that red and angry face, then, with ignominious haste, hurried after his guide.

Dr Obispo halted at last. 'Here we are,' he said, opening a door. A smell of mice and absolute alcohol floated out into the corridor. 'Come on in,' he said cordially.

Jeremy entered. There were the mice all right – cage upon cage of them, in tiers along the wall directly in front of him. To the left, three windows, hewn in the rock, gave on to the tennis-court and a distant panorama of orange trees and mountains. Seated at a table in front of one of these windows, a man was looking through a microscope. He raised his fair, tousled head as they approached, and turned towards them a face of almost child-like candour and openness. 'Hullo, doc,' he said with a charming smile.

'My assistant,' Dr Obispo explained. 'Peter Boone. Pete, this is Mr Pordage.' Pete rose and revealed himself an athletic young giant.

'Call me Pete,' he said, when Jeremy had called him Mr Boone. 'Everyone calls me Pete.'

Jeremy wondered whether he ought to invite the young man to call him Jeremy – but wondered, as usual, so long that the appropriate moment for doing so passed, irrevocably.

'Pete's a bright boy,' Dr Obispo began again in a tone that was affectionate in intention, but a little patronizing in fact. 'Knows his physiology. Good with his hands, too. Best mouse surgeon I ever saw.' He patted the young man on the shoulder.

Pete smiled – a little uncomfortably, it seemed to Jeremy, as though he found it rather difficult to make the right response to the other's cordiality.

'Takes his politics a bit too seriously,' Dr Obispo went on. 'That's his only defect. I'm trying to cure him of that. Not very successfully so far, I'm afraid. Eh, Pete?'

The young man smiled again, more confidently; this time he knew exactly where he stood and what to do.

'*Not* very successfully,' he repeated. Then, turning to Jeremy, 'Did you see the Spanish news this morning?' he asked. The expression on his large, fair, open face changed to one of concern.

Jeremy shook his head.

'It's something awful,' said Pete gloomily. 'When I think of those poor devils without planes or artillery or . . .'

'Well, don't think of them,' Dr Obispo cheerfully advised. 'You'll feel better.'

The young man looked at him, then looked away again without saying anything. After a moment of silence he pulled out his watch. 'I think I'll go and have a swim before lunch,' he said, and walked towards the door.

Dr Obispo picked up a cage of mice and held it within a few inches of Jeremy's nose. 'These are the sex-hormone boys,' he said with a jocularity that the other found curiously offensive. The animals squeaked as he shook the cage. 'Lively enough while the effect lasts. The trouble is that the effects are only temporary.'

Not that temporary effects were to be despised, he added, as he replaced the cage. It was always better to feel temporarily good than temporarily bad. That was why he was giving old Jo a course of that testosterone stuff. Not that the old bastard had any great need of it with that Maunciple girl around. . . .

Dr Obispo suddenly put his hand over his mouth and looked round towards the window. 'Thank God,' he said, 'he's out of the room. Poor old Pete!' A derisive smile appeared on his face. 'Is he in love!' He tapped his forehead. 'Thinks she's like something in the Works of Tennyson. You know, chemically pure. Last month he nearly killed a man for suggesting that she and the old boy . . . Well, you know. God knows what he figures the girl is doing here. Telling Uncle Jo about the spiral nebulae, I suppose. Well, if it makes him happy to think that way, I'm not the one that's going to spoil his fun.' Dr Obispo laughed indulgently. 'But to come back to what I was saying about Uncle Jo. . . .'

Just having that girl around the house was the equivalent of a hormone treatment. But it wouldn't last. It never did. Brown-Séquard and Voronoff and all the rest of them – they'd been on the wrong track. They'd thought that the decay of sexual power was the cause of senility. Whereas it was only one of the symptoms. Senescence started somewhere else and involved the sex mechanism along with the rest of the body. Hormone treatments were just palliatives and pick-me-ups. Helped you for a time, but didn't prevent your growing old.

Jeremy stifled a yawn.

For example, Dr Obispo went on, why should some animals live much longer than human beings and yet show so few signs of old age? Somehow, somewhere we had made a biological mistake. Crocodiles had avoided that mistake; so had tortoises. The same was true of certain species of fish.

'Look at this,' he said; and, crossing the room, he drew back a rubber curtain, revealing as he did so the glass front of a large aquarium recessed into the wall. Jeremy approached and looked in.

In the green and shadowy translucence, two huge fish hung suspended, their snouts almost touching, motionless except for the occasional ripple of a fin and the rhythmic panting of their gills. A few inches from their staring eyes a rosary of bubbles streamed ceaselessly up towards the light, and all around them the water was spasmodically silver with the dartings of smaller fish. Sunk in their mindless ecstasy, the monsters paid no attention.

Carp, Dr Obispo explained; carp from the fishponds of a castle in Franconia – he had forgotten the name; but it was somewhere near Bamberg. The family was impoverished; but the fish were heirlooms, unpurchasable. Jo Stoyte had had to spend a lot of money to have these two stolen and smuggled out of the country in a specially constructed automobile with a tank under the back seats. Sixty-pounders they were; over four feet long; and those rings in their tails were dated 1761.

'The beginning of my period,' Jeremy murmured in a sudden access of interest. 1761 was the year of *Fingal*. He smiled to himself; the juxtaposition of carp and Ossian, carp and Napoleon's favourite poet, carp and the first premonitions of the Celtic Twilight, gave him a peculiar pleasure. What a delightful subject for one of his little essays! Twenty pages of erudition and absurdity – of sacrilege in lavender – of a scholar's delicately *canaille* irreverence for the illustrious or unillustrious dead.

But Dr Obispo would not allow him to think his thoughts in peace. Indefatigably riding his own hobby, he began again. There they were, he said, pointing at the huge fish; nearly two hundred years old; perfectly healthy; no symptoms of senility; no apparent reason why they shouldn't go on for another three or four centuries. There they were; and there were you. He turned back accusingly towards Jeremy. Here were you; no more than middle-aged, but already bald, already long-sighted and short-winded; already more or less edentate; incapable of prolonged physical exertion; chronically constipated (could you deny it?); your memory already not so good as it was; your digestion capricious; your potency falling off – if it hadn't, indeed, already disappeared for good.

Jeremy forced himself to smile, and at every fresh item nodded his head in what was meant to look like an amused assent. Inwardly, he was writhing with a mixture of distress at this all too truthful diagnosis and anger against the diagnostician for the ruthlessness of his scientific detachment. Talking with a humorous self-deprecation about one's own advancing senility was very different from being bluntly told about it by someone who took no interest in you except as an animal that happened to be unlike a fish. Nevertheless, he continued to nod and smile.

Here you were, Dr Obispo repeated at the end of his diagnosis, and there were the carp. How was it that you didn't manage your physiological affairs as well as they did? Just where and how and why did you make the mistake that had already robbed you of your teeth and hair and would bring you in a very few years to the grave?

Old Metchnikoff had asked those questions and made a bold attempt to answer. Everything he said happened to be wrong: phagocytosis didn't occur; intestinal autointoxication wasn't the sole cause of senility; neuronophages were mythological monsters; drinking sour milk didn't materially prolong life; whereas the removal of the large gut *did* materially shorten it. Chuckling, he recalled those operations that were so fashionable just before the

War! Old ladies and gentlemen with their colons cut out, and in consequence being forced to evacuate every few minutes, like canaries! All to no purpose, needless to say, because of course the operation that was meant to make them live to a hundred killed them all off within a year or two. Dr Obispo threw back his glossy head and uttered one of those peals of brazen laughter which were his regular response to any tale of human stupidity resulting in misfortune. Poor old Metchnikoff, he went on, wiping the tears of merriment from his eyes. Consistently wrong. And yet almost certainly not nearly so wrong as people had thought. Wrong, yes, in supposing that it was all a matter of intestinal stasis and auto-intoxication. But probably right in thinking that the secret was somewhere down there, in the gut. Somewhere in the gut, Dr Obispo repeated; and, what was more, he believed that he was on its track.

He paused and stood for a moment in silence, drumming with his fingers on the glass of the aquarium. Poised between mud and air, the two obese and aged carp hung in their greenish twilight, serenely unaware of him. Dr Obispo shook his head at them. The worst experimental animals in the world, he said in a tone of resentment mingled with a certain gloomy pride. Nobody had a right to talk about technical difficulties who hadn't tried to work with fish. Take the simplest operation; it was a nightmare. Had you ever tried to keep its gills properly wet while it was anaesthetized on the operating-table? Or, alternatively, to do your surgery under water? Had you ever set out to determine a fish's basal metabolism, or take an electro-cardiograph of its heart action, or measure its blood-pressure? Had you ever wanted to analyse its excreta? And, if so, did you know how hard it was even to collect them? Had you ever attempted to study the chemistry of a fish's digestion and assimilation? To determine its blood-pressure under different conditions? To measure the speed of its nervous reactions?

No, you had not, said Dr Obispo contemptuously. And until you had, you had no right to complain about anything.

He drew the curtain on his fish, took Jeremy by the arm and led him back to the mice.

'Look at those,' he said, pointing to a batch of cages on an upper shelf.

Jeremy looked. The mice in question were exactly like all other mice. 'What's wrong with them?' he asked.

Dr Obispo laughed. 'If those animals were human beings,' he said dramatically, 'they'd all be over a hundred years old.'

And he began to talk, very rapidly and excitedly, about fatty alcohols and the intestinal flora of carp. For the secret was there, the key to the whole problem of senility and longevity. There, between the sterols and the peculiar flora of the carp's intestine.

Those sterols! (Dr Obispo frowned and shook his head over them.) Always linked up with senility. The most obvious case, of course, was cholesterol. A senile animal might be defined as one with an accumulation of cholesterol in the wall of its arteries. Potassium thiocyanate seemed to dissolve those accumulations. Senile rabbits would show signs of rejuvenation under a treatment with potassium thiocyanate. So would senile humans. But, again, not for very long. Cholesterol in the arteries was evidently only one of the troubles. But then cholesterol was only one of the sterols. They were a closely related group, those fatty alcohols. It didn't take much to transform one into another. But if you'd read old Schneeglock's work and the stuff they'd been publishing at Upsala, you'd know that some of the sterols were definitely poisonous – much more than cholesterol, even in large accumulations. Longbotham had even suggested a connexion between fatty alcohols and neoplasms. In other words, cancer might be regarded, in a final analysis, as a symptom of sterol-poisoning. He himself would go even further and say that such sterol-poisoning was responsible for the entire degenerative process of senescence in man and the other mammals. What nobody had done hitherto was to look into the part played by fatty alcohols in the life of such animals as carp. That was the work he had been doing for the last year. His researches had convinced him of two or three things: first, that the fatty alcohols in carp did not accumulate in excessive quantity; second, that they did not undergo transformation into the more poisonous sterols; and third, that both these immunities were due to the peculiar nature of the carp's intestinal flora. What a flora! Dr Obispo cried enthusiastically. So rich, so wonderfully varied! He had not yet succeeded in isolating the organism responsible for the carp's immunity to old age, nor did he fully understand the nature of the chemical mechanisms involved. Nevertheless, the main fact was certain. In one way or another, in combination or in isolation, these organisms contrived to keep the fish's sterols from turning into poisons. That was why a carp could live a couple of hundred years and show no signs of senility.

Could the intestinal flora of a carp be transferred to the gut of a mammal? And, if transferable, would it achieve the same chemical and biological results? That was what he had been trying, for the past few months, to discover. With no success, to begin with. Recently, however, they had experimented with a new technique – a technique that protected the flora from the process of digestion, gave it time to adapt itself to the unfamiliar conditions. It had taken root. The effect on the mice had been immediate and significant. Senescence had been halted, even reversed. Physiologically, the animals were younger than they had been for at least eighteen months – younger at the equivalent of a hundred than they had been at the equivalent of sixty.

Outside in the corridor an electric bell began to ring. It was lunch-time. The two men left the room and walked towards the elevator. Dr Obispo went on talking. Mice, he said, were apt to be a bit deceptive. He had now begun to try the thing out on larger animals. If it worked all right on dogs and baboons, it ought to work on Uncle Jo.

Chapter Six

In the small dining-room, most of the furnishings came from the Pavilion at Brighton. Four gilded dragons supported the red lacquered table, and two more served as caryatids on either side of a chimney-piece in the same material. It was the Regency's dream of the Gorgeous East. The kind of thing, Jeremy reflected, as he sat down on his scarlet and gold chair, the kind of thing that the word 'Cathay' would have conjured up in Keats's mind, for example, or Shelley's, or Lord Byron's – just as that charming 'Leda' by Etty, over there, next to the Fra Angelico's 'Annunciation', was an accurate embodiment of their fancies on the subject of pagan mythology; was an authentic illustration (he chuckled inwardly at the thought) to the Odes to Psyche and the Grecian Urn, to *Endymion* and *Prometheus Unbound*. An age's habits of thought and feeling and imagination are shared by all who live and work within that age – by all, from the journeyman up to the genius. Regency is always Regency, whether you take your sample from the top of the basket or from the bottom. In 1820, the man who shut his eyes and tried to visualize magic casements opening on the foam of faery seas would see – what? The turrets of Brighton Pavilion. At the thought, Jeremy smiled to himself with pleasure. Etty and Keats, Brighton and Percy Bysshe Shelley – what a delightful subject! Much better than carp and Ossian; better inasmuch as Nash and the Prince Regent were funnier than even the most aged fish. But for conversational purposes and at the luncheon-table, even the best of subjects is worthless if there is nobody to discuss it with. And who was there, Jeremy asked himself, who was there in this room desirous or capable of talking with him on such a theme? Not Mr Stoyte; not, certainly, Miss Maunciple, nor the two young women who had come over from Hollywood to have lunch with her; not Dr Obispo, who cared more for mice than books; nor Peter Boone, who probably didn't even know that there were any books to care for. The only person who might conceivably be expected to take an interest in the manifestations of the later-Georgian time spirit was the individual who had been introduced to him as Dr Herbert Mulge, PH.D., D.D., Principal of Tarzana College. But at the moment Dr Mulge was talking in a rich vein of something that sounded almost like pulpit eloquence about the new Auditorium which Mr Stoyte had just presented to the College and which was shortly to be given its formal opening. Dr Mulge was a large and handsome man with a voice to match – a voice at once sonorous and suave, unctuous and ringing. The flow of his language was slow, but steady and apparently stanchless. In phrases full of the audible equivalents of Capital Letters, he now went on to assure Mr Stoyte and anyone else who cared to listen that it would be a Real Inspiration for the boys and girls of Tarzana to come together in the beautiful new building for their Community Activities. For Non-Denominational Worship, for example; for the Enjoyment of the Best in Drama and Music. Yet, what an inspiration! The name of Stoyte would be remembered with love and reverence by successive generations of the College's Alumni and Alumnae – would be remembered, he might say, for ever; for the Auditorium was a *monumentum aere perennius*, a Footprint on the Sands of Time – definitely a Footprint. And now, Dr Mulge continued, between the mouthfuls of creamed chicken, now Tarzana's crying need was for a new Art School. Because, after all, Art, as we were now discovering, was one of the most potent of educational forces. Art was the aspect under which, in this twentieth century of ours, the Religious Spirit most clearly manifested itself. Art was the means by which Personalities could best achieve Creative Self-Expression and ...

'Cripes!' Jeremy said to himself; and then: 'Golly!' He smiled ruefully at the thought that he hoped to talk to this imbecile about the relation between Keats and Brighton Pavilion.

*

Peter Boone found himself separated from Virginia by the blonder of her two young friends from Hollywood, so that he could only look at her past a foreground of rouge and eyelashes, of golden curls and a thick, almost visible perfume of gardenias. To anyone else, this foreground might have seemed a bit distracting; but for Pete it was of no more significance than the equivalent amount of mud. He was interested only in what was beyond the foreground

– in that exquisitely abbreviated upper lip, in the little nose that made you want to cry when you looked at it, it was so elegant and impertinent, so ridiculous and angelic; in that long Florentine bob of lustrous auburn hair; in those wide-set, widely opened eyes with their twinkling surface of humour and their dark blue depths of what he was sure was an infinite tenderness, a plumbless feminine wisdom. He loved her so much that where his heart should have been he could feel only an aching breathlessness, a cavity which she alone could fill.

Meanwhile, she was talking to the blonde Foreground about that new job which the Foreground had landed with the Cosmopolitan-Perlmutter Studio. The picture was called 'Say it with Stockings', and the Foreground was to play the part of a rich débutante who runs away from home to make a career of her own, becomes a strip-tease dancer in a Western mining-camp and finally marries a cow-puncher, who turns out to be the son of a millionaire.

'Sounds like a swell story,' said Virginia. 'Don't you think so, Pete?'

Pete thought so; he was ready to think almost anything if she wanted him to.

'That reminds me of Spain,' Virginia announced. And while Jeremy, who had been eavesdropping on the conversation, frantically tried to imagine what train of associations had taken her from 'Say it with Stockings' to the civil war – whether it had been Cosmopolitan-Perlmutter, Anti-Semitism, Nazis, Franco; or débutante, class war, Moscow, Negrin; or strip-tease, modernity, radicalism, Republicans – while he was vainly speculating thus, Virginia went on to ask the young man to tell them about what he had done in Spain; and when he demurred, insisted – because it was so thrilling, because the Foreground had never heard about it, because, finally, she wanted him to.

Pete obeyed. Only half-articulately, in a vocabulary composed of slang and clichés, and adorned by expletives and grunts – the vocabulary, Jeremy reflected as he listened surreptitiously through the booming of Dr Mulge's eloquence, the characteristically squalid and poverty-stricken vocabulary to which the fear of being thought unsocially different or undemocratically superior, or unsportingly highbrow, condemns most young Englishmen and Americans – he began to describe his experiences as a volunteer in the International Brigade during the heroic days of 1937. It was a touching narrative. Through the hopelessly inadequate language, Jeremy could divine the young man's enthusiasm for liberty and justice; his courage; his love for his comrades; his nostalgia, even in the neighbourhood of that short upper lip, even in the midst of an absorbing piece of scientific research, for the life of men united in devotion to a cause, made one in the face of hardship and shared danger and impending death.

'Gee,' he kept repeating, 'they were swell guys.'

They were all swell – Knud, who had saved his life one day, up there in Aragon; Anton and Mack and poor little Dino, who had been killed; André, who had lost a leg; Jan, who had a wife and two children; Fritz, who'd had six months in a Nazi concentration camp; and all the others – the finest bunch of boys in the world. And what did he do, but go and get rheumatic fever on them, and then myocarditis – which meant no more active service; no more anything except sitting around. That was why he was here, he explained apologetically. But, gee, it had been good while it lasted! That time, for example, when he and Knud had gone out at night and climbed a precipice in the dark and taken a whole platoon of Moors by surprise and killed half a dozen of them and come back with a machine-gun and three prisoners. . . .

'And what is *your* opinion of Creative Work, Mr Pordage?'

Surprised in flagrant inattention, Jeremy started guiltily. 'Creative work?' he mumbled, trying to gain a little time. 'Creative work? Well, of course one's all for it. Definitely,' he insisted.

'I'm glad to hear you say so,' said Dr Mulge. 'Because *that's* what I want at Tarzana. Creative work – ever more and more Creative. Shall I tell you what is my highest ambition?' Neither Mr Stoyte nor Jeremy made any reply. But Dr Mulge proceeded, nevertheless, to tell them. 'It is to make of Tarzana the living Centre of the New Civilization that is coming to blossom here in the West.' He raised a large fleshy hand in solemn asseveration. 'The Athens of the twentieth century is on the point of emerging here, in the Los Angeles Metropolitan Area. I want Tarzana to be its Parthenon and its Academe, its Stoa and its Temple of the Muses. Religion, Art, Philosophy, Science – I want them all to find their home in Tarzana, to radiate their influence from our campus, to . . .'

In the middle of his story about the Moors and the precipice, Pete became aware that only the Foreground was listening to him. Virginia's attention had wandered, surreptitiously at first, then frankly and avowedly – had wandered to where, on her left, the less blonde of her two friends was having something almost whispered to her by Dr Obispo.

'What's that?' Virginia asked.

Dr Obispo leaned towards her and began again. The three heads, the oil-smooth black, the elaborately curly brown, the lustrous auburn, were almost touching. By the expression on their faces Pete could see that the doctor was telling one of his dirty stories. Alleviated for a moment by the smile she had given him when she asked him to tell them about Spain, the anguish in that panting void where his heart ought to have been came back with redoubled intensity. It was a complicated pain, made up of jealousy and a despairing sense of loss and personal unworthiness, of a fear that his angel was being corrupted and another, deeper fear, which his conscious mind refused to formulate, a fear that there wasn't much further corruption to be done, that the angel was not as angelic as his love had made him assume. The flow of his narrative suddenly dried up. He was silent.

'Well, what happened then?' the Foreground inquired with an eagerness and an expression of hero-worshipping admiration that any other young man would have found delightfully flattering.

He shook his head. 'Oh, nothing much.'

'But those Moors . . .'

'Hell!' he said impatiently. 'What does it matter, anyhow?'

His words were drowned by a violent explosion of laughter that sent the three conspiratorial heads, the black, the brown, the lovely auburn, flying apart from one another. He looked up at Virginia and saw a face distorted with mirth. At what? he asked himself in agony, trying to measure the extent of her corruption; and a kind of telescoped and synthetic memory of all the schoolboy stories, all the jokes and limericks he had ever heard, rushed in upon him.

Was it at that one that she was laughing? Or at that? Or, God, perhaps at *that*? He hoped and prayed it wasn't at *that*; and the more he hoped and prayed, the more insanely sure he became that *that* was the one it had been.

'. . . above all,' Dr Mulge was saying, 'Creative Work in the Arts. Hence the crying need for a new Art School, an Art School worthy of Tarzana, worthy of the highest traditions of . . .

The girls' shrill laughter exploded with a force of hilarity proportionate to the strength of the surrounding social taboos. Mr Stoyte turned sharply in the direction from which the noise had come.

'What's the joke?' he asked suspiciously. He wasn't going to have his Baby listen to smut. He disapproved of smut in mixed company almost as whole-heartedly as his grandmother, the Plymouth Sister, had done. 'What's all that noise about?'

It was Dr Obispo who answered. He'd been telling them a funny story he'd heard over the radio, he explained with that suave politeness that was like a sarcasm. Something delightfully amusing. Perhaps Mr Stoyte would like to have him repeat it.

Mr Stoyte grunted ferociously and turned away.

A glance at his host's scowling face convinced Dr Mulge that it would be better to postpone discussion of the Art School to another more propitious occasion. It was disappointing; for it seemed to him that he had been making good progress. But, there! such things would happen. Dr Mulge was a college president chronically in quest of endowments; he knew all about the rich. Knew, for example, that they were like gorillas, creatures not easily domesticated, deeply suspicious, alternately bored and bad-tempered. You had to approach them with caution, to handle them gently and with a boundless cunning. And even then they might suddenly turn savage on you and show their teeth. Half a lifetime of experience with bankers and steel-magnates and retired meat-packers had taught Dr Mulge to take such little setbacks as today's with a truly philosophic patience. Brightly, with a smile on his large, imperial-Roman face, he turned to Jeremy. 'And what do you think of our Californian weather, Mr Pordage?' he asked.

Meanwhile, Virginia had noticed the expression on Pete's face and immediately divined the causes of his misery. Poor Pete! But really, if he thought she had nothing better to do than always be listening to his talk about that silly old war in Spain – or if it wasn't

Spain, it was the laboratory; and they did vivisection there, which was just awful; because, after all, when you were hunting, the animals had a chance of getting away, particularly if you were a bad shot, like she was; besides, hunting was full of thrills and you got such a kick from being up there in the mountains in the good air; whereas Pete cut them up underground in that cellar place. . . . No, if he thought she had nothing better to do than that, he made a big mistake. All the same, he was a nice boy; and talk about being in love! It was nice having people around who felt that way about you; made you feel kind of good. Though it could be rather a nuisance sometimes. Because they got to feel they had some claim on you; they figured they had a right to tell you things and interfere. Pete didn't do that in so many words; but he had a way of looking at you – like a dog would do if it suddenly started criticizing you for taking another cocktail. Saying it with eyes, like Hedy Lamarr – only it wasn't the same thing as Hedy was saying with *her* eyes; in fact, just the opposite. It was just the opposite now – and what had she done? Got bored with that silly old war and listened in to what Sig was saying to Mary Lou. Well, all she could say was that she wasn't going to have anyone interfering with the way she chose to live her own life. That was her business. Why, he was almost as bad, the way he looked at her, as Uncle Jo, or her mother, or Father O'Reilly. Only, of course, they didn't just look; they said things. Not that he meant badly, of course, poor Pete; he was just a kid, just unsophisticated and, on top of everything, in love the way a kid is – like the high-school boy in Deanna Durbin's last picture. Poor Pete, she thought again. It was tough luck on him; but the fact was she never had been attracted by that big, fair, Cary Grant sort of boy. They just didn't appeal to her; that was all there was to it. She liked him; and she enjoyed his being in love with her. But that was all.

Across the corner of the table she caught his eye, gave him a dazzling smile and invited him, if he had half an hour to spare after lunch, to come and teach her and the girls how to pitch horseshoes.

Chapter Seven

THE meal was over at last; the party broke up. Dr Mulge had an appointment in Pasadena to see a rubber-goods manufacturer's widow, who might perhaps give thirty thousand dollars for a new girls' dormitory. Mr Stoyte drove into Los Angeles for his regular Friday afternoon board meetings and business consultations. Dr Obispo was going to operate on some rabbits and went down to the laboratory to prepare his instruments. Pete had a batch of scientific journals to look at, but gave himself, meanwhile, a few minutes of happiness in Virginia's company. And for Jeremy, of course, there were the Hauberk Papers. It was with a sense of almost physical relief, a feeling that he was going home to where he belonged, that he returned to his cellar. The afternoon slipped past – how delightfully, how profitably! Within three hours, another batch of letters from Molinos had turned up among the account books and the business correspondence. So had the third and fourth volumes of *Félicia*. So had an illustrated edition of *Le Portier des Carmes*; and, bound like a prayer-book, so had a copy of that rarest of all works of the Divine Marquis, *Les Cent-Vingt Jours de Sodome*. What a treasure! What unexpected fortune! Or perhaps, Jeremy reflected, not so unexpected if one remembered the history of the Hauberk family. For the date of the books made it likely that they had been the property of the Fifth Earl – the one who had held the title for more than half a century and died at more than ninety, under William IV, completely unregenerate. Given the character of that old gentleman, one had no reason to feel surprised at the finding of a store of pornography – one had every reason, indeed, to hope for more.

Jeremy's spirits mounted with each new discovery. Always, with him, a sure sign of happiness, he began to hum the tunes that had been popular during his childhood. Molinos evoked 'Tara-rara Boom-de-ay!' *Félicia* and the *Portier des Carmes* shared the romantic lilt of 'The Honeysuckle and the Bee'. As for the '*Cent-Vingt Jours*', which he had never previously read or even seen a copy of – the finding of that delighted him so much that when, as a matter of bibliographical routine, he raised the ecclesiastical cover and, expecting the Anglican ritual, found instead the coldly elegant prose of the Marquis de Sade, he broke out into that rhyme from 'The Rose and the Ring', the rhyme his mother had taught him to repeat when he was only three years old and which had remained with him as the symbol of childlike wonder and delight, as the only completely adequate reaction to any sudden blessing, any providentially happy surprise.

> Oh, what fun to have a plum bun!
> How I wish it never was done!

And fortunately it wasn't done, wasn't even begun; the book was still unread, the hours of entertainment and instruction still lay before him. Remembering that pang of jealousy he had felt up there, in the swimming-pool, he smiled indulgently. Let Mr Stoyte have all the girls he wanted; a well-written piece of eighteenth-century pornography was better than any Maunciple. He closed the volume he was holding. The tooled morocco was austerely elegant; on the back, the words 'The Book of Common Prayer' were stamped in a gold which the years had hardly tarnished. He put it down with the other *curiosa* on a corner of the table. When he had finished for the afternoon, he would take the whole collection up to his bedroom.

'Oh, what fun to have a plum bun!' he chanted to himself, as he opened another bundle of papers, and then, 'On a summer's afternoon, where the honeysuckles bloom and all Nature seems at rest.' The Wordsworthian touch about Nature always gave him a special pleasure. The new batch of papers turned out to be a correspondence between the Fifth Earl and a number of prominent Whigs regarding the enclosure, for his benefit, of three thousand acres of common land in Nottinghamshire. Jeremy slipped them into a file, wrote a brief preliminary description of the contents on a card, put the file in a cupboard and the card in its cabinet, and, dipping again into the bran pie, reached down for another bundle. He cut the string. 'You are my honey, honey, honeysuckle, I am the bee.' What would Dr Freud have thought of that, he wondered? Anonymous pamphlets against deism were a bore; he threw them aside. But here was a copy of Law's *Serious Call* with manuscript notes by Edward Gibbon; and here were some accounts rendered to the Fifth Earl by Mr Rogers of Liverpool: accounts of the expenses and profits of three slave-trading expeditions which the Earl had helped finance. The second voyage, it appeared, had been particularly auspicious; less than a fifth of the cargo had perished on the way, and the prices realized at Savannah were gratifyingly high. Mr Rogers begged to enclose his draft for seventeen thousand two hundred and twenty-four pounds eleven shillings and four-pence. Written from Venice, in Italian, another letter announced to the same Fifth Earl the appearance upon the market of a half-length 'Mary Magdalen' by Titian, at a price which the Italian correspondent described as derisory. Other offers had already been made; but out of respect for the not less learned than illustrious English *cognoscente*, the vendor would wait until a reply had been received from his lordship. In spite of which, his lordship would be well advised not to delay too long; for otherwise . . .

*

It was five o'clock; the sun was low in the sky. Dressed in white shoes and socks, white shorts, a yachting-cap and a pink silk sweater, Virginia had come to see the feeding of the baboons.

Its engine turned off, her rose-coloured motor-scooter stood parked at the side of the road thirty or forty feet above the cage. In company with Dr Obispo and Pete, she had gone down to have a closer look at the animals.

Just opposite the point at which they were standing, on a shelf of artificial rock, sat a baboon mother, holding in her arms the withered and disintegrating corpse of the baby she would not abandon even though it had been dead for a fortnight. Every now and then, with an intense, automatic affection, she would lick the little cadaver. Tufts of greenish fur and even pieces of skin detached themselves under the vigorous action of her tongue. Delicately, with black fingers, she would pick the hairs out of her mouth, then begin again. Above her, at the mouth of a little cave, two young males suddenly got into a fight. The air was filled with screams and barks and the gnashing of teeth. Then one of the two combatants ran away and, in a moment, the other had forgotten all about the fight and was searching for pieces of dandruff on his chest. To the right, on another shelf of rock, a formidable old male, leather-snouted, with the grey bobbed hair of a seventeenth-century Anglican divine, stood guard over his submissive female. It was a vigilant watch; for if she ventured to move without his leave, he turned and bit her; and meanwhile the small black eyes, the staring nostrils at the end of the truncated snout, kept glancing this way and that with an unsleeping suspicion. From the basket he was carrying, Pete threw a potato in his direction, then a carrot and another potato. With a vivid flash of magenta buttocks the old baboon darted down from his perch on the artificial mountain, seized the carrot and, while he was eating it, stuffed one potato into his left cheek, the other into the right; then, still biting at the carrot, advanced toward the wire and looked up for more. The coast was clear. The young male who had been looking for dandruff suddenly saw his opportunity. Chattering with excitement, he bounded down to the shelf on which, too frightened to follow her master, the little female was still squatting. Within ten seconds they had begun to copulate.

Virginia clapped her hands with pleasure. 'Aren't they cute!' she cried. 'Aren't they *human*!'

Another burst of screaming and barking almost drowned her words.

Pete interrupted his distribution of food to say that it was a long while since he had seen Mr Propter. Why shouldn't they all go down the hill and pay a call on him?

'From the monkey cage to the Propter paddock,' said Dr Obispo, 'and from the Propter paddock back to the Stoyte house and the Maunciple kennel. What do you say, angel?'

Virginia was throwing potatoes to the old male – throwing them in such a way as to induce him to turn, to retrace his steps towards the shelf on which he had left his female. Her hope was that, if she got him to go back far enough, he'd see how the girl friend passed the time when he was away. 'Yes, let's go and see old Proppy,' she said without turning round. She tossed another potato into the enclosure. With a flutter of grey bobbed hair the baboon pounced on it; but instead of looking up and catching Mrs B. having her romance with the ice-man, the exasperating animal immediately turned round towards the wire, asking for more. 'Stupid old fool!'

Virginia shouted, and this time threw the potato straight at him; it caught him on the nose. She laughed and turned towards the others. 'I like old Proppy,' she said. 'He scares me a bit; but I like him.'

'All right then,' said Dr Obispo, 'let's go and rout out Mr Pordage while we're about it.'

'Yes, let's go and fetch old Ivory,' Virginia agreed, patting her own auburn curls in reference to Jeremy's baldness. 'He's kind of cute, don't you think?'

Leaving Pete to go on with the feeding of the baboons, they climbed back to the road and up a flight of steps on the farther side, leading directly to the rock-cut windows of Jeremy's room. Virginia pushed open the glass door.

'Ivory,' she called, 'we've come to disturb you.'

Jeremy began to murmur something humorously gallant; then broke off in the middle of a sentence. He had suddenly remembered that pile of curious literature on the corner of the table. To get up and put the books into a cupboard would be to invite attention to them; he had no newspaper with which to cover them, no other books to mix them up with. There was nothing to be done. Nothing, except to hope for the best. Fervently he hoped for it; and almost immediately the worst happened. Idly, out of the need to perform some muscular action, however pointless, Virginia picked up a volume of Nerciat, opened it at one of its conscientiously detailed engravings, looked, then with wider eyes looked again and let out a whoop of startled excitement. Dr Obispo glanced and yelled in turn; then both broke out into enormous laughter.

Jeremy sat in a misery of embarrassment, sicklily smiling, while they asked him if *that* was how he spent his time, if *this* was the sort of thing he was studying. If only people weren't so wearisome, he was thinking, so deplorably unsubtle!

Virginia turned over the pages until she found another illustration. Once more there was an outcry of delight, astonishment and, this time, incredulity. Was it possible? Could it really be done? She spelled out the caption under the engraving: '*La volupté frappait à toutes les portes*' then petulantly shook her head. It was no good; she couldn't understand it. Those French lessons at High School – just lousy; that was all you could say about them. They hadn't taught her anything except a lot of nonsense about *le crayon de mon oncle* and *savez-vous planter le chou*. She'd always said that studying was mostly a waste of time; this proved it. And why did they have to print this stuff in French anyhow? At the thought that the deficiencies in the educational system of the State of Oregon might for ever prevent her from reading André de Nerciat, the tears came into Virginia's eyes. It was really *too* bad!

A brilliant idea occurred to Jeremy. Why shouldn't he offer to translate the book for her – *viva voce* and sentence by sentence, like an interpreter at a Council Meeting of the League of Nations? Yes, why not? The more he thought of it, the better the idea seemed to him to be. His decision was made and he had begun to consider how most felicitously to phrase his offer, when Dr Obispo quietly took the volume Virginia was holding, picked up the three companion volumes from the table, along with *Le Portier des Carmes* and the *Cent-Vingt Jours de Sodome*, and slipped the entire collection into the side-pocket of his jacket.

'Don't worry,' he said to Virginia. 'I'll translate them for you. And now let's go back to the baboons. Pete'll be wondering what's happened to us. Come on, Mr Pordage.'

In silence, but boiling inwardly with self-reproach for his own inefficiency and indignation at the doctor's impudence, Jeremy followed them out of the french window and down the steps.

Pete had emptied his basket and was leaning against the wire, intently following with his eyes the movements of the animals within. At their approach he turned towards them. His pleasant young face was bright with excitement.

'Do you know, doc,' he said, 'I believe it's working.'

'What's working?' asked Virginia.

Pete's answering smile was beautiful with happiness. For, oh, how happy he was! Doubly and trebly happy. By the sweetness of her subsequent behaviour, Virginia had more than made up for the pain she had inflicted by turning away to listen to that smutty story. And after all it probably wasn't a smutty story; he had been maligning her, thinking gratuitous evil of her. No, it certainly hadn't been a smutty story – not smutty because, when she turned back to him, her face had looked like the face of that child in the illustrated Bible at home, that child who was gazing so innocently and cutely while Jesus said, 'Of such is the Kingdom of Heaven.' And that was not the only reason for his happiness. He was happy, too, because it looked as though those cultures of the carp's intestinal flora were really having an effect on the baboons they had tried them on.

'I believe they're livelier,' he explained. 'And their fur – it's kind of glossier.'

The fact gave him almost as great a satisfaction as did Virginia's presence here in the transfiguring richness of the evening sunlight, as did the memory of her sweetness, the uplifting conviction of her essential innocence. Indeed, in some obscure way, the rejuvenation of the baboons and Virginia's adorableness seemed to him to have a profound connexion – a connexion not only with one another, but also and at the same time with Loyalist Spain and anti-fascism. Three separate things, and yet one thing . . . There was a bit of poetry he had been made to learn at school – how did it go?

> I could not love thee, dear, so much,
> Loved I not some or other (*he could not at the moment remember what*) more.

He did not love anything *more* than Virginia. But the fact that he cared so enormously much for science and justice, for this research and the boys back in Spain, did something to make his love for her more profound and, though it seemed a paradox, more whole-hearted.

'Well, what about moving on?' he suggested at last.

Dr Obispo looked at his wrist-watch. 'I'd forgotten,' he said. 'I've got some letters I ought to write before dinner. Guess I'll have to see Mr Propter some other time.'

'That's too bad!' Pete did his best to impart to his tone and expression the cordiality of regret he did not feel. In fact, he was delighted. He admired Dr Obispo, thought him a remarkable research worker – but not the sort of person a young innocent girl like Virginia ought to associate with. He dreaded for her the influence of so much cynicism and hardboiledness. Besides, so far as his own relations to Virginia were concerned, Dr Obispo was always in the way. 'That's too bad!' he repeated, and the intensity of his pleasure was such that he fairly ran up the steps leading from the baboon-enclosure to the drive – ran so fast that his heart began palpitating and missing beats. Damn that rheumatic fever!

Dr Obispo stepped back to allow Virginia to pass and, as he did so, gave a little tap to the pocket containing *Les Cent-Vingt Jours de Sodome* and tipped her a wink. Virginia winked back and followed Pete up the steps.

A few moments later, Dr Obispo was walking up the drive, the others down. Or, to be more exact, Pete and Jeremy were walking, while Virginia, to whom the idea of using one's legs to get from anywhere to anywhere else was practically unthinkable, sat on her strawberry-and-cream coloured scooter and, with one hand affectionately laid on Pete's shoulder, allowed herself to be carried down by the force of gravity.

The noise of the baboons faded behind them, and at the next turn of the road there was Giambologna's nymph, still indefatigably spouting from her polished breasts. Virginia suddenly interrupted a conversation about Clark Gable to say, in the righteously indignant tone of a vice crusader, 'I just can't figure why Uncle Jo allows that thing to stand there. It's disgusting!'

'Disgusting?' Jeremy echoed in astonishment.

'Disgusting!' she repeated emphatically.

'Do you object to her not having any clothes on?' he asked, remembering, as he did so, those two little satin asymptotes to nudity which she herself had worn up there, in the swimming-pool.

She shook her head impatiently. 'It's the way the water comes out.' She made the grimace of one who had tasted something revolting. 'I think it's horrible.'

'But why?' Jeremy insisted.

'Because it's horrible,' was all the explanation she could give. A child of her age, which was the age, in this context, of bottle-feeding and contraception, she felt herself outraged by this monstrous piece of indelicacy from an earlier time. It was just horrible; that was all that could be said about it. Turning back to Pete, she went on talking about Clark Gable.

Opposite the entrance to the Grotto, Virginia packed her scooter. The masons had finished their work on the tomb and were gone; the place was empty. Virginia straightened her rakishly tilted yachting-cap as a sign of respect; then ran up the steps, paused on the threshold to cross herself and, entering, knelt for a few moments before the image. The others waited silently, in the roadway.

'Our Lady was so wonderful to me when I had sinus trouble last summer,' Virginia explained to Jeremy when she emerged again. 'That's why I got Uncle Jo to make this grotto for her. Wasn't it gorgeous when the Archbishop came for the consecration?' she added, turning to Pete.

Pete nodded affirmatively.

'I haven't even had a cold since She's been here,' Virginia went on, as she took her seat on the scooter. Her face fairly shone with triumph; every victory for the Queen of Heaven was also a personal success for Virginia Maunciple. Then abruptly and without warning, as though she were doing a screen test and had received the order to register fatigue and self-pity, she passed a hand across her forehead, sighed profoundly and, in a tone of utter dejection and discouragement, said, 'All the same, I'm feeling pretty tired this evening. Guess I was in the sun too much right after lunch. Maybe I'd better go and lie down a bit.' And affectionately but very firmly rejecting Pete's offer to go back with her to the castle, she wheeled her scooter round, so that it faced uphill, gave the young man a last, particularly charming, almost amorous smile and look, said, 'Goodbye, Pete darling,' and, opening the throttle of the engine, shot off with gathering momentum and an accelerating roll of explosions up the steep curving road, out of sight. Five minutes later she was in her boudoir, fixing a chocolate-and-banana split at the soda-fountain. Seated in a gilded arm-chair upholstered in satin *couleur fesse de nymphe*, Dr Obispo was reading aloud and translating as he went along from the first volume of *Les Cent-Vingt Jours*.

Chapter Eight

Mr Propter was sitting on a bench under the largest of his eucalyptus trees. To the west the mountains were already a flat silhouette against the evening sky, but in front of him, to the north, the upper slopes were still alive with light and shadow, with rosy gold and depths of indigo. In the foreground, the castle had put on a garment of utterly improbable splendour and romance. Mr Propter looked at it and at the hills and up through the motionless leaves of the eucalyptus at the pale sky; then closed his eyes and noiselessly repeated Cardinal Bérulle's answer to the question: 'What is man?' It was more than thirty years before, when he was writing his study of the Cardinal, that he had first read those words. They had impressed him even then by the splendour and precision of their eloquence. With the lapse of time and the growth of his experience they had come to seem more than eloquent, had come to take on ever richer connotations, ever profounder significances. 'What is man?' he whispered to himself. '*C'est un néant environné de Dieu, indigent de Dieu, capable de Dieu, et rempli de Dieu, s'il veut.*' 'A nothingness surrounded by God, indigent and capable of God, filled with God, if he so desires.' And what is this God of which men are capable? Mr Propter answered with the definition given by John Tauler in the first paragraph of his *Following of Christ*: 'God is a being withdrawn from creatures, a free power, a pure working.' Man, then, is as nothingness surrounded by, and indigent of, a being withdrawn from creatures, a nothingness capable of free power, filled with a pure working if he so desires. *If* he so desires, Mr Propter was distracted into reflecting with a sudden, rather bitter sadness. But how few men ever so desire or, desiring, ever know what to wish for or how to get it! Right knowledge is hardly less rare than the sustained goodwill to act on it. Of those few who look for God, most find, through ignorance, only such reflections of their own self-will as the God of battles, the God of the chosen people, the Prayer-Answerer, the Saviour.

Having deviated thus far into negativity, Mr Propter was led on, through a continuing failure of vigilance, into an even less profitable preoccupation with the concrete and particular miseries of the day. He remembered his interview that morning with Hansen, who was the agent of Jo Stoyte's estates in the valley. Hansen's treatment of the migrants who came to pick the fruit was worse even than the average. He had taken advantage of their number and their desperate need to force down wages. In the groves he managed, young children were being made to work all day in the sun at the rate of two or three cents an hour. And when the day's work was finished, the homes to which they returned were a row of verminous sties in the waste land beside the bed of the river. For these sties, Hansen was charging a rent of ten dollars a month. Ten dollars a month for the privilege of freezing or suffocating; of sleeping in a filthy promiscuity; of being eaten up by bed-bugs and lice; of picking up ophthalmia and perhaps hookworm and amoebic dysentery. And yet Hansen was a very decent, kindly man: one who would be shocked and indignant if he saw you hurting a dog; one who would fly to the protection of a maltreated woman or a crying child. When Mr Propter drew this fact to his attention, Hansen had flushed darkly with anger.

'That's different,' he had said.

Mr Propter had tried to find out why it was different.

It was his duty, Hansen had said.

But how could it be his duty to treat children worse than slaves and inoculate them with hookworm?

It was his duty to the estates. He wasn't doing anything for himself.

But why should doing wrong for someone else be different from doing wrong on your own behalf? The results were exactly the same in either case. The victims didn't suffer any less when you were doing what you called your duty than when you were acting in what you imagined might be your own interests.

This time the anger had exploded in violent abuse. It was the anger, Mr Propter had perceived, of the well-meaning but stupid man who is compelled against his will to ask himself indiscreet questions about what he has been doing as a matter of course. He doesn't want to ask these questions, because he knows that if he does he will be forced either to go on with what he is doing, but with the cynic's awareness that he is doing wrong, or else, if he doesn't want to be a cynic, to change the entire pattern of his life so as to bring his desire to do right into harmony with the real facts as revealed in the course of self-interrogation. To most people any radical change is even more odious than cynicism. The only way between the horns of the dilemma is to persist at all costs in the ignorance which permits one to go on doing wrong in the comforting belief that by doing so one is accomplishing one's duty – one's duty to the company, to the shareholders, to the family, the city, the state, the fatherland, the church. For, of course, poor Hansen's case wasn't in any way unique; on a smaller scale, and therefore with less power to do evil, he was acting like all those civil servants and statesmen and prelates who go through life spreading misery and destruction in the name of their ideals and under orders from their categorical imperatives.

Well, he hadn't got very far with Hansen, Mr Propter sadly concluded. He'd have to try again with Jo Stoyte. In the past, Jo had always refused to listen, on the ground that the estates were Hansen's business. The alibi was so convenient that it would be hard, he foresaw, to break it down.

From Hansen and Jo Stoyte his thoughts wandered to that newly arrived family of transients from Kansas, to whom he had given one of his cabins. The three under-nourished children, with the teeth already rotting in their mouths; the woman, emaciated by God knew what complication of diseases, deep-sunken already in apathy and weakness; the husband, alternately resentful and self-pitying, violent and morose.

He had gone with the man to get some vegetables from the garden plots and a rabbit for the family supper. Sitting there, skinning the rabbit, he had had to listen to outbursts of incoherent complaint and indignation. Complaint and indignation against the wheat market, which had broken each time he had begun to do well. Against the banks he had borrowed money from and been unable to repay. Against the droughts and winds that had reduced his farm to a hundred and sixty acres of dust and wilderness. Against the luck that had always been against *him*. Against the folks who had treated him so meanly, everywhere, all his life.

Dismally familiar story! With inconsiderable variations, he had heard it a thousand times before. Sometimes they were sharecroppers from further south, dispossessed by the owners in a desperate effort to make the farming pay. Sometimes, like this man, they had owned their own place and been dispossessed, not by financiers, but by the forces of nature – forces of nature which they themselves had made destructive by tearing up the grass and planting nothing but wheat. Sometimes they had been hired men, displaced by the tractors. All of them had come to California as to a promised land; and California had already reduced them to a condition of wandering peonage and was fast transforming them into Untouchables. Only a saint, Mr Propter reflected, only a saint, could be a peon and a pariah with impunity, because only a saint would accept the position gladly and as though he had chosen it of his own free will. Poverty and suffering ennoble only when they are voluntary. By involuntary poverty and suffering men are made worse. It is easier for a camel to pass through the eye of a needle than for an involuntarily poor man to enter the kingdom of heaven. Here, for example, was this poor devil from Kansas. How had he reacted to involuntary poverty and suffering? So far as Mr Propter could judge, he was compensating himself for his misfortunes by brutality to those weaker than himself. The way he yelled at the children. . . . It was an all too familiar symptom.

When the rabbit was skinned and gutted, Mr Propter had interrupted his companion's monologue.

'Do you know which is the stupidest text in the Bible?' he had suddenly asked.

Startled, and evidently a bit shocked, the man from Kansas had shaken his head.

'It's this,' Mr Propter had said, as he got up and handed him the carcase of the rabbit. ' "They hated me without a cause." '

Under the eucalyptus tree, Mr Propter wearily sighed. Pointing out to unfortunate people that, in part at any rate, they were pretty certainly responsible for their own misfortunes; explaining to them that ignorance and stupidity are no less severely punished by the nature of things than deliberate malice – these were never agreeable tasks. Never agreeable, but, so far as he could see, always necessary. For what hope, he asked himself, what faintest glimmer of hope is there for a man who really believes that 'they hated me without a cause' and that he had no part in his own disasters?

Obviously, no hope whatever. We see, as matter of brute fact, that disasters and hatreds are never without causes; we also see that some at least of those causes are generally under the control of the people who suffer the disasters or are the object of the hatred. In some measure they are directly or indirectly responsible. Directly, by the commission of stupid or malicious acts. Indirectly, by the omission to be as intelligent and compassionate as they might be. And if they make this omission, it is generally because they choose to conform unthinkingly to local standards, and the current way of living. Mr Propter's thoughts returned to the poor fellow from Kansas. Self-righteous, no doubt disagreeable to the neighbours, an incompetent farmer, but that wasn't the whole story. His gravest offence had been to accept the world in which he found himself as normal, rational and right. Like all the others, he had allowed the advertisers to multiply his wants; he had learned to equate happiness with possessions, and prosperity with money to spend in a shop. Like all the others, he had abandoned any idea of subsistence farming to think exclusively in terms of a cash crop; and he had gone on thinking in those terms, even when the crop no longer gave him any cash. Then, like all the others, he had got into debt with the banks. And finally, like all the others, he had learned that what the experts had been saying for a generation was perfectly true: in a semi-arid country it is grass that holds down the soil; tear up the grass, the soil will go. In due course, it had gone.

The man from Kansas was now a peon and a pariah; and the experience was making a worse man of him.

St Peter Claver was another of the historical personages to whom Mr Propter had devoted a study. When the slave-ships came into the harbour of Cartagena, Peter Claver was the only white man to venture down into the holds. There, in the unspeakable stench and heat, in the vapours of pus and excrement, he tended the sick, he dressed the ulcers of those whom their manacles had wounded, he held in his arms the men who had given way to despair and spoke to them words of comfort and affection – and in the intervals talked to them about their sins. *Their* sins! The modern humanitarian would laugh, if he were not shocked. And yet – such was the conclusion to which Mr Propter had gradually and reluctantly come – and yet St Peter Claver was probably right.

Not completely right, of course; for, acting on wrong knowledge, no man, however well-intentioned, can be more than partially right. But as nearly right, at any rate, as a good man with a counter-Reformation Catholic philosophy could expect to be. Right in insisting that, whatever the circumstances in which he finds himself, a human being always has omissions to make good, commissions whose effects must, if possible, be neutralized. Right in believing that it is well even for the most brutally sinned against to be reminded of their own shortcomings.

Peter Claver's conception of the world had the defect of being erroneous, but the merit of being simple and dramatic. Given a personal God, dispenser of forgiveness, given heaven and hell and the absolute reality of human personalities, given the meritoriousness of mere good intentions and of unquestioning faith in a set of incorrect opinions, given the one true church, the efficacy of priestly mediation, the magic of sacraments – given all these, it was really quite easy to convince even a newly imported slave of his sinfulness and to explain exactly what he ought to do about it. But if there is no single inspired book, no uniquely holy church, no mediating priesthood nor sacramental magic, if there is no personal God to be placated into forgiving offences, if there are, even in the moral world, only causes and effects and the enormous complexity of inter-relationships – then, clearly the task of telling people what to do about their shortcomings is much more difficult. For every individual is called upon to display not only unsleeping good-will but also unsleeping intelligence. And this is not all. For, if individuality is not absolute, if personalities are illusory figments of a self-will disastrously blind to the reality of a more-than-personal consciousness, of which it is the limitation and denial, then all of every human being's efforts must be directed, in the last resort, to the actualization of that more-than-personal consciousness. So that even intelligence is not sufficient as an adjunct to good-will; there must also be the recollection which seeks to transform and transcend intelligence. Many are called, but few are chosen – because few even know in what salvation consists. Consider again this man from Kansas. ... Mr Propter sadly shook his head. Everything was against the poor fellow – his fundamentalist orthodoxy, his wounded and inflamed egotism, his nervous irritability, his low intelligence. The first three disadvantages might perhaps be removed. But could anything be done about the fourth? The nature of things is implacable towards weakness. 'From him that hath not shall be taken away even that which he hath.' And what were those words of Spinoza's? 'A man may be excusable and nevertheless be tormented in many ways. A horse is excusable for not being a man; but nevertheless he must needs be a horse, and not a man.' All the same, there must surely be something to be done for people like the man from Kansas – something that didn't entail telling harmful untruths about the nature of things. The untruth, for example, that there is a person up aloft, or the other more modern untruth to the effect that human values are absolute and that God is the nation or the party or the human race as a whole. Surely, Mr Propter insisted, surely there was something to be done for such people. The man from Kansas had begun by resenting what he had said about the chain of cause and effect, the network of relationships – resenting it as a personal insult. But afterwards, when he saw that he was not being blamed, that no attempt was being made to come it over him, he had begun to take an interest, to see that after all there was something in it. Little by little it might be possible to make him think a bit more realistically, at least about the world of everyday life, the outside world of appearances. And when he had done that, then it mightn't be so overwhelmingly difficult for him to think a bit more realistically about himself – to conceive of that all-important ego of his as a fiction, a kind of nightmare, a frantically agitated nothingness capable, when once its frenzy had been quieted, of being filled with God, with a God conceived and experienced as a more than personal consciousness, as a free power, a pure working, a being withdrawn. . . . Suddenly, as he thus returned to his starting-point, Mr Propter became aware of the long, circuitous, unprofitable way he had travelled in order to reach it. He had come to this bench under the eucalyptus tree in order to recollect himself, in order to realize for a moment the existence of that other consciousness behind his private thoughts and feelings, that free, pure power greater than his own. He had come for this; but memories had slipped in while he was off his guard; speculations had started up, cloud upon cloud, like sea-birds rising from their nesting-place to darken and eclipse the sun. Bondage is the life of personality, and for bondage the personal self will fight with tireless resourcefulness and the most stubborn cunning. The price of freedom is eternal vigilance; and he had failed to be vigilant. It wasn't a case, he reflected ruefully, of the spirit being willing and the flesh weak. That was altogether the wrong antithesis. The spirit is always willing; but the person, who is a mind as well as a body, is always unwilling – and the person, incidentally, is not weak but extremely strong.

He looked again at the mountains, at the pale sky between the leaves, at the soft russet pinks and purples and greys of the eucalyptus trunks; then shut his eyes once more.

'A nothingness surrounded by God, indigent of God, capable of God and filled with God if man so desires. And what is God? A being withdrawn from creatures, a free power, a pure working.' His vigilance gradually ceased to be an act of the will, a deliberate thrusting back of irrelevant personal thoughts and wishes and feelings. For little by little these thoughts and wishes and feelings had settled like a muddy sediment in a jar of water, and as they settled, his vigilance was free to transform itself into a kind of effortless unattached awareness, at once intense and still, alert and passive – an awareness whose object was the words he had spoken and at the same time that which surrounded the words. But that which surrounded the words was the awareness itself; for this vigilance which was now an effortless awareness – what was it but an aspect, a partial expression, of that impersonal and untroubled consciousness into which the words had been dropped and through which they were slowly sinking? And as they sank they took a new significance for the awareness that was following them down into the depths of itself – a significance new not in respect to the entities connoted by the words, but rather in the mode of their comprehension, which, from being intellectual in character, had become intuitive and direct, so that the nature of man in his potentiality and of God in actuality were realized by an analogue of sensuous experience, by a kind of unmediated participation.

The busy nothingness of his being experienced itself as transcended in the felt capacity for peace and purity, for the withdrawal from revulsion and desires, for the blissful freedom from personality. . . .

The sound of approaching footsteps made him open his eyes. Peter Boone and that Englishman he had sat with in the car were advancing up the path towards his seat under the eucalyptus trees. Mr Propter raised his hand in welcome and smiled. He was fond of young Pete. There was native intelligence there and native kindliness; there was sensitiveness, generosity, a spontaneous decency of impulse and reaction. Charming and beautiful qualities! The pity was that by themselves, and undirected as they were by a right knowledge of the nature of things, they should be so impotent for good, so inadequate to anything a reasonable man could call salvation. Fine gold, but still in the ore, unsmelted, unworked. Some day, perhaps, the boy would learn to use his gold. He would have to wish to learn first – and wish also to unlearn a lot of the things he now regarded as self-evident and right. It would be hard for him – as hard, but for other reasons, as it would be for that poor fellow from Kansas.

'Well, Pete,' he called, 'come and sit with me here. And you've brought Mr Pordage; that's good.' He moved to the middle of the bench so that they could sit, one on either side of him. 'And did you meet the Ogre?' he said to Jeremy, pointing in the direction of the castle.

Jeremy made a grimace and nodded. 'I remembered the name you used to call him at school,' he said. 'That made it a little easier.'

'Poor Jo,' said Mr Propter. 'Fat people are always supposed to be so happy. But who ever enjoyed being laughed at? That jolly manner they sometimes have, and the jokes they make at their own expense – it's just a case of alibis and prophylactics. They vaccinate themselves with their own ridicule so that they shan't react too violently to other people's.'

Jeremy smiled. He knew all about that. 'It's a good way out of an unpleasant predicament,' he said.

Mr Propter nodded. 'But unfortunately,' he said, 'it didn't happen to be Jo's way. Jo was the kind of a fat boy who bluffs it out. The kind that fights. The kind that bullies or patronizes. The kind that boasts and shows off. The kind that buys popularity by treating the girls to ice-creams, even if he has to steal a dime from his grandmother's purse to do it. The kind that goes on stealing even if he's found out and gets beaten and believes it when they tell him he'll go to hell. Poor Jo, he's been that sort of fat boy all his life.' He pointed once again in the direction of the castle. 'That's his monument to a faulty pituitary. And talking of pituitaries,' he went on, turning to Pete, 'how's the work been going?'

Pete had been thinking gloomily of Virginia – wondering for the hundredth time why she had left them, whether he had done anything to offend her, whether she was really tired or if there might be some other reason. At Mr Propter's mention of work he looked up, and his face brightened. 'It's going just fine,' he answered, and, in quick, eager phrases, strangely compounded of slang and technical terms, he told Mr Propter about the results they had already got with their mice and were beginning to get, so it seemed, with the baboons and the dogs.

'And if you succeed,' Mr Propter asked, 'what happens to your dogs?'

'Why, their life's prolonged,' Pete answered triumphantly.

'Yes, yes, I know that,' said the older man. 'What I meant to ask was something different. A dog's a wolf that hasn't fully developed. It's more like the foetus of a wolf than an adult wolf; isn't that so?'

Pete nodded.

'In other words,' Mr Propter went on, 'it's a mild, tractable animal because it has never grown up into savagery. Isn't that supposed to be one of the mechanisms of evolutionary development?'

Pete nodded again. 'There's a kind of glandular equilibrium,' he explained. 'Then a mutation comes along and knocks it sideways. You get a new equilibrium that happens to retard the development rate. You grow up; but you do it so slowly that you're dead before you've stopped being like your great-great-grandfather's foetus.'

'Exactly,' said Mr Propter. 'So what happens if you prolong the life of an animal that has evolved that way?'

Pete laughed and shrugged his shoulders. 'Guess we'll have to wait and see,' he said.

'It would be a bit disquieting,' said Mr Propter, 'if your dogs grew back in the process of growing up.'

Pete laughed again delightedly. 'Think of the dowagers being chased by their own Pekingese,' he said.

Mr Propter looked at him curiously and was silent for a moment, as though waiting to see whether Pete would make any further comment. The comment did not come. 'I'm glad you feel so happy about it,' he said. Then, turning to Jeremy, ' "It is not," if I remember rightly, Mr Pordage,' he went on, ' "it is not growing like a tree in bulk doth make men better be." '

' "Or standing long an oak, three hundred years," ' said Jeremy, smiling with the pleasure which an apt quotation always gave him.

'What shall we all be doing at three hundred?' Mr Propter speculated. 'Do you suppose you'd still be a scholar and a gentleman?'

Jeremy coughed and patted his bald head. 'One will certainly have stopped being a gentleman,' he answered. 'One's begun to stop even now, thank heaven.'

'But the scholar will stay the course?'

'There's a lot of books in the British Museum.'

'And you, Pete?' said Mr Propter. 'Do you suppose you'll still be doing scientific research?'

'Why not? What's to prevent you from going on with it for ever?' the young man answered emphatically.

'For ever?' Mr Propter repeated. 'You don't think you'd get a bit bored? One experiment after another. Or one book after another,' he added in an aside to Jeremy. 'In general, one damned thing after another. You don't think that would prey on your mind a bit?'

'I don't see why,' said Pete.

'Time doesn't bother you, then?'

Pete shook his head. 'Why should it?'

'Why shouldn't it?' said Mr Propter, smiling at him with an amused affection. 'Time's a pretty bothersome thing, you know.'

'Not if you aren't scared of dying, or growing old.'

'Yes, it is,' Mr Propter insisted; 'even if you're not scared. It's nightmarish in itself – intrinsically nightmarish, if you see what I mean.'

'Intrinsically?' Pete looked at him perplexed. 'I don't get it,' he said. 'Intrinsically nightmarish . . .?'

'Nightmarish in the present tense, of course,' Jeremy put in. 'But if one takes it in the fossil state – in the form of the Hauberk Papers, for example . . .' He left the sentence unfinished.

'Oh, pleasant enough,' said Mr Propter, agreeing with his implied conclusion. 'But, after all, history isn't the real thing. Past time is only evil at a distance; and, of course, the study of past time is itself a process in time. Cataloguing bits of fossil evil can never be more than an *Ersatz* for the experience of eternity.' He glanced curiously at Pete, wondering how the boy would respond to what he was saying. Plunging like this into the heart of the matter, beginning at the very core and centre of the mystery – it was risky; there was a danger of evoking nothing but bewilderment, or alternatively nothing but angry decision. Pete's, he could see, was more nearly the first reaction; but it was a bewilderment that seemed to be tempted by interest; he looked as though he wanted to find out what it was all about.

Meanwhile, Jeremy had begun to feel that this conversation was taking a most undesirable turn. 'What precisely are we supposed to be talking about?' he asked acidulously. 'The New Jerusalem?'

Mr Propter smiled at him good-humouredly. 'It's all right,' he said. 'I won't say a word about harps or wings.'

'Well, that's something,' said Jeremy.

'I never could get much satisfaction out of meaningless discourse,' Mr Propter continued. 'I like the words I use to bear some relation to facts. That's why I'm interested in eternity – psychological eternity. Because it's a fact.'

'For you, perhaps,' said Jeremy in a tone which implied that more civilized people didn't suffer from these hallucinations.

'For anyone who chooses to fulfil the conditions under which it can be experienced.'

'And why should anyone choose to fulfil them?'

'Why should anyone choose to go to Athens to see the Parthenon? Because it's worth the bother. And the same is true of eternity. The experience of timeless good is worth all the trouble it involves.'

' "Timeless good," ' Jeremy repeated with distaste. 'I don't know what the words mean.'

'Why should you?' said Mr Propter. 'One doesn't know the full meaning of the word "Parthenon" until one has actually seen the thing.'

'Yes, but at least I've seen photographs of the Parthenon; I've read descriptions.'

'You've read descriptions of timeless good,' Mr Propter answered. 'Dozens of them. In all the literatures of philosophy and religion. You've read them; but you've never bought your ticket for Athens.'

In a resentful silence, Jeremy had to admit to himself that this was true. The fact that it was true made him disapprove of the conversation even more profoundly than he had done before.

'As for time,' Mr Propter was saying to Pete, 'what is it, in this particular context, but the medium in which evil propagates itself, the element in which evil lives and outside of which it dies? Indeed, it's more than the element of evil, more than merely its medium. If you carry your analysis far enough, you'll find that time is evil. One of the aspects of its essential substance.'

Jeremy listened with growing discomfort and a mounting irritation. His fears had been justified; the old boy was launching out into the worst kind of theology. Eternity, timeless experience of good, time as the substance of evil – it was bad enough, God knew, in books; but, fired at you like this, point-blank, by somebody who really took it seriously, why, it was really frightful. Why on earth couldn't people live their lives in a rational, civilized way? Why couldn't they take things as they came? Breakfast at nine, lunch at one-thirty, tea at five. And conversation. And the daily walk with Mr Gladstone, the Yorkshire terrier. And the library; the Works of Voltaire in eighty-three volumes; the inexhaustible treasure of Horace Walpole; and for a change the *Divine Comedy*; and then, in case you might be tempted to take the Middle Ages too seriously, Salimbene's autobiography and the Miller's Tale. And sometimes calls in the afternoon – the Rector, Lady Fredegond with her ear-trumpet, Mr Veal. And political discussions – except that in these last months, since the *Anschluss* and Munich, one had found that political discussion was one of the unpleasant things it was wise to avoid. And the weekly journey to London, with lunch at the Reform, and always dinner with old Thripp of the British Museum; and a chat with one's poor brother Tom at the Foreign Office (only that too was rapidly becoming one of the things to be avoided). And then, of course, the London Library; the Vespers at Westminster Cathedral, if they happened to be singing Palestrina; and every alternate week, between five and six-thirty, an hour and a half with Mae or Doris in their flat in Maida Vale. Infinite squalor in a little room, as he liked to call it; abysmally delightful. Those were the things that came; why couldn't they take them, quietly and sensibly? But no, they had to gibber about eternity and all the rest. That sort of stuff always made Jeremy want to be blasphemous – to ask whether God had a *boyau rectum*, to protest, like the Japanese in the anecdote, that he was altogether flummoxed and perplexed by position of Honourable Bird. But, unfortunately, the present was one of those peculiarly exasperating cases where such reactions were out of place. For, after all, old Propter had written *Short Studies*; what he said couldn't just be dismissed as the vapourings of a deficient mind. Besides, he hadn't talked Christianity, so that jokes about anthropomorphism were beside the point. It was really too exasperating! He assumed an expression of haughty detachment and even started to hum 'The Honeysuckle and the Bee'. The impression he wanted to give was that of a superior being who really couldn't be expected to waste his time listening to stuff like this.

A comic spectacle, Mr Propter reflected as he looked at him; except, of course, that it was so extremely depressing.

Chapter Nine

'TIME and craving,' said Mr Propter, 'craving and time – two aspects of the same thing; and that thing is the raw material of evil. So you see, Pete,' he added in another tone, 'you see what a queer sort of present you'll be making us, if you're successful in your work. Another century or so of time and craving. A couple of extra lifetimes of potential evil.'

'*And* potential good,' the young man insisted with a note of protest in his voice.

'*And* potential good,' Mr Propter agreed. 'But only at a far remove from that extra time you're giving us.'

'Why do you say that?' Pete asked.

'Because potential evil is *in* time; potential good isn't. The longer you live, the more evil you automatically come into contact with. Nobody comes automatically into contact with good. Men don't find more good by merely existing longer. It's curious,' he went on reflectively, 'that people should always have concentrated on the problem of evil. Exclusively. As though the nature of good were something self-evident. But it isn't self-evident. There's a problem of good at least as difficult as the problem of evil.'

'And what's the solution?' Pete asked.

'The solution is very simple and profoundly unacceptable. Actual good is outside time.'

'Outside time? But then how . . .?'

'I told you it was unacceptable,' said Mr Propter.

'But if it's outside time, then . . .'

'. . . then nothing within time can be actual good. Time is potential evil, and craving converts the potentiality into actual evil. Whereas a temporal act can never be more than potentially good, with a potentiality, what's more, that can't be actualized except out of time.'

'But inside time, here – you know, just doing the ordinary things – hell! we do sometimes do right. What acts *are* good?'

'Strictly speaking, none,' Mr Propter answered. 'But, in practice, I think one's justified in applying the word to certain acts. Any act

that contributes towards the liberation of those concerned in it —
I'd call it a good act.'

'Liberation?' the young man repeated dubiously. The words, in
his mind, carried only economic and revolutionary connotations.
But it was evident that Mr Propter wasn't talking about the necessity for getting rid of capitalism. 'Liberation from what?'

Mr Propter hesitated before replying. Should he go on with this?
he wondered. The Englishman was hostile; the time short; the boy
himself entirely ignorant. But it was an ignorance evidently mitigated by good-will and a touching nostalgia for perfection. He
decided to take a chance and go on.

'Liberation from time,' he said. 'Liberation from craving and
revulsions. Liberation from personality.'

'But heck,' said Pete, 'you're always talking about democracy.
Doesn't that mean respecting personality?'

'Of course,' Mr Propter agreed. 'Respecting it in order that it
may be able to transcend itself. Slavery and fanaticism intensify the
obsession with time and evil and the self. Hence the value of democratic institutions and a sceptical attitude of mind. The more you
respect a personality, the better its chance of discovering that all
personality is a prison. Potential good is anything that helps you to
get out of prison. Actualized good lies outside the prison, in timelessness, in the state of pure, disinterested consciousness.'

'I'm not much good at abstractions,' said the young man. 'Let's
take some concrete examples. What about science, for instance? Is
that good?'

'Good, bad and indifferent, according to how it's pursued and
what it's used for. Good, bad, and indifferent, first of all, for the
scientists themselves – just as art and scholarship may be good, bad,
or indifferent for artists and scholars. Good if it facilitates liberation; indifferent if it neither helps nor hinders; bad if it makes
liberation more difficult by intensifying the obsession with personality. And, remember, the apparent selflessness of the scientist, or
the artist, is not necessarily a genuine freedom from the bondage of
personality. Scientists and artists are men devoted to what we
vaguely call an ideal. But what is an ideal? An ideal is merely the
projection, on an enormously enlarged scale, of some aspect of
personality.'

'Say that again,' Pete requested, while even Jeremy so far forgot his pose of superior detachment to lend his most careful attention.

Mr Propter said it again. 'And that's true,' he went on, 'of every ideal except the highest, which is the ideal of liberation – liberation from personality, liberation from time and craving, liberation into union with God, if you don't object to the word, Mr Pordage. Many people do,' he added. 'It's one of the words that the Mrs Grundys of the intellect find peculiarly shocking. I always try to spare their sensibilities, if I can. Well, to return to our idealist,' he continued, glad to see that Jeremy had been constrained, in spite of himself, to smile. 'If he serves any ideal except the highest – whether it's the artist's ideal of beauty, or the scientist's ideal of truth, or the humanitarian's ideal of what currently passes for goodness – he's not serving God; he's serving a magnified aspect of himself. He may be completely devoted; but in the last analysis his devotion turns out to be directed towards an aspect of his own personality. His apparent selflessness is really not a liberation from his ego, but merely another form of bondage. This means that science may be bad for scientists, even when it appears to be a deliverer. And the same holds good of art, of scholarship, of humanitarianism.'

Jeremy thought nostalgically of his library at The Araucarias. Why couldn't this old madman be content to take things as they came?

'And what about other people?' Pete was saying. 'People who aren't scientists. Hasn't it helped to set them free?'

Mr Propter nodded. 'And it has also helped to tie them more closely to themselves. And what's more, I should guess that it has increased bondage more than it has diminished it – and will tend to go on increasing it, progressively.'

'How do you figure that out?'

'Through its applications,' Mr Propter answered. 'Applications to warfare, first of all. Better planes, better explosives, better guns and gases – every improvement increases the sum of fear and hatred, widens the incidence of nationalistic hysteria. In other words, every improvement in armaments makes it more difficult for people to escape from their egos, more difficult to forget those horrible projections of themselves they call their ideals of patriotism, heroism, glory and all the rest. And even the less destructive applications of science aren't really much more satisfactory. For what do such applications result in? The multiplication of possessable objects; the invention of new instruments of stimulation; the dissemination of new wants through propaganda aimed at equating possession with well-being and incessant stimulation with happiness.

'But incessant stimulation from without is a source of bondage; and so is the preoccupation with possessions. And now you're threatening to prolong our lives, so that we can go on being stimulated, go on desiring possessions, go on waving flags and hating our enemies and being afraid of air attack – go on and on, generation after generation, sinking deeper and deeper into the stinking slough of our personality.' He shook his head. 'No, I can't quite share your optimism about science.'

There was a silence while Pete debated with himself whether to ask Mr Propter about love. In the end he decided he wouldn't. Virginia was too sacred. But why, why had she turned back at the Grotto? What could he have said or done to offend her? As much to prevent himself from brooding over these problems as because he wanted to know the old man's opinions on the last of the three things that seemed to him supremely valuable, he looked up at Mr Propter and asked, 'What about social justice? I mean, take the French Revolution. Or Russia. And what about this Spanish business – fighting for liberty and democracy against fascist aggression?' He had tried to remain perfectly calm and scientific about the whole thing; but his voice trembled a little as he spoke the last words. In spite of their familiarity (perhaps because of their familiarity), phrases like 'fascist aggression' still had power to move him to the depths.

'Napoleon came out of the French Revolution,' said Mr Propter after a moment's silence. 'German nationalism came out of Napoleon. The war of 1870 came out of German nationalism. The war of 1914 came out of the war of 1870. Hitler came out of the war of 1914. Those are the bad results of the French Revolution. The good results were the enfranchisement of the French peasants and the spread of political democracy. Put the good results in one scale of your balance and the bad ones in the other, and try which set is the heavier. Then perform the same operation with Russia. Put the abolition of tsardom and capitalism in one scale; and in the other put Stalin, put the secret police, put the famines, put twenty years of hardship for a hundred and fifty million people, put the liquidation of intellectuals and kulaks and old bolsheviks, put the hordes of slaves in prison camps; put the military conscription of everybody, male and female, from childhood to old age, put the revolutionary propaganda which spurred the bourgeoisie to invent fascism.' Mr Propter shook his head. 'Or take the fight for democracy in Spain,' he went on. 'There was a fight for democracy all over Europe not so long ago. Rational prognosis can only be based on past experience. Look at the results of 1914 and then ask yourself what chance the loyalists ever had of establishing a liberal régime at the end of a long war. The others are winning; so we shall never have the opportunity of seeing what circumstances and their own passions would have driven those well-intentioned liberals to become.'

'But hell!' Pete broke out, 'what do you expect people to do when they're attacked by the fascists? Sit down and let their throats be cut?'

'Of course not,' said Mr Propter. 'I *expect* them to fight. And the expectation is based on my previous knowledge of human behaviour. But the fact that people generally do react to that kind of situation in that kind of way doesn't prove that it's the best way of reacting. Experience makes me expect that they'll behave like that. But experience also makes me expect that, if they do behave like that, the results will be disastrous.'

'Well, how do you want us to act? Do you want us to sit still and do nothing?'

'Not nothing,' said Mr Propter. 'Merely something appropriate.'

'But what is appropriate?'

'Not war, anyhow. Not violent revolution. Nor yet politics, to any considerable extent, I should guess.'

'Then what?'

'That's what we've got to discover. The main lines are clear enough. But there's still a lot of work to be done on the practical details.'

Pete was not listening. His mind had gone back to that time in Aragon when life had seemed supremely significant. 'But those boys, back there in Spain,' he burst out. 'You didn't know them, Mr Propter. They were wonderful, really they were. Never mean to you, and brave, and loyal and . . . and everything.' He wrestled with the inadequacies of his vocabulary, with the fear of making an exhibition of himself by talking big, like a highbrow. 'They weren't living for themselves, I can tell you that, Mr Propter.' He looked into the old man's face almost supplicatingly, as though imploring him to believe. 'They were living for something much bigger than themselves – like what you were talking about just now; you know, something more than just personal.'

'And what about Hitler's boys?' Mr Propter asked. 'What about Mussolini's boys? What about Stalin's boys? Do you suppose they're not just as brave, just as kind to one another, just as loyal to their cause and just as firmly convinced that it's the cause of justice, truth, freedom, right and honour?' He looked at Pete inquiringly; but Pete said nothing. 'The fact that people have a lot of virtues,' Mr Propter went on, 'doesn't prove anything about the goodness of their actions. You can have all the virtues – that's to say, all except the two that really matter, understanding and compassion – you can have all the others, I say, and be a thoroughly bad man. Indeed, you can't be really bad unless you *do* have most of the virtues. Look at Milton's Satan for example. Brave, strong, generous, loyal, prudent, temperate, self-sacrificing. And let's give the dictators the credit that's due to them; some of them are nearly as virtuous as Satan. Not quite, I admit, but nearly. That's why they can achieve so much evil.'

His elbows on his knees, Pete sat in silence, frowning. 'But that feeling,' he said at last. 'That feeling there was between us. You know — the friendship; only it was more than just ordinary friendship. And the feeling of being there all together – fighting for the same thing – and the thing being worth while – and then the danger, and the rain, and that awful cold at nights, and the heat in summer, and being thirsty, and even those lice and the dirt – share and share alike in everything bad or good – and knowing that tomorrow it might be your turn, or one of the other boys – your turn for the field hospital (and the chances were they wouldn't have enough anaesthetics, except maybe for an amputation or something like that), or your turn for the burial-party. All those feelings, Mr Propter – I just can't believe they didn't mean something.'

'They meant themselves,' said Mr Propter.

Jeremy saw the opportunity for a counter-attack and, with a promptitude unusual in him, immediately took it. 'Doesn't the same thing apply to your feelings about eternity, or whatever it is?' he asked.

'Of course it does,' said Mr Propter.

'Well, in that case, how can you claim any validity for it? The feeling means itself, and that's all there is to it.'

'It means itself,' Mr Propter agreed. 'But what precisely is this "itself"? In other words, what is the nature of the feeling?'

'Don't ask me,' said Jeremy with a shake of the head and a comically puzzled lift of the eyebrows. 'I really don't know.'

Mr Propter smiled. 'I know you don't want to know,' he said. 'And I won't ask you. I'll just state the facts. The feeling in question is a non-personal experience of timeless peace. Accordingly, non-personality, timelessness and peace are what it means. Now let's consider the feeling that Pete had been talking about. These are all personal feelings, evoked by temporal situations, and characterized by a sense of excitement. Intensification of the ego within the world of time and craving – that's what these feelings meant.'

'But you can't call self-sacrifice an intensification of the ego,' said Pete.

'I can and I do,' Mr Propter insisted. 'For the good reason that it generally is. Self-sacrifice to any but the highest cause is sacrifice to an ideal, which is simply a projection of the ego. What is commonly called self-sacrifice is the sacrifice of one part of the ego to another part, one set of personal feelings and passions for another set – as when the feelings connected with money or sex are sacrificed in order that the ego may have the feelings of superiority, solidarity, and hatred which are associated with patriotism, or any kind of political or religious fanaticism.'

Pete shook his head. 'Sometimes,' he said, with a smile of rueful perplexity, 'sometimes you almost talk like Dr Obispo. You know – cynically.'

Mr Propter laughed. 'It's good to be cynical,' he said. 'That is, if you know when to stop. Most of the things that we're all taught to respect and reverence – they don't deserve anything but cynicism. Take your own case. You've been taught to worship ideals like patriotism, social justice, science, romantic love. You've been told that such virtues as loyalty, temperance, courage, and prudence are good in themselves, in any circumstances. You've been assured that self-sacrifice is always splendid and fine feelings invariably good. And it's all nonsense, all a pack of lies that people have made up in order to justify themselves in continuing to deny God and wallow in their own egotism. Unless you're steadily and unflaggingly cynical about the solemn twaddle that's talked by bishops and bankers and professors and politicians and all the rest of them, you're lost. Utterly lost. Doomed to perpetual imprisonment in your ego – doomed to be a personality in a world of personalities; and a world of personalities is *this* world, the world of greed and fear and hatred, of war and capitalism and dictatorship and slavery. Yes, you've got to be cynical, Pete. Specially cynical about all the actions and feelings you've been taught to suppose were good. Most of them are not good. They're merely evils which happen to be regarded as creditable. But, unfortunately, creditable evil is just as bad as discreditable evil. Scribes and Pharisees aren't any better, in the last analysis, than publicans and sinners. Indeed, they're often much worse. For several reasons. Being well thought of by others, they think well of themselves; and nothing so confirms an egotism as thinking well of oneself. In the next place, publicans and sinners are generally just human animals, without enough energy or self-control to do much harm. Whereas the Scribes and Pharisees have all the virtues, except the only two which count, and enough intelligence to understand everything except the real nature of the world. Publicans and sinners merely fornicate and overeat, and get drunk. The people who make wars, the people who reduce their fellows to slavery, the people who kill and torture and tell lies in the name of their sacred causes, the really evil people, in a word – these are never the publicans and the sinners. No, they're the virtuous, respectable men, who have the finest feelings, the best brains, the noblest ideals.'

'So what it all boils down to,' Pete concluded in a tone of angry despair, 'is that there just isn't anything you can do. Is that it?'

'Yes and no,' said Mr Propter, in his quiet judicial way. 'On the strictly human level, the level of time and craving, I should say that it's quite true: in the last resort, there isn't anything you can do.'

'But that's just defeatism!' Pete protested.

'Why is it defeatism to be realistic?'

'There *must* be something to do!'

'I see no "must" about it.'

'Then what about the reformers and all those people? If you're right, they're just wasting their time.'

'It depends what they think they're doing,' said Mr Propter. 'If they think they're just temporarily palliating particular distresses, if they see themselves as people engaged in laboriously deflecting evil from old channels into new and slightly different channels, then they can justifiably claim to be successful. But if they think they're making good appear where evil was before, why, then, all history clearly shows that they *are* wasting their time.'

'But why can't they make good appear where evil was before?'

'Why do we fall when we jump out of a tenth-story window? Because the nature of things happens to be such that we do fall. And the nature of things is such that, on the strictly human level of time and craving, you can't achieve anything but evil. If you choose to work exclusively on that level, and exclusively for the ideals and causes that are characteristic of it, then you're insane if you expect to transform evil into good. You're insane, because experience should have shown you that, on that level, there doesn't happen to be any good. There are only different degrees and different kinds of evil.'

'Then what do you want people to *do*?'

'Don't talk as though it were all my fault,' said Mr Propter. 'I didn't invent the universe.'

'What ought they to do, then?'

'Well, if they want fresh varieties of evil, let them go on with what they're doing now. But if they want good, they'll have to change their tactics. And the encouraging thing,' Mr Propter added in another tone, 'the encouraging thing is that there *are* tactics which will produce good. We've seen that there's nothing to be done on the strictly human level – or rather there are millions of things to be done, only none of them will achieve any good. But there *is* something effective to be done on the levels where good actually exists. So you see , Pete, I'm not a defeatist. I'm a strategist. I believe that if a battle is to be fought, it had better be fought under conditions in which there's at least some chance of winning . I believe that, if you want the golden fleece, it's more sensible to go to the place where it exists than to rush round performing prodigies of valour in a country where all the fleeces happen to be coal-black.'

'Then where ought we to fight for good?'

'Where good is.'

'But where is it?'

'On the level below the human and on the level above. On the animal level and on the level . . . well, you can take your choice of names: the level of eternity; the level, if you don't object, of God; the level of the spirit – only that happens to be about the most ambiguous word in the language. On the lower level, good exists as the proper functioning of the organism in accordance with the laws of its own being. On the higher level, it exists in the form of a knowledge of the world without desire or aversion; it exists as the experience of eternity, as the transcendence of personality, the extension of consciousness beyond the limits imposed by the ego. Strictly human activities are activities that prevent the manifestation of good on the other two levels. For, in so far as we're human, we're obsessed with time, we're passionately concerned with our personalities and with those magnified projections of our personalities which we call our policies, our ideals, our religions. And what are the results? Being obsessed with time and our egos, we are for ever craving and worrying. But nothing impairs the normal functioning of the organism like craving and revulsion, like greed and fear and worry. Directly or indirectly, most of our physical ailments and disabilities are due to worry and craving. We worry and crave ourselves into high blood-pressure, heart disease, tuberculosis, peptic ulcer, low resistance to infection, neurasthenia, sexual aberrations, insanity, suicide. Not to mention all the rest.' Mr Propter waved his hand comprehensively. 'Craving even prevents us from seeing properly,' he went on. 'The harder we try to see, the graver our error of accommodation. And it's the same with bodily posture: the more we worry about doing the thing immediately ahead of us in time, the more we interfere with our correct body posture and the worse, in consequence, becomes the functioning of the entire organism. In a word, in so far as we're human beings, we prevent ourselves from realizing the physiological and instinctive good that we're capable of as animals. And, *mutatis mutandis*, the same thing is true in regard to the sphere above. In so far as we're human beings, we prevent ourselves from realizing the spiritual and timeless good that we're capable of as potential inhabitants of eternity, as potential enjoyers of the beatific vision. We worry and crave ourselves out of the very possibility of transcending personality and knowing, intellectually at first and then by direct experience, the true nature of the world.'

Mr Propter was silent for a moment; then, with a sudden smile, 'Luckily,' he went on, 'most of us don't manage to behave like human beings all the time. We forget our wretched little egos and those horrible great projections of our egos in the ideal world – forget them and relapse for a while into harmless animality. The organism gets a chance to function according to its own laws; in other words, it gets a chance to realize such good as it's capable of. That's why we're as healthy and sane as we are. Even in great cities, as many as four persons out of five manage to go through life without having to be treated in a lunatic asylum. If we were consistently human, the percentage of mental cases would rise from twenty to a hundred. But fortunately most of us are incapable of consistency – the animal always resuming its rights. And to some people fairly frequently, perhaps occasionally to all, there come little flashes of illumination – momentary glimpses into the nature of the world as it is for a consciousness liberated from appetite and time, of the world as it might be if we didn't choose to deny God by being our personal selves. Those flashes come to us when we're off our guard; then craving and worry come rushing back and the light is eclipsed once more by our personality and its lunatic ideals, its criminal policies and plans.'

There was silence. The sun had gone. Behind the mountains to the west, a pale yellow light faded through green into a blue that deepened as it climbed. At the zenith, it was all night.

Pete sat quite still, staring into the dark but still transparent sky above the northern peaks. That voice, so calm at first and then at the end so powerfully resonant, those words, now mercilessly critical of all the things to which he had given his allegiance, now charged with the half-comprehended promise of things incommensurably worthier of loyalty, had left him profoundly moved and at the same time perplexed and at a loss. Everything he saw would have to be brought out again, from the beginning – science, politics, perhaps even love, even Virginia. He was appalled by the prospect and yet, in another part of his being, attracted; he felt resentful at the thought of Mr Propter, but at the same time loved the disquieting old man; loved him for what he did and, above all, for what he so admirably and, in Pete's own experience, uniquely was – disinterestedly friendly, at once serene and powerful, gentle and strong, self-effacing and yet intensely *there*, more present, so to speak, radiating more life than anyone else.

Jeremy Pordage had also found himself taking an interest in what the old man said, had even, like Pete, experienced the stirrings of a certain disquiet – a disquiet none the less disquieting for having stirred in him before. The substance of what Mr Propter had said was familiar to him. For, of course, he had read all the significant books on the subject – would have thought himself barbarously uneducated if he hadn't – had read Sankara and Eckhart, the Pali texts and John of the Cross, Charles de Condren and the Bardo, and Patanjali and the Pseudo-Dionysius. He had read them and been moved by them into wondering whether he oughtn't to do something about them; and, because he had been moved in this way, he had taken the most elaborate pains to make fun of them, not only to other people, but also and above all to himself. 'You've never bought your ticket to Athens,' the man had said – damn his eyes! Why did he want to go putting these things over on one? All one asked was to be left in peace, to take things as they came. Things as they came – one's books, one's little articles, and Lady Fredegond's ear-trumpet, and Palestrina, and steak-and-kidney pudding at the Reform, and Mae and Doris. Which reminded him that to-day was Friday; if he were in England it would be his afternoon at the flat in Maida Vale. Deliberately he turned his attention away from Mr Propter and thought instead of those alternate Friday afternoons; of the pink lampshades; the smell of talcum powder and perspiration; the Trojan women, as he called them because they worked so hard, in their kimonos from Marks and

Spencer's; the framed reproductions of pictures by Poynter and Alma Tadema (delicious irony, that works which the Victorians had regarded as art should have come to serve, a generation later, as pornography in a trollop's bedroom!); and, finally, the erotic routine, so matter-of-factly sordid, so conscientiously and professionally low, with a lowness and a sordidness that constituted, for Jeremy, their greatest charm, that he prized more highly than any amount of moonlight and romance, any number of lyrics and *Liebestods*. Infinite squalor in a little room! It was the apotheosis of refinement, the logical conclusion of good taste.

Chapter Ten

THIS Friday, Mr Stoyte's afternoon in town had been exceptionally uneventful. Nothing untoward had occurred during the preceding week. In the course of his various meetings and interviews nobody had said or done anything to make him lose his temper. The reports on business conditions had been very satisfactory. The Japs had bought another hundred thousand barrels of oil. Copper was up two cents. The demand for bentonite was definitely increasing. True, applications for bank credit had been rather disappointing; but the influenza epidemic had raised the weekly turnover of the Pantheon to a figure well above the average.

Things went so smoothly that Mr Stoyte was through with all his business more than an hour before he had expected. Finding himself with time to spare, he stopped on the way home at his agent's, to find out what was happening on the estate. The interview lasted only a few minutes – long enough, however, to put Mr Stoyte in a fury that sent him rushing out to the car.

'Drive to Mr Propter's,' he ordered with a peremptory ferocity as he slammed the door.

What the hell did Bill Propter think he was doing? he kept indignantly asking himself. Shoving his nose into other people's business. And all on account of those lousy bums who had come to pick the oranges! All for those tramps, those stinking, filthy hobos! Mr Stoyte had a peculiar hatred for the ragged hordes of transients on whom he depended for the harvesting of his crops, a hatred that was more than the rich man's ordinary dislike of the poor. Not that he didn't experience that complex mixture of fear and physical disgust, of stifled compassion and shame transformed by repression into chronic exasperation. He did. But over and above this common and generic dislike for poor people, he was moved by other hatreds of his own. Mr Stoyte was a rich man who had been poor. In the six years between the time when he ran away from his father and grandmother in Nashville and the time when he had been adopted by the black sheep of the family, his Uncle Tom, in

California, Jo Stoyte had learned, as he imagined, everything there was to be known about being poor. Those years had left him with an ineradicable hatred for the circumstances of poverty and at the same time an ineradicable contempt for all those who had been too stupid, or too weak, or too unlucky, to climb out of the hell into which they had fallen or been born. The poor were odious to him, not only because they were potentially a menace to his position in society, not only because their misfortunes demanded a sympathy he did not wish to give, but also because they reminded him of what he himself had suffered in the past, and at the same time because the fact that they were still poor was a sufficient proof of their contemptibleness and his own superiority. And since he had suffered what they were now suffering, it was only right that they should go on suffering what he had suffered. Also, since their continued poverty proved them contemptible, it was proper that he, who was now rich, should treat them in every way as the contemptible creatures they had shown themselves to be. Such was the logic of Mr Stoyte's emotions. And here was Bill Propter, running counter to this logic by telling the agent that they oughtn't to take advantage of the glut of transient labour to force down wages; that they ought, on the contrary, to raise them – raise them, if you please, at a time when these bums were swarming over the State like a plague of Mormon crickets! And not only that; they ought to build accommodation for them – cabins, like the ones that crazy fool Bill had built for them himself; two-roomed cabins at six or seven hundred dollars apiece – for bums like that, and their women, and those disgusting children who were so filthy dirty he wouldn't have them in his hospital; not unless they were really dying of appendicitis or something – you couldn't refuse them then, of course. But meanwhile, what the hell did Bill Propter think he was doing? And it wasn't the first time either that he'd tried to interfere. Gliding through the twilight of the orange groves, Mr Stoyte kept striking the palm of his left hand with his clenched right fist.

'I'll let him have it,' he whispered to himself. 'I'll let him have it.'

Fifty years before, Bill Propter had been the only boy in the school who, even though he was the older and stronger, didn't make fun of him for being fat. They had met again when Bill was

104

teaching at Berkeley and he himself had made good in the real estate game and had just gone into oil. Partly in gratitude for the way Bill Propter had acted when they were boys, partly also in order to display his power, to redress the balance of superiority in his own favour, Jo Stoyte had wanted to do something handsome for the young assistant professor. But in spite of his modest salary and the two or three miserable thousand dollars a year his father had left him, Bill Propter hadn't wanted anything done for him. He had seemed genuinely grateful, he had been perfectly courteous and friendly; but he just didn't want to come in on the ground floor of Consol Oil – didn't want to because, as he kept explaining, he had all he needed and preferred not to have anything more. Jo's effort to redress the balance of superiority had failed. Failed disastrously because, by refusing his offer, Bill had done something which, though he called him a fool for doing it, compelled Jo Stoyte secretly to admire him more than ever. Extorted against his will, this admiration bred a corresponding resentment towards its object. Jo Stoyte felt aggrieved that Bill had given him so many reasons for liking him. He would have preferred to like him without a reason, in spite of his shortcomings. But Bill had few shortcomings and many merits, merits which Jo himself did not have and whose presence in Bill he therefore regarded as an affront. Thus it was that all the reasons for liking Bill Propter were also, in Jo's eyes, equally valid reasons for disliking him. He continued to call Bill a fool; but he felt him as a standing reproach. And yet the nature of this standing reproach was such that he liked to be in Bill's company. It was because Bill had settled down on a ten-acre patch of land in this part of the valley that Mr Stoyte had decided to build his castle on the site where it now stood. He wanted to be near Bill Propter, even though, in practice, there was almost nothing that Bill could do or say that didn't annoy him. Today, this chronic exasperation had been fanned by Mr Stoyte's hatred of the transients into a passion of fury.

'I'll let him have it,' he repeated again and again.

The car came to a halt, and before the chauffeur could open the door for him, Mr Stoyte had darted out and was hurrying in his determined way, looking neither to right nor left, up the path that led from the road to his old friend's bungalow.

'Hullo, Jo,' a familiar voice called from the shadow under the eucalyptus trees.

Mr Stoyte turned, peered through the twilight, then, without a word, hurried towards the bench on which the three men were sitting. There was a chorus of 'Good evenings', and, as he approached, Pete rose politely and offered him his place. Ignoring his gesture and his very presence, Mr Stoyte addressed himself immediately to Bill Propter.

'Why the hell can't you leave my man alone?' he almost shouted.

Mr Propter looked at him with only a moderate astonishment. He was used to these outbursts from poor Jo; he had long since divined their fundamental cause and knew by experience how to deal with them.

'Which man, Jo?' he asked.

'Bob Hansen, of course. What do you mean by going to him behind my back?'

'When I went to you,' said Mr Propter, 'you told me it was Hansen's business. So I went to Hansen.'

This was so infuriatingly true that Mr Stoyte could only resort to roaring. He roared. 'Interfering with him in his work! What's the idea?'

'Pete's offering you a seat,' Mr Propter put in. 'Or, if you prefer it, there's an iron chair behind you. You'd better sit down, Jo.'

'I'm not going to sit down,' Mr Stoyte bellowed. 'And I want an answer. What's the idea?'

'The idea?' Mr Propter repeated in his slow quiet way. 'Well, it's quite an old one, you know. I didn't invent it.'

'Can't you answer me?'

'It's the idea that men and women are human beings. Not vermin.'

'Those bums of yours!'

Mr Propter turned to Pete. 'You may as well sit down again,' he said.

'Those lousy bums! I tell you I won't stand it.'

'Besides,' Mr Propter went on, 'I'm a practical man. You're not.'

'Me not practical?' Mr Stoyte echoed with indignant amazement. 'Not *practical*? Well, look at the place I live in and then look at this dump of yours.'

'Exactly. That proves the point. You're hopelessly romantic, Jo; so romantic, you think people can work when they haven't had enough to eat.'

'You're trying to make communists of them.' The word 'communist' renewed Mr Stoyte's passion and at the same time justified it; his indignation ceased to be merely personal and became righteous. 'You're nothing but a communist agitator.' His voice trembled, Mr Propter sadly noticed, just as Pete's had trembled half an hour before at the words 'fascist aggression'. He wondered if the boy had noticed or, having noticed, would take the hint. 'Nothing but a communist agitator,' Mr Stoyte repeated with a crusader's zeal.

'I thought we were talking about eating,' said Mr Propter.

'You're stalling!'

'Eating and working – wasn't that it?'

'I've put up with you all these years,' Mr Stoyte went on. 'For old times' sake. But now I'm through. I'm sick of you. Talking communism to those bums! Making the place dangerous for decent people to live in.'

'Decent?' Mr Propter echoed, and was tempted to laugh, but immediately checked the impulse. Being laughed at in the presence of Pete and Mr Pordage might goad the poor fellow into doing something irreparably stupid.

'I'll have you run out of the valley,' Mr Stoyte was roaring. 'I'll see that you're . . .' He broke off in the middle of the sentence and stood there for a few seconds in silence, his mouth still open and working, his eyes staring. That drumming in his ears, that tingling heat in the face – they had suddenly reminded him of his blood-pressure, of Dr Obispo, of death. Death and that flame-coloured text in his bedroom at home. Terrible to fall into the hands of the living God – not Prudence's God, of course; the other one, the *real* one, the God of his father and his grandmother.

Mr Stoyte drew a deep breath, pulled out his handkerchief, wiped his face and neck, then, without uttering another word, turned and began to walk away.

Mr Propter got up, hurried after him and, in spite of the other's angry motion of recoil, took Mr Stoyte's arm and walked along beside him.

'I want to show you something, Jo,' he said. 'Something that'll interest you, I think.'

'I don't want to see it,' said Mr Stoyte between his false teeth.

Mr Propter paid no attention, but continued to lead him towards the back of the house. 'It's a gadget that Abbot of the Smithsonian has been working on for some time,' he continued. 'A thing for making use of solar energy.' He interrupted himself for a moment to call back to the others to follow him; then turned again to Mr Stoyte and resumed the conversation. 'Much more compact than anything of the kind that's ever been made before,' he said. 'Much more efficient, too.' And he went on to describe the system of trough-shaped reflectors, the tubes of oil heated to a temperature of four or five hundred degrees Fahrenheit; the boiler for raising steam, if you wanted to run a low-pressure engine; the cooking-range and water-heater, if you were using it only for domestic purposes. 'Pity the sun's down,' he said, as they stood in front of the machine. 'I'd have liked to show you the way it works the engine. I've had two horse-power, eight hours a day, ever since I got the thing working last week. Not bad considering we're still in January. We'll have her working overtime all summer.'

Mr Stoyte had intended to persist in his silence – just to show Bill that he was still angry, that he hadn't forgiven him; but his interest in the machine and, above all, his exasperated concern with Bill's idiotic, crackpot notions were too much for him. 'What the hell do you want with two horse-power, eight hours a day?' he asked.

'To run my electric generator.'

'But what do you want with an electric generator? Haven't you got your current wired in from the city?'

'Of course. And I'm trying to see how far I can be independent of the city.'

'But what for?'

Mr Propter uttered a little laugh. 'Because I believe in Jeffersonian democracy.'

'What the hell has Jeffersonian democracy got to do with it?' said Mr Stoyte with mounting irritation. 'Can't you believe in Jefferson and have your current wired in from the city?'

'That's exactly it,' said Mr Propter; 'you almost certainly can't.'

'What do you mean?'

'What I say,' Mr Propter answered mildly.

'*I* believe in democracy too,' Mr Stoyte announced with a look of defiance.

'I know you do. And you also believe in being the undisputed boss in all your businesses.'

'I should hope so!'

'There's another name for an undisputed boss,' said Mr Propter. ' "Dictator".'

'What are you trying to get at?'

'Merely at the facts. You believe in democracy; but you're at the head of businesses which have to be run dictatorially. And your subordinates have to accept your dictatorship because they're dependent on you for their living. In Russia they'd depend on government officials for their living. Perhaps you think that's an improvement,' he added, turning to Pete.

Pete nodded. 'I'm all for the public ownership of the means of production,' he said. It was the first time he had openly confessed his faith in the presence of his employer; he felt happy at having dared to be a Daniel.

' "Public ownership of the means of production," ' Mr Propter repeated. 'But unfortunately governments have a way of regarding the individual producers as being parts of the means. Frankly, I'd rather have Jo Stoyte as my boss than Jo Stalin. This Jo,' (he laid his hand on Mr Stoyte's shoulder), 'this Jo can't have you executed; he can't send you to the Arctic; he can't prevent you from getting a job under another boss. Whereas the other Jo . . .' he shook his head. 'Not that,' he added, 'I'm exactly longing to have even this Jo as my boss.'

'You'd be fired pretty quick,' growled Mr Stoyte.

'I don't want *any* boss,' Mr Propter went on. 'The more bosses, the less democracy. But unless people can support themselves, they've got to have a boss who'll undertake to do it for them. So the less self-support, the less democracy. In Jefferson's day, a great many Americans did support themselves. They were economically independent. Independent of governments and independent of big business. Hence the Constitution.'

'We've still got the Constitution,' said Mr Stoyte.

'No doubt,' Mr Propter agreed. 'But if we had to make a new Constitution today, what would it be like? A Constitution to fit the facts of New York and Chicago and Detroit; of United States Steel and the Public Utilities and General Motors and the C.I.O. and the government departments. What on earth would it be like?' he repeated. 'We respect our old Constitution, but in fact we live under a new one. And if we want to live under the first, we've got to re-create something like the conditions under which the first was made. That's why I'm interested in this gadget.' He patted the frame of the machine. 'Because it may help to give independence to anyone who desires independence. Not that many do desire it,' he added parenthetically. 'The propaganda in favour of dependence is too strong. They've come to believe that you can't be happy unless you're entirely dependent on government or centralized business. But for the few who do care about democracy, who really want to be free in the Jeffersonian sense, this thing may be a help. If it makes them independent of fuel and power, that's already a great deal.'

Mr Stoyte looked anxious. 'Do you really think it'll do that?'

'Why not?' said Mr Propter. 'There's a lot of sunshine running to waste in this part of the country.'

Mr Stoyte thought of his presidency of the Consol Oil Company. 'It won't be good for the oil business,' he said.

'I should hate it to be good for the oil business,' Mr. Propter answered cheerfully.

'And what about coal?' He had an interest in a group of West Virginia mines. 'And the railroads?' There was that big block of Union Pacific shares that had belonged to Prudence. 'The railroads can't get on without long hauls. And steel,' he added disinterestedly; for his holdings in Bethlehem Steel were almost negligible. 'What happens to steel if you hurt the railroads and cut down trucking? You're going against progress,' he burst out in another access of righteous indignation. 'You're turning back the clock.'

'Don't worry, Jo,' said Mr Propter. 'It won't affect your dividends for quite a long while. There'll be plenty of time to adjust to the new conditions.'

With an admirable effort, Mr Stoyte controlled his temper. 'You seem to figure I can't think of anything but money,' he said with dignity. 'Well, it may interest you to know that I've decided to give Dr Mulge another thirty thousand dollars for his Art School.' (The decision had been made there and then, for the sole purpose of serving as a weapon in the perennial battle with Bill Propter.) 'And if you think,' he added as an afterthought, 'if you think I'm only concerned with my own interests, read the special World's Fair number of the *New York Times*. Read that,' he insisted with the solemnity of a fundamentalist recommending the Book of Revelation. 'You'll see that the most forward-looking men in the country think as I do.' He spoke with unaccustomed and incongruous unction, in the phraseology of after-dinner eloquence. 'The way of progress is the way of better organization, more service from business, more goods for the consumer!' Then, incoherently, 'Look at the way a housewife goes to her grocer,' he added, 'and buys a package of some nationally advertised cereal or something. *That's* progress. Not your crackpot idea of doing everything at home with this idiotic contraption.' Mr Stoyte had reverted completely to his ordinary style. 'You always were a fool, Bill, and I guess you always will be. And remember what I told you about interfering with Bob Hansen. I won't stand for it.' In dramatic silence he walked away ; but after taking a few steps he halted and called back over his shoulder, 'Come up to dinner, if you feel like it.'

'Thanks,' said Mr Propter. 'I will.'

Mr Stoyte walked briskly towards his car. He had forgotten about high blood-pressure and the living God and felt all of a sudden unaccountably and unreasonably happy. It was not that he had scored any notable success in his battle with Bill Propter. He hadn't; and, what was more, in the process of not scoring a success he had made, and was even half aware that he had made, a bit of a fool of himself. The source of his happiness was elsewhere. He was happy, though he would never have admitted the fact, because, in spite of everything, Bill seemed to like him.

In the car, as he drove back to the castle, he whistled to himself.

Entering (with his hat on, as usual; for even after all these years he still derived a childish pleasure from the contrast between the palace in which he lived and the proletarian manners he affected),

Mr Stoyte crossed the great hall, stepped into the elevator and, from the elevator, walked directly into Virginia's boudoir.

When he opened the door, the two were sitting at least fifteen feet apart. Virginia was at the soda-counter, pensively eating a chocolate-and-banana split; seated in an elegant pose on one of the pink satin armchairs, Dr Obispo was in process of lighting a cigarette.

On Mr Stoyte the impact of suspicion and jealousy was like the blow of a fist directed (for the shock was physical and localized in the midriff) straight to the solar plexus. His face contracted as though with pain. And yet he had seen nothing; there was no apparent cause for jealousy, no visible reason, in their attitudes, their actions, their expressions, for suspicion. Dr Obispo's manner was perfectly easy and natural; and the Baby's smile of startled and delighted welcome was angelic in its candour.

'Uncle Jo!' She ran to meet him and threw her arms round his neck. 'Uncle Jo!'

The warmth of her tone, the softness of her lips, had a magnified effect on Mr Stoyte. Moved to a point at which he was using the word to the limit of its double connotation, he murmured, 'My Baby!' with a lingering emphasis. The fact that he should have felt suspicious, even for a moment, of this pure and adorable, this deliciously warm, resilient and perfumed child, filled him with shame. And even Dr Obispo now heaped coals of fire on his head.

'I was a bit worried,' he said, as he got up from his chair, 'by the way you coughed after lunch. That's why I came up here, to make sure of catching you the moment you got in.' He put a hand in his pocket and, after half drawing out and immediately replacing a little leather-bound volume, like a prayer-book, extracted a stethoscope. 'Prevention's better than cure,' he went on. 'I'm not going to let you get influenza if I can help it.'

Remembering what a good week they had had at the Beverly Pantheon on account of the epidemic, Mr Stoyte felt alarmed. 'I don't *feel* bad,' he said. 'I guess that cough wasn't anything. Only my old – you know: the chronic bronchitis.'

'Maybe it was only that. But all the same, I'd like to listen in.' Briskly professional, Dr Obispo hung the stethoscope round his neck.

'He's right, Uncle Jo,' said the Baby.

Touched by so much solicitude, and at the same time rather disturbed by the thought that it might perhaps be influenza, Mr Stoyte took off his coat and waistcoat and began to undo his tie. A moment later he was standing stripped to the waist under the crystals of the chandelier. Modestly, Virginia retired again to her soda-fountain. Dr Obispo slipped the ends of the curved nickel tubes of the stethoscope into his ears. 'Take a deep breath,' he said as he pressed the muzzle against Mr Stoyte's chest. 'Again,' he ordered. 'Now cough.' Looking past that thick barrel of hairy flesh, he could see, on the wall behind the inhabitants of Watteau's mournful paradise as they prepared to set sail for some other paradise, doubtless yet more heartbreaking.

'Say ninety-nine,' Dr Obispo commanded, returning from the embarkation for Cythera to a near view of Mr Stoyte's thorax and abdomen.

'Ninety-nine,' said Mr Stoyte. 'Ninety-nine. Ninety-nine.'

With professional thoroughness, Dr Obispo shifted the muzzle of his stethoscope from point to point on the curving barrel of flesh before him. There was nothing wrong, of course, with the old buzzard. Just the familiar set of râles and wheezes he always had. Perhaps it would make things a bit more realistic if he were to take the creature down to his office and stick him up in front of the fluoroscope. But, no; he really couldn't be bothered. And, besides, this farce would be quite enough.

'Cough again,' he said, planting his instrument among the grey hairs on Mr Stoyte's left pap. And among other things, he went on to reflect, while Mr Stoyte forced out a succession of artificial coughs, among other things, these old sacks of guts didn't smell too good. How any young girl could stand it, even for money, he really couldn't imagine. And yet the fact remained that there were thousands of them who not only stood it, but actually enjoyed it. Or, perhaps, 'enjoy' was the wrong word. Because in most cases there probably wasn't any question of enjoyment in the proper, physiological sense of the word. It all happened in the mind, not in the body. They loved their old gut-sacks with their heads; loved them because they admired them, because they were impressed by the gut-sack's position in the world, or his knowledge, or his celebrity. What they slept with wasn't the man; it was a reputation, it was the embodiment of a function. And then, of course, some of the girls were future models for Mother's Day advertisements; some were little Florence Nightingales, on the look-out for a Crimean War. In those cases, the very infirmities of their gut-sacks were added attractions. They had the satisfaction of sleeping not only with a reputation or a stock of wisdom, not only with a federal judgeship, for example, or the presidency of a chamber of commerce, but also and simultaneously with a wounded soldier, with an imbecile child, with a lovely stinking little baby who still made messes in its bed. Even this cutie (Dr Obispo shot a sideways glance in the direction of the soda-fountain), even this one had something of the Florence Nightingale in her, something of the Gold Star Mother. (And that in spite of the fact that, with her conscious mind, she felt a kind of physical horror of physical maternity.) Jo Stoyte was a little bit her baby and her patient; and at the same time, of course, he was a great deal her own private Abraham Lincoln. Incidentally, he also happened to be the man with the cheque-book. Which was a consideration, of course. But if he were only that, Virginia wouldn't have been so nearly happy as she obviously was. The cheque-book was made more attractive by being in the hands of a demi-god who had to have a nanny to change his diapers.

'Turn round, please.'

Mr Stoyte obeyed. The back, Dr Obispo reflected, was perceptibly less revolting than the front. Perhaps because it was less personal.

'Take a deep breath,' he said; for he was going to play the farce all over again on this new stage. 'Another.'

Mr Stoyte breathed enormously, like a cetacean.

'And another,' said Dr Obispo. '*And* again,' said Dr Obispo, reflecting as the old man snorted that his own chief asset was a refreshing unlikeness to this smelly old gut-sack. She would take him, and take him, what was more, on his own terms. No Romeo-and-Juliet acts, no nonsense about Love with a large L, none of that popular-song claptrap with its skies of blue, dreams come true, heaven with you. Just sensuality for its own sake. The real, essential concrete thing; no less, it went without saying, but also (and this most certainly didn't go without saying; for the bitches were always trying to get you to stick them on pedestals, or be their soul-mates), also no more. No more, to begin with, out of respect for scientific truth. He believed in scientific truth. Facts were facts; accept them as such. It was a fact, for example, that young girls in the pay of rich old men could be seduced without much difficulty. It was also a fact that rich old men, however successful at business, were generally so frightened, ignorant and stupid that they could be bamboozled by any intelligent person who chose to try.

'Say ninety-nine again,' he said aloud.

'Ninety-nine. Ninety-nine.'

Ninety-nine chances out of a hundred that they would never find out anything. That was the fact about old men. The fact about love was that it consisted essentially of tumescence and detumescence. So why embroider the fact with unnecessary fictions? Why not be realistic? why not treat the whole business scientifically?

'Ninety-nine,' Mr Stoyte went on repeating, 'Ninety-nine.'

And then, Dr Obispo went on to reflect, as he listened without interest to the whisperings and crepitations inside the warm, smelly barrel before him, then there were the more personal reasons for preferring to take love unadorned, in the chemically pure condition. Personal reasons that were also, of course, a fact that had to be accepted. For it was a fact that he personally found an added pleasure in the imposition of his will upon the partner he had chosen. To be pleasurable, this imposition of will must never be too easy, too much a matter of course. Which ruled out all professionals. The partner had to be an amateur and, like all amateurs, committed to the thesis that tumescence and detumescence should always be associated with LOVE, PASSION, SOUL-MATING – all in upper-case letters. In imposing his will, he imposed the contradictory doctrine, the doctrine of tumescence and detumescence for tumescence's and detumescence's sake. All he asked was that a partner should give the thesis a practical try-out – however reluctantly, however experimentally, for just this once only; he didn't care. Just a single try-out. After that it was up to him. If he couldn't make a permanent and enthusiastic convert of her, at any rate so far as he was concerned, then the fault was his.

'Ninety-nine, ninety-nine,' said Mr. Stoyte with exemplary patience.

'You can stop now,' Dr Obispo told him graciously.

Just one try-out; he could practically guarantee himself success. It was a branch of applied physiology; he was an expert, a specialist. The Claude Bernard of the subject. And talk of imposing one's will! You began by forcing the girl to accept a thesis that was in flat contradiction to all the ideas she had been brought up with, all the dreams-come-true rigmarole of popular ideology. Quite a pleasant little victory, to be sure. But it was only when you got down to the applied physiology that the series of really satisfying triumphs began. You took an ordinarily rational human being, a good hundred-per-cent American with a background, a position in society, a set of conventions, a code of ethics, a religion (Catholic in the present instance, Dr Obispo remembered parenthetically); you took this good citizen, with rights fully and formally guaranteed by the Constitution, you took her (and perhaps she had come to the place of assignation in her husband's Packard limousine and direct from a banquet, with speeches in honour, say, of Dr Nicholas Murray Butler or the retiring Archbishop of Indianapolis), you took her and you proceeded, systematically and scientifically, to reduce this unique personality to a mere epileptic body, moaning and gibbering under the excruciations of a pleasure for which you, the Claude Bernard of the subject, were responsible and of which you remained the enjoying, but always detached, always ironically amused, spectator.

'Just a few more deep breaths, if you don't mind.'

Wheezily Mr Stoyte inhaled, then with a snorting sigh emptied his lungs.

Chapter Eleven

THERE was silence after Mr Stoyte's departure. A long silence, while each of the three men thought his own private thoughts. It was Pete who spoke first.

'Things like that,' he said gloomily, 'they get me kind of wondering if I ought to go on taking his money. What would you do, Mr Propter, if you were me?'

'What would I do?' Mr Propter reflected for a moment. 'I'd go on working in Jo's laboratory,' he said. 'But only so long as I felt fairly certain that what I was doing wouldn't cause more harm than good. One has to be a utilitarian in these matters. A utilitarian with a difference,' he qualified. 'Bentham crossed with Eckhart, say, or Nagarjuna.'

'Poor Bentham!' said Jeremy, horrified by the thought of what was being done to his namesake.

Mr Propter smiled. 'Poor Bentham, indeed! Such a good, sweet, absurd, intelligent man! So nearly right; but so enormously wrong! Deluding himself with the notion that the greatest happiness of the greatest number could be achieved on the strictly human level – the level of time and evil, the level of the absence of God. Poor Bentham!' he repeated. 'What a great man he would have been if only he could have grasped that good can't be had except where it exists!'

'That sort of utilitarian you're talking about,' said Pete, 'what would he feel about the job I'm doing now?'

'I don't know,' Mr Propter answered. 'I haven't thought about it enough to guess what he'd say. And, anyhow, we haven't yet got the empirical material on which a reasonable judgement could be based. All I know is that if I were in on this I'd be cautious. Infinitely cautious,' he insisted.

'And what about the money?' Pete went on. 'Seeing where it comes from and who it belongs to, do you think I ought to take it?'

'All money's pretty dirty,' said Mr Propter. 'I don't know that poor Jo's is appreciably dirtier than anyone else's. You may think it is; but that's only because, for the first time, you're seeing money at its source – its personal, human source. You're like one of these city children who have been used to getting their milk in sterilized bottles from a shiny white delivery wagon. When they go into the country and see it being pumped out of a big, fat, smelly old animal, they're horrified, they're disgusted. It's the same with money. You've been used to getting it from behind a bronze grating in a magnificent marble bank. Now you've come out into the country and are living in the cowshed with the animal that actually secretes the stuff. And the process doesn't strike you as very savoury or hygienic. But the same process was going on, even when you didn't know about it. And if you weren't working for Jo Stoyte, you'd probably be working for some college or university. But where do colleges and universities get their money from? From rich men. In other words, from people like Jo Stoyte. Again it's dirt served out in sterile containers – by a gentleman in a cap and gown this time.'

'So you figure it's all right for me to go on like I am now?' said Pete.

'All right,' Mr Propter answered, 'in the sense that it's not conspicuously worse than anything else.' Suddenly smiling, 'I was glad to hear that Dr Mulge had got his Art School,' he said in another, lighter tone. 'Immediately after the Auditorium, too. It's a lot of money. But I suppose the prestige of being a patron of learning is worth it. And, of course, there's an enormous social pressure on the rich to make them become patrons of learning. They're being pushed by shame as well as pulled by the longing to believe they're the benefactors of humanity. And, happily, with Dr Mulge a rich man can have his kudos with safety. No amount of art schools at Tarzana will ever disturb the *status quo*. Whereas if I were to ask Jo for fifty thousand dollars to finance research into the technique of democracy, he'd turn me down flat. Why? Because he knows that sort of thing is dangerous. He likes speeches about democracy. (Incidentally, Dr Mulge is really terrific on the subject.) But he doesn't approve of the coarse materialists who try to find out how to put those ideals into practice. You saw how angry he got about my poor little sun-machine. Because, in its tiny way, it's a menace to the sort of big business he makes his money from.

And it's the same with these other little gadgets that I've talked to him about from time to time. Come and look, if it doesn't bore you.'

He took them into the house. Here was the little electric mill, hardly larger than a coffee-machine, in which he ground his own flour as he needed it. Here was the loom at which he had learnt and was now teaching others to weave. Next he took them out to the shed in which, with a few hundred dollars' worth of electrically operated tools, he was equipped to do any kind of carpentry and even some light metal-work. Beyond the shed were the still unfinished greenhouses; for the vegetable plots weren't adequate to supply the demands of his transients. There they were, he added, pointing through the increasing darkness to the lights of a row of cabins. He could put up only a few of them; the rest had to live in a sort of garbage-heap down in the dry bed of the river – paying rent to Jo Stoyte for the privilege. Not the best material to work with, of course. But such misery as theirs left one no choice. They simply had to be attended to. A few had come through undemoralized; and, of these, a few could see what had to be done, what you had to aim at. Two or three were working with him here; and he had been able to raise money to settle two or three more on some land near Santa Susanna. Mere beginning – unsatisfactory at that. Because, obviously, you could not even start experimenting properly until you had a full-fledged community working under the new conditions. But to set a community on its feet would require money. A lot of money. But rich men wouldn't touch the work; they preferred art schools at Tarzana. The people who were interested had no money; that was one of the reasons why they were interested. Borrowing at the current commercial rates was dangerous. Except in very favourable circumstances, the chances were that you'd merely be selling yourself into slavery to a bank.

'It isn't easy,' said Mr Propter, as they walked back to the house. 'But the great point is that, easy or not easy, it's there, waiting to be done. Because, after all, Pete, there *is* something to do.'

Mr Propter went into the bungalow for a moment to turn out the lights, then emerged again on to the porch. Together, the three men walked down the path to the road. Before them the castle was a vast black silhouette punctured by occasional lights.

'There *is* something you can do,' Mr Propter resumed; 'but only on condition that you know what the nature of the world happens to be. If you know that the strictly human level is the level of evil, you won't waste your time trying to produce good on that level. Good manifests itself only on the animal level and on the level of eternity. Knowing that, you'll realize that the best you can do on the human level is preventive. You can see that purely human activities don't interfere too much with the manifestation of good on the other levels. That's all. But politicians don't know the nature of reality. If they did, they wouldn't be politicians. Reactionary or revolutionary, they're all humanists, all romantics. They live in a world of illusion, a world that's a mere projection of their own human personalities. They act in ways which would be appropriate if such a world as they think they live in really existed. But, unfortunately, it doesn't exist except in their imaginations. Hence nothing that they do is appropriate to the real world. All their actions are the actions of lunatics, and all, as history is there to demonstrate, are more or less completely disastrous. So much for the romantics. The realists, who have studied the nature of the world, know that an exclusively humanistic attitude towards life is always fatal, and that all strictly human activities must therefore be made instrumental to animal and spiritual good. They know, in other words, that men's business is to make the human world safe for animals and spirits. Or perhaps,' he added, turning to Jeremy, 'perhaps, as an Englishman, you prefer Lloyd George's phrase to Wilson's: "A home fit for heroes to live in" – wasn't that it? A home fit for animals and spirits, for physiology and disinterested consciousness. At present, I'm afraid, it's profoundly unfit. The world we've made for ourselves is a world of sick bodies and insane or criminal personalities. How shall we make this world safe for ourselves as animals and as spirits? If we can answer that question, we've discovered what to do.'

Mr Propter halted at what appeared to be a wayside shrine, opened a small steel door with a key he carried in his pocket, and, lifting the receiver of the telephone within, announced their presence to an invisible porter, somewhere on the other side of the moat. They walked on.

'What are the things that make the world unsafe for animals and spirits?' Mr Propter continued. 'Obviously greed and fear, lust for power, hatred, anger . . .'

At this moment, a dazzling light struck them full in the face and was almost immediately turned out.

'What in heaven's name . . .?' Jeremy began.

'Don't worry,' said Peter. 'They only want to make sure it's us, not a set of gangsters. It's just the searchlight.'

'Just our old friend Jo expressing his personality,' said Mr Propter taking Jeremy's arm. 'In other words, proclaiming to the world that he's afraid because he's been greedy and domineering. And he's been greedy and domineering, among other reasons, because the present system puts a premium on those qualities. Our problem is to find a system that will give the fewest possible opportunities for unfortunate people, like Jo Stoyte, to realize their potentialities.'

The bridge had swung down as they approached the moat, and now the boards rang hollow under their feet.

'You'd like socialism, Pete,' Mr Propter continued. 'But socialism seems to be fatally committed to centralization and standardized urban mass production all round. Besides, I see too many occasions for bullying there – too many opportunities for bossy people to display their bossiness, for sluggish people to sit back and be slaves.'

The portcullis rose, the gates slid back to receive them.

'If you want to make the world safe for animals and spirits, you must have a system that reduces the amount of fear and greed and hatred and domineering to their minimum. Which means that you must have enough economic security to get rid at least of that source of worry. Enough personal responsibility to prevent people from wallowing in sloth. Enough property to protect them from being bullied by the rich, but not enough to permit them to bully. And the same thing with political rights and authority – enough of the first for the protection of the many, too little of the second for domination by the few.'

'Sounds like peasants to me,' said Pete dubiously.

'Peasants plus small machines and power. Which means that they're no longer peasants, except in so far as they're largely self-sufficient.'

'And who makes the machines? More peasants?'

'No; the same sort of people as make them now. What can't be made satisfactorily except by mass-production methods, obviously has to go on being made that way. About a third of all production – that's what it seems to amount to. The other two-thirds are more economically produced at home or in a small workshop. The immediate, practical problem is to work out the technique of that small-scale production. At present, all the research is going to the discovery of new fields for mass production.'

❖

In the Grotto a row of twenty-five-feet electric candles burned in perpetual adoration before the Virgin. Above, on the tennis-court, the second butler, two maids and the head electrician were playing mixed doubles by the light of arc lamps.

'And do you figure people will want to leave the cities and live the way you're telling us, on little farms?'

'Ah, now you're talking, Pete!' said Mr Propter approvingly. 'Frankly, then, I don't expect them to leave the cities, any more than I expect them to stop having wars and revolutions. All I expect is that, if I do my work and it's reasonably good, there'll be a few people who will want to collaborate with me. That's all.'

'But if you're not going to get more than just a few, what's the point? Why not try to do something with the cities and the factories seeing that that's where most people are going to stay? Wouldn't that be more practical?'

'It depends how one defines the word,' said Mr Propter. 'For example, *you* seem to think that it's practical to help a great many people to pursue a policy which is known to be fatal; but that it isn't practical to help a very few people to pursue a policy which there is every reason to regard as sound. I don't agree with you.'

'But the many are there. You've got to do something about them.'

'You've got to do something about them,' Mr Propter agreed. 'But at the same time there are circumstances when you can't do anything. You can't do anything effective about anyone if he doesn't choose or isn't able to collaborate with you in doing the right thing. For example, you've *got* to help people who are being killed off by malaria. But in practice you can't help them if they refuse to screen their windows and insist on taking walks near stagnant water in the twilight. It's exactly the same with the diseases of the body politic. You've got to help people if they're faced by war or ruin or enslavement, if they're under the menace of sudden revolution or slow degeneration. You've got to help. But the fact remains, nevertheless, that you can't help if they persist in the course of behaviour which originally got them into their trouble. For example, you can't preserve people from the horrors of war if they won't give up the pleasures of nationalism. You can't save them from slumps and depressions so long as they go on thinking exclusively in terms of money and regarding money as the supreme good. You can't avert revolution and enslavement if they *will* identify progress with the increase of centralization and prosperity with the intensifying of mass production. You can't preserve them from collective madness and suicide if they persist in paying divine honours to ideals which are merely projections of their own personalities – in other words, if they persist in worshipping themselves rather than God. So much for conditional clauses. Now let's consider the actual facts of the present situation. For our purposes, the most significant facts are these: the inhabitants of every civilized country are menaced; all desire passionately to be saved from impending disaster; the overwhelming majority refuse to change the habits of thought, feeling and action which are directly responsible for their present plight. In other words, they can't be helped, because they are not prepared to collaborate with any helper who proposes a rational and realistic course of action. In these circumstances, what ought the would-be helper to do?'

'He's got to do *something*,' said Pete.

'Even if he thereby accelerates the process of destruction?' Mr Propter smiled sadly. 'Doing for doing's sake,' he went on. 'I prefer Oscar Wilde. Bad art can't do so much harm as ill-considered political action. Doing good on any but the tiniest scale requires more intelligence than most people possess. They ought to be content with keeping out of mischief; it's easier and it doesn't have such frightful results as trying to do good in the wrong way. Twiddling the thumbs and having good manners are much more helpful, in most cases, than rushing about with good intentions, *doing* things.'

Floodlighted, Giambologna's nymph was still indefatigably spouting away against the velvet background of the darkness. Electricity and sculpture, Jeremy was thinking as he looked at her – predestined partners. The things that old Bernini could have done with a battery of projectors! The startling lights, the rich fantastic shadows! The female mystics in orgasm, the conglobulated angels, the skeletons whizzing up out of papal tombs like sky-rockets, the saints in their private hurricane of flapping draperies and wind-blown marble curls! What fun! What splendour! What self-parodying emphasis! What staggering beauty! What enormous bad taste! And what a shame that the man should have had to be content with mere daylight and tallow candles!

'No,' Mr Propter was saying in answer to a protesting question from the young man, 'no, I certainly wouldn't advise their abandonment. I'd advise the constant reiteration of the truths they've been told again and again during the past three thousand years. And, in the intervals, I'd do active work on the technics of a better system, and active collaboration with the few who understand what the system is and are ready to pay the price demanded for its realization. Incidentally, the price, measured in human terms, is enormously high. Though, of course, much lower than the price demanded by the nature of things from those who persist in behaving in the standard human way. Much lower than the price of war, for example – particularly war with contemporary weapons. Much lower than the price of economic depression and political enslavement.'

'And what happens,' Jeremy asked in a fluting voice, 'what happens when you've had your war? Will the few be any better off than the many?'

'Oddly enough,' Mr Propter answered, 'there's just a chance they may be. For this reason. If they've learnt the technique of self-sufficiency they'll find it easier to survive a time of anarchy than the people who depend for their livelihood on a highly centralized and specialized organization. You can't work for the good without incidentally preparing yourself for the worst.'

He stopped speaking, and they walked on through a silence broken only by the sound, from somewhere high overhead in the castle, of two radios tuned to different stations. The baboons, on the contrary, were already asleep.

Chapter Twelve

I N the columned Lady Chapel, with its hat-racks and its Magnascos, its Brancusi and its Etruscan sarcophagus used as an umbrella-stand, Jeremy Pordage began, all of a sudden, to feel himself more cheerful and at home.

'It's as though one were walking into the mind of a lunatic,' he said, smiling happily, as he hung up his hat and followed the others into the great hall. 'Or, rather, an idiot,' he qualified. 'Because I suppose a lunatic's a person with a one-track mind. Whereas this . . .' – he made a circular gesture – 'this is a no-track mind. No-track because infinity-track. It's the mind of an idiot of genius. Positively stuffed with the best that has been thought and said.' He pronounced the phrase with a kind of old-maidish precision that made it sound entirely ludicrous. 'Greece, Mexico, backsides, cruci-fixions, machinery, George IV, Amida Buddha, science, Christian Science, Turkish baths – anything you like to mention. And every item is perfectly irrelevant to every other item.' He rubbed his hands together, he twinkled delightedly through his bifocals. 'Dis-quieting at first. But, do you know? I'm beginning to enjoy it. I find I really rather like living inside an idiot.'

'I don't doubt it,' said Mr Propter, matter-of-factly. 'It's a common taste.'

Jeremy was offended. 'One wouldn't have thought this sort of thing was very common,' he said, nodding in the direction of the Greco.

'It isn't,' Mr Propter agreed. 'But you can live in an idiot-universe without going to the expense of actually constructing it out of ferro-concrete and filling it with works of art.'

There was a pause while they entered the lift.

'You can live inside a cultural idiot,' Mr Propter went on. 'Inside a patchwork of mutually irrelevant words and bits of information. Or, if you're a lowbrow, you can live in the idiot world of the *homme moyen sensuel* – the world where the irrelevances consist of newspapers and baseball, of sex and worry, of advertising and money and halitosis and keeping up with the Joneses. There's a hierarchy of idiocies. Naturally, you and I prefer the classiest variety.'

The elevator came to a halt. Pete opened the gate, and they stepped out into the whitewashed corridor of the sub-sub-basement.

'Nothing like an idiot-universe if you want a quiet irresponsible life. That is, provided you can stand the idiocy,' Mr Propter added. 'A lot of people can't. After a time, they get tired of their no-track world. They feel the need of being concentrated and directed. They want their lives to have some sense. That's when they go communist, or join the Church of Rome, or take up with the Oxford Group. Anything, provided it will make them one-trackers. And, of course, in the overwhelming majority of cases they choose the wrong track. Inevitably. Because there are a million wrong tracks and only one right – a million ideals, a million projections of personality, and only one God and one beatific vision. From no-track idiocy most of them pass on to some one-track lunacy, generally criminal. It makes them feel better, of course; but pragmatically, the last state is always worse than the first. If you don't want the only thing worth having, my advice is: Stick to idiocy. – Is this where you work?' he went on in another tone, as Jeremy opened the door of his vaulted study. 'And those are the Hauberk Papers, I take it. Plenty of them. The title's extinct, isn't it?'

Jeremy nodded. 'And so's the family – or very nearly. Nothing left but two old maids in a haunted house without any money.' He twinkled, uttered his little preparatory cough and, patting his bald crown, said with an exaggerated precision: 'Decayed gentle-women.' Exquisite locution! It was one of his favourites. 'And the decay must have gone pretty far,' he added. 'Otherwise they wouldn't have sold the papers. They've refused all previous offers.'

'How fortunate one is, not to belong to an ancient family!' said Mr Propter. 'All those inherited loyalties to bricks and mortar, all those obligations to tombstones and bits of paper and painted can-vases!' He shook his head. 'What's a dismal form of compulsory idolatry.'

Jeremy, meanwhile, had crossed the room, opened a drawer and returned with a file of papers which he handed to Mr Propter. 'Look at these.'

Mr Propter looked. 'From Molinos!' he said in surprise.

'I thought that would be your cup of tea,' said Jeremy, deriving a sly pleasure from talking about mysticism in the most absurdly unappropriate language.

Mr Propter smiled. 'My cup of tea,' he repeated. 'But not my favourite blend. There was something not quite right about poor Molinos. A strain of – how shall I put it? – of negative sensuality. He enjoyed suffering. Mental suffering, the dark night of the soul – he really wallowed in it. No doubt, poor fellow, he sincerely believed he was destroying self-will; but, without his being aware of it, he was always turning the process of destruction into another affirmation of self-will. Which was a pity,' Mr Propter added, taking the letters to the light, to look at them more closely. 'Because he certainly did have some first-hand experience of reality. Which only shows that you're never certain of getting there, even when you've come near enough to see what sort of thing you're going to. Here's a fine sentence,' he put in parenthetically. ' "*Ame a Dios*," ' he read aloud, ' "*como es en sí y no como se lo dice y forma su imaginacion.*" '

Jeremy almost laughed. The coincidence that Mr Propter should have picked on the same passage as had caught Dr Obispo's eye that morning gave him a peculiar satisfaction. 'Pity he couldn't have read a little Kant,' he said. '*Dios en sí* seems to be much the same as *Ding an sich*. Unknowable by the human mind.'

'Unknowable by the *personal* human mind,' Mr Propter agreed, 'because personality is self-will, and self-will is the negation of reality, the denial of God. So far as the ordinary human personality is concerned, Kant is perfectly right in saying that the thing in itself is unknowable. *Dios en sí* can't be comprehended by a consciousness dominated by an ego. But now suppose there were some way of eliminating the ego from consciousness. *If* you could do this, you'd get close to reality, you'd be in a position to comprehend *Dios en sí*. Now, the interesting thing is that, as a matter of brute fact, this thing can be done, has been done again and again. Kant's blind alley is for people who choose to remain on the human level. If you choose to climb on to the level of eternity, the *impasse* no longer exists.'

There was a silence. Mr Propter turned over the sheets, pausing every now and then to decipher a line or two of the fine calligraphy. ' "*Tres maneras hay de silencio*," ' he read aloud after a moment. ' "*La primera es de palabras, la segunda de deseos, y la tercera de pensamientos.*" He writes nicely, don't you think? Probably that had a lot to do with his extraordinary success. How disastrous when a man knows how to say the wrong things in the right way! Incidentally,' he added, looking up with a smile into Jeremy's face, 'how few great stylists have ever said any of the right things. That's one of the troubles about education in the humanities. The best that has been thought and said. Very nice. But best in which way? Alas, only in form. The context is generally deplorable.' He turned back to the letters. After a moment, another passage caught his attention. ' "*Oirá y leerá el hombre racional estas espirituales materias, pero no llegará, dice San Pablo, a comprenderlas: Animalis homo non percipit ea quae sunt spiritus.*" And not merely *animalis homo*,' Mr Propter commented. 'Also *humanus homo*. Indeed, above all *humanus homo*. And you might even add that *humanus homo non percipit ea quae sunt animalis*. In so far as we think as strictly human beings, we fail to understand what is below us no less than what is above. And then there's a further trouble. Suppose we stop thinking in a strictly human fashion; suppose we make it possible for ourselves to have direct intuitions of the non-human realities in which, so to speak, we're imbedded. Well and good. But what happens when we try to pass on the knowledge so acquired? We're floored. The only vocabulary at our disposal is a vocabulary primarily intended for thinking strictly human thoughts about strictly human concerns. But the things *we* want to talk about are non-human realities and non-human ways of thinking. Hence the radical inadequacy of all statements about our animal nature and, even more, of all statements about God, or spirit, or eternity.'

Jeremy uttered a little cough. 'I can think of some pretty adequate statements about . . .' he paused, beamed, caressed his polished scalp; 'well, about the more *intime* aspects of our animal nature,' he concluded demurely. His face suddenly clouded; he had remembered his treasure-trove and Dr Obispo's impudent theft.

'But what does their adequacy depend on?' Mr Propter asked. 'Not so much on the writer's skill as the reader's response. The direct, animal intuitions aren't rendered by words; the words merely remind you of your memories of similar experiences. *Notus calor* is what Virgil says when he's talking about the sensations experienced by Vulcan in the embrace of Venus. Familiar heat. No attempts at description or analysis; no effort to get any kind of verbal equivalence to the facts. Just a reminder. But that reminder is enough to make the passage one of the most voluptuous affairs in Latin poetry. Virgil left the work to his readers. And, by and large, that's what most erotic writers are content to do. The few who try to do the work themselves have to flounder about with metaphors and similes and analogies. You know the sort of stuff: fire, whirlwinds, heaven, darts.'

' "The vale of lilies," ' Jeremy quoted. ' "And the bower of bliss." '

'Not to mention the expense of spirit in a waste of shame,' said Mr Propter; 'and all the other figures of speech. An endless variety, with only one feature in common – they're all composed of words which don't connote any aspect of the subject they're supposed to describe.'

'Saying one thing in order to mean another,' Jeremy put in. 'Isn't that one of the possible definitions of imaginative literature?'

'Maybe,' Mr Propter answered. 'But what chiefly interests me at the moment is the fact that our immediate animal intuitions have never been given any but the most summary and inadequate labels. We say "red", for example, or "pleasant", and just leave it at that, without trying to find verbal equivalents for the various aspects of perceiving redness or experiencing pleasure.'

'Well, isn't that because you can't go beyond "red" or "pleasant"?' said Pete. 'They're just facts, ultimate facts.'

'Like giraffes,' Jeremy added. ' "There ain't no such animal" is what the rationalist says, when he's shown its portrait. And then in it walks, neck and all!'

'You're right,' said Mr Propter. 'A giraffe is an ultimate fact. You've got to accept it, whether you like it or not. But accepting the giraffe doesn't prevent you from studying and describing it. And the same applies to redness or pleasure or *notus calor*. They can be analysed, and the results of the analysis can be described by means of suitable words. But as a matter of historical fact, this hasn't been done.'

Pete nodded slowly. 'Why do you figure that should be?' he asked.

'Well,' said Mr Propter, 'I should say it's because men have always been more interested in doing and feeling than in understanding. Always too busy making good and having thrills and doing what's "done" and worshipping the local idols – too busy with all this even to feel any desire to have an adequate verbal instrument for elucidating their experiences. Look at the languages we've inherited – incomparably effective in rousing violent and exciting emotions; an ever-present help for those who want to get on in the world; worse than useless for anyone who aspires to disinterested understanding. Hence, even on the strictly human level, the need for special impersonal languages like mathematics and the technical vocabularies of the various sciences. Wherever men have felt the wish to understand, they've given up the traditional language and substituted for it another special language, more precise and, above all, less contaminated with self-interest. Now, here's a very significant fact. Imaginative literature deals mainly with the everyday life of men and women; and the everyday life of men and women consists, to a large extent, of immediate animal experiences. But the makers of imaginative literature have never forged an impersonal, uncontaminated language for the elucidation of immediate experiences. They're content to use the bare, unanalysed names of experiences as mere aids to their own and their reader's memory. Every direct intuition is *notus calor*, with the connotation of the words left open, so to speak, for each individual reader to supply according to the nature of his or her particular experiences in the past. Simple, but not exactly scientific. But then people don't read literature in order to understand; they read it because they want to re-live the feelings and sensations which they found exciting in the past. Art can be a lot of things; but in actual practice most of it is merely the mental equivalent of alcohol and cantharides.'

Mr Propter looked down again at the close-set lines of Molinos's epistle. ' "*Oirá y leerá el hombre racional estas espirituales materias,*" ' he read out once more. ' "*Pero no llegará a comprenderlas.*" He'll hear and read these things, but he won't succeed in understanding them. And he won't succeed,' said Mr Propter, closing the file and handing it back to Jeremy, 'he won't succeed for one of two excellent reasons. Either he has never seen the giraffes in question, and so, being an *hombre racional*, knows quite well that there ain't no such animal. Or else he has had glimpses of the creatures, or has some other reason for believing in their existence, but can't understand what the experts say about them; can't understand because of the inadequacy of the language in which the fauna of the spiritual world is ordinarily described. In other words, he either hasn't had the immediate experience of eternity and so has no reason to believe that eternity exists; or else he *does* believe that eternity exists, but can't make head or tail of the language in which it's talked about by those who have had experience of it. Furthermore, when he wants to talk about eternity himself – and he may wish to do so, either in order to communicate his own experiences to others or to understand them better, from the human point of view, himself – he finds himself on the horns of a dilemma. For either he recognizes that the existing language is unsuitable – in which case he has only two rational choices: to say nothing at all, or to invent a new and better technical language of his own, a calculus of eternity, so to speak, a special algebra of spiritual experience – and if he does invent it, nobody who hasn't learnt it will know what he's talkimg about. So much for the first horn of the dilemma. The second horn is reserved for those who don't recognize the inadequacy of the existing language; or else who do recognize it, but are irrationally hopeful enough to take a chance with an instrument which they know to be worthless. These people will write in the existing language, and their writing will be, in consequence, more or less completely misunderstood by most of their readers. Inevitably, because the words they use don't correspond to the things they're talking about. Most of them are words taken from the language of everyday life.... But the language of everyday life refers almost exclusively to strictly human affairs. What happens when you apply words derived from that language to experiences on the plane of the spirit, the plane of timeless experience? Obviously, you create a misunderstanding; you say what you didn't mean to say.'

Pete interrupted him. 'I'd like an example, Mr Propter,' he said.

'All right,' the other answered. 'Let's take the commonest word in all religious literature: "love". Love on the human level means –

what? Practically everything from Mother to the Marquis de Sade.'

The name reminded Jeremy yet again of what had happened to the *Cent-Vingt Jours de Sodome*. Really it was too insufferable! the impudence of it . . .!

'We don't even make the simple Greek distinction between *erao* and *philo*, *eros* and *agape*. With us everything is just love, whether it's self-sacrificing or possessive, whether it's friendship or lust or homicidal lunacy. It's all just love,' he repeated. 'Idiotic word! Even on the human level it's hopelessly ambiguous. And when you begin using it in relation to experiences on the level of eternity – well, it's simply disastrous. "The love of God." "God's love for us." "The saint's love for his fellows." What does the word stand for in such phrases? And in what way is this related to what it stands for when it's applied to a young mother suckling her baby? or to Romeo climbing into Juliet's bedroom? or to Othello as he strangles Desdemona? or to the research worker who loves his science? or to the patriot who's ready to die for his country – to die and, in the meantime, to kill, steal, lie, swindle and torture for it? Is there really anything in common between what the word stands for in these contexts and what it stands for when one talks, let us say, of the Buddha's love for all sentient beings? Obviously, the answer is: No, there isn't. On the human level, the word stands for a great many different states of mind and ways of behaving. Dissimilar in many respects, but alike at least in this: they're all accompanied by emotional excitement and they all contain an element of craving. Whereas the most characteristic features of the enlightened person's experience are serenity and disinterestedness. In other words, the absence of excitement and the absence of craving.'

' "The absence of excitement and the absence of craving," ' Pete said to himself, while the image of Virginia in her yachting-cap, riding her pink scooter, kneeling in her shorts under the arch of the grotto, swam before his inward eye.

'Distinctions in fact ought to be represented by distinctions in language,' Mr Propter was saying. 'If they're not, you can't expect to talk sense. In spite of which, we insist on using one word to connote entirely different things. "God is love," we say. The word's the same as the one we use when we talk about "being in love", or "loving one's children", or "being inspired by love of country". Consequently we tend to think that the thing we're talking about must be more or less the same. We imagine in a vague, reverential way, that God is composed of a kind of immensely magnified yearning.' Mr Propter shook his head. 'Creating God in our own image. It flatters our vanity, and of course we prefer vanity to understanding. Hence those confusions of language. If we wanted to understand the word, if we wanted to think about it realistically, we should say that we were in love, but that God was x-love. In this way, people who had never had any first-hand experience on the level of eternity would at least be given a chance of knowing intellectually that what happens on that level is not the same as what happens on the strictly human level. They'd know, because they'd seen it in print, that there was some kind of difference between love and x-love. Consequently, they'd have less excuse than people have today for imagining that God was like themselves, only a bit more so on the side of respectability and a bit less so, of course, on the other side. And, naturally, what applies to the word "love", applies to all the other words taken over from the language of everyday life and used to describe spiritual experience. Words like "knowledge", "wisdom", "power", "mind", "peace", "joy", "freedom", "good". They stand for certain things on the human level. But the things that writers force them to stand for when they describe events on the level of eternity are quite different. Hence the use of them merely confuses the issue. They just make it all but impossible for anyone to know what's being talked about. And, meanwhile, you must remember that these words from the language of everyday life aren't the only trouble-makers. People who write about experiences on the level of eternity also make use of technical phrases borrowed from various systems of philosophy.'

'Isn't that your algebra of spiritual experience?' said Pete. 'Isn't that the special, scientific language you've been talking about?'

'It's an attempt at such an algebra,' Mr Propter answered. 'But, unfortunately, a very unsuccessful attempt. Unsuccessful because this particular algebra is derived from the language of metaphysics – bad metaphysics, incidentally. The people who use it are committing themselves, whether they like it or no, to an explanation of the facts as well as a description. An explanation of actual experiences in terms of metaphysical entities, whose existence is purely hypothetical and can't be demonstrated. In other words, they're describing the facts in terms of figments of the imagination; they're explaining the known in terms of the unknown. Take a few examples. Here's one: "ecstasy". It's a technical term that refers to the soul's ability to stand outside the body – and of course it carries the further implication that we know what the soul is and how it's related to the body and the rest of the universe. Or take another instance, a technical term that is essential to the Catholic theory of mysticism: "infused contemplation". Here the implication is that there's somebody outside us who pours a certain kind of psychological experience into our minds. The further implication is that we know who that somebody is. Or consider even "union with God". What it means depends on the upbringing of the speaker. It may mean "union with the Jehovah of the Old Testament". Or it may mean "union with the personal deity of orthodox Christianity". It may mean what it probably would have meant, say, to Eckhart, "union with the impersonal Godhead of which the God of orthodoxy is an aspect and a particular limitation". Similarly, if you were an Indian, it may mean "union with Isvara" or "union with Brahman". In every case, the term implies a previous knowledge about the nature of things which are either completely unknowable, or at best only to be inferred from the nature of the experiences which the term is supposed to describe. So there,' Mr Propter concluded, 'you have the second horn of the dilemma – the horn on which all those who use the current religious vocabulary to describe their experiences on the level of eternity inevitably impale themselves.'

'And the way between the horns?' Jeremy questioned. 'Isn't it the way of the professional psychologists who have written about mysticism? They've evolved a pretty sensible language. You haven't mentioned them.'

'I haven't mentioned them,' said Mr Propter, 'for the same reason as in talking about beauty I shouldn't mention professional aestheticians who had never been inside a picture gallery.'

'You mean, they don't know what they're talking about?'

Mr Propter smiled. 'I'd put it another way,' he said. 'They talk about what they know. But what they know isn't worth talking about. For what they know is only the literature of mysticism – not the experience.'

'Then there's *no* way between the horns,' Jeremy concluded. His eyes twinkled behind his spectacles; he smiled like a child, taking a sly triumph in some small consummation of naughtiness. 'What fun it is when there isn't a way between!' he went on. 'It makes the world seem so deliciously cosy, when all the issues are barred and there's nowhere to go to with all your brass bands and shining armour. Onward, Christian soldiers! Forward, the Light Brigade! Excelsior! And all the time you're just going round and round – head to tail, follow-my-fuehrer – like Fabre's caterpillars. That really gives me a *great* deal of pleasure!'

This time Mr Propter laughed outright. 'I'm sorry to have to disappoint you,' he said. 'But unfortunately there is a way between the horns. The practical way. You can go and find out what it means for yourself, by first-hand experience. Just as you can find out what El Greco's "Crucifixion of St. Peter" looks like by taking the elevator and going up to the hall. Only, in this case, I'm afraid, there isn't any elevator. You have to go up on your own legs. And make no mistakes,' he added, turning to Pete, 'there's an awful lot of stairs.'

❉

Dr Obispo straightened himself up, took the tubes of the stethoscope out of his ears and stowed the instrument away in his pocket along with the *Cent-Vingt Jours de Sodome*.

'Anything bad?' Mr Stoyte asked anxiously.

Dr Obispo shook his head and gave him a smile of reassurance. 'No influenza anyhow,' he said. 'Just a slight intensification of the bronchial condition. I'll give you something for it tonight before you go to bed.'

Mr Stoyte's face relaxed into cheerfulness. 'Glad it was only a false alarm,' he said, and turned away to get his clothes, which were lying in a heap on the sofa, under the Watteau.

From her seat at the soda-counter, Virginia let out a whoop of triumph. 'Isn't that just swell!' she cried. Then, in another, graver tone: 'You know, Uncle Jo,' she added, 'he'd got me panicked about that cough of yours. Panicked,' she repeated.

Uncle Jo grinned triumphantly and slapped his chest so hard that its hairy, almost female accumulations of flesh shivered like jellies under the blow. 'Nothing wrong with *me*,' he boasted.

Virginia watched him over the top of her glass, as he got into his shirt and knotted his tie. The expression on her innocent young face was one of perfect serenity. But behind those limpid blue eyes her mind was simmering with activity. 'Was that a close call!' she kept saying to herself. 'Gee, was it close!' At the recollection of that sudden violent start at the sound of the elevator gate being opened, of that wild scramble as the footsteps approached along the corridor, she felt herself tingling with a delicious mixture of fear and amusement, of apprehension and triumph. It was the sensation she used to have as a child, playing hide-and-seek in the dark. A close call! And hadn't Sig been wonderful! What presence of mind! And that stethoscope thing he pulled out of his pocket – what a brainwave! That had saved the situation. Because, without the stethoscope, Uncle Jo would have put on one of his jealousy acts. Though what right he had to be jealous, Virginia went on to reflect, with a strong sense of injury, she really didn't know. Seeing that nothing had happened except just a little reading aloud. And, anyhow, why shouldn't a girl be allowed to read that sort of thing if she wanted to? Especially as it was in French. And, besides, who was Uncle Jo to be prudish, she'd like to know? Getting mad with people only for telling you a funny story, when just look what he himself was *doing* all the time – and then expecting you to talk like Louisa M. Alcott, and thinking you ought to be protected from hearing so much as a dirty word! And the way he simply wouldn't allow her to tell the truth about herself, even if she had wanted to. Making a build-up of her as somebody quite different from what she really was. Acting almost as though she were Daisy Mae in the comic strip and he a sort of Little Abner rescuing her in the nick of time. Though, of course, she had to admit that it had happened at least once before he came along, because if it hadn't, there'd have been no excuse for *him*. It had happened, but quite unwillingly – you know, practically a rape – or else some fellow taking advantage of her being so dumb and innocent – at Congo Club with nothing on but a G-string and some talcum powder. And naturally she was always supposed to have hated it; crying her eyes out all the time until Uncle Jo came along; and then everything was different. But in that case, it now suddenly occurred to Virginia, if that was the way he thought about her, what the hell did he mean by coming home like this at seven-fifteen, when he'd told her he wouldn't be back till eight? The old double-crosser! Was he trying to spy on her? Because, if so, she wasn't going to stand for it; if so, then it just served him right that that was what Sig had been reading to her. He was just getting what he deserved for snooping around, trying to catch her doing something that wasn't right. Well, if *that* was how he was going to act, she'd tell Sig to come every day and read another chapter. Though how on earth the man who wrote the book was going to keep it up for a hundred and twenty days she really couldn't imagine. Considering what had happened already in the first week – and here was she, figuring that there wasn't anything she didn't know! Well, one lived and learned. Though there was some of it she really hadn't in the least wanted to learn. Things that made you feel sick to your stomach. Horrible! As bad as having babies! (She shuddered.) Not that there weren't a lot of funny things in the book too. The piece she had made Sig read over again – that was grand, that had given her a real kick. And that other bit where the girl . . .

'Well, Baby,' said Mr Stoyte, as he did up the last button of his waistcoat. 'You're not saying much, are you? A penny for your thoughts.'

Virginia raised that childishly short upper lip in a smile that made his heart melt with tenderness and desire. 'I was thinking about you, Uncle Jo,' she said.

Chapter Thirteen

If thou appear untouch'd by solemn thought,
Thy nature is not therefore less divine;
Thou liest in Abraham's bosom all the year;
And worship'st at the Temple's inner shrine,
God being with thee when we know it not.

'AND very nice too,' Jeremy said aloud. *Transparent* was the word, he reflected. The meaning was there like a fly in amber. Or, rather, there was no fly; there was only the amber; and the amber was the meaning. He looked at his watch. Three minutes to midnight. He closed his Wordsworth – and to think, he went on bitterly to remind himself, to think that he might have been refreshing his memory of *Félicia*! – laid the volume down on the table beside his bed and took off his glasses. Deprived of their six and a half diopters of correction, his eyes were instantly reduced to a state of physiological despair. Curved crystal had become their element; unspectacled, they were like a pair of jellied sea-creatures suddenly taken out of water. Then the light went out; and it was as though the poor things had been mercifully dropped, for safe keeping, into an aquarium.

Jeremy stretched under the bedclothes and yawned. What a day! But now, thank God, the paradise of bed. The Blessed Damozel leaned out from the gold bed of heaven. But these sheets were cotton ones, not linen; which was really a bit discreditable in a house like this! A house full of Rubenses and Grecos – and your sheets were cotton! But that 'Crucifixion of St Peter' – what a really staggering machine! At least as good as the 'Assumption' at Toledo. Which had probably been blown up by this time, incidentally. Just to demonstrate what happened when people took things too seriously. Not but that, he went on to reflect, there wasn't something rather impressive about that old Propter-Object. (For that was what he had decided to call the man in his own mind and when he wrote to his mother: the Propter-Object.) A bit of an Ancient Mariner, perhaps. The wedding guest, he beat his breast on occasions; ought perhaps to have beaten it more often than he had done, seeing what a frightful subversion of all the common decencies and, *a fortiori*, the common indecencies (such as *Félicia*, such as every other Friday afternoon in Maida Vale) the creature was inculcating. Not without a considerable persuasiveness, damn his glittering eyes! For this particular Mariner not only held you with that eye of his; he was also and simultaneously the loud bassoon you wanted to hear. One listened without reluctance – though, of course, one had no intention of permitting one's own particular little structures of decencies and indecencies to be subverted. One was not going to allow religion (of all things!) to invade the sanctities of private life. An Englishman's home is his castle; and, curiously enough, an American's castle, as he had discovered after the first shock began to wear off, was turning out to be this particular Englishman's home. His spiritual home. Because it was the embodiment of an imbecile's no-track mind. Because there were no issues and nothing led anywhere and the dilemmas had an infinity of horns and you went round and round, like Fabre's caterpillars, in a closed universe of utter cosiness – round and round among the Hauberk Papers, from St Peter to La Petite Morphil to Giambologna to the gilded Bodhisattvas in the cellar to the baboons to the Marquis de Sade to St François de Sales to Félicia and round again in due course to St Peter. Round and round, like caterpillars inside the mind of an imbecile; round and round in an infinite cosiness of issueless thoughts and feelings and actions, of hermetically bottled art and learning, of culture for its own sake, of self-sufficient little decencies and indecencies, of impassable dilemmas and moral questions sufficiently answered by the circumambient idiocy.

Round and round, round and round, from Peter's feet to Morphil's little buttocks to the baboon's, from the beautiful Chinese spiral of the folds in the Buddha's robe to the humming-bird drinking in mid-air to Peter's feet again with the nails in them … His drowsiness darkened into sleep.

In another room on the same floor of the donjon Pete Boone was not even trying to get to sleep; he was trying, on the contrary, to figure things out. To figure out science and Mr Propter, social justice and eternity and Virginia and anti-fascism. It wasn't easy. Because, if Mr Propter was right, then you'd have to start thinking quite differently about almost everything. 'Disinterested quest for truth' – that was what you said (if you were ever forced to say anything so embarrassing about why you were a biologist). And in the case of socialism it was 'humanity', it was 'the greatest happiness of the greatest number', it was 'progress' – and, of course, that linked up with biology again: happiness and progress through science as well as socialism. And while happiness and progress were on the way there was loyalty to the cause. He remembered a piece about loyalty by Josiah Royce, a piece he had had to read in his sophomore year at college. Something about all loyal people grasping in their own way some form of religious truth – winning some kind of genuine religious insight. It had made a big impression on him at the time. He had just lost his faith in that old Blood-of-the-Lamb business he'd been brought up in, and this had come as a kind of reassuran ce, had made him feel that, after all, he *was* religious even if he didn't go to church any more – religious because he was loyal. Loyal to causes, loyal to friends. He had been religious, it had always seemed to him, over there in Spain. Religious, again, when he felt that way about Virginia. And yet, if Mr Propter was right, old Royce's ideas about loyalty were all wrong. Being loyal didn't of itself give you religious insight. On the contrary, it might prevent you from having insight – indeed, was absolutely certain to prevent you, if you gave your loyalty to anything less than the highest cause of all; and the highest cause of all (if Mr Propter was right) was almost terrible in its farness and strangeness. Almost terrible; and yet the more he thought about it, the more dubious he felt about everything else. Perhaps it really was the highest. But if it was, then socialism wasn't enough. And it wasn't enough, because humanity wasn't enough. Because the greatest happiness didn't happen to be in the place where people had thought it was, because you couldn't make it come by doing things in the sort of fields you worked in if you were a social reformer. The best you could do in those fields was to make it easier for people to go on to where the greatest happiness could be had. And, of course, what applied to socialism would apply to biology or any other science, if you thought of it as a means to progress. Because, if Mr Propter was right, then what people called progress wasn't progress. That is, it wouldn't be progress unless it had made it easier for people to go on to where the greatest happiness actually was. Easier, in other words, to be loyal to the highest cause of all. And, obviously, if that was your standard, you had to think twice about using progress as a justification for science. And then there was that disinterested quest for truth. But again, if Mr Propter was right, biology and the rest were the disinterested quest for only one aspect of truth. But a half-truth was a falsehood, and it remained a falsehood even when you'd told it in the belief that it was the whole truth. So it looked as though *that* justification wouldn't do either – or at any rate as though it wouldn't do unless you were at the same time disinterestedly trying to discover the other aspect of truth, the aspect you were looking for when you gave your loyalty to the highest cause of all. And meanwhile what about Virginia, he asked himself in mounting anguish, what about Virginia? For, if Mr Propter were right, then even Virginia wasn't enough, even Virginia might actually be an obstacle to prevent him from giving his loyalty to the highest cause of all. Even those eyes and her innocence and that utterly adorable mouth; even what he felt about her; even love itself, even the best kind of love (for he could honestly say that he hated the other kind – that dreadful brothel in Barcelona, for example, and here, at home, those huggings after the third or fourth cocktail, those gropings by the roadside in a parked car) – yes, even the best kind of love might be inadequate, might actually be worse than inadequate. 'I could not love thee, dear, so much, loved I not something or other more.' Hitherto, something or other had been his biology, his socialism. But now these had turned out to be inadequate, or even, taken as ends in themselves, worse than inadequate. No loyalty was good in itself, or brought religious insight except loyalty to the highest cause of all. 'I could not love thee, dear, so much, loved I not the highest cause of all more.' But the question, the agonizing question, was this: Could you love the highest cause of all and go on feeling as you did about Virginia? The worst love was obviously incompatible with loyalty to the highest cause of all. Obviously so; because the worst love was just being loyal to your own physiology, whereas, if Mr Propter was right, you couldn't be loyal to the highest cause of all without denying such loyalties to yourself. But was the best love so fundamentally different, after all, from the worst? The worst was being loyal to your physiology. It was hateful to admit it; but so too was the best: being loyal to your physiology and at the same time (which was its distinguishing mark) loyal also to your higher feelings – to that empty ache of longing, to that infinity of tenderness, to that adoration, that happiness, those pains, that sense of solitude, that longing for identity. You were loyal to these, and being loyal to these was the definition of the best kind of love, of what people called romance and praised as the most wonderful thing in life. But being loyal to these was being loyal to yourself; and you couldn't be loyal to yourself and loyal at the same time to the highest cause of all. The practical conclusion was obvious. But Pete refused to draw it. Those eyes were blue and limpid, that mouth adorable in its innocence. And then, how sweet she was, how beautifully thoughtful! He remembered the conversation they had had on the way into dinner. He had asked her how her headache was. 'Don't talk about it,' she had whispered; 'it might upset Uncle Jo. Doc's been going over him with his stethoscope; doesn't think he's so good this evening. I don't want to have him worrying about *me*. And anyhow, what is a headache?' No: only beautiful, not only innocent and sweet, but brave too, and unselfish. And how adorable she had been to him all the evening, asking him about his work, telling him about her home in Oregon, making him talk about his home down in El Paso. In the end, Mr Stoyte had come and sat down beside them – in silence, and his face black as thunder. Pete had glanced inquiringly at Virginia, and she had given him a look that said, 'Please go,' and another when he rose to say good-night, so pleadingly apologetic, so full of gratitude, so understanding, so sweet and affectionate, that the recollection of it was enough to bring the tears into his eyes. Lying there in the darkness, he cried with happiness.

That niche in the wall between the windows in Virginia's bedroom had been intended, no doubt, for a book-shelf. But Virginia was not very keen on books; the recess had been fitted up, instead, as a little shrine. You drew back a pair of short white velvet curtains (everything in the room was white), and there, in a bower of artificial flowers, dressed in real silk clothes, with the cutest little gold crown on her head and six strings of seed pearls round her neck, stood Our Lady, brilliantly illuminated by an ingenious system of concealed electric bulbs. Barefooted and in white satin pyjamas, Virginia was kneeling before this sacred doll's house, saying her evening prayers. Our Lady, it seemed to her, was looking particularly sweet and kind tonight. Tomorrow, she decided, while her lips pronounced the formulas of praise and supplications, tomorrow morning, first thing, she'd go right down to the sewing-room and get one of the girls to help her make a new mantle for Our Lady out of that lovely piece of blue brocade she had bought last week at the junk shop in Glendale. A blue brocade mantle, fastened in front with a gold button – or, better still, with a little gold cord that you could tie in a bow, with the ends hanging down, almost to Our Lady's feet. Oh, that would be just gorgeous! She wished it were morning so that she could start right away.

The last prayer had been said; Virginia crossed herself and rose from her knees. Happening to look down as she did so, she saw to her horror that some of the cyclamen-coloured varnish had scaled off the nails of the second and third toes of her left foot. A minute later she was squatting on the floor beside the bed, the right leg outstretched, the other foot drawn across it, making ready to repair the damage. An open bottle stood beside her; she held a small paint-brush in her hand, and a horribly industrial aura of acetone had enveloped the Schiaparelli 'Shocking' with which her body was impregnated. She started to work, and as she bent forward, two strands of auburn hair broke loose from their curly pattern and fell across her forehead. Under frowning brows, the large blue eyes intently stared. To aid concentration, the tip of a pink tongue was held between the teeth. 'Hell!' she suddenly said aloud, as the little brush made a false stroke. Then, immediately, the teeth clamped down again.

Interrupting her work to allow the first coat of varnish to dry, she shifted her scrutiny from the toes to the calf and shin of her left leg. The hairs were beginning to grow again, she noticed with annoyance; it would soon be time for another of those wax treatments. Still pensively caressing the leg, she let her mind travel back over the events of the day. The memory of that close call with Uncle Jo still gave her shivers of apprehensive excitement. Then she thought of Sig with his stethoscope, and the upper lip lifted ravishingly in a smile of amusement. And then there was that book, which it served Uncle Jo right that she should have had Sig read to her. And Sig getting fresh with her between the chapters and making passes: that also served Uncle Jo right for trying to spy on her. She remembered how mad she had got at Sig. Not so much for what he actually did; for besides serving Uncle Jo right (of course it was only *afterwards* that she discovered quite how right it served him), what he actually did had been rather thrilling than otherwise; because, after all, Sig was terribly attractive and in those ways Uncle Jo didn't hardly count – in fact, you might almost say that he counted the other way; in the red, so to speak; counted less than nobody, so that anybody else who *was* attractive seemed still more attractive when Uncle Jo had been around. No, it wasn't what he actually did that had made her mad at him. It was the way he did it. Laughing at her, like that. She didn't mind a bit of kidding at ordinary times. But kidding while he was actually making passes—that was treating her like she was a tart on Main Street. No romance, or anything; just that sniggering sort of laugh and a lot of dirty cracks. Maybe it was sophisticated; but she didn't like it. And didn't he see that it was just plain dumb to act that way? Because, after all, when you'd been reading that book with someone so attractive as Sig – well, you felt you'd like a bit of romance. Real romance, like in the pictures, with moonlight, and swing music, or perhaps a torch singer (because it was nice to feel sad when you were happy), and a boy saying lovely things to you, and a lot of kissing, and at the end of it, almost without your knowing it, almost as if it weren't happening to you, so that you never felt there was anything wrong, anything that Our Lady would really mind . . . Virginia sighed deeply and shut her eyes; her face took on an expression of seraphic tranquillity. Then she sighed again, shook her head and frowned. Instead of that, she was thinking angrily, instead of that, Sig had to go and spoil it all by acting hard-boiled and sophisticated. It just shot all the romance to pieces and made you feel mad at him. And what was the sense in that? Virginia concluded resentfully. What was the sense in that, either from his point of view or from hers?

The first coat of varnish seemed to be dry. Bending over her foot, she blew on her toes for a little, then started to apply the second coat. Behind her, all of a sudden, the door of the bedroom was opened and as gently closed again.

'Uncle Jo?' she said inquiringly and with a note of surprise in her voice, but without looking up from her enamelling.

There was no answer, only the sound of an approach across the room.

'Uncle Jo?' she repeated and, this time, interrupted the painting of her toes to turn round.

Dr Obispo was standing over her. 'Sig!' Her voice dropped to a whisper. 'What *are* you doing?'

Dr Obispo smiled his smile of ironic admiration, of intense and at the same time amused and mocking concupiscence. 'I thought we might go on with our French lesson,' he said.

'You're crazy!' She looked apprehensively towards the door. 'He's just across the hall. He might come in. . . .'

Dr Obispo's smile broadened to a grin. 'Don't worry about Uncle Jo,' he said.

'He'd kill you if he found you here.'

'He won't find me here,' Dr Obispo answered. 'I gave him a capsule of Nembutal before he went to bed. He'll sleep through the Last Trump.'

'I think you're awful!' said Virginia emphatically; but she couldn't help laughing, partly out of relief and partly because it really was rather funny to think of Uncle Jo snoring away next door while Sig read her that stuff.

Dr Obispo pulled the Book of Common Prayer out of his pocket. 'Don't let me interrupt your labours,' he said with the parody of chivalrous politeness. ' "A woman's work is never done." Just go on as though I weren't there. I'll find the place and start reading.' Smiling at her with imperturbable impudence, he sat down on the edge of the rococo bed and turned over the pages of the book.

Virginia opened her mouth to speak; then, catching hold of her left foot, closed it again under the compulsion of a need even more urgent than that of telling him exactly where he got off. The varnish was drying in lumps; her toes would look just awful if she didn't go on with them at once. Hastily dipping her little brush in the bottle of acetone enamel, she started painting again with the focussed intensity of a Van Eyck at work on the microscopic details of the 'Adoration of the Lamb'.

Dr Obispo looked up from the book. 'I admired the way you acted with Pete this evening,' he said. 'Flirting with him all through dinner, so that you got the old man hopping jealous of him. That was masterly. Or should one say mistressly?'

Virginia released her tongue to say emphatically, 'Pete's a nice boy.'

'But dumb,' Dr Obispo qualified, as he sprawled with conscious elegance and a maddeningly insolent assumption of being at home across the bed.

'Otherwise he wouldn't be in love with you the way he is.' He uttered a snort of laughter. 'The poor chump thinks you're an angel, a heavenly little angel, complete with wings, harp and genuine eighteen-carat, fully jewelled, Swiss-made virginity. Well, if that isn't being dumb . . .'

'You just wait till I get time for you,' said Virginia menacingly. but without looking up; for she had reached a critical phase in the execution of her work of art.

Dr Obispo ignored the remark. 'I used to under-estimate the value of an education in the humanities,' he said after a little silence. 'Now, I make that mistake no longer.' In a tone of deep solemnity, a tone, one might imagine, like Whittier's in a reading from his own works.

'The lessons of great literature!' he went on. 'The deep truths! The gems of wisdom!'

'Oh, shut up!' said Virginia.

'When I think what I owe Dante and Goethe,' said Dr Obispo in the same prophetic style. 'Take the case of Paolo reading aloud to Francesca. With the most fruitful results, if you remember. "*Noi leggevamo un giorno, per diletto, di Lancilotto, come amor lo strinse. Soli eravamo e senz' alcun sospetto. Senz' alcun sospetto,*"' Dr Obispo repeated with emphasis, looking, as he did so, at one of the engravings in the *Cent-Vingt Jours*. 'Not the smallest suspicion, mark you, of what was going to happen.'

'Hell!' said Virginia, who had made another slip.

'No, not even a suspicion of hell,' Dr Obispo insisted. 'Though, of course, they ought to have been on the look-out for it. They ought to have had the elementary prudence to guard against being sent there by the accident of sudden death. A few simple precautions, and they could have made the best of both worlds. Could have had their fun while the brother was out of the way and, when the time for having fun was over, could have repented and died in the odour of sanctity. But then it must be admitted that they hadn't the advantage of reading Goethe's *Faust*. They hadn't learnt that inconvenient relatives could be given sleeping-draughts. And even if they had learnt, they wouldn't have been able to go to the drugstore and buy a bottle of Nembutal. Which shows that education in the humanities isn't enough; there must also be education in science. Dante and Goethe to teach you what to do. And the professor of pharmacology to show you how to put the old buzzard into a coma with a pinch of barbiturate.'

The toes were finished. Still holding her left foot, so as to keep it from any damaging contact until the varnish should be entirely dry, Virginia turned on her visitor. 'I won't have you calling him an old buzzard,' she said hotly.

'Well, shall we say "bastard"?' Dr Obispo suggested.

'He's a better man than you'll ever be!' Virginia cried; and her voice had the ring of sincerity. 'I think he's wonderful.'

'You think he's wonderful,' Dr Obispo repeated. 'But all the same, in about fifteen minutes you'll be sleeping with me.' He laughed as he spoke and, leaning forward from his place on the bed, caught her two arms from behind, a little below the shoulders. 'Look out for your toes,' he said, as Virginia cried out and tried to wrench herself away from him.

The fear of ruining her masterpiece made her check the movement before it was more than barely initiated. Dr Obispo took advantage of her hesitation to stoop down, through the aura of acetone towards the nape of that delicious neck, towards the perfume of 'Shocking', towards a firm warmth against the mouth, a touch of hair like silk upon the cheeks. Swearing, Virginia furiously jerked her head away. But a fine tingling of agreeable sensation was running parallel, so to speak, with her indignation, was incorporating itself in it.

This time, Dr Obispo kissed her behind the ear. 'Shall I tell you,' he whispered, 'what I'm going to do to you?' She answered by calling him a lousy ape-man. But he told her all the same, in considerable detail.

Less than fifteen minutes had elapsed when Virginia opened her eyes and, across the now darkened room, caught sight of Our Lady smiling benignantly from among the flowers of her illuminated doll's house. With a cry of dismay she jumped up and, without waiting to put on any clothes, ran to the shrine and drew the curtains. The lights went out automatically. Stretching out her hands in the thick darkness, she groped her way cautiously back to bed.

PART TWO

•

Chapter One

'AGAIN, no dearth of news,' Jeremy wrote to his mother three weeks later. 'News of every kind and from all the centuries. Here's a bit of news, to begin with, about the Second Earl. In the intervals of losing battles for Charles I, the Second Earl was a poet. A bad poet, of course (for the chances are always several thousands to one against any given poet being good), but with occasional involuntary deviations into charm. What about this, for example, which I found in manuscript only yesterday?

> One taper burns, but 'tis too much;
> Our loves demand complete eclipse.
> Let sight give place to amorous touch,
> And candle-light to limbs and lips!

Rather pretty, don't you think? But, alas, almost the only nugget so far unearthed from the alluvium. If only the rest were silence! But that's the trouble with poets, good no less than bad. They will not keep their traps shut, as we say in the Western hemisphere. What joy if the rest of Wordsworth had been silence, the rest of Coleridge, the rest of Shelley!

'Meanwhile, the Fifth Earl sprang a surprise on me yesterday in the form of a notebook full of miscellaneous jottings. I have only just started on them (for I mustn't spend all my time on any one item till I have the whole collection unpacked and roughly catalogued); but the fragments I've read are decidedly appetizing. I found this on the first page: "Lord Chesterfield writes to his Son that a Gentleman never speaks to his footman, nor even the beggar in the street, *d'un ton brusque*, but 'corrects the one coolly and refuses the other with humanity. . . .' His lordship should have added that there is an Art by which such coolness may be rendered no less formidable than Anger and such humanity more wounding than Insult.

' "Furthermore, footmen and beggars are not the only objects on whom this Art may be exercised. His lordship has been ungallant enough in this instance to forget the Sex, for there is also an

Art of coolly outraging a devoted female, and of abusing her Person, with all the *bienséance* befitting the most accomplished Gentleman."

'Not a bad beginning! I will keep you posted of any subsequent discoveries in this field.

'Meanwhile, contemporary news is odd, confused and a bit disagreeable. To begin with, Uncle Jo is chronically glum and ill-tempered these days. I suspect the green-eyed monster; for the blue-eyed monster (in other words, Miss Maunciple, the Baby) has been rolling them, for some time now, in the direction of young Pete. Whether she rolls more than the eyes, I don't know; but suspect the fact; for she has that inward, dreamy look, that far-away sleep-walker's expression, which one often remarks on the faces of young ladies who have been doing a lot of strenuous love-making. You know the expression I mean: exquisitely spiritual and pre-Raphaelitish. One has only to look at such a face to *know* that God Exists. The one incongruous feature in the present instance is the costume. A pre-Raphaelite expression demands pre-Raphaelite clothes: long sleeves, square yokes, yards and yards of Liberty velveteen. When you see it, as I did today in combination with white shorts, a bandana and a cowboy hat, you're disturbed, you're all put out. Meanwhile, in defence of Baby's Honour, I must insist that all this is mere hypothesis and guess-work. It may be, of course, that this new, spiritual expression of hers is not the result of amorous fatigue. For all I know to the contrary, Baby may have been converted by the teachings of the Propter-Object and is now walking about in a state of perpetual *samadhi*. On the other hand, I *do* see her giving the glad eye to Pete. What's more, Uncle Jo exhibits all the symptoms of being suspicious of them and extremely cross with everybody else. With me among others, of course. Perhaps even more with me than with others, because I happen to have read more books than the rest and am therefore more of a symbol of Culture. And Culture, of course, is a thing for which he has positively a Tartar's hatred. Only, unlike the Tartars, he doesn't want to burn the monuments of Culture, he wants to buy them up. He expresses his superiority to talent and education by means of possession rather than destruction; by hiring and then insulting the talented and educated rather than by killing them.

(Though perhaps he would kill them if he had the Tartar's opportunities and power.) All this means that, when I am not in bed or safely underground with the Hauberks, I spend most of my time grinning and bearing, thinking of Jelly-Belly and my nice salary, in order not to think too much of Uncle Jo's bad manners. It's all very unpleasant; but fortunately not unbearable – and the Hauberks are an immense consolation and compensation.

'So much for the erotic and cultural fronts. On the scientific front, the news is that we're all perceptibly nearer to living as long as crocodiles. At the time of writing, I haven't decided whether I really want to live as long as a crocodile.' (With the penning of the second 'crocodile', Jeremy was seized by a sudden qualm. His mother would be seventy-seven in August. Under that urbanity of hers, under the crackled glaze of the admirable conversation, there was a passionate greed for life. She would talk matter-of-factly enough about her own approaching extinction; she would make little jokes about her death and funeral. But behind the talk and the little jokes there lurked, as Jeremy knew, a fierce determination to hold on to what was left, to go on doing what she had always done, in the teeth of death, in defiance of old age. This talk of crocodiles might give pain; this expression of doubt as to the desirability of prolonging life might be interpreted as an unfavourable criticism. Jeremy took a new sheet of paper and started the paragraph afresh.)

'So much for the erotic and cultural fronts,' he wrote. 'On the scientific front, *rien de nouveau*, except that the Obispo is being more bumptious than ever; which isn't news, because he's always more bumptious than ever. Not one of my favourite characters, I'm afraid: though not unamusing when one feels inclined for a few moments of ribaldry. Longevity, it appears, is making headway. Old Parr and the Countess of Desmond are on the march.

'And what of the religious front? Well, our Propter-Object has given up his attempts at edification, at any rate so far as I'm concerned. Thank heaven! for when he dismounts from his hobby-horse, what excellent company he is! A mind full of all kinds of oddments; and the oddments are pigeon-holed in apple-pie order. One rather envies him his intellectual coherence; but consoles oneself by thinking that, if one had them, they'd spoil one's own particular little trick. When one has a gift for standing gracefully on one's head, one is foolish and ungrateful to envy the Marathon-runner. A funny little literary article in the hand is worth at least three Critiques of Pure Reason in the bush.

'My final item is from the home front and refers to your last letter from Grasse. What a feast! Your account of Mme de Ville-momble was really Proustian. And as for the description of your drive to Cap d'Ail and your day with what remains of the Princess and *ce pauvre Hunyadi* – well, all I can say is that it was worthy of Murasaki: the essence of all tragedy refined to a couple of table-spoonfuls of amber-coloured tea in a porcelain cup no bigger than a magnolia flower. What an admirable lesson in the art of literary chastity! My own tendencies – only in the world of letters, I am thankful to say – are towards a certain exhibitionism. This vestal prose of yours puts me to shame.

'Well, there is nothing more to say, as I used to write when I was at school – very large, do you remember? in an effort to make the words fill up half a page of notepaper. There is nothing more to say, except, of course, the unsayable, which I leave unsaid because you know it already.'

Jeremy sealed up his letter, addressed it – to The Araucarias, for his mother would be back from Grasse by the time it had crossed the Atlantic – and slipped the envelope into his pocket. All around him the Hauberk Papers clamoured for his attention; but for some time he remained idle. His elbow on the desk, in an attitude of prayer, he meditatively scratched his head; scratched it with both hands where little spots had formed the dry scabs at the roots of the hair that still remained to him, scabs which it was an exquisite pleasure to prise up with the finger-nails and carefully detach. He was thinking of his mother and how curious it was, after all, that one should have read all the Freudian literature about the Oedipus business, all the novels, from *Sons and Lovers* downwards, about the dangers of too much filial devotion, the menace of excessive maternal love – that one should have read them all, and still, with one's eyes open, go on being what one was: the victim of a greedy, possessive mother. And perhaps even odder was the fact that this possessive mother had also read all the relevant literature and was also perfectly aware of what she was and what she had done to her son. And yet she too went on being and doing what she had always been and done, just as he did, and with eyes no less open than his own. (There! the scab under the right hand had come loose. He pulled it out through the thick tufted hair above his ears and, as he looked at the tiny desiccated shred of tissue, was suddenly reminded of the baboons. But, after all, why not? The most certain and abiding pleasures are the tiniest, the simplest, the rudimentarily animal – the pleasure of lying in a hot bath, for example, or under the bedclothes, between waking and sleeping, in the morning; the pleasure of answering the calls of nature, the pleasure of being rubbed by a good masseur, the pleasure finally of scratching when one itched. Why be ashamed? He dropped the scab into the waste-paper basket and continued to scratch with the left hand.)

Nothing like self-knowledge, he reflected. To know why you do a thing that is wrong or stupid is to have an excuse for going on doing it. Justification by psycho-analysis – the modern substitute for justification by faith. You know the distant causes which made you a sadist or a money-grubber, a mother-worshipper or a son-cannibal; therefore you are completely justified in continuing to be a son-cannibal, mother-worshipper, money-grubber or sadist. No wonder if whole generations had risen up to bless the name of Freud! Well, that was how he and his mother managed things. 'We blood-sucking matriarchs!' Mrs Pordage used to say of herself – in the presence of the Rector, what was more. Or else it was into Lady Fredegond's ear-trumpet that she proclaimed her innocence. 'Old Jocastas like me, with a middle-aged son in the house,' she would shout. And Jeremy would play up to her by coming across the room and bellowing into that tomb of intelligent conversation some feeble waggery about his being an old maid, for example, or about erudition as a substitute for embroidery; any rot would do. And the old harridan would utter that deep gangster's laugh of hers and wag her head till the stuffed sea-gulls, or the artificial petunias, or whatever it was that she happened to be wearing in her always extraordinary hat, nodded like the plumes of a horse in a French *pompe funèbre* of the first class. Yes, how curious it was, he said to himself again; but how sensible, considering that they both, his mother and he, desired nothing better than to go on being just what they were. Her reasons for wanting to go on being a matriarch were obvious enough; it's fun to be a queen, it's delightful to receive homage and have a faithful subject. Less obvious, perhaps, at any rate to an outsider, were his own reasons for preferring the *status quo*. But, looked into, they turned out to be cogent enough. There was affection to begin with; for, under a certain superficial irony and airiness, he was deeply attached to his mother. Then there was habit – habit so long standing that his mother had come to be for him almost like an organ of his own body, hardly less dispensable than his pancreas or his liver. There was even a feeling of gratitude towards her for having done to him the things which, at the time she did them, had seemed the most cruelly unjustifiable. He had fallen in love when he was thirty; he had wanted to marry. Without making a single scene, without being anything but sympathetically loving towards himself and charming in all her dealings with dear little Eileen, Mrs Pordage had set to work to undermine the relationship between the two young people; and had succeeded so well that, in the end, the relationship just fell in on itself, like a house sapped from beneath. He had been very unhappy at the time, and with a part of himself he had hated his mother for what she had done. But as the years passed he had felt less and less bitterly about the whole business, until now he was positively grateful to her for having delivered him from the horrors of responsibility, of a family, of regular and remunerative labour, of a wife who would probably have turned out to be a worse tyrant than his mother – indeed, who would certainly have turned out to be a worse tyrant; for the bulging, bustling matron into whom Eileen had by degrees transformed herself was one of the most disastrous females of his acquaintance: a creature passionately conventional, proud of her obtuseness, ant-like in her efficiency, tyrannically benevolent. In short, a monster. But for his mother's strategy he would now be the unfortunate Mr Welkin who was Eileen's husband and the father of no less than four little Welkins as dreadful even in childhood and adolescence as Eileen had become in her middle age. His mother was doubtless speaking the truth when she jokingly called herself an old Jocasta, a blood-sucking matriarch; and doubtless, too, his brother Tom was right when he called him, Jeremy, a Peter Pan, and talked contemptuously of apron-strings. But the fact remained that he had had the opportunity to read what he liked and write his little articles; and that his mother saw to all the practical aspects of life, demanded in return an amount of devotion which it really wasn't very difficult to give, and left him free, on alternate Friday afternoons, to savour the refined pleasures of an infinite squalor in Maida Vale. Meanwhile, look what had happened to poor Tom! Second Secretary at Tokyo; First Secretary at Oslo; Counsellor at La Paz; and now back, more or less for good, in the Foreign Office, climbing slowly up the hierarchy, towards posts of greater responsibility and tasks of increasing turpitude. And as the salary rose and the morality of what he was called upon to do correspondingly sank, the poor fellow's uneasiness had increased, until at last, with the row over Abyssinia, he just hadn't been able to stand it any longer. On the brink of resignation or a nervous breakdown, he had managed, in the nick of time, to get himself converted to Catholicism. Thenceforward, he had been able to pack up the moral responsibility for his share in the general iniquity, take it to Farm Street and leave it there, in camphor, so to speak, with the Jesuit Fathers. Admirable arrangement! It had made a new man of him. After fourteen years of childlessness, his wife had suddenly had a baby – conceived, Jeremy had calculated, on the very night that the Spanish civil war began. Then, two days after the sack of Nanking, Tom had published a volume of comic verses. (Curious how many English Catholics take to comic versifying.) Meanwhile, he was steadily gaining weight; between the *Anschluss* and Munich he had put on eleven pounds. Another year or two of Farm Street and power-politics, and Tom would turn the scale at fourteen stone and have written the libretto of a musical comedy. No! Jeremy said to himself with decision. No! it simply wasn't admissible. Better Peter Pan and apron-strings and infinite squalor in a little room. Better a thousand times. Better to begin with, aesthetically; for this getting fat on *Realpolitik*, this scribbling of comic verses on the margins of an engraving of the Crucifixion – really, it was too inelegant. And that wasn't all: it was better even ethically; for, of course, the old Propter-Object was right: if you can't be sure of doing positive good, at least keep out of mischief. And there was poor old Tom, as busy as a beaver and, now that he was a Papist, as happy as a lark, working away at the precise spot where he could do the maximum amount of harm to the greatest possible number of people.

(The other scab came loose. Jeremy sighed and leaned back in his chair.)

One scratched like a baboon, he concluded; one lived, at fifty-four, in the security of one's mother's shadow; one's sexual life was simultaneously infantile and corrupt; by no stretch of the imagination could one's work be described as useful or important. But when one compared oneself with other people, with Tom, for example, or even with the eminent and august, with cabinet ministers and steel-magnates and bishops and celebrated novelists – well, really, one didn't come out so badly after all. Judged by the negative criterion of harmlessness, one even came out extremely well. So that, taking all things into consideration, there was really no reason why one should do anything much about anything. Having decided which, it was time to get back to the Hauberks.

Chapter Two

VIRGINIA did not wake up that morning till nearly ten; and even after having had her bath and eaten her breakfast she remained in bed for another hour or more, her eyes closed, leaning back motionless against the heaped-up pillows, like a beautiful young convalescent newly emerged from the valley of the shadow.

The valley of the shadow of death; of the greater deaths and all the little deaths. Through deaths come transfigurations. He who would save his life must lose it. Men and women are continually trying to lose their lives, the stale, unprofitable, senseless lives of their ordinary personalities. For ever trying to get rid of them, and in a thousand different ways. In the frenzies of gambling and revivalism; in the monomanias of avarice and perversion, of research and sectarianism and ambition; in the compensatory lunacies of alcohol, of reading, of day-dreaming, of morphia; in the hallucinations of opium and the cinema and ritual; in the wild epilepsies of political enthusiasm and erotic pleasure; in the stupors of veronal and exhaustion. To escape; to forget one's own, old, wearisome identity; to become someone else or, better, some other *thing* – a mere body, strangely numbed or more than ordinarily sentient; or else just a state of impersonal mind, a mode of unindividualized consciousness. What happiness, what a blissful alleviation! Even for such as were not previously aware that there was anything in their condition that needed to be alleviated. Virginia had been one of those, happy in limitation, not sufficiently conscious of her personal self to realize its ugliness and inadequacy, or the fundamental wretchedness of the human state. And yet, when Dr Obispo had scientifically engineered her escape into an erotic epilepsy more excruciatingly intense than anything she had known before or even imagined possible, Virginia had realized that, after all, there was something in her existence that required alleviating, and that this head-long plunge through an intenser, utterly alien consciousness into the darkness of a total oblivion was precisely the alleviation it required.

But, like the other addictions, whether to drugs or books, to power or applause, the addiction to pleasure tends to aggravate the condition it temporarily alleviates. The addict goes down into the valley of the shadow of his own particular little death – down indefatigably, desperately down in search of something else, something not himself, something other and better than the life he miserably lives as a human person in the hideous world of human persons. He goes down and, either violently or in delicious inertia, he dies and is transfigured; but dies only for a little while, is transfigured only momentarily. After the little death is a little resurrection, a resurrection out of unconsciousness, out of self-annihilating excitement, back into the misery of knowing oneself alone and weak and worthless, back into a completer separateness, an acuter sense of personality. And the acuter the sense of separate personality, the more urgent the demand for yet another experience of assuaging death and transfiguration. The addiction alleviates, but in doing so increases the pains demanding alleviation.

Lying there, propped up against her pillows, Virginia was suffering her daily resurrection from the valley of the shadow of her nocturnal deaths. From having been epileptically something else, she was becoming her own self again – a self, it was true, still somewhat numbed and bewildered by fatigue, still haunted by the memory of strange scenes and overpowering sensations, but none the less recognizably the old Virginia; the Virginia who admired Uncle Jo for his success and was grateful to him for having given her such a wonderful time, the Virginia who had always laughed and thought life grand and never bothered about things, the Virginia who had made Uncle Jo build the Grotto and had loved Our Lady ever since she was a kid. And now this Virginia was double-crossing her poor old, admired Uncle Jo – not just telling a few little fibs, which might happen to anyone, but deliberately and systematically double-crossing him. And not only him; she was also double-crossing poor Pete. Talking to him all the time; giving him the glad eye (as glad an eye, at any rate, as she was capable of giving in the circumstances); practically making love to him in public, so that Uncle Jo wouldn't suspect Sig. Not that she wouldn't be glad in some ways if Uncle Jo did suspect him. She'd love to see him getting a punch on the jaw and being thrown out. Just love it! But meanwhile she was doing everything she could to cover him up; and in the process making that poor, idiot boy imagine she was stuck on him. A double-crosser – that was all she was. A double-crosser. The knowledge of this worried her, it made her feel unhappy and ashamed; it prevented her laughing at things the way she used to; it kept her thinking, and feeling bad about what she was doing, and resolving not to do it again; resolving, but not being able to prevent herself doing it again, even though she really hated herself for doing it and hated Sig for making her and, above all, for telling her, in that horrible, hard-boiled, cynical way, just how he made her and why she couldn't resist it. And one of the reasons why she had to do it again was that it stopped her feeling bad about having done it before. But then, afterwards, she felt bad again. Felt so bad, indeed, that she had been ashamed to look Our Lady in the face. For more than a week now the white velvet curtains across the front of the sacred doll's house had remained drawn. She simply didn't dare to open them, because she knew that if she did, and if she made a promise there, on her knees, to Our Lady, it just wouldn't be any good. When that awful Sig came along again, she'd just go all funny inside, like her bones had all turned into rubber, and the strength would go out of her and, before she knew where she was, it would all be happening again. And that would be much worse than the other times, because she'd made a promise about it to Our Lady. So that it was better not to make any promise at all – not now, at any rate; not until there seemed to be some chance of keeping it. Because it just couldn't last this way for ever; she simply refused to believe she'd always have that awful rubber feeling in her bones. Some day she'd feel strong enough to tell Sig to go to hell. And when she did, she'd make that promise. Till then, better not.

Virginia opened her eyes, and looked with a nostalgic expression at the niche between the windows and the drawn white curtains that concealed the treasure within – the cunning little crown, the seed pearls, the mantle of blue silk, the benignant face, the adorable little hands. Virginia sighed profoundly and, closing her eyes again, tried, by a simulation of sleep, to recapture the happy oblivion from which the light of morning had forced her unwillingly to emerge.

Chapter Three

Mr Stoyte had spent his morning at the Beverly Pantheon. Very reluctantly; for he had a horror of cemeteries, even his own. But the claims of money-making were sacred; business was a duty to which all merely personal considerations had to be sacrificed. And talk of business! The Beverly Pantheon was the finest real estate proposition in the country. The land had been bought during the War at five hundred dollars an acre, improved (with roads, Tiny Tajes, Columbariums and statuary) to the tune of about ten thousand an acre, and was now selling, in grave-sites, at the rate of a hundred and sixty thousand an acre – selling so fast that the entire capital outlay had already been amortized, so that everything from now on would be pure jam. And, of course, as the population of Los Angeles increased, the jam would become correspondingly more copious. And the population *was* increasing, at the rate of nearly ten per cent per annum – and, what was more, the main accessions consisted of elderly retired people from other States of the Union; the very people who would bring the greatest immediate profit to the Pantheon. And so, when Charlie Habakkuk sent that urgent call for him to come over and discuss the latest plans of improvements and extensions, Mr Stoyte had found it morally impossible to refuse. Repressing his antipathies, he had done his duty. All that morning the two men had sat with their cigars in Charlie's office at the top of the Tower of Resurrection; and Charlie had waved those hands of his, and spouted cigar-smoke from his nostrils, and talked – God, how he had talked! As though he were one of those men in a red fez trying to make you buy an Oriental carpet – and incidentally, Mr Stoyte reflected morosely, that was what Charlie looked like; only he was better fed than most of those carpet boys, and therefore greasier.

'Cut the sales talk,' he growled out loud. 'You seem to forget I own the place.'

Charlie looked at him with an expression of pained surprise. Sales talk? But this wasn't sales talk. This was real, this was earnest. The Pantheon was his baby; for all practical purposes he had in-

vented the place. It was he who had thought up the Tiny Taj and
the Church of the Bard; he who, on his own initiative, had bought
that bargain lot of statues at Genoa; he who had first clearly formu-
lated the policy of injecting sex-appeal into death; he who had
resolutely resisted every attempt to introduce into the cemetery any
representation of grief or age, any symbol of mortality, any image
of the sufferings of Jesus. He had had to fight for his ideas, he had
had to listen to a lot of criticism; but the results had proved him
right. Anyone who complained that there was no Crucifixion in the
place could be referred to the published accounts. And here was
Mr Stoyte talking sarcastically about sales talk. Sales talk, indeed,
when the demand for space in the Pantheon was so great that existing accommodation would soon be inadequate. There would have
to be enlargements. More space, more buildings, more amenities.
Bigger and better; progress; service.

In the top of the Tower of Resurrection, Charlie Habakkuk un-
folded his plans. The new extension was to have a Poets' Corner,
open to any bona fide writer – though he was afraid they'd have to
draw the line at the authors of advertising copy, which was a pity,
because a lot of them made good money and might be persuaded to
pay extra for the prestige of being buried with the moving-picture
people. But that cut both ways – because the scenario writers
wouldn't feel that the Poets' Corner was exclusive enough if you
let in the advertising boys. And seeing that the moving-picture
fellows made so much more than the others . . . well, it stood to
reason, Charlie had concluded, it stood to reason. And, of course,
they'd have to have a replica of Westminster Abbey in the Poets'
Corner. Wee Westminster – it would sound kind of cute. And as
they needed a couple of extra mortuary furnaces anyhow, they'd
have them installed there in the Dean's Yard. And they'd put a new
automatic record-player in the crypt, so that there'd be more
variety in the music. Not that people didn't appreciate the Perpetual
Wurlitzer; they did. But all the same it got a bit monotonous. So
he'd thought they might have some recordings of a choir singing
hymns and things, and perhaps, every now and then, just for a
change, some preacher giving an inspirational message, so that
you'd be able to sit in the Garden of Contemplation, for example,
and listen to the Wurlitzer for a few minutes, and then the choir

singing 'Abide with Me', and then a nice sort of Barrymore voice saying some piece, like the Gettysburg Address, or 'Laugh and the World Laughs with You', or maybe some nice juicy bit by Mrs Eddy or Ralph Waldo Trine – anything would do so long as it was inspirational enough. And then there was his idea of the Catacombs. And, boy, it was the best idea he'd ever had. Leading Mr Stoyte to the south-eastern window, he had pointed across an intervening valley of tombs and cypresses and the miniature monuments of bogus antiquity, to where the land sloped up again to a serrated ridge on the farther side. There, he had shouted excitedly, there, in that hump in the middle; they'd tunnel down into that. Hundreds of yards of catacombs. Lined with reinforced concrete to make them earthquake-proof. The only class-A catacombs in the world. And little chapels, like the ones in Rome. And a lot of phoney-looking murals, looking like they were real old. You could get them done cheap by one of those W.P.A. art projects. Not that those guys knew how to paint, of course; but that was quite O.K. seeing that the murals had to look phoney anyhow. And they wouldn't have anything but candles and little lamps for people to carry around – no electric light at all, except right at the very end of all those winding passages and stairs, where there'd be a great big sort of underground church, with one of those big nude statues that were going up at the San Francisco Fair and that they'd be glad to sell for a thousand bucks or even less when the show was over – one of those modernistic broads with muscles on them – and they'd have her standing right in the middle there, with maybe some fountain spouting all around her and concealed pink lighting in the water so she'd look kind of real. Why, the tourists would come a thousand miles to see it. Because there was nothing people liked so much as caves. Look at those Carlsbad Caverns, for example; and all those caves in Virginia. And those were just common-or-garden natural caves, without murals or anything. Whereas these would be catacombs. Yes, sir; real catacombs, like the things the Christian Martyrs lived in – and, by gum, that was another idea! Martyrs! Why wouldn't they have a Chapel of the Martyrs with a nice plaster group of some girls with no clothes on, just going to be eaten by a lion? People wouldn't stand for the Crucifixion; but they'd get a real thrill out of that.

Mr Stoyte had listened wearily and with repugnance. He loathed his Pantheon and everything to do with it. Loathed it because in spite of statues and Wurlitzer, it spoke to him of nothing but disease and death and corruption and final judgement; because it was here, in the Pantheon, that they would bury him – at the foot of the pedestal of Rodin's '*Le Baiser*'. (An assistant manager had once inadvisedly pointed out the spot to him and been immediately fired; but there was no dismissing the memory of his offence.) Charlie's enthusiasm for catacombs and Wee Westminsters elicited no answering warmth; only occasional grunts and a final sullen O.K. for everything except the Chapel of the Martyrs. Not that the Chapel of the Martyrs seemed to Mr Stoyte a bad idea; on the contrary, he was convinced that the public would go crazy over it. If he rejected it, it was merely on principle – because it would never do to allow Charlie Habakkuk to think he was always right.

'Get plans and estimates for everything else,' he ordered in a tone so gruff that he might have been delivering a reprimand. 'But no martyrs. I won't have any martyrs.'

Almost in tears, Charlie pleaded for just one lion, just one Early Christian Virgin with her hands tied behind her back – because people got such a kick out of anything to do with ropes or handcuffs. Two or three Virgins would have been much better, of course; but he'd be content with one. 'Just one, Mr Stoyte,' he implored, clasping his eloquent hands. 'Only one.'

Obstinately deaf to all his entreaties, Mr Stoyte shook his head. 'No martyrs here,' he said. 'That's final.' And to show that it was final, he threw away the butt of his cigar and got up to go.

Five minutes later, Charlie Habakkuk was letting off steam to his secretary. The ingratitude of people! The stupidity! He'd a good mind to resign, just to show the old buzzard that they couldn't get on without him. Not for five minutes. Who was it that had made the place what it was: the uniquest cemetery in the world? Absolutely the uniquest. Who? (Charlie slapped himself on the chest.) And who made all the money? Jo Stoyte. And what had *he* done to make the place a success? Absolutely nothing at all. It was enough to make you want to be a communist. And the old devil wasn't grateful or even decently polite. Pushing you around as though you were a bum off the streets! Well, there was one comfort: Old Jo hadn't been looking any too good this morning. One of these days, maybe, they'd have the pleasure of burying him. Down there in the vestibule of the Columbarium, eight foot underground. And serve him right!

It was not only that he didn't look too good; leaning back in the car which was taking him down to Beverly Hills on his way to see Clancy, Mr Stoyte was thinking, as he had thought so often during these last two or three weeks, that he didn't feel too good. He'd wake up in the morning feeling kind of sluggish and heavy; and his mind didn't seem to be as clear as it was. Obispo called it suppressed influenza and made him take those pills every night; but they didn't seem to do him any good. He went on feeling that way just the same. And on top of everything else he was worrying himself sick about Virginia. The Baby was acting strange, like someone that wasn't really there; so quiet, and not noticing anything, and starting when you spoke to her and asking what you said. Acting for all the world like one of those advertisements for Sal Hepatica or California Syrup of Figs; and that was what he'd have thought it was, if it hadn't been for the way she went on with that Peter Boone fellow. Always talking to him at meals; and asking him to come and have a swim; and wanting to take a squint down his microscope – and what sort of a damn did *she* give for microscopes, he'd like to know? Throwing herself at him – that was what it had looked like on the surface. And that kind of syrup-of-figs way of acting (like people at those Quaker Meetings that Prudence used to make him go to before she took up with Christian Science) – that all fitted in. You'd say she was kind of stuck on the fellow. But then why should it have happened so suddenly? Because she'd never shown any signs of being stuck on him before. Always treated him like you'd treat a great big dog – friendly and all that, but not taking him too seriously; just a pat on the head and then, when he'd wagged his tail, thinking of something else. No, he couldn't understand it; he just couldn't figure it out. It looked like she was stuck on him; but then, at the same time, it looked like she just didn't notice if he was a boy or a dog. Because that was how she was acting even now. She paid a lot of attention to him – only the way you'd pay attention to a nice big retriever. And that was what had thrown him out. If she'd been stuck on Pete in the ordinary way, then he'd have got mad, and raised hell, and thrown the boy out of the house. But how could you raise hell over a dog? How could you get mad with a girl for telling a retriever she'd like to have a squint down his microscope? You couldn't even if you tried; because getting mad didn't make any sense. All he'd been able to do was just worry, trying to figure things out and not being able to. There was only one thing that was clear, and that was that the Baby meant more to him than he had thought, more than he had ever believed it possible that anyone should mean to him. It had begun by his just wanting her – wanting her to touch, to hold, to handle, to eat; wanting her because she was warm and smelt good; wanting her because she was young and he was old, because she was so innocent and he too tired for anything not innocence to excite. That was how it had begun; but almost immediately something else had happened. That youth of hers, that innocence and sweetness – they were more than just exciting. She was so cute and lovely and childish, he almost felt like crying over her, even while he wanted to hold and handle and devour. She did the strangest things to him – made him feel good, like you felt when you'd tanked up a bit on Scotch, and at the same time made him feel *good*, like you felt when you were at church, or listening to William Jennings Bryan, or making some poor kid happy by giving him a doll or something. And Virginia wasn't just anybody's kid, like the ones at the hospital; she was *his* kid, his very own. Prudence wasn't able to have children; and at the time he'd been sore about it. But now he was glad. Because if he'd had a row of kids, they'd be standing in the way of the Baby. And Virginia meant more to him than any daughter could mean. Because even if she were *only* a daughter, which she wasn't, she was probably a lot nicer than his own flesh-and-blood daughter would have been – seeing that, after all, the Stoytes were all a pretty sour-faced lot and Prudence had been kind of dumb even if she was a good woman, which she certainly was – maybe a bit too good. Whereas with the Baby everything was just right, just perfect. He had been happier since he'd known her than he'd ever been in years. With her around, things had seemed worth doing again. You didn't have to go through life asking 'Why?' The reason for everything was there in front of you, wearing that cunning little yachting-cap,

169

maybe, or all dressed up with her emeralds and everything for some party with the moving-picture crowd.

And now something had happened. The reason for carrying on was being taken away from him. The Baby had changed; she was fading away from him; she had gone somewhere else. Where had she gone? And why? Why did she want to leave him? To leave him all alone. Absolutely alone, and he was an old man, and the white slab was there in the vestibule of the Columbarium, waiting for him.

'What's the matter, Baby?' he had asked. Time and again he had asked, with anguish in his heart, too miserable to be angry, too much afraid of being left alone to care about his dignity, or his rights, about anything except keeping her, at whatever cost: 'What's the matter, Baby?'

And all she ever did was to look at him as though she were looking at him from some place a million miles away – to look at him like that and say: Nothing; she was feeling fine; she hadn't got anything on her mind; and, no, there wasn't anything he could do for her, because he'd given her everything already, and she was perfectly happy.

And if he mentioned Pete (kind of casually, so she shouldn't think he suspected anything) she wouldn't even bat an eyelid; just say: Yes, she liked Pete; he was a nice boy, but unsophisticated – and that made her laugh; and she liked laughing.

'But, Baby, you're different,' he would say; and it was difficult for him to keep his voice from breaking, he was so unhappy. 'You don't act like you used to, Baby.'

And all she'd answer was, that that was funny because she felt just the same.

'You don't feel the same about me,' he would say.

And she'd say she did. And he'd say no. And she'd say it wasn't true. Because what reasons did he have for saying she felt different about him? And of course she was quite right; there weren't any reasons you could lay your finger on. He couldn't honestly say she acted less affectionate, or didn't want to let him kiss her, or anything like that. She was different because of something you couldn't put a name to. Something in the way she looked and moved and sat around. He couldn't describe it except by saying it

was like she wasn't really there where you thought you were looking at her, but some place else; some place where you couldn't
touch her, or talk to her, or even really see her. That was how it
was. But whenever he had tried to explain it to her, she had just
laughed at him and said he must be having some of those feminine
intuitions you read about in stories – only his feminine intuitions
were all wrong.

And so there he'd be, back where he started from, trying to
figure it out and not being able to, and worrying himself sick. Yes,
worrying himself sick. Because when he'd got over feeling sluggish
and heavy, like he always did in the mornings now, he felt so
worried about the Baby that he'd start bawling at the servants and
being rude to that god-damned Englishman and getting mad with
Obispo. And the next thing that happened was that he couldn't
digest his meals. He was getting heartburn and sour stomach; and
one day he had such a pain that he'd thought it was appendicitis.
But Obispo had said it was just gas; because of his suppressed
influenza. And then he'd got mad and told the fellow he must be
a lousy doctor if he couldn't cure a little thing like that. Which
must put the fear of God into Obispo, because he'd said, 'Just give
me two or three days more. That's all I need to complete the
treatment.' And he'd said that suppressed influenza was a funny
thing; didn't seem to be anything, but poisoned the whole system,
so you couldn't think straight any more; and you'd get to imagining things that weren't really there, and worrying about them.

Which might be true in a general way; but in this case he just
knew it wasn't all imagination. The Baby *was* different; he had a
reason for being worried.

Sunk in his mood of perplexed and agitated gloom, Mr Stoyte
was carried down the windings of the mountain road, through the
bowery oasis of Beverly Hills, and eastward (for Clancy lived in
Hollywood) along Santa Monica Boulevard. Over the telephone,
that morning, Clancy had put on one of his melodramatic con-
spirator acts. From the rigmarole of hints and dark allusions and
altered names, Mr Stoyte had gathered that the news was good.
Clancy and his boys had evidently succeeded in buying up most of
the best land in the San Felipe Valley. At another time, Mr Stoyte
would have exulted in his triumph; today, even the prospect of

making a million or two of easy money gave him no sort of pleasure. In the world he had been reduced to inhabiting, millions were irrelevant. For what could millions do to allay his miseries? The miseries of an old, tired, empty man; of a man who had no end in life but himself, no philosophy, no knowledge but of his own interests, no appreciations, not even any friends – only a daughter-mistress, a concubine-child, frantically desired, cherished to the point of idolatry. And now this being, on whom he had relied to give significance to his life, had begun to fail him. He had come to doubt her fidelity – but to doubt without tangible reasons, to doubt in such a way that none of the ordinary satisfying re-actions, of rage, of violence, of recrimination, was appropriate. The sense was going out of his life and he could do nothing; for he was in a situation with which he did not know how to deal, hopelessly bewildered. And always, in the background of his mind, there floated an image of that circular marble room, with Rodin's image of desire at the centre, and that white slab in the pavement at its base – the slab that would some day have his name engraved upon it: Joseph Panton Stoyte, and the dates of his birth and death. And along with that inscription went another, in orange letters on a coal-black ground: 'It is a terrible thing to fall into the hands of the living God.' And meanwhile here was Clancy, conspiratorially announcing victory. Good news! Good news! A year or two from now he would be richer by another million. But the millions were in one world and the old, unhappy, frightened man was in another, and there was no communication between the two.

Chapter Four

JEREMY worked for a couple of hours, unpacking, examining, provisionally cataloguing, filing. There were no finds this morning – merely accounts and legal documents and business letters. Stuff for Coulton and Tawney and the Hammonds; not at all his cup of tea.

By half past twelve the weight of boredom had become too much for him. He broke off and, in search of a little spiritual refreshment, turned to the Fifth Earl's vellum-bound notebook.

'July 1780,' he read. 'Sensuality is close allied with Sorrow, and it sometimes happens that, on account of the very sincerity of her Grief, the weeping Widow is betrayed by her own Feelings and finds herself unable to resist the importunities of the funeral Guest, who knows the Art of passing imperceptibly from Condolence to Familiarity. I myself have posthumously cuckolded a Duke and two Viscounts (one of them no later than last night) upon the very Beds from which, but a few hours before, they had been borne in Pomp to the ancestral Sepulchre.'

That was something for his mother, Jeremy reflected. The sort of thing she really adored! He had a good mind, if it wasn't too horribly expensive, to cable it to her in a night letter.

He returned to the notebook.

'One of the Livings in my Gift having unexpectedly fallen vacant, my Sister sent to me today a young Divine whom she commends, and I believe her, for his singular Virtue. I will have no Parsons around me but such as drink deep, ride to Hounds and caress the Wives and daughters of their Parishioners. A Virtuous Parson does nothing to test or exercise the Faith of his Flock; but as I have written to my Sister, it is by Faith that we come to Salvation.'

The next entry was dated March 1784.

'In old Tombs newly opened a kind of ropy Slime depends from the roof and coats the walls. It is the condensation of decay.'

'January 1786. Half a dozen pensées in as many years. If I am to fill a volume at this rate, I must outlast the patriarchs. I regret my sloth, but console myself with the thought that my fellow men are too contemptible for me to waste my time instructing or entertaining them.'

Jeremy hurried over three pages of reflections on politics and economics. Under the date of March 12th, 1787, he found a more interesting entry:

'Dying is almost the least spiritual of our acts, more strictly carnal even than the act of love. There are Death Agonies that are like the strainings of the Costive at stool. Today I saw M. B. die.'

'January 11th, 1788. This day fifty years ago I was born. From solitude in the Womb, we emerge into solitude among our Fellows, and return again to solitude within the Grave. We pass our lives in the attempt to mitigate that solitude. But Propinquity is never fusion. The most populous City is but an agglomeration of wildernesses. We exchange Words, but exchange them from prison to prison, and without hope that they will signify to others what they mean to ourselves. We marry, and there are two solitudes in the house instead of one; we beget children, and there are many solitudes. We reiterate the act of love; but again propinquity is never fusion. The most intimate contact is only of Surfaces, and we couple, as I have seen the condemned Prisoners at Newgate coupling with their Trulls, between the bars of our cages. Pleasure cannot be shared; like Pain, it can only be experienced or inflicted, and when we give Pleasure to our Lovers or bestow Charity upon the Needy, we do so, not to gratify the object of our Benevolence, but only ourselves. For the Truth is that we are kind for the same reason as we are cruel, in order that we may enhance the sense of our own Power; and this we are for ever trying to do, despite the fact that by doing it we cause ourselves to feel more solitary than ever. The reality of Solitude is the same in all men, there being no mitigation of it, except in Forgetfulness, Stupidity or Illusion; but a man's sense of Solitude is proportionate to the sense and fact of his Power. In any set of circumstances, the more Power we have, the more intensely do we feel our solitude. I have enjoyed much Power in my life.'

'June 1788. Captain Pavey came to pay his respects today, a round, jovial, low man, whom even his awe of me could not entirely prevent from breaking out into the vulgar Mirth which is native to him. I questioned him concerning his last Voyage, and he very minutely described for me the mode of packing the Slaves in the holds; the chains used to secure them; the feeding of them and, in calm weather, the exercising on deck, though always with Nets about the bulwarks, to prevent the more desperate from casting themselves into the sea; the Punishments for the refractory; the schools of hungry sharks accompanying the vessel; the scurvy and other diseases, the wearing away of the negroes' Skin by the hardness of the planks on which they lie and the continual Motion of the waves; the Stench so horrible that even the hardiest seaman will turn pale and swoon away, if he ventures into the hold; the frequent Deaths and almost incredibly rapid Putrefaction, especially in damp Weather near the Line. When he took his leave, I made him a present of a gold snuff box. Anticipating no such favour, he was so coarsely loud in his expression of thanks and future devotion to my Interests, that I was forced to cut him short. The snuff box cost me sixty guineas; Captain Pavey's last three Voyages have brought me upwards of forty thousand. Power and wealth increase in direct proportion to a man's distance from the material objects from which wealth and power are ultimately derived. For every risk taken by the General Officer, the private soldier takes a hundred; and for every guinea earned by the latter the General earns a hundred. So with myself and Pavey and the Slaves. The Slaves labour in the Plantation for nothing but blows and their diet; Captain Pavey undergoes the hardships and dangers of the Sea and lives not so well as a Haberdasher or Vintner; I put my hands to nothing more material than a Banker's draft, and a shower of gold descends upon me for my pains. In a world such as ours, a man is given but three choices. In the first place, he may do as the multitudes have always done and, too stupid to be wholly a knave, mitigate his native baseness with a no less native folly. Second, he may imitate those more consummate fools who painfully deny their native Baseness in order to practise Virtue. Third, he may choose to be a man of sense – one who, knowing his native Baseness, thereby learns to make use of it and, by the act of knowledge, rises superior to it and to his more foolish Fellows. For myself, I have chosen to be a man of sense.'

'March 1789. Reason promises happiness; Feeling protests that it is Happiness; Sense alone gives Happiness. And Happiness itself is like dust in the mouth.'

'July 1789. If Men and Women took their Pleasures as noisily as the Cats, what Londoner could ever hope to sleep of nights?'

'July 1789. The Bastille is fallen. Long live the Bastille!'

The next few pages were devoted to the Revolution. Jeremy skipped them. In 1794 the Fifth Earl's interest in the Revolution gave place to interest in his own health.

'To those who visit me,' he had written, 'I say that I have been sick and am now well again. The words are quite untrue; for it was not I who lay at Death's door, nor is it I who am recovered. The first was a special creation of Fever, an embodiment of Pain and Lassitude; the second is not I, but an old man, weak, shrunken and without desires. My name and some memories are all that remain to me of the Being I once was. It is as if a Man had died and willed to some surviving Friend a handful of worthless trinkets to remember him by.'

'1794. A sick, rich Man is like one who lies wounded and alone in the deserts of Egypt; the Vultures hover lower and lower above his head and the Jackals and Hyenas prowl in ever-narrowing circles about the place where he lies. Not even a rich Man's Heirs could be more unsleepingly attentive. When I look into my Nephew's face and read there, behind the mask of Solicitude, his impatient longing for my Death and his disappointment that I am not already gone, I feel an influx of new Life and Strength. If for no other reason, I will live on to rob Him of the Happiness which he still believes (for he is confident of my Relapse) to be within his Grasp.'

'1794. The World is a Mirror, reflecting his image to the Beholder.'

'January 1795. I have tried King David's remedy against old age and found it wanting. Warmth cannot be imparted, but only evoked; and where no lingering spark persists, even tinder will not raise a flame.

'It may be as the Parsons say, that we are saved by another's vicarious suffering; but I can vouch for the fact that vicarious pleasure is without efficacity, except only to enhance the sentiments of Superiority and Power in him who inflicts it.'

'1795. As the Satisfactions of Sense decay, we compensate ourselves for their loss by cultivating the sentiments of Pride and Vanity. The love of Domination is independent of the bodily faculties and therefore, when the body loses its powers, may easily take the place of vanished Pleasure. For myself, I was never without the love of Dominion even when in the Throes of Pleasure. Since my late Death, the Phantom that remains of me is forced to content itself with the first, less substantial, and above all, less harmless of these two Satisfactions.'

'July 1796. The fishponds at Gonister were dug in the Ages of Superstition by the monks of the Abbey upon whose foundations the present House is built. Under King Charles I, my great-great-grandfather caused a number of leaden Disks engraved with his cypher and the date, to be attached by silver rings to the tails of fifty well-grown carp. Not less than twenty of these fish are alive today, as one may count whenever the bell is rung that calls the Creatures to be fed. With them come others even larger than they – survivors, it may be, from the monkish times before King Henry's Dissolution of the Religious Houses. Watching them through the pellucid Water, I marvel at the strength and unimpaired agility of these great Fishes, of which the oldest were perhaps alive when the Utopia was written, while the youngest are co-eval with the author of Paradise Lost. The latter attempted to justify God's ways to Man. He would have done a more useful Work in undertaking to explain the ways of God to Fish. Philosophers have wasted their own and their readers' time in speculations upon the Immortality of the Soul; the Alchemists have pored for centuries over their crucibles in the vain hope of discovering the Elixir or the Stone. Meanwhile, in every pond and river, one may find Carps that have outlived three Platos and half a dozen Paracelsuses. The Secret of eternal Life is not to be found in old Books, nor in liquid Gold, nor even in Heaven; it is to be found in the Mud and only awaits a skilful Angler.'

Outside the corridor the bell rang for lunch. Jeremy rose, put the Fifth Earl's notebook away and walked towards the lift, smiling to himself at the thought of the pleasure he would derive from telling that bumptious ass, Obispo, that all his best ideas about longevity had been anticipated in the eighteenth century.

Chapter Five

Luncheon, in the absence of Mr Stoyte, was a very cheerful meal. The servants went about their business unreprimanded. Jeremy could talk without the risk of being snubbed or insulted. Dr Obispo was able to tell the story about the chimney-sweep who applied for life-insurance after going on his honeymoon, and, from the far-away depths of that almost trance-like state of fatigue – that state which she deliberately fostered, so as not to have to think too much and feel too badly about what was happening – Virginia was at liberty to laugh at it as loudly as she liked. And though with one part of herself she would have liked not to laugh at all, because she didn't want to make Sig think she was encouraging him in any way, with another part she wanted to laugh, indeed couldn't help laughing, because, after all, the story was really very funny. Besides, it was such a relief not to have to put on that act with Pete for the benefit of uncle Jo. No double-crossing. For once, she could be herself. The only fly in the ointment was that this self she was being was such a miserable specimen: a self with bones that would go like rubber whenever that horrible Sig chose to come along; a self without the strength to keep a promise even to Our Lady. Her laughter abruptly ceased.

Only Pete was consistently unhappy – about the chimney-sweep, of course, and Virginia's burst of merriment; but also because Barcelona had fallen and, with it, all his hopes of a speedy victory over fascism, all prospect of ever seeing any of his old comrades again. And that wasn't all. Laughing at the story of the chimney-sweep was only a single painful incident among many. Virginia had allowed the first two courses of the meal to come and go without once paying any attention to him. But why, why? His distress was aggravated by bitter bewilderment. Why? In the light of what had been happening during the past three weeks it was inexplicable. Ever since the evening of the day she had turned back at the Grotto, Virginia had been simply wonderful to him – going out of her way to talk to him, inviting him to tell her things about Spain and even about biology. Why, she had actually asked to look at something under the microscope. Trembling with happiness, so that he could hardly adjust the slide, he had focused the instrument on a preparation of the carp's intestinal flora. Then she had sat down in his place, and as she bent over the eyepiece her auburn curls had swung down on either side of the microscope and, above the edge of her pink sweater, the nape of her neck had been uncovered, so white, so tangibly inviting, that the enormous effort he had had to make to prevent himself from kissing it had left him feeling almost faint.

There had been times during the ensuing days when he wished that he hadn't made that effort. But then his better self would reassert its rule and he was glad again that he had. Because, of course, it wouldn't have been right. For, though he had long since given up the family belief in that Blood-of-the-Lamb business, he still remembered what his pious and conventional mother had said about kissing anyone you weren't engaged to; he was still at heart the earnest adolescent whom Reverend Schlitz's eloquence had fired during the perplexities of puberty with a passionate determination to be continent, a conviction of the Sacredness of Love, an enthusiasm for something wonderful called Christian marriage. But at the moment, unfortunately, he wasn't earning enough to feel justified in asking Virginia to accept his sacred love and enter into Christian marriage with him. And there was the added complication that on his side the Christian marriage wouldn't be Christian except in substance, whereas Virginia was attached to the institution which Reverend Schlitz sometimes called the Whore of Babylon and the Marxists regarded as pre-eminently detestable. An institution, moreover, that would think as poorly of him as he thought of it – though he thought rather less poorly of it now that Hitler was persecuting it in Germany and since he had been looked after by those Sisters of Mercy in Spain. And even if those religious and financial difficulties could somehow be miraculously smoothed away, there remained the dreadful fact of Mr Stoyte. He *knew*, of course, that Mr Stoyte was nothing more than a father to Virginia, or at most an uncle – but knew it with that excessive certainty that is born of desire; knew it in the same way as Don Quixote knew that the pasteboard vizor of his helmet was as strong as steel. It was the kind of knowledge about which it is prudent to make no inquiries; and of course, if he asked Virginia to marry him, such inquiries, or the information such inquiries might be expected to elicit, would almost inevitably be forced upon him.

Yet another complicating factor in the situation was Mr Propter. For if Mr Propter was right, as Pete was coming to feel more and more certain that he was, then it was obviously unwise to do something that would make more difficult the passage from the human level to the level of eternity. And though he loved Virginia, he found it difficult to believe that marriage to her would be anything but an obstacle to the enlightenment of everybody concerned.

Or rather, he *had* thought this; but in the course of the last week or two his opinion had changed. Or, to be more exact, he no longer had an opinion; he was just uncertain and bewildered. For Virginia's character seemed almost suddenly to have changed. From being childlike, loud and extraverted, her innocence had become quiet and inscrutable. In the past, she had treated him with the jocular and casual friendliness of mere good-fellowship; but recently there had been a strange alteration. The jokes had stopped and a kind of earnest solicitude had taken their place. She had been simply wonderful to him – but not in the way a girl is wonderful to a man she wants to fall in love with her. No, Virginia had been wonderful like a sister – and not an ordinary sister, either: almost a Sister of Mercy. Not just any Sister of Mercy: that particular Sister who had nursed him when he was in hospital at Gerona; the young Sister with the big eyes and the pale oval face, like the face of the Virgin Mary in a picture; the one who always seemed to be secretly happy, not because of anything that was going on around her, but because of something inside, something extraordinary and beautiful behind her eyes that she could look in at; and when she'd looked at it, there was no reason any more why she should feel scared by an air-raid, for example, or upset by an amputation. She evidently saw things from what Mr Propter called the level of eternity; they didn't affect her in the way they'd affect a person living on the human level. On the human level you were scared and angry; or, if you were calm, you made yourself calm by an effort of will. But the Sister was calm without making an effort of will. At the time, he had admired without comprehension. Now, thanks to Mr Propter, he could begin to understand as well as admire.

Well, that was the face that Virginia's had reminded him of during the past weeks. There had been a kind of sudden conversion from the outward-looking life to the inward, from open responsiveness to secret and mysterious abstraction. The cause of this conversion was beyond his comprehension; but the fact was manifest, and he had respected it. Respected it by not kissing her neck as she bent over the microscope; by never even touching her arm or taking her hand; by not saying to her one word of all he felt about her. In the strange, inexplicable circumstances of her transformation, such actions, he had felt, would have been inappropriate to the point positively of sacrilege. It was as a sister that she had chosen to be wonderful to him; it was therefore as a brother that he had responded. And now, for no known reason, she seemed suddenly to have become unaware of his existence.

The sister had forgotten her brother; and the Sister of Mercy had forgotten herself – forgotten herself so far as to listen to Dr Obispo's ignoble anecdote about the chimney-sweep, even to laugh at it. And yet, Pete noticed in bewilderment, the moment she stopped laughing, her face resumed its expression of inwardness and secrecy and detachment. The Sister of Mercy remembered herself as promptly as she had forgotten. It was beyond him; he simply couldn't figure it out.

With the arrival of the coffee, Dr Obispo announced that he proposed to take the afternoon off and, as there was nothing that urgently needed doing in the laboratory, he advised Pete to do the same. Pete thanked him and, pretending to be in a hurry (for he didn't want to go through the humiliation of being ignored when Virginia discussed her plans for the afternoon), swallowed his coffee and, mumbling excuses, left the room. A little later he was out in the sunshine, walking down towards the plain.

As he went, he thought of some of the things Mr Propter had said to him in the course of his recent visits.

Of what he had said about the silliest text in the Bible and the most sensible. 'They hated me without a cause' and 'God is not mocked; as a man sows, so shall he reap.'

Of what he had said about nobody ever getting something for nothing – so that a man would pay for too much money, for example, or too much power, or too much sex, by being shut up more tightly inside his own ego; so that a country that moved too quickly and violently would fall under a tyranny, like Napoleon's, or Stalin's, or Hitler's; and a people that was prosperous and internally peaceful would pay for it by being smug and self-satisfied and conservative, like the English.

The baboons were gibbering as he passed. Pete recalled some of Mr Propter's remarks about literature. About the wearisomeness, to an adult mind, of all those merely descriptive plays and novels which critics expected one to admire. All the innumerable, interminable anecdotes and romances and character-studies, but no general theory of anecdotes, no explanatory hypothesis of romance or character. Just a huge collection of facts about lust and greed, fear and ambition, duty and affection; just facts, and imaginary facts at that, with no coordinating philosophy superior to common sense and the local system of conventions, no principle of arrangement more rational than simple aesthetic expediency. And then the astonishing nonsense talked by those who undertake to elucidate and explain this hodge-podge of prettily patterned facts and fancies! All that solemn tosh, for example, about Regional Literature – as though there were some special and outstanding merit in recording uncoordinated facts about the lusts, greeds and duties of people who happen to live in the country and speak in dialect! Or else the facts were about the urban poor and there was an effort to coordinate them in terms of some post-Marxian theory that might be partly true, but was always inadequate. And in that case it was the great Proletarian Novel. Or else somebody wrote yet another book proclaiming that Life is Holy; by which he always meant that anything people do in the way of fornicating, or getting drunk, or losing their tempers, or feeling maudlin, is entirely O.K. with God and should therefore be regarded as permissible and even virtuous. In which case it was up to the critics to talk about the author's ripe humanity, his deep and tender wisdom, his affinities with the great Goethe, and his obligations to William Blake.

Pete smiled as he remembered, but with a certain ruefulness as well as amusement; for he too had taken this sort of thing with the seriousness its verbiage seemed to demand.

Misplaced seriousness – the source of some of our most fatal errors. One should be serious, Mr Propter had said, only about what deserves to be taken seriously. And, on the strictly human level, there was nothing that deserved to be taken seriously except the suffering men inflicted upon themselves by their crimes and follies. But, in the last analysis, most of these crimes and follies arose from taking too seriously things which did not deserve it. And that, Mr Propter had continued, was another of the enormous defects of so-called good literature; it accepted the conventional scale of values; it respected power and position; it admired success; it treated as though they were reasonable the mainly lunatic pre-occupations of statesmen, lovers, business men, social climbers, parents. In a word, it took seriously the causes of suffering as well as the suffering. It helped to perpetuate misery by explicitly or implicitly approving the thoughts and feelings and practices which could not fail to result in misery. And this approval was bestowed in the most magnificent and persuasive language. So that even when a tragedy ended badly, the reader was hypnotized by the eloquence of the piece into imagining that it was all somehow noble and worth while. Which of course it wasn't. Because, if you considered them dispassionately, nothing could be more silly and squalid than the themes of *Phèdre*, or *Othello*, or *Wuthering Heights*, or the *Agamemnon*. But the treatment of these themes had been in the highest degree sublime and thrilling, so that the reader or the spectator was left with the conviction that, in spite of the catastrophe, all was really well with the world, the all too human world, which had produced it. No, a good satire was much more deeply truthful and, of course, much more profitable than a good tragedy. The trouble was that so few good satires existed, because so few satirists were prepared to carry their criticism of human values far enough. *Candide*, for example, was admirable as far as it went; but it went no further than debunking the principal human activities in the name of the ideal of harmlessness. Now, it was perfectly true that harmlessness was the highest ideal most people could aspire to; for, though few had the power to do much positive good, there was nobody who could not refrain, if he so desired, from evil. Nevertheless, mere harmlessness, however excellent, most certainly didn't represent the highest possible ideal. *Il faut cultiver notre jardin* was not the last word in human wisdom; at the best it was only the last but one.

The sun was in such a position that, as he walked down the hill, Pete saw two little rainbows spouting from the nipples of Giambologna's nymph. Thoughts of Noah immediately arose in conjunction with thoughts of Virginia in her white satin bathing-costume. He tried to repress the latter as incompatible with the new thoughts he was trying to cultivate about the Sister of Mercy; and since Noah was not a subject that would bear much thinking about, he proceeded instead to concentrate on that talk he had had with Mr Propter about sex. It had begun with his own puzzled questionings as to what sort of sexual behaviour was normal – not statistically normal, of course, but normal in that absolute sense in which perfect vision or unimpaired digestion may be called normal. What sort of sexual behaviour was normal in that sense of the word? And Mr Propter had answered: None. But there must be, he had protested. If good could be manifested on the animal level, then there must be some kind of sexual behaviour that was absolutely normal and natural, just as there was an absolutely normal and natural sort of digestive activity. But man's sexual behaviour, Mr Propter had answered, wasn't on the same level as digestion. A rat's love-making – yes, that *was* on the same level as digestion; for the entire process was instinctive; in other words, was controlled by the physiological intelligence of the body – the same physiological intelligence as correlated the actions of heart and lungs and kidneys, as regulated temperature, as nourished the muscles and made them do the work demanded of them by the central nervous system. Men's bodily activities were controlled by the same physiological intelligence; and it was that intelligence which, on the animal level, manifested good. In human beings, sexual behaviour was almost completely outside the jurisdiction of this physiological intelligence. It controlled only the cellular activities which made sexual behaviour possible. All the rest was non-instinctive and took place on the strictly human level of self-consciousness. Even when men thought that they were being most exclusively animal in their sexuality, they were still on the human level. Which meant that they were still self-conscious, still dominated by words – and where there were words, there, of necessity, were memories and wishes, judgements and imaginations. There, inevitably, were the past and the future, the actual and the fantastic; regret and anticipation; good and evil; the creditable and the discreditable; the beautiful and the ugly. Among men and women, even the most apparently bestial acts of eroticism were associated with some or all of these non-animal factors – factors which were injected into every human situation by the existence of language. This meant that there was no one type of human sexuality that could be called 'normal' in the sense in which one could say that there was a normality of vision or digestion. In *that* sense, all kinds of human sexuality were strictly abnormal. The different kinds of sexual behaviour could not be judged by referring them to an absolute natural norm. They could only be judged in reference to the ultimate aims of each individual and the results observed in each case. Thus, if an individual wanted to be well thought of in any given society, he or she could safely regard as 'normal' the type of sexual behaviour currently tolerated by that local religion and approved by the 'best people'. But there were some individuals who cared little for the judgement of an angry God or even of the best people. Their principal desire was for intense and reiterated stimulation of their senses and their feelings. For these, it was obvious, 'normality' in sexual behaviour would be quite different from what it was for the more social-minded. Then there would be all the kinds of sexuality 'normal' to those desirous of making the best of both worlds – the personal world of sensations and emotions, and the social world of moral and religious conventions. The 'normalities' of Tartuffe and Pecksniff; of the clergymen who can't keep away from schoolgirls, the cabinet ministers with a secret mania for handsome youths. And, finally, there were those who were concerned neither to get on in society, nor to placate the local deity, nor to enjoy repeated emotional and sensuous stimulations, but whose chief preoccupation was with enlightenment and liberation, with the problem of transcending personality, of passing from the human level to the level of eternity. Their conceptions of 'normality' in sexual behaviour would not resemble those of the men and women in any of the other categories.

From the concrete tennis-court the children of the Chinese cook were flying kites in the shape of birds and equipped with little whistles, so that they warbled plaintively in the wind. The cheerful quacking sound of Cantonese drifted down to Pete's ears. Across the Pacific, he reflected, millions upon millions of such children had died already or were dying. Below them, in the Sacred Grotto, stood the plaster figure of Our Lady. Pete thought of Virginia kneeling in white shorts and a yachting-cap, of the abusive eloquence of Reverend Schlitz, of Dr Obispo's jokes, of Alexis Carrel on the subject of Lourdes, of Lee's *History of the Inquisition*, of Tawney on the relationship between Protestantism and Capitalism, of Niemöller and John Knox and Torquemada and that Sister of Mercy and again of Virginia, and finally of Mr Propter as the only person he knew who could make some sense out of the absurd, insane, diabolical confusion of it all.

Chapter Six

SOMEWHAT to Jeremy's disappointment, Dr Obispo was not at all mortified by the information that his ideas had been anticipated in the eighteenth century.

'I'd like to hear some more about your Fifth Earl,' he said, as they glided down into the cellars with the Vermeer. 'You say he lived to ninety?'

'More than ninety,' Jeremy answered. 'Ninety-six or seven, I forget which. And died in the middle of a scandal, what's more.'

'What sort of a scandal?'

Jeremy coughed and patted the top of his head. 'The usual sort,' he fluted.

'You mean, the old bozo was still at it?' Dr Obispo asked incredulously.

'Still at it,' Jeremy repeated. 'There's a passage about the affair in the unpublished papers of Greville. He died just in time. They were actually on the point of arresting him.'

'What for?'

Jeremy twinkled again and coughed. 'Well,' he said slowly and in his most Cranford-like manner, 'it seems that he had a tendency to take his pleasures rather homicidally.'

'You mean, he'd killed someone.'

'Not actually killed,' Jeremy answered: 'just damaged.'

Dr Obispo was rather disappointed, but consoled himself almost immediately by the reflection that, at ninety-six, even damage was pretty creditable. 'I'd like to look into this a little further,' he added.

'Well, the notebook's at your disposal,' said Jeremy politely.

Dr Obispo thanked him. Together they walked towards Jeremy's work-room.

'The handwriting's rather difficult,' said Jeremy as they entered. 'I think it might be easier if I read it aloud to you.'

Dr Obispo protested that he didn't want to waste Jeremy's time; but as the other was anxious to find an excuse for putting off to another occasion the wearisome task of sorting papers that didn't interest him, the protest was out-protested. Jeremy insisted on being altruistic. Dr Obispo thanked him and settled down to listen. Jeremy took his eyes out of their native element for long enough to polish his spectacles, then began to re-read aloud the passage he had been reading that morning when the bell rang for lunch.

' "It is to be found in the Mud," ' he concluded, ' "and only awaits a skilful Angler." '

Dr Obispo chuckled. 'You might almost use it as a definition of science,' he said. 'What is science? Science is angling in the mud – angling for immortality and for anything else that may happen to turn up.' He laughed again and added that he liked the old bastard.

Jeremy went on reading.

' "August 1796. Today my gabbling niece Caroline reproached me with what she called the Inconsistency of my Conduct. A man who is humane with the Horses in his stables, the Deer in his park and the Carp in his fishponds should show his Consistency by being more sociable than I am, more tolerant of the company of Fools, more charitable towards the poor and humble. To which I answered by remarking that the word, Man, is the general Name applied to successions of inconsistent Conduct, having their source within a two-legged and featherless Body, and that such words as Caroline, John and the like are the proper names applied to particular successions of inconsistent Conduct within particular Bodies. The only Consistency exhibited by the mass of Mankind is a Consistency of Inconsistency. In other words, the nature of any particular succession of inconsistent Conduct depends upon the history of the individual and his ancestors. Each succession of Inconsistencies is determined and obeys the Laws imposed upon it by its own antecedent Circumstances. A Character may be said to be consistent in the sense that its Inconsistencies are predestined and cannot pass beyond the boundaries ordained for it. The Consistency demanded by such Fools as Caroline is of quite another kind. These reproach us because our successive Acts are not consistent with some arbitrarily selected set of Prejudices, or ridiculous code of rules, such as the Hebrew, the Gentleman-like, the Iroquois or the Christian. Such Consistency is not to be achieved, and the attempt to achieve it results only in Imbecility or Hypocrisy. Consider, I said to Caroline, your own Conduct. What Consistency, pray, do you find between your conversations with the Dean upon Redemption and your Draconian birchings of the young Maids? between your conspicuous charities and the setting of man-traps on your estates? between your appearance at Court and your *chaise percée*? or between divine service on Sunday morning and the pleasures enjoyed on Saturday night with your husband and on Friday or Thursday, as all the world suspects, with a certain Baronet who shall be nameless? But before I had concluded my final question, Caroline had left the room." '

'Poor Caroline,' said Dr Obispo, with a laugh. 'Still, she got what she asked for.'

Jeremy read out the next entry.

' "December 1796. After this second attack of pulmonary congestion, Convalescence has come more slowly than before and advanced less far. I hang here suspended above the pit as though by a single thread, and the substance of that thread is Misery." '

With an elegantly bent little finger, Dr Obispo flicked the ash of his cigarette on to the floor.

'One of those pharmaceutical tragedies,' he commented. 'With a course of thiamin chloride and some testosterone I could have made him as happy as a sand-boy. Has it ever struck you,' he added, 'what a lot of the finest romantic literature is the result of bad doctoring?

> I could lie down like a tired child
> And weep away this life of care.

Lovely! But if they'd known how to clear up poor Shelley's chronic tuberculous pleurisy it would never have been written. Lying down like a tired child and weeping life away happens to be one of the most characteristic symptoms of chronic tuberculous pleurisy. And most of the other *Weltschmerz* boys were either sick men or alcoholics or dope addicts. I could have prevented every one of them from writing as he did.' Dr Obispo looked at Jeremy with a wolfish smile that was almost childlike in the candour of its triumphant cynicism. 'Well, let's hear how the old boy gets over his troubles.'

' "December 1796," ' Jeremy read out. ' "The prowlings of my attendant hyaenas became so intolerable to me that yesterday I resolved to put an end to them. When I asked them to leave me alone in the future, Caroline and John protested their more than filial Affection. In the end I was forced to say that, unless they were gone by noon today, I would order my Steward to bring a score of men and eject them from my House. This morning, from my window, I watched them take their departure." '

The next note was dated January 11th, 1797. ' "This year the anniversary of my birth calls up Thoughts more gloomy than ever before. I am too weary to record them. The day being fine and remarkably warm for the Season, I had myself carried in my chair to the fishponds. The bell was rung, and the Carp at once came hurrying to be fed. The spectacle of the brute Creation provides me with almost my sole remaining pleasure. The stupidity of the Brutes is without pretensions and their malignity depends on Appetite and is therefore only intermittent. Men are systematically and continuously cruel, while their Follies are justified in the names of Religion and Politics, and their Ignorance is muffled up in the pompous garments of Philosophy.

' "Meanwhile, as I watched the fishes pushing and jostling for their dinner, like a crowd of Divines in search of Preferment, my Thoughts returned to the perplexing Question upon which I have so often speculated in the past. Why should a man die at three-score years and ten, when a Fish can retain its Youth for two or three centuries? I have debated with myself a number of possible answers. There was a time, for example, when I thought that the longer life of Carp and Pike might be due to the superiority of their Watery Element over our Air. But the lives of some subaqueous Creatures are short, while those of certain Birds exceed the human span.

' "Again, I have asked myself if the Fish's longer years might not be due to its peculiar mode of begetting and bearing its young. But again I am met by fatal Objections. The Males of Parrots and Ravens do not onanize, but copulate; the females of Elephants do not lay eggs but bear their young, if we are to believe M. de Buffon, for a period of not less than four and twenty months. But Parrots, Ravens and Elephants are long-lived Creatures; from which we must conclude that the Brevity of human Life is due to other Causes than the manner in which Men beget and Females reproduce their Kind.

' "The only Hypotheses to which I can see no manifest Objections are these: the Diet of such fish as Carp and Pike contains some substance which preserves their Bodies from the Decay which overtakes the greater number of Creatures even while they are alive; alternatively the substance which prevents Decay is to be found within the Body of the Fish, especially, it would be reasonable to guess, in the Stomach, Liver, Bowels and other Organs of Concoction and Assimilation. In the short-lived animals, such as Man, the Substances preventive of Decay must be presumed to be lacking. The question then arises whether these Substances can be introduced into the human Body from that of the Fish. History does not record any remarkable instances of longevity among the Ichthyophagi, nor have I ever observed that the Inhabitants of sea ports and other places where there is an abundance of Fish were specially long-lived. But we need not conclude from this that the Substance preventive of Decay can never be conveyed from Fish to Man. For Man cooks his Food before eating it, and we know by a thousand instances that the application of Heat profoundly modifies the nature of many Substances; moreover, he throws away, as unfit for his Consumption, precisely those Organs of the Fish in which it is most reasonable to assume that the Substance preventive of Decay is contained." '

'Christ!' said Dr Obispo, unable to contain himself any longer. 'Don't tell me that the old buzzard is going to eat raw fish-guts!'

Bright behind their bifocals, Jeremy's eyes had darted down to the bottom of the page and were already at the top of the next. 'That's exactly what he is doing,' he cried delightedly. 'Listen to this: "My first three attempts provoked an uncontrollable retching; at the fourth I contrived to swallow what I had placed in my mouth, but within two or three minutes my triumph was cut short by an access of vomiting. It was only after the ninth or tenth essay that I was able to swallow and retain even a few spoonfuls of the nauseating mince meat." '

'Talk of courage!' said Dr Obispo. 'I'd rather go through an air-raid than that.'

Jeremy, meanwhile, had not so much as raised his eyes from the book.

' "It is now a month," ' he read, ' "since I began to test the truth of my Hypothesis, and I am now ingesting each day not less than six ounces of the raw, triturated Viscera of freshly opened Carp." '

'And the fish,' said Dr Obispo, slowly shaking his head, 'has a greater variety of parasitic worms than any other animal. It makes my blood run cold even to hear about it.'

'You needn't worry,' said Jeremy, who had gone on reading. 'His Lordship does nothing but get better and better. Here's a "singular accession of Strength and Vigour during the month of March." Not to mention "Revival of appetite and Improved memory and powers of ratiocination." I like that ratiocination,' Jeremy put in appreciatively. 'Such a nice period piece, don't you think? A real Chippendale word!' He went on reading to himself, and after a little silence announced triumphantly: 'By April he's riding again "an hour on the bay gelding every afternoon". And the dose of what he calls his "visceral and stercoraceous pap" has been raised to ten ounces a day.'

Dr Obispo jumped up from his chair and began to walk excitedly up and down the room. 'Damn it all!' he shouted. 'This is more than a joke. This is serious. Raw fish-guts; intestinal flora; prevention of sterol poisoning; and rejuvenation. Rejuvenation!' he repeated.

'The Earl's more cautious than you are,' said Jeremy. 'Listen to this. "Whether I owe my recovery to the Carp, to the Return of Spring, or to the *Vis medicatrix Naturæ*, I am not yet able to determine." '

Dr Obispo nodded approvingly. 'That's the right spirit,' he said.

' "Time," ' Jeremy continued, ' "will show; that is, if I can force it to show, which I intend to do by persisting in my present Regimen. For I take it that my Hypothesis will be substantiated if, after persisting in it for some time longer, I shall have recovered not only my former state of Health, but a measure of Vigour not enjoyed since the passing of Youth." '

'Good for him!' Dr Obispo exclaimed. 'I only wish old Uncle Jo could look at things in that scientific way. Or, maybe,' he added, suddenly remembering the Nembutal and Mr Stoyte's childlike faith in his medical omniscience, 'maybe I don't wish it. It might have its inconveniences.' He chuckled to himself over his private joke. 'Well, let's go on with our case history,' he added.

'In September he can ride for three hours at a stretch without fatigue,' said Jeremy. 'And he's renewing his acquaintance with Greek literature, and thinks very poorly of Plato, I notice. After which we have no entry till 1799.'

'No entry till 1799!' Dr Obispo repeated indignantly. 'The old bastard! Just when his case is getting really interesting, he goes and leaves us in the dark.'

Jeremy looked up from the notebook, smiling. 'Not entirely in the dark,' he said. 'I'll read you his first entry after the two years of silence, and you can draw your own conclusions about the state of his intestinal flora.' He uttered a little cough and began to read in his Mrs Gaskell manner. ' "May 1799. The most promiscuously abandoned Females, especially among Women of Quality, are often those to whom an unkind Nature has denied the ordinary Reason and Excuse for Gallantry. Cut off by a constitutional Frigidity from the enjoyments of Pleasure, they are in everlasting rebellion against their Fate. The power which drives them on to multiply the number of their Gallantries is not Sensuality, but Hope; not the wish to reiterate the experience of a familiar Bliss, but rather the aspiration towards a common and much vaunted Felicity which they themselves have had the misfortune never to know. To the Voluptuary, the woman of easy Virtue is often no less obnoxious, though for other reasons, than she seems to the severe Moralist. God preserve me in Future from any such Conquests as that which I made this Spring at Bath!" ' Jeremy put down the book. 'Do you still feel that you've been left in the dark?' he asked.

Chapter Seven

WITH a deafening shriek the electric smoothing-tool whirled its band of sandpaper against the rough surface of the wood. Bent over the carpenter's bench, Mr Propter did not hear the sound of Pete's entrance and approach. For a long half-minute the young man stood in silence, watching him while he moved the smoothing-tool back and forth over the board before him. There was sawdust, Pete noticed, in the shaggy eyebrows, and on the sunburnt forehead a black smear where he had touched his face with oily fingers.

Pete felt a sudden twinge of compunction. It wasn't right to spy on a man if he didn't know you were there. It was underhand: you might be seeing something he didn't want you to see. He called Mr Propter's name.

The old man looked up, smiled, and stopped the motor of his little machine.

'Well, Pete,' he said. 'You're just the man I want. That is, if you'll do some work for me. Will you? But I'd forgotten,' he added, interrupting Pete's affirmative answer, 'I'd forgotten about that heart of yours. These miserable rheumatic fevers! Do you think you ought to?'

Pete blushed a little; for he had not yet had time to live down a certain sense of shame in regard to his disability. 'You're not going to make me run the quarter-mile, are you?'

Mr Propter ignored the jocular question. 'You're sure it's all right?' he insisted, looking with an affectionate earnestness into the young man's face.

'Quite sure, if it's only this sort of thing.' Pete waved his hand in the direction of the carpenter's bench.

'Honest?'

Pete was touched and warmed by the other's solicitude. 'Honest!' he affirmed.

'Very well then,' said Mr Propter, reassured. 'You're hired. Or rather you're not *hired*, because you'll be lucky if you get as much as a Coca-Cola for your work. You're conscribed.'

All the other people round the place, he went on to explain, were busy. He had been left to run the entire furniture factory single-handed. And the trouble was that it had to be run under pressure; three of the migrant families down at the cabins were still without any chairs or tables.

'Here are the measurements,' he said, pointing to a typewritten sheet of paper pinned to the wall. 'And there's the lumber. Now, I'll tell you what I'd like you to do first,' he added, as he picked up a board and laid it on the bench.

The two men worked for some time without trying to speak against the noise of their electric tools. Then there was an interim of less noisy activity. Too shy to embark directly upon the subject of his own perplexities, Pete started to talk about Professor Pearl's new book on population. Forty inhabitants to the square mile for the entire land area of the planet Sixteen acres per head. Take away at least half for unproductve land, and you were left with eight acres. And with average agricultural methods a human being could be supported on the produce of two and a half acres. With five and a half acres to spare for every person, why should a third of the world be hungry?

'I should have thought you'd have discovered the answer in Spain,' said Mr Propter. 'They're hungry because man cannot live by bread alone.'

'What has that got to do with it?'

'Everything,' Mr Propter answered. 'Men can't live by bread alone, because they need to feel that their life has a point. That's why they take to idealism. But it's a matter of experience and observation that most idealism leads to war, persecution and mass insanity. Man cannot live by bread alone; but if he chooses to nourish his mind on the wrong kind of spiritual food, he won't even get bread. He won't even get bread, because he'll be so busy killing or preparing to kill his neighbours in the name of God, or Country, or Social Justice, that he won't be able to cultivate his fields. Nothing could be simpler or more obvious. But at the same time,' Mr Propter concluded, 'nothing is unfortunately more certain than that most people will go on choosing the wrong spiritual food and thereby indirectly choosing their own destruction.'

He turned on the current, and once more the smoothing-tool set up its rasping shriek. There was another cessation of talk.

'In a climate like this,' said Mr Propter, in the next interval of silence, 'and with all the water that'll be available when the Colorado River aqueduct starts running next year, you could do practically anything you liked.' He unplugged the smoothing-tool and went to fetch a drill. 'Take a township of a thousand inhabitants; give it three or four thousand acres of land and a good system of producers' and consumers' co-operatives: it could feed itself completely; it could supply about two-thirds of its other needs on the spot; and it could produce a surplus to exchange for such things as it couldn't produce itself. You could cover the State with such townships. That is,' he added, smiling rather mournfully, 'that is, if you could get the permission from the banks and a supply of people intelligent and virtuous enough to run a genuine democracy.'

'You certainly wouldn't get the banks to agree,' said Pete.

'And you probably couldn't find more than quite a few of the right people,' Mr Propter added. 'And of course nothing's more disastrous than starting a social experiment with the wrong people. Look at all the efforts to start communities in this country. Robert Owen, for example, and the Fourierists and the rest of them. Dozens of social experiments and they all failed. Why? Because the men in charge didn't choose their people. There was no entrance examination and no novitiate. They accepted anyone who came along. That's what comes of being unduly optimistic about human beings.'

He started the drill and Pete took his turn with the smoothing-tool.

'Do you think one oughtn't to be optimistic?' the young man asked.

Mr Propter smiled. 'What a curious question!' he answered. 'What would you say about a man who installed a vacuum pump in a fifty-foot well? Would you call him an optimist?'

'I'd call him a fool.'

'So would I,' said Mr Propter. 'And that's the answer to your question; a man's a fool if he's optimistic about any situation in which experience has shown that there's no justification for optimism. When Robert Owen took in a crowd of defectives and incompetents and habitual crooks, and expected them to organize themselves into a new and better sort of human society, he was just a damned fool.'

There was silence for a time while Pete did some sawing.

'I suppose I've been too optimistic,' the young man said reflectively, when it was over.

Mr Propter nodded. 'Too optimistic in certain directions,' he agreed. 'And at the same time too pessimistic in others.'

'For instance?' Pete questioned.

'Well, to begin with,' said Mr Propter, 'too optimistic about social reforms. Imagining that good can be fabricated by mass-production methods. But, unfortunately, good doesn't happen to be that sort of commodity. Good is a matter of moral craftsmanship. It can't be produced except by individuals. And, of course, if individuals don't know what good consists in, or don't wish to work for it, then it won't be manifested, however perfect the social machinery. There!' he added, in another tone, and blew the sawdust out of the hole he had been drilling. 'Now for these chair-legs and battens.' He crossed the room and began to adjust the lathe.

'And what do you think I've been too pessimistic about?' Pete asked.

Mr Propter answered, without looking up from his work: 'About human nature.'

Pete was surprised. 'I'd have expected you to say I was too optimistic about human nature,' he said.

'Well, of course, in certain respects that's true,' Mr Propter agreed. 'Like most people nowadays, you're insanely optimistic about people as they are, people living exclusively on the human level. You seem to imagine that people can remain as they are and yet be the inhabitants of a world conspicuously better than the world we live in. But the world we live in is a consequence of what men have been and a projection of what they are now. If men continue to be like what they are now and have been in the past, it's obvious that the world they live in can't become better. If you imagine it can, you're wildly optimistic about human nature. But, on the other hand, you're wildly pessimistic if you imagine that men and women are condemned by their nature to pass their whole lives on the strictly human level. Thank God,' he said emphatically, 'they're not. They have it in their power to climb out and up, on to the level of eternity. No human society can become conspicuously better than it is now, unless it contains a fair proportion of individuals who know that their humanity isn't the last word and who consciously attempt to transcend it. That's why one should be profoundly pessimistic about the things most people are optimistic about – such as applied science, and social reform, and human nature as it is in the average man or woman. And that's also why one should be profoundly optimistic about the thing they're so pessimistic about that they don't even know it exists – I mean, the possibility of transforming and transcending human nature. Not by evolutionary growth, not in some remote future, but at any time – here and now, if you like – by the use of properly directed intelligence and good-will.'

Tentatively he started the lathe, then stopped it again for further adjustments.

'It's the kind of pessimism and the kind of optimism you find in all the great religions,' he added. 'Pessimism about the world at large and human nature as it displays itself in the majority of men and women. Optimism about the things that can be achieved by anyone who wants to and knows how.' He started the lathe again and, this time, kept it going.

'You know the pessimism of the New Testament,' he went on through the noise of the machine. 'Pessimism about the mass of mankind: many are called, few chosen. Pessimism about weakness and ignorance: from those that have not shall be taken away even that which they have. Pessimism about life as lived on the ordinary human level; for that life must be lost if the other eternal life is to be gained. Pessimism about even the highest forms of worldly morality: there's no access to the kingdom of heaven for anyone whose righteousness fails to exceed that of the Scribes and Pharisees. But who are the Scribes and Pharisees? Simply the best citizens; the pillars of society; all right-thinking men. In spite of which, or rather because of which, Jesus calls them a generation of vipers. Poor dear Dr Mulge!' he added parenthetically. 'How pained he'd be if he ever had the misfortune to meet his Saviour!' Mr Propter smiled to himself over his work. 'Well, that's the pessimistic side of the Gospel teaching,' he went on. 'And, more systematically and philosophically, you'll find the same things set forth in the Buddhist and Hindu scriptures. The world as it is and people on the strictly human level – they're beyond hope: that's the universal verdict. Hope begins only when human beings start to realize that the kingdom of heaven, or whatever other name you care to give it, is within and can be experienced by anybody who's prepared to take the necessary trouble. That's the optimistic side of Christianity and the other-world religions.'

Mr Propter stopped the lathe, took out the chair-leg he had been turning and put another in its place.

'It isn't the sort of optimism they teach you in the liberal churches,' said Pete, thinking of his transition period between Reverend Schlitz and militant anti-fascism.

'No, it isn't,' Mr Propter agreed. 'What they teach you in liberal churches hasn't got anything to do with Christianity or any other realistic religion. It's mainly drivel.'

'Drivel!'

'Drivel,' Mr Propter repeated. 'Early twentieth-century humanism seasoned with nineteenth-century evangelicalism. What a combination! Humanism affirms that good can be achieved on a level where it doesn't exist and denies the fact of eternity. Evangelicalism denies the relationship between causes and effects by affirming the existence of a personal deity who forgives offences. They're like Jack Spratt and his wife: between the two of them, they lick the platter clean of all sense whatsoever. No, I'm wrong,' Mr Propter added, through the buzz of the machine, 'not *all* sense. The humanists don't talk of more than one race, and the evangelicals only worship one God. It's left to the patriots to polish off that last shred of sense. The patriots and the political sectarians. A hundred mutually exclusive idolatries. "There are many gods and the local bosses are their respective prophets." The amiable silliness of the liberal churches is good enough for quiet times; but note that it's always supplemented by the ferocious lunacies of nationalism for use in times of crisis. And those are the philosophies young people are brought up on. The philosophies your optimistic elders expect you to reform the world with.' Mr Propter paused for a moment, then added, ' "As a man sows, so shall he reap. God is not mocked." Not mocked,' he repeated. 'But people simply refuse to believe it. They go on thinking they can cock a snook at the nature of things and get away with it. I've sometimes thought of writing a little treatise, like a cook-book, "One Hundred Ways of Mocking God" I'd call it. And I'd take a hundred examples from history and contemporary life, illustrating what happens when people undertake to do things without paying regard to the nature of reality. And the book would be divided into sections, such as "Mocking God in Agriculture", "Mocking God in Politics", "Mocking God in Education", "Mocking God in Philosophy", "Mocking God in Economics". It would be an instructive little book. But a bit depressing,' Mr Propter added.

Chapter Eight

THE news that the Fifth Earl had had three illegitimate children at the age of eighty-one was announced in the notebook with a truly aristocratic understatement. No boasting, no self-congratulation. Just a brief, quiet statement of the facts between the record of a conversation with the Duke of Wellington and a note on the music of Mozart. One hundred and twenty years after the event, Dr Obispo, who was not an English gentleman, exulted noisily, as though the achievement had been his own.

'Three of them,' he shouted in his proletarian enthusiasm. '*Three!* What do you think of that?'

Brought up in the same tradition as the Fifth Earl, Jeremy thought that it wasn't bad, and went on reading.

In 1820 the Earl had been ill again, but not severely; and a three months' course of raw carps' entrails had restored him to his normal health, 'the health,' as he put it, 'of a man in the flower of his age.'

A year later, for the first time in a quarter of a century, he visited his nephew and niece, and was delighted to find that Caroline had become a shrew, that John was already bald and asthmatic, and that their eldest daughter was so monstrously fat that nobody would marry her.

On the news of the death of Bonaparte he had written philosophically that a man must be a great fool if he could not satisfy his desire for glory, power and excitement except by undergoing the hardships of war and the tedium of civil government. ' "The language of polite conversation," he concluded, "reveals with a sufficient clarity that such exploits as those of Alexander and Bonaparte have their peaceful and domestic equivalents. We speak of amorous *Adventure*, of the *Conquest* of a desired Female and the *Possession* of her Person. For the Man of sense, such tropes are eloquent indeed. Considering their significance, he perceives that war and the pursuit of Empire are wrong because foolish, foolish because unnecessary, and unnecessary because the satisfactions derivable from Victory and Dominion may be obtained with vastly less trouble, pain and ennui behind the silken curtains of the Duchess's Alcove or on the straw Pallet of the Dairy Maid. And if at any time such simple Pleasures should prove insipid, if, like the antique Hero, he should find himself crying for new Worlds to conquer, then by the offer of a supplementary guinea, or in very many instances, as I have found, gratuitously, by the mere elicitation of a latent Desire for Humiliation and even Pain, a man may enjoy the privilege of using the Birch, the Manacles, the Cage and any such other Emblems of absolute Power as the Fancy of the Conqueror may suggest and the hired Patience of the Conquered will tolerate or her consenting Taste approve. I recall a remark by Dr Johnson to the effect that a man is seldom more innocently employed than when making Money. Making Love is an even more innocent employment than making Money. If Bonaparte had had the Wisdom to vent his Desire for Domination in the Saloons and Bed Chambers of his native Corsica, he would have expired in Freedom among his own people, and many hundreds of thousands of men now dead or maimed or blind would be alive and enjoying the use of their faculties. True, they would doubtless be employing their Eyes, Limbs and Lives as foolishly and malignantly as those whom Bonaparte did not murder are employing them today. But though a Superior Being might applaud the one-time Emperor for having removed so great a quantity of Vermin from the Earth, the Vermin themselves will always be of another Opinion. As a mere Man of Sense, and not a Superior Being, I am on the side of the Vermin." '

'Have you ever noticed,' said Dr Obispo reflectively, 'the way even the most hard-boiled people always try to make out they're really good. Even this old buzzard – you'd think *he* wouldn't care how he rated, so long as he got his fun. But no; he has to write a long screed proving what a much better man he is than Napoleon. Which, of course, he is by any reasonable standard. But you wouldn't expect him to go out of his way to say so.'

'Well, nobody else was likely to say so,' Jeremy put in.

'So he had to do it himself,' Dr Obispo concluded. 'Which just proves my point. Iagos don't exist. People will do everything Iago did; but they'll never say they're villains. They'll construct a beautiful verbal world in which all their villainies are right and reasonable. I'd hoped that old carp-guts would be an exception. But he isn't. It's really rather a disappointment.'

Jeremy giggled with a certain patronizing disdain. 'You'd have liked him to do the Don-Juan-in-hell-act. The *calme héros courbé sur sa rapière*. You're more romantic than I thought.' He turned back to the notebook and, after a pause, announced that in 1823 the Fifth Earl had spent some hours with Coleridge and found his conversation deep, but singularly muddy – 'characteristics,' he had added, 'which are admirable in Fish Ponds, but deplorable in rational Discourse, which should be pellucid and always shallow enough for a man to wade through without risk of drowning himself in an abyss of nonsense.' Jeremy beamed with pleasure. Coleridge was not a favourite of his. 'When I think of the rot people are still talking about the rubbish that old dope-addict wrote . . .'

Dr Obispo cut him short. 'Let's hear some more about the Earl,' he said.

Jeremy returned to the notebook.

In 1824 the old gentleman was lamenting the passage of the Bill which assimilated the transportation of slaves to piracy and so made the trade a capital offence. Henceforward, he would be a matter of eight or nine thousand a year the poorer. But he consoled himself by thinking of Horace living in philosophic tranquillity on his Sabine farm.

In 1826 he was deriving his keenest pleasure from a reperusal of Theocritus and the company of a young female, called Kate, whom he had made his housekeeper. In the same year, despite the curtailment of his income, he had been unable to resist the temptation of purchasing an exquisite 'Assumption of the Virgin' by Murillo.

1827 had been a year of financial reverses; reverses that were connected, apparently, with the death, following an abortion, of a very young maid employed by the housekeeper as her personal attendant. The entry in the notebook was brief and obscure; but it seemed to imply that the girl's parents had had to be paid a very substantial sum.

A little later, he was unwell again and wrote a long and minute description of the successive stages of decay in the human corpse, with special reference to the eyes and lips. A short course of triturated carp restored him to a more cheerful frame of mind, and in 1828 he made a voyage to Athens, Constantinople and Egypt.

In 1831 he was in negotiations for the purchase of a house near Farnham.

'That must be Selford,' Jeremy put in. 'The house where these things came from.' He indicated the twenty-seven packing-cases. 'Where the two old ladies are living.' He continued his reading. ' "The house is old, dark and inconvenient, but stands in sufficiently extensive Grounds upon an Eminence above the River Wey, whose southern bank at this point rises almost perpendicularly in a Cliff of yellow sandstone, to the height of perhaps one hundred and twenty feet. The Stone is soft and easily worked, a Circumstance which accounts for the existence beneath the house of very extensive Cellars which were dug, it would seem, about a Century ago, when the Vaults were used for the storage of smuggled Spirits and other goods on their way from the coasts of Hampshire and Sussex to the Metropolis. To allay the fears of his Wife, who dreads to lose a child in their subterranean meanders, the Farmer who now owns the House has walled off the greater part of his Cellarage; but even that which remains presents the appearance of a veritable Catacomb. In Vaults such as these a man could be assured of all the Privacy required for the satisfaction of even the most eccentric Tastes." ' Jeremy looked up over the top of his book. 'That sounds a bit sinister, don't you think?'

Dr Obispo shrugged his shoulders. 'Nobody can have enough privacy,' he said emphatically. 'When I think of all the trouble I've had for want of some nice cellars like the ones you've been reading about . . .' He left the sentence unfinished, and a shadow crossed his face: he was thinking that he couldn't go on giving Jo Stoyte those Nembutal capsules indefinitely, damn him!

'Well, he buys the house,' said Jeremy, who had been reading to himself. 'And he has repairs and additions made in the Gothic manner. And an apartment is fitted up in the cellars, forty-five feet underground and at the end of a long passage. And, to his delight, he finds that there's a subterranean well, and another shaft that goes down to a great depth and can be used as a privy. And the place is perfectly dry and has an ample supply of air, and . . .'

'But what does he do down there?' Dr Obispo asked impatiently.

'How should I know?' Jeremy answered. He ran his eyes down the page. 'At the moment,' he went on, 'the old boy's making a speech to the House of Lords in favour of the Reform Bill.'

'In favour of it?' said Obispo in surprise.

' "In the first days of the French Revolution," ' Jeremy read out, ' "I infuriated the adherents of every political Party by saying: 'The Bastille is fallen; long live the Bastille.' Forty-three years have elapsed since the occurrence of that singularly futile Event, and the correctness of my Prognostications has been demonstrated by the rise of new Tyrannies and the restoration of old ones. It is therefore with perfect Confidence that I now say: 'Privilege is dead; long live Privilege.' The masses of mankind are incapable of Emancipation and too inept to direct their own Destinies. Government must always be by Tyrants or Oligarchs. My opinion of the Peerage and the landed Gentry is exceedingly low; but their own opinion of themselves must be even lower than mine. *They* believe that the Ballot will rob them of their Power and Privileges, whereas *I* am sure that, by the exercise of even such little Prudence and Cunning as parsimonious Nature has endowed them with, they can with ease maintain themselves in their present pre-eminence. This being so, let the Rabble amuse itself by voting. An Election is no more than a gratuitous Punch and Judy Show, offered by the Rulers in order to distract the attention of the Ruled." ' "

'How he'd have enjoyed a modern communist or fascist election!' said Dr Obispo. 'By the way, how old was he when he made this speech?'

'Let me see.' Jeremy paused for a moment to make the calculation, then answered: 'Ninety-four.'

'Ninety-four!' Dr Obispo repeated. 'Well, if it wasn't those fish-guts, I don't know what it was.'

Jeremy turned back to the notebook. 'At the beginning of 1833 he sees his nephew and niece again, on the occasion of Caroline's sixty-fifth birthday. Caroline now wears a red wig, her eldest daughter is dead of cancer, the younger is unhappy with her husband and is addicted to piety, the son, who is now a Colonel, has gambling debts which he expects his parents to pay. Altogether, as the Earl remarks, "a most enjoyable evening." '

'Nothing about those cellars?' Dr Obispo complained.

'No; but his housekeeper, Kate, has been ill and he's giving her the carp diet.'

Dr Obispo showed a renewal of interest. 'And what happens?' he asked.

Jeremy shook his head. 'The next entry's about Milton,' he said.

'Milton?' exclaimed Dr Obispo in a tone of indignant disgust.

'He says that Milton's writings prove that religion depends for its existence upon the picturesque use of intemperate language.'

'He may be right,' said Dr Obispo irritably. 'But what I want to know is what happened to that housekeeper.'

'She's evidently alive,' said Jeremy. 'Because here's a little note in which he complains about the tediousness of too much female devotion.'

'Tedious!' Dr Obispo repeated. 'That's putting it mildly. I've known women who were like fly-paper.'

'He doesn't seem to have objected to an occasional infidelity. There's a reference here to a young mulatto girl.' He paused; then, smiling, 'Delicious creature,' he said. " 'She combines the brutish imbecility of the Hottentot with the malice and cupidity of the European.'' After which the old gentleman goes out to dinner at Farnham Castle with the Bishop of Winchester and finds his claret poor, his port execrable, and his intellectual powers beneath contempt.'

'Nothing about Kate's health?' Dr Obispo persisted.

'Why should he talk about it? He takes it for granted.'

'I'd hoped he was a man of science,' said Dr Obispo almost plaintively.

Jeremy laughed. 'You must have very odd ideas about fifth earls and eleventh barons. Why on earth should they be men of science?' Dr Obispo was unable to answer. There was a silence, while Jeremy started a new page. 'Well, I'm damned!' he broke out. 'He's been reading James Mill's *Analysis of the Human Mind*. At ninety-five. I think that's even more remarkable than having a rejuvenated housekeeper and a mulatto. "The Common Fool is merely stupid and ignorant. To be a Great Fool a man must have much learning and high abilities. To the everlasting credit of Mr Bentham and his Lieutenants it must be said that *their* Folly has always been upon the grandest scale. Mr Mill's *Analysis* is a veritable Coliseum of silliness." And the next note is about the Marquis de Sade. By the way,' Jeremy interpolated, looking up at Dr Obispo, 'when are you going to return me my books?'

Dr Obispo shrugged his shoulders. 'Whenever you like,' he answered. 'I'm through with them.'

Jeremy tried not to show his delight and, with a cough, returned to the notebook. ' "The Marquis de Sade," ' he read aloud, ' "was a man of powerful genius, unhappily deranged. In my opinion, an Author would achieve Perfection if he combined the qualities of the Marquis with those of Bishop Butler and Sterne." ' Jeremy paused. 'The Marquis, Bishop Butler and Sterne,' he repeated slowly. 'My word, you'd have a pretty remarkable book!' He went on reading. ' "October 1833. To degrade oneself is pleasurable in proportion to the height of the worldly and intellectual Eminence from which one descends and to which one returns when the act of Degradation is concluded." That's pretty good,' he commented, thinking of the Trojan Women and alternate Friday afternoons in Maida Vale. 'Yes, that's pretty good. Let me see, where are we? Oh yes. "The Christians talk much of Pain, but nothing of what they say is to the point. For the most remarkable Characteristics of Pain are these: the Disproportion between the enormity of physical suffering and its often trifling causes; and the manner in which, by annihilating every faculty and reducing the body to helplessness, it defeats the Object for which it was apparently devised by Nature: viz. to warn the sufferer of the approach of Danger, whether from within or without. In relation to Pain, that empty word, Infinity, comes near to having a meaning. This is not the case with Pleasure; for Pleasure is strictly finite and any attempt to extend its boundaries results in its transformation into Pain. For this reason, the infliction of Pleasure can never be so delightful to the aspiring Mind as the infliction of Pain. To give a finite quantity of Pleasure is a merely human act; the infliction of the Infinity we call Pain is truly god-like and divine." '

'The old bastard's going mystical in his old age,' Dr Obispo complained. 'Almost reminds me of Mr Propter.' He lit a cigarette. There was a silence.

'Listen to this,' Jeremy suddenly cried in a tone of excitement. ' "March 11th, 1834. By the criminal negligence of Kate, Priscilla has been allowed to escape from the subterranean place of confinement. Bearing as she does upon her Person the evidence that she has been for some weeks past the subject of my Investigations, she holds in her hands my Reputation and perhaps even my Liberty and Life." '

'I suppose this is what you were talking about before we started reading,' said Dr Obispo. 'The final scandal. What happened?'

'Well, I suppose the girl must have told her story,' Jeremy answered, without looking up from the page before him. 'Otherwise how do you account for the presence of this "hostile Rabble" he's suddenly started talking about? "The Humanity of men and women is inversely proportional to their Numbers. A Crowd is no more human than an Avalanche or a Whirlwind. A rabble of men and women stands lower in the scale of moral and intellectual being than a herd of Swine or of jackals." '

Dr Obispo threw back his head and uttered a peal of his surprisingly loud, metallic laughter. 'That's exquisite!' he said. 'Exquisite! You couldn't have a better example of typically human behaviour. *Homo* conducting himself like *sub-homo* and then being *sapiens* in order to prove that he's really *super-homo*.' He rubbed his hands together. 'This is really heavenly!' he said; then added: 'Let's hear what happens now.'

'Well, as far as I can make out,' said Jeremy, 'they have to send a company of militia from Guildford to protect the house from the rabble. And a magistrate has issued a warrant for his arrest; but they're not doing anything for the time being, on account of his age and position and the scandal of a public trial. Oh, and now they've sent for John and Caroline. Which makes the old gentleman wildly angry. But he's helpless. So they arrive at Selford; "Caroline in her orange wig, and John, at seventy-two, looking at least twenty years older than I, who was already twenty-four when my Brother, then scarcely of age, had the imprudence to marry an attorney's Daughter and the richly merited misfortune to beget this Attorney's Grandson whom I have always treated with the Contempt which his low origin and feeble Intellect deserve, but to whom the negligence of a Strumpet has now given the Power to impose his Will upon me." '

'One of those delightful family reunions,' said Dr Obispo. 'But I suppose he doesn't give us any of the details?'

Jeremy shook his head. 'No details,' he said. 'Just an outline of the negotiations. On March the seventeenth they tell him that he can avoid prosecution if he makes over his unentailed property by deed of gift, assigns them the revenues of the entailed estates, and consents to enter a private asylum.'

'Pretty stiff conditions!'

'Which he refuses,' Jeremy continued, 'on the morning of the eighteenth.'

'Good for him!'

' "Private madhouses," ' Jeremy read out, ' "are private prisons in which, uncontrolled by Parliament or Judiciary, subject to no inspection by the Police and closed even to the humanitarian visitations of Philanthropists, hired Torturers and Gaolers execute the dark designs of family Vengeance and personal Spite." '

Dr Obispo clapped his hands with delight. 'There's another beautiful human touch!' he cried. 'Those humanitarian visitations of philanthropists!' he laughed aloud. 'And hired torturers! It's like a speech by one of the Founding Fathers. Magnificent! And then one thinks of those slave-ships and little Miss Priscilla. It's almost as good as Field-Marshal Goering denouncing unkindness to animals. Hired torturers and gaolers,' he repeated with relish, as though the phrase were a delicious sweetmeat, slowly melting upon the palate. 'What's the next move?' he asked.

'They tell him he'll be tried, condemned and transported. To which he answers that he prefers transportation to a private asylum. "At this it was evident that my precious nephew and niece were nonplussed. They swore that my treatment in the Madhouse should be humane. I answered that I would not accept their word. John talked of his honour. I said, An Attorney's honour, no doubt, and spoke of the manner in which a lawyer sells his convictions for a Fee. They then implored me for the good name of the Family to accept their offers. I answered that the good name of the Family was indifferent to me, but that I had no desire to undergo the Humiliations of a Public Trial or the pains and discomforts of Transportation. I was ready, I said, to accept any reasonable alternative to Trial and Transportation; but I would regard no Alternative as reasonable which did not in some sort guarantee my proper treatment at their hands. Their word of honour I did not regard as such a Guarantee; nor could I accept to be placed in an Institution where I should be entrusted to the care of Doctors and Keepess in the pay of those whose Interest it was that I should perish with all possible Celerity. I therefore refused to subscribe to any Arrangement which left me at their Mercy without placing them to a corresponding extent at mine." '

'The principles of diplomacy in a nutshell!' said Dr Obispo. 'If only Chamberlain had understood them a little better before he went to Munich! Not that it would have made much difference in the long run,' he added. 'Because, after all, it doesn't really matter what the politicians do: nationalism will always produce at least one war each generation. It has done in the past, and I suppose we can rely on it to do the same in the future. But how does the old gentleman propose to put his principles into practice? He's at their mercy all right. How's he going to put them at his?'

'I don't know yet,' Jeremy answered from the depths of the recorded past. 'He's gone off on one of his philosophizing jaunts again.'

'Now?' said Dr Obispo in astonishment. 'When he's got a warrant out against him?'

' "There was a time," ' Jeremy read, ' "when I believed that all the Efforts of Humanity were directed towards a Point located approximately at the Centre of the female Person. Today I am inclined to think that Vanity and Avarice play a more considerable part even than Lust in shaping the course of men's Actions and determining the nature of their Thoughts." And so on. Where the devil does he get back to the point again? Perhaps he never does; it would be just like him. No, here's something: "March 20th. Today, Robert Parsons, my Factor, returned from London bringing with him in the Coach, three strong boxes containing Gold coin and Bank Notes to the value of two hundred and eighteen thousand pounds, the product of the sale of my Securities and such Jewels, Plate and works of Art as it was possible to dispose of at such short notice and for cash. With more time I could have realized at least three hundred and fifty thousand pounds. This loss I can bear philosophically; for the sum I have in hand is amply sufficient for my purposes." '

'What purposes?' asked Dr Obispo.

Jeremy did not answer for a little while. Then he shook his head in bewilderment. 'What on earth is happening now?' he said. 'Listen to this: "My funeral will be conducted with all the Pomp befitting my exalted Rank and the eminence of my Virtues. John and Caroline were miserly and ungrateful enough to object to the expense; but I have insisted that my Obsequies shall cost not a penny less than Four Thousand Pounds. My only Regret is that I shall be unable to leave my subterranean Retreat to see the Pageantry of Woe and to study the expression of grief upon the withered faces of the new Earl and his Countess. Tonight I shall go down with Kate to our Quarters in the Cellarage; and tomorrow morning the World will hear the news of my death. The body of an aged Pauper has already been conveyed hither in Secret from Haslemere, and will take my place in the Coffin. After the Interment the New Earl and Countess will proceed at once to Gonister, where they will take up their Residence, leaving this house untenanted except for Parsons, who will serve as Caretaker and provide for our material wants. The Gold and Bank Notes brought by Parsons from London are already bestowed in a subterranean hiding-place known only to myself, and it has been arranged that, every First of June, so long as I live, five thousand pounds in cash shall be handed over by myself to John, or to Caroline, or, in the event of their predeceasing me, to their Heir, or to some duly authorized Representative of the Family. By this arrangement, I flatter myself, I fill the Place left vacant by the Affection they most certainly do not feel." And that's all,' said Jeremy, looking up. 'There's nothing else. Just two more blank pages, and that's the end of the book. Not another word of writing.'

There was a long silence. Once more Dr Obispo got up and began to walk about the room.

'And nobody knows how long the old buzzard lived on?' he said at last.

Jeremy shook his head. 'Not outside the family. Perhaps those two old ladies . . .'

Dr Obispo halted in front of him, and banged the table with his fist. 'I'm taking the next boat to England,' he announced dramatically.

Chapter Nine

TODAY, even the Children's Hospital brought Mr Stoyte no consolations. The nurses had welcomed him with their friendliest smiles. The young house physician encountered in the corridor was flatteringly deferential. The convalescents shouted 'Uncle Jo!' with all their customary enthusiasm, and, as he paused beside their beds, the faces of the sick were momentarily illuminated with pleasure. His gifts of toys were received as usual, sometimes with noisy rapture, sometimes (more touchingly) in the silence of a happiness speechless with amazement and incredulity. On his round of the various wards, he saw, as on other days, the pitiful succession of small bodies distorted by scrofula and paralysis, of small emaciated faces resigned to suffering, of little angels dying, and martyred innocents and snub-faced imps of mischief tortured into a reluctant stillness.

Ordinarily it all made him feel good – like he wanted to cry, but at the same time like he wanted to shout and be proud: proud of just being human, because these kids were human and you'd never seen anything so brave as they were; and proud that he had done this thing for them, giving them the finest hospital in the State, and all the best that money could buy. But today his visit brought none of the customary reactions. He had no impulsion either to cry or to shout. He felt neither pride, nor the anguish of sympathy, nor the exquisite happiness that resulted from their combination. He felt nothing – nothing except the dull, gnawing misery which had been with him all that day, at the Pantheon, with Clancy, in his downtown office. Driving out from the city, he had looked forward to his visit to the hospital as an asthma patient might look forward to a dose of adrenalin or an opium-smoker to a long-postponed pipe. But the looked-for relief had not come. The kids had let him down.

Taking his cue from what had happened at the end of previous visits, the porter smiled at Mr Stoyte as he left the hospital and said something about it being the finest bunch of great little kids he ever knew. Mr Stoyte looked at him blankly, nodded without speaking, and passed on.

The porter watched him go. 'Jeepers Creepers!' he said to himself, remembering the expression on Mr Stoyte's face.

❀

Mr Stoyte drove back to the castle feeling as unhappy as he had felt when he left it in the morning. He went up with the Vermeer to the fourteenth floor; Virginia was not in her boudoir. He went down to the tenth; but she was not in the billiard-room. He dropped to the second; but she was being neither manicured nor massaged. In a sudden access of suspicion he descended to the sub-sub-basement and almost ran to see if she were in the laboratory with Pete; the laboratory was empty. A mouse squeaked in its cage, and behind the glass of the aquarium one of the aged carp glided slowly from shadow into light and from light once more into green shadow. Mr Stoyte hurried back to the elevator, shut himself in with the Dutchman's dream of everyday life mysteriously raised to the pitch of mathematical perfection, and pressed the topmost of the twenty-three buttons.

Arrived at his destination, Mr Stoyte slid back the gate of the elevator and looked out through the glass panel in the second door.

The water of the swimming-pool was perfectly still. Between the battlements, the mountains had taken on their evening richness of golden light and indigo shadow. The sky was cloudless and transparently blue. A tray with bottles and glasses had been set on the iron table at the further side of the pool, and behind the table stood one of the low couches on which Mr Stoyte was accustomed to take his sun-baths. Virginia was lying on this couch, as though anaesthetized, her lips parted, her eyes closed, one arm dropped limply and its hand lying palm upwards on the floor, like a flower carelessly thrown aside and forgotten. Half concealed by the table, Dr Obispo, the Claude Bernard of his subject, was looking down into her face with an expression of slightly amused scientific curiosity.

In its first irrepressible uprush, Mr Stoyte's fury came near to defeating its own homicidal object. With a great effort, he checked the impulse to shout, to charge headlong out of the elevator, waving his fists and foaming at the mouth. Trembling under the internal pressure of pent-up rage and hatred, he groped in the pocket of his jacket. Except for a child's rattle and two packets of chewing-gum left over from his distribution of gifts at the hospital, it was empty. For the first time in months he had forgotten his automatic.

For a few seconds Mr Stoyte stood hesitating, undecided what to do. Should he rush out, as he had first been moved to do, and kill the man with his bare hands? Or should he go down and fetch his gun? In the end, he decided to get the gun. He pressed the button, and the lift dropped silently down its shaft. Unseeing, Mr Stoyte glared at the Vermeer; and from her universe of perfected geometrical beauty the young lady in blue satin turned her head from the open harpsichord and looked out, past the draped curtain, over the black-and-white tessellated floor – out through the window of the picture-frame into that other universe in which Mr Stoyte and his fellow-creatures had their ugly and untidy being.

Mr Stoyte ran to his bedroom, opened the drawer in which his handkerchiefs were kept, rummaged furiously among the silks and cambrics, and found nothing. Then he remembered. Yesterday morning he had worn no jacket. The gun had been in his hippocket. Then Pedersen had come to give him his Swedish exercises. But a gun in the hip-pocket was uncomfortable if you did things on your back, on the floor. He had taken it out and put it away in the writing-desk in his study.

Mr Stoyte ran back to the elevator, went down four floors and ran to the study. The gun was in the top left-hand drawer of the writing-table; he remembered exactly.

The top left-hand drawer of the writing-table was locked. So were all the other drawers.

'God damn that old bitch!' Mr Stoyte shouted as he tugged at the handles.

Thoughtful and conscientious in every detail, Miss Grogram, his secretary, always locked up everything before she went home.

Still cursing Miss Grogram, whom he hated at the moment almost as bitterly as he hated that swine there on the roof, Mr Stoyte hurried back to the elevator. The gate was locked. During his absence in the study, somebody must have pressed the recall button on some other floor. Through the closed door he could hear the faint hum of the machinery. The elevator was in use. God only knew how long he would have to wait.

Mr Stoyte let out an inarticulate bellow, rushed along the corridor, turned to the right, opened a swing-door, turned to the right again and was at the gate of the service lift. He seized the handle and pulled. It was locked. He pressed the recall button. Nothing happened. The service elevator was also in use.

Mr Stoyte ran back along the corridor, through the swing-door, then through another swing-door. Spiral round a central well that went down two hundred feet into the depth of the cellars, the staircase mounted and descended. Mr Stoyte started to climb. Breathless after only two floors, he ran back to the elevators. The service elevator was still in use; but the other responded to the call of the button. Dropping from somewhere overhead, it came to a halt in front of him. The locked door unlocked itself. He pulled it open and stepped in. The young lady in satin still occupied her position of equilibrium in a perfectly calculated universe. The distance of her left eye from the left side of the picture was to its distance from the right side as one is to the square root of two minus one; and the distance of the same eye from the bottom of the picture was equal to its distance from the left side. As for the knot of ribbons on her right shoulder – that was precisely at the corner of an imaginary square with the sides equal to the longer of the two golden sections into which the base of the picture was divisible. A deep fold in the satin skirt indicated the position of the right side of this square, and the lid of the harpsichord marked the top. The tapestry in the upper right-hand corner stretched exactly one-third of the way across the picture and had its lower edge at a height equal to the base. Pushed forward by the browns and dusky ochres of the background, the blue satin encountered the black-and-white marble slabs of the floor and was pushed back, to be held suspended in mid picture-space, like a piece of steel between two magnets of opposite sign. Within the frame nothing could have been different; the stillness of that world was not the mere immobility of old paint and canvas; it was also the spirited repose of consummated perfection.

'The old bitch!' Mr Stoyte kept growling to himself, and then, turning in memory from his secretary to Dr Obispo, 'The swine!'

The elevator came to a stop. Mr Stoyte darted out and hurried along the corridor to Miss Grogram's empty office. He thought he knew where she kept the keys; but it turned out that he was wrong.

They were somewhere else. But where? where? where? Frustration churned up his rage into a foam of frenzy. He opened drawers and flung their contents on the floor, he scattered the neatly filed papers about the room, he overturned the dictaphone, he even went to the trouble of emptying the bookshelves and upsetting the potted cyclamen and the bowl of Japanese goldfish which Miss Grogram kept on the window-sill. Red scales flashed among the broken glass and the reference-books. One gauzy tail was black with spilt ink. Mr Stoyte picked up a bottle of glue and, with all his might, threw it down among the dying fish.

'Bitch!' he shouted. 'Bitch!'

Then suddenly he saw the keys, hanging in a neat little bunch on a hook near the mantelpiece, where, he suddenly remembered, he had seen them a thousand times before.

'Bitch!' he shouted with redoubled fury as he seized them. He hurried towards the door, pausing only to push the typewriter off its table. It fell with a crash into the chaos of torn paper and glue and goldfish. That would serve the old bitch right, Mr Stoyte reflected with a kind of maniacal glee as he ran towards the elevator.

Chapter Ten

BARCELONA had fallen.

But even if it had not fallen, even if it had never been besieged, what then?

Like every other community, Barcelona was part machine, part sub-human organism, part nightmare-huge projection and embodiment of men's passions and insanities – their avarice, their pride, their lust for power, their obsession with meaningless words, their worship of lunatic ideals.

Captured, or uncaptured, every city and nation has its being on the plane of the absence of God. Has its being on the plane of the absence of God, and is therefore foredoomed to perpetual self-stultification, to endlessly reiterated attempts at self-destruction.

Barcelona had fallen. But even the prosperity of human societies is a continual process of gradual or catastrophic falling. Those who build up the structures of civilization are the same as those who undermine the structures of civilization. Men are their own termites, and must remain their own termites for just so long as they persist in being only men.

The towers rise, the palaces, the temples, the dwellings, the workshops; but the heart of every beam is gnawed to dust as it is laid, the joists are riddled, the floors eaten away under the feet.

What poetry, what statues – but on the brink of the Peloponnesian War! And now the Vatican is painted – just in time for the sack of Rome. And the Eroica is composed – but for a hero who turns out to be just another bandit. And the nature of the atom is elucidated – by the same physicists as volunteer in war-time to improve the arts of murder.

On the plane of the absence of God, men can do nothing else except destroy what they have built – destroy even while they build – build with the elements of destruction.

Madness consists in not recognizing the facts; in making wishes the fathers of thoughts; in conceiving things to be other than they really are; in trying to realize desired ends by means which countless previous experiments have shown to be inappropriate.

Madness consists, for example, in thinking of oneself as a soul, a coherent and enduring human entity. But, between the animal below and the spirit above there is nothing on the human level except a swarm of constellated impulses and sentiments and notions; a swarm brought together by the accidents of heredity and language; a swarm of incongruous and often contradictory thoughts and desires. Memory and the slowly changing body constitute a kind of spatio-temporal cage, within which the swarm is enclosed. To talk of it as though it were a coherent and enduring 'soul' is madness. On the strictly human level there is no such thing as a soul.

Thought-constellations, feeling-arrangements, desire-patterns. Each of these has been built up and is strictly conditioned by the nature of its fortuitous origin. Our 'souls' are so little 'us' that we cannot even form the remotest conception how 'we' should react to the universe, if we were ignorant of language in general, or even of our own particular language. The nature of our 'souls' and of the world they inhabit would be entirely different from what it is, if we had never learnt to talk, or if we had learnt to talk Eskimo instead of English. Madness consists, among other things, in imagining that our 'soul' exists apart from the language our nurses happen to have taught us.

Every psychological pattern is determined; and, within the cage of flesh and memory, the total swarm of such patterns is no more free than any of its members. To talk of freedom in connexion with acts which in reality are determined is madness. On the strictly human level no acts are free. By their insane refusal to recognize facts as they are, men and women condemn themselves to have their desires stultified and their lives distorted or extinguished. No less than the cities and nations of which they are members, men and women are for ever falling, for ever destroying what they have built and are building. But whereas cities and nations obey the laws that come into play whenever large numbers are involved, individuals do not. Or rather need not; for though in actual fact most individuals allow themselves to be subjected to these laws, they are under no necessity to do so. For they are under no necessity to remain exclusively on the human level of existence. It is in their power to pass from the level of the absence of God to that of God's presence. Each member of the psychological swarm is determined; and so is the conduct of the total swarm. But beyond the swarm, and yet containing and interpenetrating it, lies eternity, ready and waiting to experience itself. But if eternity is to experience itself within the temporal and spatial cage of any individual human being, the swarm we call the 'soul' must voluntarily renounce the frenzy of its activity, must make room, as it were, for the other timeless consciousness, must be silent to render possible the emergence of profounder silence. God is completely present only in the complete absence of what we call our humanity. No iron necessity condemns the individual to the futile torment of being merely human. Even the swarm we call the soul has it in its power temporarily to inhibit its insane activity, to absent itself, if only for a moment, in order that, if only for a moment, God may be present. But let eternity experience itself, let God be sufficiently often present in the absence of human desires and feelings and pre-occupations: the result will be a transformation of the life which must be lived, in the intervals, on the human level. Even the swarm of our passions and opinions is susceptible to the beauty of eternity; and, being susceptible, becomes dissatisfied with its own ugliness; and, being dissatisfied, undertakes to change itself. Chaos gives place to order – not the arbitrary, purely human order that comes from the sub-ordination of the swarm to some lunatic 'ideal', but an order that reflects the real order of the world. Bondage gives place to liberty – for choices are no longer dictated by the chance occurrences of earlier history, but are made teleologically and in the light of a direct insight into the nature of things. Violence and mere inertia give place to peace – for violence is the manic, and inertia the depressive, phase of that cyclic insanity, which consists in regarding the ego or its social projections as real entities. Peace is the serene activity which springs from the knowledge that our 'souls' are illusory and their creations insane, that all beings are potentially united in eternity. Compassion is an aspect of peace and a result of the same act of knowledge.

Walking at sunset up the castle hill, Pete kept thinking with a kind of tranquil exultation of all the things Mr Propter had said to him. Barcelona had fallen. Spain, England, France, Germany, America – all were falling; falling even at such times as they seemed to be rising; destroying what they built in the very act of building. But any individual has it in his power to refrain from falling, to stop destroying himself. The solidarity with evil is optional, not compulsory.

On their way out of the carpenter's shop Pete had brought himself to ask Mr Propter if he would tell him what he ought to do.

Mr Propter had looked at him intently. 'If you want it,' he had said, 'I mean, if you *really* want it . . .'

Pete had nodded without speaking.

The sun had set; and now the twilight was like the embodiment of peace – the peace of God, Pete said to himself, as he looked across the plain to the distant mountains, the peace that passes all understanding. To part with such loveliness was unbearable. Entering the castle, he went straight to the elevator, recalled the cage from somewhere up aloft, shut himself up with the Vermeer and pressed the highest of the buttons. Up there, at the top of the keep, he would be at the very heart of this celestial peace.

The elevator came to a halt. He opened the gates and stepped out. The swimming-pool reflected a luminous tranquillity. He turned his eyes from the water to the sky, and from the sky to the mountains; then walked round the pool in order to look down over the battlements on the further side.

'Go away!' a muffled voice suddenly said.

Pete started violently, turned and saw Virginia lying in the shadow almost at his feet.

'Go away,' the voice repeated. 'I hate you.'

'I'm sorry,' he stammered. 'I didn't know . . .'

'Oh, it's you.' She opened her eyes, and in the dim light he was able to see that she had been crying. 'I thought it was Sig. He went to get a comb for my hair.' She was silent for a little; then suddenly she burst out, 'I'm so unhappy, Pete.'

'Unhappy?' The word and her tone had utterly shattered the peace of God. In an anguish of love and anxiety he sat down beside her on the couch. (*Under her bath-robe, he couldn't help noticing, she didn't seem to be wearing anything at all.*) 'Unhappy?'

Virginia covered her face with her hands and began to sob. 'Not even Our Lady,' she gasped in an incoherency of grief. 'I can't even tell *her*. I feel so mean . . .'

'Darling!' he said in a voice of entreaty, as though imploring her to be happy. He began to stroke her hair. 'My darling!'

Suddenly there was a violent commotion on the further side of the pool; a crash as the elevator gates were flung back; a rush of feet; an inarticulate yell of rage. Pete turned his head and was in time to see Mr Stoyte rushing towards them, holding something in his hand, something that might almost have been an automatic pistol.

He had half risen to his feet, when Mr Stoyte fired.

Arriving two or three minutes later with the comb for Virginia's hair, Dr Obispo found the old man on his knees, trying, with a pocket-handkerchief, to stanch the blood that was still pouring out of the two wounds, one clean and small, the other cavernous, which the bullet had made as it passed through Pete's head.

Crouching in the shadow of the battlements, the Baby was praying. 'Holy-Mary-Mother-of-God-pray-for-us-sinners-now-and-in-the-hour-of-our-death-Amen,' she repeated, again and again, as fast as her sobs would permit her. Every now and then she would be seized and shaken by an access of nausea, and the praying would be interrupted for a moment. Then it began again where she had left off '. . . us-sinners-now-and-in-the-hour-of-our-death-Amen-Holy-Mary-Mother-of-God . . .'

Dr Obispo opened his mouth to make an exclamation, then closed it again, whispered, 'Christ!' and walked quickly and silently round the pool. Before making his presence known, he took the precaution of picking up the pistol and slipping it into his pocket. One never knew. Then he called Mr Stoyte's name. The old man started, and a hideous expression of terror appeared on his face. Fear gave place to relief as he turned round and saw who it was that had spoken to him.

'Thank God it's you,' he said; then suddenly remembered that this was the man he had meant to kill. But all that had been a million years ago, a million miles away. The near, immediate, urgent fact was not the Baby, not love or anger; it was fear and this thing that lay here on the ground.

'You got to save him,' he said in a hoarse whisper. 'We can say it was an accident. I'll pay him anything he likes. Anything in reason,' an old reflex impelled him to add. 'But you got to save him.'

Laboriously he heaved himself to his feet and motioned Dr Obispo to his vacated place.

The only movement Dr Obispo made was one of withdrawal. The old man was covered with blood, and he had no wish to spoil a ninety-five-dollar suit. 'Save *him*?' he repeated. 'You're mad. Look at all the brain lying there on the floor.'

From the shadows behind him, Virginia interrupted the sobbing mutter of her prayers to scream. 'On the floor,' she kept wailing. 'On the floor.'

Dr Obispo turned on her savagely. 'Shut up, do you hear?'

The screams abruptly ceased; but a few seconds later there was a sound of violent retching; then 'Holy-Mary-Mother-of-God-pray-for-us-sinners-now-and-in-the-hour-of-our-death-Amen-Holy-Mary-Mother-of-God-pray-for-us-sinners . . .'

'If we're going to try and save anybody,' Dr Obispo went on, 'it had better be you. And believe me,' he added emphatically, throwing all his weight on his left leg and using the toe of his right shoe to point at the body, 'you need some saving. It's either the gas chamber or St Quentin for life.'

'But it was an accident.' Mr Stoyte began to protest with a breathless eagerness. 'I mean, it was all a mistake. I never wanted to shoot him. I meant to . . .' He broke off and stood in silence, his mouth working, as though he were trying to swallow some unspoken words.

'You meant to kill me,' said Dr Obispo, completing the sentence for him and smiling, as he did so, with the expression of wolfish good-humour which was characteristic of him in any situation where the joke was at all embarrassing or painful. Secure in the knowledge that the old buzzard was much too scared to be angry, and that anyhow the gun was in his own pocket, he prolonged the joke by saying, 'Well,' sententiously, 'that's what comes of snooping.'

'. . . now-and-in-the-hour-of-our-death-Amen,' Virginia gabbled in the ensuing silence. 'Holy-Mary-Mother . . .'

'I never meant it,' Mr Stoyte reiterated. 'I just got mad. Guess I didn't really figure out what I was doing. . . .'

'Tell that to the jury,' said Dr Obispo sarcastically.

'But I swear it: I didn't really know,' Mr Stoyte protested. His harsh voice broke grotesquely into a squeak. His face was white with fear.

The doctor shrugged his shoulders. 'Maybe,' he said. 'But not knowing doesn't make any difference to that.' He stood on one leg again to point an elegantly shod foot in the direction of the body.

'But what shall I *do*?' Mr Stoyte almost screamed in the anguish of his terror.

'Don't ask me.'

Mr Stoyte initiated the gesture of laying his hand imploringly on the other's sleeve; but Dr Obispo quickly drew back. 'No, don't touch me,' he said. 'Just look at your hands.'

Mr Stoyte looked. The thick, carrot-like fingers were red; under the horny nails the blood was already caked and dry, like clay. 'God!' he whispered. 'Oh my God!'

'. . . and-at-the-hour-of-our-death-Amen-Holy-Mary . . .'

At the word 'death' the old man started as though he had been struck with a whip. 'Obispo,' he began again, breathless with apprehension. 'Obispo! Listen here – you got to help me out of this. You got to help me,' he entreated.

'After you did your best to do *that* to me?' The white-and-tan shoe shot out again.

'You wouldn't let them get me?' Mr Stoyte wheedled, abject in his terror.

'Why wouldn't I?'

'But you can't,' he almost shouted. 'You can't.'

Dr Obispo bent down to make quite sure, in the fading light, that there was no blood on the couch; then, pulling up his fawn-coloured trousers, sat down. 'One gets tired of standing,' he said in a pleasant conversational tone.

Mr Stoyte went on pleading. 'I'll make it worth your while,' he said. 'You can have anything you care to ask for. Anything,' he repeated without any qualifying reference, this time, to reason.

'Ah,' said Dr Obispo, 'now you're talking turkey.'

'. . . Mother-of-God,' muttered the Baby, 'pray-for-us-sinners-now-and-in-the-hour-of-our-death-Amen-Holy-Mary-Mother-of-God-pray-for-us-sinners-now . . .'

'You're talking turkey,' Dr Obispo repeated.

PART THREE

Chapter One

THERE was a tap at the door of Jeremy's work-room; it was Mr Propter who entered. He was wearing, Jeremy noticed, the same dark-grey suit and black tie as he had worn at Pete's funeral. The urban costume diminished him; he seemed smaller than in his working clothes, and at the same time less himself. That weather-beaten, emphatically featured face of his – that face of a statue high up on the west front of a cathedral – looked curiously incongruous above a starched collar.

'You've not forgotten?' he said, when they had shaken hands.

For all reply, Jeremy pointed to his own black jacket and sponge-bag trousers. They were expected at Tarzana for the ceremonial opening of the new Stoyte Auditorium.

Mr Propter looked at his watch. 'We've got another few minutes before we need think of starting.' He sat down. 'What's the news?'

'Couldn't be better,' Jeremy answered.

Mr Propter nodded. 'Now that poor Jo and the others have gone, it must be quite agreeable here.'

'All alone with twelve million dollars' worth of bric-à-brac,' said Jeremy. 'I have the most enormous fun.'

'How little fun you'd be having,' said Mr Propter meditatively, 'if you'd been left in company with the people who actually made the bric-à-brac. With Greco, and Rubens, and Turner, and Fra Angelico.'

'God preserve us!' said Jeremy, throwing up his hands.

'That's the charm of art,' Mr Propter went on. 'It represents only the most amiable aspects of the most talented human beings. That's why I've never been able to believe that the art of any period threw much light on the life of that period. Take a Martian; show him a representative collection of Botticellis, Peruginos and Raphaels. Could he infer from them the conditions described by Machiavelli?'

'No, he couldn't,' Jeremy agreed. 'But meanwhile, here's another question. The conditions described by Machiavelli – were they the real conditions? Not that Machiavelli didn't tell the truth. The things he described really happened. But did contemporaries think them as awful as they seem to us when we read about them now? *We* think they ought to have been miserable about what was happening. But were they?'

'Were they?' Mr Propter repeated. 'We ask the historians; and of course they can't answer – because obviously there's no way of compiling statistics about the sum of happiness, nor any way of comparing the feelings of people living under one set of conditions with the feelings of people living under another and quite different set. The real conditions at any given moment are the subjective conditions of the people then alive. And the historian has no way of finding out what those conditions were.'

'No way except through looking at works of art,' said Jeremy. 'I'd say they do throw light on the subjective conditions. Take one of your examples. Perugino's a contemporary of Machiavelli. That means that at least one person contrived to be cheerful all through an unpleasant period. And if one could be, why not many?' He cleared the way for a quotation with a little cough. ' "The state of the country never put a man off his dinner." '

'Massive wisdom!' said Mr Propter. 'But remember that the state of Dr Johnson's England was excellent, even at its worst. What about the state of a country like China, say, or Spain – a country where a man can't be put off his dinner, for the simple reason that there isn't any dinner? And conversely, what about all the losses of appetite at times when everything's going well?' He paused, smiled inquiringly at Jeremy, then shook his head. 'Sometimes there's a lot of cheerfulness as well as a lot of misery; sometimes there seems to be almost nothing but misery. That's all the historian can say in so far as he's a historian. In so far as he's a theologian, of course, or a metaphysician, he can maunder on indefinitely, like Marx or St Augustine or Spengler.' Mr Propter made a little grimace of distaste. 'God, what a lot of bosh we've managed to talk in the last few thousand years!' he said.

'But it has its charm,' Jeremy insisted. 'Really *good* bosh . . .'

'I'm barbarous enough to prefer sense,' said Mr Propter. 'That's why, if I want a philosophy of history, I go to the psychologist.'

' "Totem and Taboo?" ' Jeremy questioned in some astonishment.

'No, no,' said Mr Propter with a certain impatience. 'Not *that* kind of psychologist. I mean the religious psychologist; the one who knows by direct experience that men are capable of liberation and enlightenment. He's the only philosopher of history whose hypothesis has been experimentally verified; therefore the only one who can make a generalization that covers the facts.'

'And what are his generalizations?' said Jeremy. 'Just the usual thing?'

Mr Propter laughed. 'Just the usual thing,' he answered: 'the old, boring, unescapable truths. On the human level, men live in ignorance, craving and fear. Ignorance, craving and fear result in some temporary pleasures, in many lasting miseries, in final frustration. The nature of the cure is obvious; the difficulties in the way of achieving it, almost insuperable. We have to choose between almost insuperable difficulties on the one hand and absolutely certain misery and frustration on the other. Meanwhile, the general hypothesis remains as the intellectual key to history. Only the religious psychologist can make any sense of Perugino and Machiavelli, for example; or of all this.' He pointed towards the Hauberk Papers.

Jeremy twinkled behind his glasses and patted his bald patch. 'Your true scholar,' he fluted, 'doesn't even *want* to make sense of it.'

'Yes, I always tend to forget that,' said Mr Propter rather sadly.

Jeremy coughed. ' "Gave us the doctrine of the enclitic *De*," ' he quoted from the 'Grammarian's Funeral'.

'Gave it for his own sake,' said Mr Propter, getting out of his chair. 'Gave it regardless of the fact that the grammar he was studying was hopelessly unscientific, riddled with concealed metaphysics, utterly provincial and antiquated. Well,' he added, 'that's what one would expect, I suppose.' He took Jeremy's arm, and they walked together towards the elevator. 'What a curious figure old Browning is!' he continued, his mind harking back to the Grammarian. 'Such a first-rate intelligence, and at the same time *such* a fool. All the preposterous stuff about romantic love! Bringing God into it, putting it into heaven, talking as though marriage and the higher forms of adultery were identical with the beatific vision. The silliness of it! But, again, that's what one has to expect.' He sighed. 'I don't know why,' he added after a pause, 'I often find myself remembering that rhyme of his – I can't even recall which poem it comes from – the one that goes: "one night he kissed My soul out in a burning mist." My soul out in a burning mist, indeed!' he repeated. 'Really, how much I prefer Chaucer on the subject. Do you remember? "Thus swivèd is this carpenterès wife." So beautifully objective and unemphatic and free of verbiage! Browning was always rambling on about God; but I suspect he was much further away from reality than Chaucer was, even though Chaucer never thought about God if he could possibly help it. Chaucer had nothing between himself and eternity but his appetites. Browning had his appetites, plus a great barrage of nonsense – nonsense, what's more, with a purpose. For, of course, that bogus mysticism wasn't merely gratuitous bosh. It had an object. It existed in order that Browning might be able to persuade himself that his appetites were identical with God. "Thus swivèd is this carpenterès wife," ' he repeated, as they entered the elevator and went up with Vermeer to the great hall. ' "My soul out in a burning mist!" It's extraordinary the way the whole quality of our existence can be changed by altering the words in which we think and talk about it. We float in language like icebergs – four-fifths under the surface and only one-fifth of us projecting into the open air of immediate, non-linguistic experience.'

They crossed the hall. Mr Propter's car was standing outside the front door. He took the wheel; Jeremy got in beside him. They drove off, down the curving road, past the baboons, past Giambologna's nymph, past the Grotto, under the portcullis and across the drawbridge.

'I so often think of that poor boy,' said Mr Propter, breaking a long silence. 'Dying so suddenly.'

'I'd no idea his heart was as bad as that,' said Jeremy.

'In a certain sense,' Mr Propter went on, 'I feel responsible for what happened. I asked him to help me in the carpenter's shop. Made him work too hard, I guess – though he insisted it was all right for him. I ought to have realized that he had his pride – that he was young enough to feel ashamed of admitting he couldn't take it. One's punished for being insensitive and unaware. And so are the people one's insensitive about.'

They drove past the hospital and through the orange groves in silence. 'There's a kind of pointlessness about sudden and premature death,' said Jeremy at last. 'A kind of specially acute irrelevance . . .'

'Specially acute?' Mr Propter questioned. 'No, I shouldn't say so. It's no more irrelevant than any other human event. If it seems more irrelevant, that's only because, of all possible events, premature death is the most glaringly out of harmony with what we imagine ourselves to be.'

'What do you mean?' Jeremy asked.

Mr Propter smiled. 'I mean what I presume *you* mean,' he answered. 'If a thing seems irrelevant, there must be something it's irrelevant to. In this case, that something is our conception of what we are. We think of ourselves as free, purposive beings. But every now and then things happen to us that are incompatible with this conception. We speak of them as accidents; we call them pointless and irrelevant. But what's the criterion by which we judge? The criterion is the picture we paint of ourselves in our own fancy – the highly flattering portrait of the free soul making creative choices and being the master of its fate. Unfortunately, the picture bears no resemblance to ordinary human reality. It's the picture of what we'd like to be, of what, indeed, we might become if we took the trouble. To a being who is in fact the slave of circumstance there's nothing specially irrelevant about premature death. It's the sort of event that's characteristic of the universe in which he actually lives – though not, of course, of the universe he foolishly imagines he lives in. An accident is the collision of a train of events on the level of determinism with another train of events on the level of freedom. We imagine that our life is full of accidents, because we imagine that our human existence is lived on the level of freedom. In fact, it isn't. Most of us live on the mechanical level, where events happen in accordance with the laws of large numbers. The things we call accidental and irrelevant belong to the very essence of the world in which we elect to live.'

Annoyed at having, by an unconsidered word, landed himself in a position which Mr Propter could show to be unwarrantably 'idealistic', Jeremy was silent. They drove on for a time without speaking.

'That funeral!' Jeremy said at last; for his chronically anec-
dotal mind had wandered back to what was concrete, particular
and odd in the situation under discussion. 'Like something out
of Ronald Firbank!' He giggled. 'I told Mr. Habakkuk he ought
to put steam heat into the statues. They're dreadfully unlifelike
to the *touch*.' He moved his cupped hand over an imaginary marble
protuberance.

Mr Propter, who had been thinking about liberation, nodded
and politely smiled.

'And Dr Mulge's reading of the service!' Jeremy went on. 'Talk
of unction! It couldn't have been oilier even in an English cathedral. Like vaseline with a flavour of port wine. And the way he
said, "I am the resurrection and the life" – as though he really
meant it, as though he, Mulge, could personally guarantee it, in
writing, on a money-back basis: the entire cost of the funeral
refunded if the next world fails to give complete satisfaction.'

'He probably even believes it,' said Mr Propter meditatively.
'In some curious Pickwickian way, of course. You know: it's true,
but you consistently act as though it weren't; it's the most important fact in the universe, but you never think about it if you can
possibly avoid it.'

'And how do *you* believe in it?' Jeremy asked. 'Pickwickianly or
unPickwickianly?' And when Mr Propter answered that he didn't
believe in that sort of resurrection and life: 'Oho!' he went on in
the tone of an indulgent father who has caught his son kissing the
housemaid, 'Oho! So there's also a Pickwickian resurrection?'

Mr Propter laughed. 'I think there may be,' he said.

'In which case, what has become of poor Pete?'

'Well, to start with,' said Mr Propter slowly, 'I should say that
Pete, *qua* Pete, doesn't exist any longer.'

'Super-Pickwickian!' Jeremy interjected.

'But Pete's ignorance,' Mr Propter went on, 'Pete's fears and
cravings – well, I think it's quite possible that they're still somehow
making trouble in the world. Making trouble for everything and
everyone, especially for themselves. Themselves in whatever form
they happen to be taking.'

'And if by any chance Pete hadn't been ignorant and concupiscent, what then?'

CHAPTER ONE

'Well, obviously,' said Mr Propter, 'there wouldn't be anything to make further trouble.' After a moment's silence, he quoted Tauler's definition of God. ' "God is a being withdrawn from creatures, a free power, a pure working." '

He turned the car off the main road, into the avenue of pepper trees that wound across the green lawns of the Tarzana Campus. The new Auditorium loomed up, austerely romanesque. Mr Propter parked his old Ford among the lustrous Cadillacs and Chryslers and Packards already lined up in front of it, and they entered. The press photographers at the entrance looked them over, saw at a glance that they were neither bankers, nor movie stars, nor corporation lawyers, nor dignitaries of any church, nor senators, and turned away contemptuously.

The students were already in their places. Under their stares, Jeremy and Mr Propter were ushered down the aisle to the rows of seats reserved for distinguished guests. And what distinction! There, in the front row, was Sol R. Katzenblum, the President of Abraham Lincoln Pictures Incorporated and a pillar of Moral Re-Armament; there, beside him, was the Bishop of Santa Monica; there too was Mr Pescecagniolo, of the Bank of the Far West. The Grand Duchess Eulalie was sitting next to Senator Bardolph and in the next row were two of the Engels Brothers and Gloria Bossom, who was chatting with Rear-Admiral Shotoverk. The orange robe and permanently waved beard belonged to Swami Yogalinga, founder of the School of Personality. Beside him sat the Vice-President of Consol Oil and Mrs Wagner . . .

Suddenly the organ burst out, full blast, into the Tarzana Anthem. The academic procession filed in. Two by two, in their gowns and hoods and tasselled mortar-boards, the Doctors of Divinity, of Philosophy, of Science, of Law, of Letters, of Music, shuffled down the aisle and up the steps on to the platform, where their seats had been prepared for them in a wide arc close to the back drop. At the centre of the stage stood a reading-desk, and at the reading-desk stood Dr Mulge. Not that he did any reading, of course; for Dr Mulge prided himself on being able to speak almost indefinitely without a note. The reading-desk was there to be intimately leant over, to be caught hold of and passionately leant back from, to be struck emphatically with the palm of the hand, to be dramatically walked away from and returned to.

The organ was silent. Dr Mulge began his address – began it with a reference, of course, to Mr Stoyte. Mr Stoyte whose generosity . . . The realization of a Dream . . . This embodiment of an ideal in Stone . . . The Man of Vision. Without Vision the people perish . . . But this Man had had Vision . . . The Vision of what Tarzana was destined to become . . . The centre, the focus, the torch-bearer . . . California . . . New Culture, richer science, higher spirituality . . . (Dr Mulge's voice modulated from bassoon to trumpet. From vaseline with a mere flavour of port wine to undiluted fatty alcohol.) But, alas (and here the voice subsided pathetically into saxophone and lanoline), alas . . . Unable to be with us today . . . A sudden distressing event . . . Carried off on the threshold of life . . . A young collaborator in those scientific fields which he ventured to say were as close to Mr Stoyte's heart as the fields of social service and culture . . . The shock . . . The exquisitely sensitive heart under the sometimes rough exterior . . . His physician had ordered a complete and immediate change of scene . . . But in spite of physical absence, his spirit . . . We feel it among us today . . . An inspiration to all, young and old alike . . . The torch of Culture . . . The Future . . . The Ideal . . . The Spirit of Man . . . Great things already accomplished . . . God had walked in power through this campus . . . Strengthened and guided . . . Forward . . . Onward . . . Upward . . . Faith and Hope . . . Democracy . . . Freedom . . . The imperishable heritage of Washington and Lincoln . . . The glory that was Greece reborn beside the waters of the Pacific . . . The flag . . . The mission . . . The manifest destiny . . . The will of God . . . Tarzana . . .

It was over at last. The organ played. The academic procession filed back up the aisle. The distinguished guests straggled after it.

Outside, in the sunshine, Mr Propter was button-holed by Mrs Pescecagniolo.

'I thought that was a wonderfully inspirational address,' she said with enthusiasm.

Mr Propter nodded. 'Almost the most inspirational address I ever listened to. And God knows,' he said, 'I've heard a lot of them in the course of my life.'

Chapter Two

EVEN in London there was a little diluted sunshine – sunshine that brightened and grew stronger as they drove through the diminishing smoke of the outer suburbs, until at last, somewhere near Esher, they had travelled into the most brilliant of early spring mornings.

Under a fur rug, Mr Stoyte sprawled diagonally across the rear seat of the car. More for his own good, this time, than for his physician's, he was back again on sedatives, and found it hard, before lunch, to keep awake. With a fitful stertorousness he had dozed almost from the moment they drove away from the Ritz.

Pale and with sad eyes, silently ruminating an unhappiness which five days of rain on the Atlantic and three more of London gloom had done nothing to alleviate, Virginia sat aloof in the front seat.

At the wheel (for he had thought it best to take no chauffeur on this expedition) Dr Obispo whistled to himself and, occasionally, even sang aloud – sang, 'Stretti, stretti, nell' estasi d'amor'; sang, 'Do you think a little drink'll do us any harm?'; sang, 'I dreamt I dwelt in marble halls'. It was partly the fine weather that made him so cheerful – spring-time, he said to himself, the only merry ring-time, not to mention the lesser celandines, the windflowers, whatever they might be, the primroses in the copse. And should he ever forget his bewilderment when English people had started talking about cops in the singular and in contexts where policemen seemed deliriously out of place? 'Let's go and pick some primroses in the cops.' Surprising intestinal flora! Better even than the carp's. Which brought him to the second reason for his satisfaction with life. They were on their way to see the two old Hauberk ladies – on their way, perhaps, to finding something interesting about the Fifth Earl, something significant about the relationship between senility and sterols and the intestinal flora of the carp.

With mock-operatic emphasis he burst again into song.

'I drea-heamt I dwe-helt in mar-harble halls,' he proclaimed, 'with vass-als and serfs at my si-hi-hide. And of all who assembled with-hin those walls, that I was the hope and the pri-hi-hide.'

Virginia, who had been sitting beside him, stony with misery, turned round in sudden exasperation. 'Oh, for heaven's sake!' she almost screamed, breaking a silence that had lasted all the way from Kingston-on-Thames. 'Can't you be quiet?'

Dr Obispo ignored her protests. 'I had riches,' he sang on (and reflected, with an inward chuckle of satisfaction as he did so, that the statement now happened to be true), 'I had riches too grea-heat to cou-hount.' No; that was an exaggeration. Not at all too great to count. Just a nice little competence. Enough to give him security and the means to continue his researches without having to waste his time on a lot of sick people who ought to be dead. Two hundred thousand dollars in cash and forty-five hundred acres of land in the San Felipe Valley – land that Uncle Jo had positively sworn was just on the point of getting its irrigation water. (And if it didn't get it, God! how he'd twist the old buzzard's tail for him!) 'Heart failure due to myocarditis of rheumatic origin.' He could have asked a lot more than two hundred thousand for that death-certificate. Particularly as it hadn't been his only service. No, sir! There had been all the mess to clear up. (The ninety-five-dollar fawn-coloured suit was ruined after all.) There had been the servants to keep away; the Baby to put to bed with a big shot of morphia; the permission to cremate the body to be obtained from the next of kin, who was a sister, living, thank God, in straitened circumstances, and at Pensacola, Florida, so that she fortunately couldn't afford to come out to California for the funeral. And then (most ticklish of all) there had been the search for a dishonest undertaker; the discovery of a possible crook; the interview, with its veiled hints of an unfortunate accident to be hushed up, of money that was, practically speaking, no object; then, when the fellow had fired off his sanctimonious little speech about its being a duty to help a leading citizen to avoid unpleasant publicity, the abrupt change of manner, the business-like statement of the unavoidable facts and the necessary fictions, the negotiations as to price. In the end, Mr Pengo had agreed not to notice the holes in Pete's skull for as little as twenty-five thousand dollars.

'I had riches too gre-heat to cou-hount, could boast of a hi-yish ancestral name.' Yes, decidedly, Dr Obispo reflected, as he sang, decidedly he could have asked for a great deal more. But what would have been the point? He was a reasonable man; almost, you might say, a philosopher; modest in his ambitions, uninterested in worldly success, and with tastes so simple that the most besetting of them, outside the sphere of scientific research, could be satisfied in the great majority of cases at practically no expense whatsoever, sometimes even with a net profit, as when Mrs Bojanus had given him that solid gold cigarette-case as a token of her esteem – and then there were Josephine's pearl studs, and the green enamel cuff-links with his monogram in diamonds from little what's-her-name . . .

'But I a-halso drea-heamt which plea-heased me most,' he sang, raising his voice for this final affirmation and putting in a passionate tremolo, 'that you lo-hoved me sti-hill the same, that you lo-hoved me sti-hill the same, that you loved me,' he repeated, turning away for a moment from the Portsmouth road to peer with raised eye-brows and a look of amused, ironical inquiry into Virginia's averted face, 'you lo-hoved me sti-hill the same,' and, for the fourth time with tremendous emphasis and pathos, 'that you lo-ho-ho-hoved me sti-hi-hill the same.'

He shot another glance at Virginia. She was staring straight in front of her, holding her lower lip between her teeth, as though she were in pain but determined not to cry out.

'Did I dream correctly?' His smile was wolfish.

The Baby did not answer. From the back seat Mr Stoyte snored like a bulldog.

'Do you lo-ho-hove sti-hi-hill the same?' he insisted, making the car swerve to the right as he spoke, and putting on speed to pass a row of Army lorries.

The Baby released her lip and said, 'I could kill you.'

'Of course you could,' Dr Obispo agreed. 'But you won't. Because you lo-ho-ho-hove me too much. Or rather,' he added, and his smile became more gleefully canine with every word, 'you don't lo-ho-ho-hove *me*; you lo-ho-ho-hove . . .' he paused for an instant: 'Well, let's put it in a more poetical way – because one can never have too much poetry, don't you agree? you're in lo-ho-hove with Lo-ho-ho-hove, so much in lo-ho-ho-hove that, when it came to the point, you simply couldn't bring yourself to bump me off. Because, whatever you may feel about me, I'm the boy that produces the lo-ho-ho-hoves.' He began to sing again: 'I dre-heamt I ki-hilled the goo-hoo-hoo-hoose that lai-haid the go-holden e-he-heggs.'

Virginia covered her ears with her hands in an effort to shut out the sound of his voice – the hideous sound of the truth. Because, of course, it was true. Even after Pete's death, even after she had promised Our Lady that it would never, never happen again – well, it had happened again.

Dr Obispo continued his improvisation. 'And that thu-hus I'd lo-host my so-hole excuse for showing the skin of my le-he-hegs.'

Virginia pressed her fingers more tightly over her ears. It had happened again, even though she'd said no, even though she'd got mad at him, fought with him, scratched him; but he'd only laughed and gone on; and then suddenly she was just too tired to fight any more. Too tired and too miserable. He got what he wanted; and the awful thing was that it seemed to be what she wanted – or, rather, what her unhappiness wanted; for the misery had been relieved for a time; she had been able to forget the blood; she had been able to sleep. The next morning she had despised and hated herself more than ever.

'I had grottoes and candles and doodahs galore,' Dr Obispo sang on; then relapsed into speech; 'not to mention fetishes, relics, mantras, prayer-wheels, gibberish, vestments. But I also dreamt which pleased me most – or rather more, seeing that we have to rhyme with galore' (he opened his mouth and let out his richest and most tremulous notes), 'that you lo-hoved me sti-hill the same, that you lo-ho-ho-ho-ho-ho-ho-ho-ho-ho-ho-ho-ho-ho-hoved me . . .'

'Stop!' Virginia shouted at the top of her voice.

Uncle Jo woke up with a start. 'What's the matter?' he asked.

'She objects to my singing,' Dr Obispo called back to him. 'Goodness knows why. I have a charming voice. Particularly well adapted to a small auditorium, like this car.' He laughed with whole-hearted merriment. The Baby's antics, as she vacillated between Priapus and the Sacred Grotto, gave him the most exquisite amusement. Along with the fine weather, the primroses in the cops and the prospect of learning something decisive about sterols and senility, they accounted for the ebullience of his good-humour.

It was about half past eleven when they reached their destination. The lodge was untenanted; Dr Obispo had to get out and open the gates himself.

Within, grass was growing over the drive and the park had sunk back towards the squalor of unmodified nature. Uprooted by past storms, dead trees lay rotting where they had fallen. On the boles of the living, great funguses grew like pale buns. The ornamental plantations had turned into little jungles, impenetrable with brambles. Perched on its knoll above the drive, the Grecian gazebo was in ruins. They rounded a curve, and there was the house, Jacobean at one end, with strange accretions of nineteenth-century Gothic at the other. The yew hedges had grown up into high walls of shaggy greenery. The position of what had once been formal flower-beds was marked by rich green circles of docks, oblongs and crescents of sow-thistles and nettles. From the tufted grass of a long untended lawn emerged the tops of rusty croquet hoops.

Dr Obispo stopped the car at the foot of the front steps and got out. As he did so, a little girl, perhaps eight or nine years old, darted out of a tunnel in the yew hedge. At the sight of the car and its occupants the child halted, made a movement of retreat, then, reassured by a second glance, came forward.

'Look what I got,' she said in sub-standard Southern English, and held out, snout downwards, a gas-mask half filled with primroses and dog's-mercury.

Gleefully, Dr Obispo laughed. 'The cops!' he cried. 'You picked them in the cops!' He patted the child's tow-coloured head. 'What's your name?'

'Millie,' the little girl answered; and then added, with a note of pride in her voice: 'I 'aven't been somewhere for five days now.'

'Five days?'

Millie nodded triumphantly. 'Granny says she'll 'ave to take me to the doctor.' She nodded again, and smiled up at him with the expression of one who has just announced his forthcoming trip to Bali.

'Well, I think your Granny's entirely right,' said Dr Obispo. 'Does your Granny live here?'

The child nodded affirmatively. 'She's in the kitchen,' she answered; and added irrelevantly, 'she's deaf.'

'And what about Lady Jane Hauberk?' Dr Obispo went on. 'Does *she* live here? And the other one – Lady Anne, isn't that it?'

Again the child nodded. Then, an expression of sly mischief appeared on her face. 'Do you know what Lady Anne does?' she asked.

'What does she do?'

Millie beckoned to him to bend down so that she could put her mouth to his ear. 'She makes noises in 'er stomick,' she whispered.

'You don't say so!'

'Like birds singing,' the child added poetically. 'She does it after lunch.'

Dr Obispo patted the tow-coloured head again and said, 'We'd like to see Lady Anne and Lady Jane.'

'See them?' the little girl repeated in a tone almost of alarm.

'Do you think you could go and ask your Granny to show us in?'

Millie shook her head. 'She wouldn't do it. Granny won't let nobody come in. Some people came about these things.' She held up the gas-mask. 'Lady Jane, she got so angry I was frightened. But then she broke one of the lamps with her stick – you know, by mistake: bang! and the glass was all in bits, all over the floor. That made me laugh.'

'Good for you,' said Dr Obispo. 'Why shouldn't we make you laugh again?'

The child looked at him suspiciously. 'What do you mean?'

Dr Obispo assumed a conspiratorial expression and dropped his voice to a whisper. 'I mean, you might let us in by one of the side-doors, and we'd all walk on tiptoes, like this'; he gave a demonstration across the gravel. 'And then we'd pop into the room where they're sitting and give them a surprise. And then maybe Lady Jane will smash another lamp, and we'll all laugh and laugh and laugh. What do you say to that?'

'Granny'd be awfully cross,' the child said dubiously.

'We won't tell her you did it.'

'She'd find out.'

'No, she wouldn't,' said Dr Obispo confidently. Then changing his tone, 'Do you like candies?' he added.

The child looked at him blankly.

'Lovely candies?' he repeated voluptuously; then suddenly re-membered that, in this damned country, candies weren't called candies. What the hell did they call them? He remembered. 'Lovely sweets!' He darted back to the car and returned with the expensive-looking box of chocolates that had been bought in case Virginia should feel hungry by the way. He opened the lid, let the child take one sniff, then closed it again. 'Let us in,' he said, 'and you can have them all.'

Five minutes later they were squeezing their way through an ogival french window at the nineteenth century end of the house. Within, there was a twilight that smelt of dust and dry-rot and moth-balls. Gradually, as the eyes became accustomed to the gloom, a draped billiard-table emerged into view, a mantelpiece with a gilt clock, a bookshelf containing the Waverley Novels in crimson leather, and the eighth edition of the *Encyclopaedia Britannica*, a large brown painting representing the baptism of the future Edward VII, the heads of five or six stags. Hanging on the wall near the door was a map of the Crimea; little flags on pins marked the position of Sevastopol and the Alma.

Still carrying the flower-filled gas-mask in one hand, and with the forefinger of the other pressed to her lips, Millie led the way on tiptoes along a corridor, across a darkened drawing-room, through a lobby, down another passage. Then she halted and, waiting for Dr Obispo to come up with her, pointed.

'That's the door,' she whispered. 'They're in there.'

Without a word, Dr Obispo handed her the box of chocolates; the child snatched it and, like an animal with a stolen tit-bit, slipped past Virginia and Mr Stoyte, and hurried away down the dark passage to enjoy her prize in safety. Dr Obispo watched her go, then turned to his companions.

There was a whispered consultation, and in the end it was agreed that Dr Obispo should go on alone.

He walked forward, quietly opened the door, slipped through and closed it behind him.

Outside, in the corridor, the Baby and Uncle Jo waited for what seemed to them hours. Then, all at once, there was a crescendo of confused noise which culminated in the sudden emergence of

Dr Obispo. He slammed the door, pushed a key into the lock and turned it.

An instant later, from within, the door-handle was violently rattled, a shrill old voice cried, 'How dare you?' Then an ebony cane delivered a series of peremptory raps and the voice almost screamed, 'Give me back those keys. Give them back at once.'

Dr Obispo put the key of the door in his pocket and came down the corridor, beaming with satisfaction.

'The two god-damnest-looking old hags you ever saw,' he said. 'One on each side of the fire, like Queen Victoria and Queen Victoria.'

A second voice joined the first; the rattling and the rapping were redoubled.

'Bang away!' Dr Obispo shouted derisively; then, pushing Mr Stoyte with one hand and with the other giving the Baby a familiar little slap on the buttocks, 'Come on,' he said. 'Come on.'

'Come on where?' Mr. Stoyte asked in a tone of resentful bewilderment. He'd never been able to figure out what this damn fool expedition across the Atlantic was for – except, of course, to get away from the castle. Oh, yes, they'd had to get away from the castle. No question about that; in fact, the only question was whether they'd ever be able to go back to it, after what happened – whether they'd ever be able to bathe in that pool again, for example. Christ! when he thought of it . . .

But, then, why go to England? At this season? Why not Florida or Hawaii? But no; Obispo had insisted it must be England. Because of his work, because there might be something important to be found out there. Well, he couldn't say no to Obispo – not now, not yet. And besides, he couldn't do without the man. His nerves, his digestion – all shot to pieces. And he couldn't sleep without dope; he couldn't pass a cop on the street without his heart missing a beat or two. And you could say, 'God is love. There is no death,' till you were blue in the face; but it didn't make any difference. He was old, he was sick; death was coming closer and closer, and unless Obispo did something quick, unless he found out something soon . . .

In the dim corridor Mr Stoyte suddenly halted. 'Obispo,' he said anxiously, while the Hauberk ladies hammered with ebony on the door of their prison, 'Obispo, are you absolutely certain there's no such thing as hell? Can you prove it?'

Dr Obispo laughed. 'Can you prove that the back side of the moon isn't inhabited by green elephants?' he asked.

'No, but seriously . . .' Mr Stoyte insisted, in anguish.

'Seriously,' Dr Obispo gaily answered, 'I can't prove anything about any assertion that can't be verified.' Mr Stoyte and he had had this sort of conversation before. There was something, to his mind, exquisitely comic about chopping logic with the old man's unreasoning terror.

The Baby listened in silence. She *knew* about hell; she *knew* what happened if you committed mortal sins – sins like letting it happen again, after you'd promised Our Lady that it wouldn't. But Our Lady was so kind and so wonderful. And, after all, it had really been all that beast Sig's fault. Her own intentions had been absolutely pure; and then Sig had come along and just made her break her word. Our Lady would understand. The awful thing was that it had happened again, when he hadn't forced her. But even then it hadn't *really* been her fault – because, after all, she'd been through that terrible experience; she wasn't well; she . . .

'But do you think hell's possible?' Mr Stoyte began again.

'Everything is possible,' said Dr Obispo cheerfully. He cocked an ear to listen to what the old hags were yelling back there behind the door.

'Do you think there's one chance in a thousand it may be true? Or one in a million?'

Grinning, Dr Obispo shrugged his shoulders. 'Ask Pascal,' he suggested.

'Who's Pascal?' Mr Stoyte inquired, clutching despairingly at any and every straw.

'He's dead,' Dr Obispo positively shouted in his glee. 'Dead as a door-nail. And now, for God's sake!' He seized Uncle Jo by the arm and fairly dragged him along the passage.

The terrible word reverberated through Mr Stoyte's imagination. 'But I want to be certain,' he protested.

'Certain about what you can't know!'

'There *must* be a way.'

'There isn't. No way except dying and then seeing what happens.

Where the hell is that child?' he added in another tone, and called, 'Millie!'

Her face smeared with chocolate, the little girl popped up from behind an umbrella-stand in the lobby. 'Did you see 'em?' she asked with her mouth full.

Dr Obispo nodded. 'They thought I was the Air Raid Precautions.'

'That's it!' the child cried excitedly. 'That was the one that made her break the lamp.'

'Come here, Millie,' Dr Obispo commanded. The child came. 'Where's the door to the cellar?'

An expression of fear passed over Millie's face. 'It's locked,' she answered.

Dr Obispo nodded. 'I know it,' he said. 'But Lady Jane gave me the keys.' He pulled out of his pocket a ring on which were suspended three large keys.

'There's bogies down there,' the child whispered.

'We don't worry about bogies.'

'Granny says they're awful,' Millie went on. 'She says they're something chronic.' Her voice broke into a whimper. 'She says if I don't go somewhere more regular-like, the bogies will come after me. But I can't 'elp it.' The tears began to flow. 'It isn't my fault.'

'Of course it isn't,' said Dr Obispo impatiently. 'Nothing is ever anybody's fault. Even constipation. But now I want you to show us the door of the cellar.'

Still in tears, Millie shook her head. 'I'm frightened.'

'But you won't have to go down into the cellar. Just show us where the door is, that's all.'

'I don't want to.'

'Won't you be a nice little girl,' Dr Obispo wheedled, 'and take us to the door?'

Stubborn with fear, Millie continued to shake her head.

Dr Obispo's hand shot out and snatched the box of chocolates out of the child's grasp. 'If you don't tell me, you won't have any candies,' he said, and added irritably, 'sweets, I mean.'

Millie let out a scream of anguish and tried to get back at the box; but he held it high up, beyond her reach. 'Only when you show us the door of the cellar,' he said; and, to show that he was in earnest, he opened the box, took a handful of chocolates and popped them one after another into his mouth. 'Aren't they good!' he said as he munched. 'Aren't they just wonderful! Do you know, I'm glad you won't show us the door, because then I can eat them all.' He took another bite, made a grimace of ecstasy. 'Ooh, goody, goody!' He smacked his lips. 'Poor little Millie! She isn't going to get any more of them.' He helped himself again.

'Oh, don't, don't!' the child entreated each time she saw one of the brown nuggets of bliss disappearing between Dr Obispo's jaws. Then a moment came when greed was stronger than fear. 'I'll show you where it is,' she screamed, like a victim succumbing to torture and promising to confess.

The effect was magical. Dr Obispo replaced in the box the three chocolates he was still holding and closed the lid. 'Come on,' he said, and held out his hand for the child to take.

'Give me the box,' she demanded.

Dr Obispo, who understood the principles of diplomacy, shook his head. 'Not till you've taken us to the door,' he said.

Millie hesitated for a moment; then, resigned to the hard necessity of keeping to her side of the bargain, took his hand.

Followed by Uncle Jo and the Baby, they made their way out of the lobby, back through the drawing-room, along the passage, past the map of the Crimea and across the billiard-room, along another passage and into a large library. The red plush curtains were drawn; but a little light filtered between them. All round the room the brown and blue and crimson strata of classic literature ran up to within three feet of the high ceiling, and at regular intervals along the mahogany cornice stood busts of the illustrious dead. Millie pointed to Dante. 'That's Lady Jane,' she whispered confidentially.

'For Christ's sake!' Mr Stoyte broke out startlingly. 'What's the big idea? What the hell do you figure we're doing?'

Dr Obispo ignored him. 'Where's the door?' he asked.

The child pointed.

'What do you mean?' he started angrily to shout. Then he saw that what he had taken for just another section of the book-filled shelves was in fact a mere false front of wood and leather simulating thirty-three volumes of the Collected Sermons of Archbishop

Stillingfleet and (he recognized the Fifth Earl's touch) the Complete Works, in seventy-seven volumes, of Donatien Alphonse François, Marquis de Sade. A keyhole revealed itself to a closer scrutiny.

'Give me my sweets,' the child demanded.

But Dr Obispo was taking no risks. 'Not till we see if the key fits.'

He tried and, at the second attempt, succeeded. 'There you are.' He handed Millie her chocolates and at the same time opened the door. The child uttered a scream of terror and rushed away.

'What's the big idea?' Mr Stoyte repeated uneasily.

'The big idea,' said Dr Obispo, as he looked down the flight of steps that descended, after a few feet, into an impenetrable darkness, 'the big idea is that you may not have to find out whether there's such a place as hell. Not yet awhile, that's to say; not for a very long time maybe. Ah, thank God!' he added. 'We shall have some light.'

Two old-fashioned bull's-eye lanterns were standing on a shelf just inside the door. Dr Obispo picked one of them up, shook it, held it to his nose. There was oil in it. He lit them both, handed one to Mr Stoyte and, taking the other himself, led the way cautiously down the stairs.

A long descent; then a circular chamber cut out of the yellow sandstone. There were four doorways. They chose one of them and passed, along a narrow corridor, into a second chamber with two more doorways. A blind alley first; then another flight of steps leading to a cave full of ancient refuse. There was no second issue; laboriously, with two wrong turnings on the way, they retraced their steps to the circular chamber from which they had started, and made trial of its second doorway. A flight of descending steps; a succession of small rooms. One of these had been plastered, and upon its walls early eighteenth century hands had scratched obscene *graffiti*. They hurried on, down another short flight of steps, into a large square room with an air-shaft leading at an angle through the rock to a tiny, far-away ellipse of white light. That was all. They turned back again. Mr Stoyte began to swear; but the doctor insisted on going on. They tried the third doorway. A passage; a suite of three rooms. Two outlets from the last, one mounting, but walled up with masonry after a little way; the other descending to a corridor on a lower level. Thirty or forty feet brought them to an opening on the left. Dr Obispo turned his lantern into it, and the light revealed a vaulted recess, at the end of which, on a stuccoed pedestal, stood a replica in marble of the Medici Venus.

'Well, I'm damned!' said Mr Stoyte, and then, on second thoughts, was seized with a kind of panic. 'How the hell did *that* get here, Obispo?' he said, running to catch up the doctor.

Dr Obispo did not answer, but hurried impatiently forward.

'It's crazy,' Mr Stoyte went on apprehensively, as he trotted behind the doctor. 'It's downright crazy. I tell you, I don't like it.'

Dr Obispo broke his silence. 'We might see if we can get her for the Beverly Pantheon,' he said with a wolfish joviality. 'Hullo, what's this?' he added.

They emerged from the tunnel into a fair-sized room. At the centre of the room was a circular drum of masonry, with two iron uprights rising from either side of it, and a cross-piece, from which hung a pulley.

'The well!' said Dr Obispo, remembering a passage in the Fifth Earl's notebook.

He almost ran towards the tunnel on the further side of the room. Ten feet from the entrance, his progress was barred by a heavy, nail-studded oak door. Dr Obispo took out his bunch of keys, chose at random and opened the door at the first trial. They were on the threshold of a small oblong chamber. His bull's-eye revealed a second door on the opposite wall. He started at once towards it.

'Canned beef!' said Mr Stoyte in astonishment, as he ran the beam of his lantern over the rows of tins and jars on the shelves of a tall dresser that occupied almost the whole of one of the sides of the room. 'Biloxi Shrimps. Sliced Pineapple. Boston Baked Beans,' he read out, then turned towards Dr Obispo. 'I tell you, Obispo, I don't like it.'

The Baby had taken out a handkerchief saturated in 'Shocking' and was holding it to her nose. 'The smell!' she said indistinctly through its folds, and shuddered with disgust. 'The smell!'

Dr Obispo, meanwhile, was trying his keys on the lock of the other door. It opened at last. A draught of warm air flowed in, and at once the little room was filled with an intolerable stench. 'Christ!' said Mr Stoyte, and behind her handkerchief the Baby let out a scream of nauseated horror.

Dr Obispo made a grimace and advanced along the stream of foul air. At the end of a short corridor was a third door, of iron bars this time, like the door (Dr Obispo reflected) of a death-cell in a prison. He flashed his lantern between the bars, into the foetid darkness beyond.

From the little room Mr Stoyte and the Baby suddenly heard an astonished exclamation and then, after a moment's silence, a violent, explosive guffaw, succeeded by peal after peal of Dr Obispo's ferocious, metallic laughter. Paroxysm upon uncontrollable paroxysm, the noise reverberated back and forth in the confined space. The hot, stinking air vibrated with a deafening and almost maniacal merriment.

Followed by Virginia, Mr Stoyte crossed the room and hastened through the open door into the narrow tunnel beyond. Dr Obispo's laughter was getting on his nerves. 'What the hell . . .?' he shouted angrily as he advanced; then broke off in the middle of the sentence. 'What's that?' he whispered.

'A foetal ape,' Dr Obispo began; but was cut short by another explosion of hilarity, that doubled him up as though with a blow in the solar plexus.

'Holy Mary,' the Baby began behind her handkerchief.

Beyond the bars, the light of the lanterns had scooped out of the darkness a narrow world of forms and colours. On the edge of a low bed, at the centre of this world, a man was sitting, staring, as though fascinated, into the light. His legs, thickly covered with coarse reddish hair, were bare. The shirt, which was his only garment, was torn and filthy. Knotted diagonally across the powerful chest was a broad silk ribbon that had evidently once been blue. From a piece of string tied round his neck was suspended a little image of St. George and the Dragon in gold and enamel. He sat hunched up, his head thrust forward and at the same time sunk between his shoulders. With one of his huge and strangely clumsy hands he was scratching a sore place that showed red between the hairs of his left calf.

'A foetal ape that's had time to grow up,' Dr Obispo managed at last to say. 'It's *too* good!' Laughter overtook him again. 'Just look at his face!' he gasped, and pointed through the bars. Above the matted hair that concealed the jaws and cheeks, blue eyes stared out of cavernous sockets. There were no eyebrows; but under the dirty, wrinkled skin of the forehead a great ridge of bone projected like a shelf.

Suddenly, out of the black darkness, another simian face emerged into the beam of the lantern – a face only lightly hairy, so that it was possible to see, not only the ridge above the eyes, but also the curious distortions of the lower jaws, the accretions of bone in front of the ears. Clothed in an old check ulster and some glass beads, a body followed the face into the light.

'It's a woman,' said Virginia, almost sick with the horrified disgust she felt at the sight of those pendulous and withered dugs.

The doctor exploded into even noisier merriment.

Mr Stoyte seized him by the shoulder and violently shook him. 'Who are they?' he demanded.

Dr Obispo wiped his eyes and drew a deep breath; the storm of his laughter was flattened to a heaving calm. As he opened his mouth to answer Mr Stoyte's question, the creature in the shirt suddenly turned upon the creature in the ulster and hit out at her head. The palm of the enormous hand struck the side of the face. The creature in the ulster uttered a scream of pain and rage, and shrank back out of the light. From the shadow came a shrill, furious gibbering that seemed perpetually to tremble on the verge of articulate blasphemy.

'The one with the Order of the Garter,' said Dr Obispo, raising his voice against the tumult, 'he's the Fifth Earl of Gonister. The other's his housekeeper.'

'But what's happened to them?'

'Just time,' said Dr Obispo airily.

'Time?'

'I don't know how old the female is,' Dr Obispo went on. 'But the Earl there – let me see, he was two hundred and one last January.'

From the shadows the shrill voice continued to scream its all but articulate abuse. Impassibly the Fifth Earl scratched the sore on his leg and stared at the light.

Dr Obispo went on talking. Slowing up of development rates ... one of the mechanisms of evolution ... the older an anthropoid, the stupider ... senility and sterol poisoning ... the intestinal flora of the carp ... the Fifth Earl had anticipated his own discovery ... no sterol poisoning, no senility ... no death, perhaps, except through an accident ... but meanwhile the foetal anthropoid was able to come to maturity ... It was the finest joke he had ever known.

Without moving from where he was sitting, the Fifth Earl urinated on the floor. A shriller chattering arose from the darkness. He turned in the direction from which it came and bellowed the guttural distortions of almost forgotten obscenities.

'No need of any further experiment,' Dr Obispo was saying. 'We know it works. You can start taking the stuff at once. At once,' he repeated with sarcastic emphasis.

Mr Stoyte said nothing.

On the other side of the bars, the Fifth Earl rose to his feet, stretched, scratched, yawned, then turned and took a couple of steps towards the boundary that separated the light from the darkness. His housekeeper's chattering became more agitated and rapid. Affecting to pay no attention, the Earl halted, smoothed the broad ribbon of his order with the palm of his hand, then fingered the jewel at his neck, making as he did so a curious humming noise that was like a simian memory of the serenade in *Don Giovanni*. The creature in the ulster whimpered apprehensively, and her voice seemed to retreat further into the shadows. Suddenly, with a ferocious yell, the Fifth Earl sprang forward, out of the narrow universe of lantern light into the darkness beyond. There was a rush of footsteps, a succession of yelps; then a scream and the sound of blows and more screams; then no more screams, but only a stertorous growling in the dark and little cries.

Mr Stoyte broke the silence. 'How long do you figure it would take before a person went like that?' he said in a slow, hesitating voice. 'I mean, it wouldn't happen at once ... there'd be a long time while a person ... well, you know; while he wouldn't change any. And once you get over the first shock — well, they look like they were having a pretty good time. I mean in their own way, of course. Don't you think so, Obispo?' he insisted.

Dr Obispo went on looking at him in silence; then threw back his head and started to laugh again.

MORE ABOUT PENGUINS

Penguinews, which appears every month, contains details of all the new books issued by Penguins as they are published. From time to time it is supplemented by *Penguins in Print*, which is a complete list of all books published by Penguins which are in print. (There are well over three thousand of these.)

A specimen copy of *Penguinews* will be sent to you free on request, and you can become a subscriber for the price of the postage. For a year's issues (including the complete lists) please send 4s. if you live in the United Kingdom, or 8s. if you live elsewhere. Just write to Dept EP, Penguin Books Ltd, Harmondsworth, Middlesex, enclosing a cheque or postal order, and your name will be added to the mailing list.

Some other books published by Penguins are described on the following pages.

Note: *Penguinews* and *Penguins in Print* are not available in the U.S.A. or Canada

JOSEPH CONRAD

'Conrad is among the very greatest novelists in the language – or any language' – F. R. Leavis in *The Great Tradition*

Six books by Conrad are now available in the Penguin Modern Classics series:

LORD JIM

The novel by which Conrad is perhaps oftenest remembered by a majority of readers, and the first considerable novel he wrote.

THE SECRET AGENT: *A Simple Tale*

Based on anarchist and terrorist activities in London, this novel has been described by Dr Leavis as 'indubitably a classic and a masterpiece'.

VICTORY: *An Island Tale*

In his critical biography of the author Jocelyn Baines places this tragic story of the Malay Archipelago 'among Conrad's best novels'.

THE NIGGER OF THE NARCISSUS, TYPHOON *and other Stories*

Conrad's first sea novel, together with 'Typhoon', 'Falk', 'Amy Foster', and 'Tomorrow'.

NOSTROMO: *A Tale of the Seaboard*

His story of revolution in South America, which Arnold Bennett regarded 'as one of the greatest novels of any age'.

and

UNDER WESTERN EYES

NOT FOR SALE IN THE U.S.A.

ALDOUS HUXLEY

The name of Aldous Huxley, which became known in the twenties, rapidly developed into a password for his generation. At cocktail parties, which were becoming fashionable in the same period, it was bandied about as if the mere mention of it were enough to show that one was brilliant, witty, and cynically up to date. To start with, as Cyril Connolly has written, 'witty, serious, observant, well-read, sensitive, intelligent, there can have been few young writers as gifted as Huxley'. But the accusations of his less perceptive critics were completely off the mark, for in spite of Huxley's brilliant sense of light comedy, he was always fundamentally serious. Too good an artist to become a preacher, he never disguised his disillusionment, which in one form or another was the basis of his satire, while he showed himself to be a mystic – a role with which he was preoccupied after he went to live in California in 1937. As a result he became more and more concerned in his books with contrasting reality and illusion. Those of his books at present available as Penguins are:

BRAVE NEW WORLD
BRIEF CANDLES
POINT COUNTER POINT
THOSE BARREN LEAVES
AFTER MANY A SUMMER
ANTIC HAY
CROME YELLOW
EYELESS IN GAZA
ISLAND

NOT FOR SALE IN THE U.S.A.